DWELLERS
OF
DARKNESS

STACEY MARIE BROWN

Edited by Hollie Westring hollietheeditor@gmail.com
Edited by Chase Nottingham www.chaseediting.com
Cover Design by Jay Aheer https://www.simplydefinedart.com
Design Layout: www.formatting4U.com

ALSO BY STACEY MARIE BROWN

Contemporary Romance

Buried Alive

Blinded Love Series
Shattered Love (#1)
Pezzi di me (Shattered Love)—Italian
Broken Love (#2)
Twisted Love (#3)

The Unlucky Ones
(Má Sorte—Portuguese)

Royal Watch Series
Royal Watch (#1)
Royal Command (#2)

Smug Bastard

Paranormal Romance

Darkness Series
Darkness of Light (#1)
(L'oscurita Della Luce—Italian)
Fire in the Darkness (#2)
(Il Fuoco Nell Oscurita—Italian)
Beast in the Darkness (An Elighan Dragen Novelette)
Dwellers of Darkness (#3)
Blood Beyond Darkness (#4)
West (A Darkness Series Novel)

Collector Series
City in Embers (#1)
The Barrier Between (#2)
Across the Divide (#3)
From Burning Ashes (#4)

Lightness Saga
The Crown of Light (#1)
Lightness Falling (#2)
The Fall of the King (#3)
Rise from the Embers (#4)

A Winterland Tale
Descending into Madness (#1)
Ascending from Madness (#2)
Beauty in Her Madness (#3)
Beast in His Madness (#4)

Savage Lands Series
Savage Lands (#1)
Wild Lands (#2)
Dead Lands (#3)
Bad Lands (#4)

For my readers.
You have made this possible.

ONE

Some days can feel like years. In my case just the opposite was true. I had only been in the Otherworld for what felt like a few days but returned to Earth's realm three years older. Age didn't really apply when you can live for thousands of years. If I were human, I would be twenty-two now.

I'm not. Human that is.

The rebuilt city of Seattle glittered below and only cemented the fact I had truly been gone so long. My last glimpse of Seattle was of piles of concrete and death. All done by my hand.

"No. This can't be. It's not possible." Kennedy's voice shuddered, breaking into my thoughts.

"Well, it is." Eli sounded detached.

I turned to face him. Everything about his demeanor was forbidding and vicious. He seemed even bigger than his 6-foot 4-inch frame, and he seemed ready to attack. His green eyes were sharp and menacing as he watched my every movement. He was more Dark Dweller than the guy I had been with a few "days" ago.

"How did you get here so fast?"

His unfeeling eyes latched on to mine. "I happened to be in the neighborhood."

"In the neighborhood? We're over an hour and a half from Olympia, in the middle of the forest." The sharp smell of pine clung to the inside of my nose. The hot sun broke through the branches, filtering across my face. When I had left it had been almost winter. Now, the air was warm causing a trickle of sweat to slide down my back.

Normally nature relaxed me. Eli was not making this possible.

His shoulders swelled; his head hunched down. "Like I said... in the area."

I forced down the nervous acid curling up my throat. Having his

1

blood was like a flare in my veins. It came to life when he was near. It was even stronger for him. He could track me anywhere.

"H-how is this possible?" Kennedy stared at the rebuilt city below, a trembling hand at her stomach. Granted, I was stunned by the evolution of Seattle, but I had known about the Otherworld a little longer—how time moved differently there. In the past couple months, or years if Earth time counted, I had learned to adapt quickly to the surreal life I was plunged into. My survival depended on it.

Even though Kennedy had been held prisoner by Queen Aneira and been given information about the Fae world, I knew it was different to experience it. She was a facts person and could handle being told things, absorbing the realities, but living it was not the same.

"You were being held by a Fairy, surrounded by magic, and you ask me how?" Eli snapped at her.

"Hey. Give her a break. Some of us weren't raised knowing about this stuff." My eyes narrowed. Eli had never been known as the nice guy, not even close, but this was unusual. His rage and irritation rippled off him, dying to be invoked.

"Well, she's gonna have to learn fast." Eli's tone hinted at what we both knew about Kennedy. What she didn't even know about herself yet—what she really was.

My head shook slightly in warning. I squinted my eyes to convey: *not yet.*

Eli jerked back and looked away from me. Anger smoldered through his eyes. Even when being an ass, he was a sight to behold. Eli's shoulder-length, light brown hair had been shaved off. He looked menacing with his tattoos and the scar cutting along his jaw-line. His piercing, green eyes were full of heated fury. But, damn, he was still so freakin' sexy it hurt to look at him. It was even more painful to recall what happened between us only a few days before. Well, a few days to me. Where his lips and hands had been. How he felt deep inside me. How his gaze had roamed greedily over my body. Now they only looked at me with cool contempt.

"Kennedy, I know this must be really hard for you to take in." My mom stepped up to her and touched her shoulder. Her dark auburn hair hung limply down her back. She was drawn and sickly looking after years of torture, but her eyes were just as gorgeous as I remembered. A deep rust color, which glinted in the sunlight.

Kennedy shook her head. "But my family... what they must be going through..." she trailed off. Her tiny frame shook.

"I know, sweetheart." My mother's voice was soothing.

I was reaching out for Kennedy when I heard a diffused pop of energy. Two tiny, winged creatures sailed through the space, a doorway from the Otherworld, and almost crashed into Eli's head.

"Oooohhh, prruutty llaady?" I heard Cal slur before Simmons spoke over him. Cal was in his pirate-like jacket with his swizzle stick sword swinging in the air.

"My lady! They are coming. The soldiers are approaching." Simmons was dressed in a 1960s fighter pilot outfit, which he had stolen off a Ken doll.

"What?" My shoulders tightened.

"Suuulders... blah blah... cooooming." Cal hiccupped. "Whaaat heee saaaid."

"We tried to divert them to another portal, but they split up and some are heading this way." Simmons's frown reflected the disappointment he felt with himself. "I am so sorry, my lady. I failed you."

The group went still with alarm, except for Cal who weaved drunkenly through the air.

"Move. I have a car down the hill." Eli waved for everyone to start running.

I pushed Kennedy to follow Eli and Jared and then turned to my mother. "Come on."

Mom set her jaw and shook her head. "Ember, we are not going with the Dark Dwellers. They are hired assassins. You don't know what they have done. They are even more dangerous than the soldiers."

"Mom, we really don't have time for this, but trust me when I say they're not."

Simmons zipped down, close to my ear. "My lady, we really need you to retreat."

I grasped her hands. "Mom, please. Whatever issues you have with them are just going to have to wait till we're safe."

"Ember, they are dangerous."

"You don't think I know? But it doesn't matter; I'm one of them now."

She missed my meaning and responded, "Don't you dare say such a thing. You are not like those killers."

The air crackled and at least a dozen of the Queen's men propelled out the realm door. "Go," I shouted. At the sight of more and more soldiers coming toward us with swords raised, my mother's stubborn nature gave in, and she ran with me. Her legs could barely keep at a jogging pace. Since being locked up in Aneira's dungeon, her once strong, petite body had become spindly and weak.

The solid block of soldiers advanced on us. I looked over my shoulder and fixated on the first united front. I drew on my powers, and with a push from my mind, a few of the men flew off their feet crashing like dominos into the ones behind them. It would only stall them for a moment. We had to move faster.

"Eli," I screamed. He whipped around. *Help*. My expression must have conveyed to him what I needed because, without a word, he sprinted back to me, picked up my mother, and took off.

"Get her," a dark-haired soldier yelled pointing at me, while more men came through the entry.

As I ran after the group, my brain rapidly evaluated the situation, maybe due to my Dark Dweller part or Alki's training. They were after me because only I really mattered to the Queen. If I split from them, my friends and mother would have more of a chance of getting away. My powers alone would not be enough to stop the soldiers. I could already feel the muscles in my legs straining to keep running. My body was too exhausted to be able to fight them all. Escape was my only option.

Not needing a second thought on the matter, I pivoted, breaking off the main trail onto another one. A wall of colossal trees and thickly dense foliage kept me on the thin gravel path. Immediately, I heard the Queen's troops shouting. As I hoped, most changed direction to follow me. Their instructions were to capture me at all costs.

"Jumpin' junipers, w-what are yoooou doin'?" Cal's hummingbird metabolism was burning off whatever liquor he'd consumed, but he still swerved as he flew down close to my head.

"Leading them away from my friends," I hissed through my teeth. "You don't happen to have any more of what made them sleepy do you?"

"Uh... no... didn't think we'd need it anymore. So... I kind of drank it."
Ah.

"My lady, what would you like us to do?" Simmons whizzed around a tree. The Queen's men were so close I could feel the vibrations from their shouts creeping up my spine. I had to get off this trail; I was too easy to follow. The steep ravines were coated in heavy brush, unstable ground, and rocks. I stopped, looking down.

"Oh, no. Are you nuts, girly?" Cal exclaimed as he darted by my ear.

I ignored Cal's boozy insult. "Simmons, please go help the others. Make sure they get out of here safely. Tell them whatever you need to get them to leave."

"No, my lady. We can't leave you here."

Cal suddenly became serious. "Simmons, do as the lady tells you. You do not question orders. I will stay with her. She will be okay, I promise."

Simmons sighed but saluted me and darted off through the trees. My chest burst with relief because Cal wasn't leaving. Simmons was always good to have at your side; he would follow orders. But Cal conveyed a fierce loyalty once he let you in. He would fight to the death for you and not follow the rules in doing it.

"You! Stop!" A voice boomed behind me.

After another panicked look down at the treacherous ravine, I let out a small whine.

"Well, think of it this way, you won't actually die in this realm." Cal buzzed in my periphery.

That wasn't completely true. A perk of being Fae was the difficulty of dying on Earth. Death here consisted of fire, decapitation, or being shot with iron bullets but not from diseases, accidents, or natural causes. Weapons made in the Otherworld could kill us here as well. Two times a year we were even more vulnerable: Samhain, known to most as Halloween, and Beltane, the first of May. Both times were when our worlds bled together and exposed us to all sorts of risks. Thank goodness this was not one of those times.

"Thanks, Cal," I retorted. "But I don't plan on getting hurt." I fixated on my powers. If I could move people and objects with my mind, why couldn't I do it to myself?

"Um... Ember... your powers don—"

"See you at the bottom." I took a deep breath and flung myself into the gulch, concentrating on images of my body floating. The first time I hit the ground, bones crunched, knocking the wind out of me. Tucking my head in, I somersaulted, flipped, rolled, and crashed down the hill. There was so much pain I couldn't decipher between hitting a bush or a stump. My body picked up speed, so I flew through the air and bounced off the ground in intervals. I am sure I screamed, but I couldn't recall even opening my mouth.

It felt like eons before coming to a stop at the bottom. I continued to lie there; my body was in too much shock to move. *Why hadn't my powers worked?*

I heard distant shouts above me. The soldiers were still at the top of the hill.

"I'll give you an eight point five. Your dismount was somewhat lacking flare." Cal fluttered to my chest.

A groan tore through my teeth. Still numb, pain had yet to fully reach me. I was not looking forward to when it did.

"I tried to stop you before you did something foolish. Too late. Next time you want to throw yourself down a gully, know your powers never function on yourself."

I grunted in response, which was my way of saying, "Good to know."

Note to self: find out if your powers work on yourself before executing a plan.

"It's probably the last thing you want to do, girly, but this is the perfect time to get away from them. They are still fiddling with themselves up there, indecisive on what to do next."

Blinking a couple of times, I forced myself to nod. I wanted to lie there and let the earth heal me, to soak in its energy. Yet time was critical, and I couldn't afford to hesitate. Another grunt broke over my lips as I pushed myself up. My ribs stabbed me, causing agony. No doubt, there were a few broken ones. The rest were fractured or bruised, along with my wrists and ankles.

Awesome. Good day so far.

Cal hovered over me as I climbed to my feet. He tugged at my shirt, pulling me forward. Working through the pain, my legs jogged slowly forward, and I let Cal lead me through the gully. I felt blood trickle down my face and knew it covered me. Almost every exposed inch of my skin was bleeding, and mounting bruises filled in the gaps. My brain felt like it had been through one of those salad spinners.

The agony from my wounds had me tripping and grumbling through the dense forest. We had lost the soldiers, but with the Queen after me, I would never be really safe until I was at the Dark Dweller's compound.

"You have to keep going. We may have lost them for now, but they will not give up easily. She will have someone track you down." Cal nudged his head into my back, bumping me to continue.

I hated being weak, but the stabbing pain took everything out of me. I stumbled forward, falling to the ground. This time I knew I couldn't get

6

up. Cal's voice hummed in my ear, but I could no longer understand him. My hands clenched the dirt, wanting it to swallow me and take the agony away. Its energy started to trickle into my veins, but I didn't have time for the earth to pump into me the quantity of healing I needed.

"Ember?" My name moved through the late afternoon air, pricking at my ear. "Brycin, where are you?" That voice was as familiar to me as my own. I moaned.

"Here!" Cal yelled, his tiny voice barely carrying. I couldn't move or respond and hoped Cal would lead Eli back to me. I must have drifted off to sleep because the next thing I felt were Eli's strong hands on me, flipping me over.

"What the hell happened?" Eli demanded. My lids tapered till he disappeared again.

"Hey, Brycin. Stay with me." He tapped his fingers roughly against my cheek. I forced my eyes to lift slightly. "Now tell me what the hell happened?" He turned to Cal.

"Don't look at me. She kind of threw herself down a ravine. I thought it was some kinky fetish she enjoyed."

Eli rubbed his shaved head in irritation.

"She's pretty much out of it. She's been mumbling gibberish about flying monkeys and a tea party with a Dormouse. Have no idea what the hell she is jabbering about." Cal's feet tickled my arm as he landed.

Eli's hand went to my face, rubbing dried blood away from my eyes. He picked me up like a baby, and I curled into his chest, letting the protection of his body calm and comfort me.

I dozed off and on to the bobbing rhythm of his steps as he walked us out of the forest. His voice drifted into my ear. "Good thing I can still feel you." I thought his lips touched the top of my head, but I slipped back to sleep, confused as to what was real and what was not.

TWO

When I opened my eyes, leaves swayed gently over my head. I thought I was dreaming until the pain throbbing up and down my body made it clear I was awake. Plants had wrapped themselves around my legs and arms, keeping a firm hold on me as they donated their vitality.

"I thought this would be better than putting you in the infirmary bed." Eli's harsh tone rammed into me. I turned the only part of me not pinned down: my head.

He sat against a tree not too far away.

"I knew you were better off here." Eli's eyes were constricted as he stared off past me. "You'll heal faster being among the plants and trees," His words did not match his brusque tone, every syllable choppy and shot at me like an accusation. "Though, Owen is salivating at having you back. His little test monkey has returned."

That didn't surprise me. Owen was the clan's medical practitioner. He preferred healing and science to killing. Not only was I one of the only living Dae's, but my DNA was now part Dark Dweller. I was a utopia of research to him.

With every word Eli spoke, my defenses went up, sensing the need for protection. "Yeah, thanks." I stiffly brought my body up to a sitting position, the plants rescinding their embrace. "Bubbles, the test monkey, would like a banana."

Cool, green eyes glared into mine.

"What? Potassium is helpful when you're trying to heal. A banana actually sounds good."

His lids only narrowed.

"Guess someone's lost his sense of humor in the last three years." My eyes were not ready for quick movement and barely caught how rapidly he was up and flying at me. I flinched and looked away, preparing

8

for his attack. Two breaths later I realized nothing had happened. I opened my eyes and turned to look at his hulking body standing over mine. Wrath shook through his taut muscles, flexing and twitching under his skin. His eyes were so bright green they were almost neon.

"You have no idea what I went through these past years," Eli breathed out heavily, "while you were off with your boyfriend..." He trailed off, stepping away from me, huffing out of his nose. "You still reek of sex. Of me."

I flushed. He could still smell himself on me? Humiliated, I pulled my jacket tighter around me. "Sorry, it was a little hard to shower when locked up in the Queen's dungeon. Plus, I only take showers every four years, not three."

The pupils of his eyes stretched out, and his nose flared. "Don't push me right now. My patience is extremely thin."

"Wait. You're mad at me? Are you kidding?" I bellowed, grimacing as I tried to stand up. My ribs still ached fiercely. "How dare you be mad at me when you were the one who had sex with me and then told me you killed my mother? Why would you do that? What kind of person does such a horrible thing?"

Like a boulder, his heavy presence loomed over me. "A person like me I guess."

Biting back my emotion, I shoved at his chest. "You are sick."

"I've never denied it." His large hands wrapped easily around my wrists.

"Why?" My words barely came out. "Why would my tattoo warn me against you, and Lorcan, if you didn't kill her? Did you lie about that, too? Tell me what involvement you had with my mother." I couldn't stop my tirade. "Your touch was never as painful as Lorcan's, but now it's almost completely gone. Please. What is going on?"

He dropped my arms, rubbing his face absently. "Brycin." He scrubbed at his face harder. "You nee—"

"Ember?" Another voice cut him off. My mom stepped out from the trees. She had dark circles under her eyes and cuts all over. Her clothes were torn and dirty. "Are you all right?" Her eyes and tone were sharp. I could tell she was more concerned about Eli's effect on me than my wounds.

"Yeah, Mom, I'm fine." I backed away from Eli.

She gave a slight nod, but her eyes darted suspiciously between Eli and me. "I wanted to check on you." She stepped closer to my side. "Also, the Dark Dwellers were anxious to gather when you woke up."

I nodded and turned to go when I realized no one was following. "Are you guys coming?"

"Give me a moment. I would like to speak with Elighan alone." Her cutting glare never fully left Eli.

Uh-oh. This can't be good.

Eli didn't flinch but crossed his arms and rolled his eyes. The hostility between them was profound, especially on my mother's side. Eli had lied about killing her, but why? I needed to know what in the hell was going on.

I hesitated, my scrutiny darting between the two. "How do you guys know each other? What happened between you two?"

My mother's attention finally turned to me. "Ember, this is really not the time."

"When is the time?" I flung out my arms in question. "Why can't anyone ever just tell me the truth for once?"

"Ember." My mom's tone hit the scary warning level I recalled from when she got angry with me. "This is *not* the time or place. Please, give me a moment alone with Elighan."

I started to complain but stopped myself. How did she do it? She had the ultimate power to instantly turn me into a five-year-old again. My mother had never needed to use glamour on me. All she had to do was give me her narrow-eyed, jaw-pinched look of disappointment and disapproval, and I was a goner.

I stomped away in a huff. Very teenage of me although, technically, I wasn't a teenager anymore at least in the Otherworld. When they were almost out of sight, I turned around. I couldn't hear them, but it was clear they were arguing, hands gesticulating, and their faces pinched by seriousness. Whatever it was, I would find out.

Walking into the ranch house felt familiar even though it had been over six months to me and over three years to them. Everything looked and smelled the same.

"Ember." Kennedy jumped off the sofa. The force of her arms wrapping around me almost caused me to fall back on my butt. "You're okay. I was so worried about you."

"I'm okay. As you know now, I'm not easy to keep down." I laughed.

"Yeah." She stepped back, frowning. "About that... part of me really wants to kill you. The months of agony you put me and Ryan through. When you disappeared from the party..." She looked away blinking. "We blamed ourselves."

"I'm so sorry."

"I understand most of it was out of your control, and you felt like you were protecting us, but don't you *ever* do it to me again."

I looked at my feet, feeling like a scolded puppy. "I won't. I promise."

"We *will* talk later." There was no question to this statement, and I nodded in response. Kennedy was small-boned and only a few inches over five feet. She had long, silky, brown hair and brown eyes usually encircled by glasses. Ken was also the sweet one in our group. She let Ryan and me vie for dominance, but she was actually our leader. With one word or look she could silence us.

"Ember, glad you're awake." Cole stepped in from the kitchen, his stubble had grown out into a full beard. All these guys were so damn sexy it was wrong. "And alive." The rest of the Dark Dwellers mulled around behind him.

"Hey, guys." Despite all the issues and complex relationships I had with the group, part of me fought wanting to run over and hug them. I was aware I had actually missed them, which generated an uncomfortable emotion within me. I had hoped the feeling I had when I saw West was a fluke—the sentiment they were my family. Dammit—it wasn't.

"Where is Eli?" Gabby scanned the room.

"He's outside talking with my mom."

Cole nodded, and his face clenched in a frown. "We'll have to start without them."

"The Queen has West," I blurted out. There was no good way to say it. I would prefer to rip the bandage off and get it over with. But none of them showed the shock I expected.

Cole bobbed his head again as fury flickered in his hazel eyes. "Jared told us you saw him in the dungeon, and Lorcan was the one who turned him over to her." He rubbed his chin harshly. "We've been searching for him for over three years. We can usually feel each other, like Eli can with you. Our awareness of West disappeared six months before you vanished. We thought Lorcan killed him." His fists tightened as they gripped together, cracking his knuckles. "We've learned through you and West our ties are cut off when you go into the Otherworld. We've never had a reason to find this out before. We were in the Otherworld till we were all banned. Then we couldn't go between the worlds. Because you have returned, we are aware of this failure."

"I tried to get him out. I hated leaving him there, but he had a spiked collar around his throat. I'm sure it's charmed. I promised him we'd come back for him... for him and my dad, Ryan, and Josh. It killed me to walk away without them."

"I know, Ember, but it was the only thing you could do. Don't worry; we do not abandon our own." Cole's lips strained into a slight smile. "Good or bad you are one of us now, and along with West, your friends and family will not be left. We will get them out."

"Thank you." His words meant more to me than anything. I had help now. I would be able to get them back.

He shifted his head, his long, auburn hair falling into his eyes. Owen, Cole, and Jared all had the same eye and hair color, and their family resemblance was strong. Cole turned to address us. "Have a seat. We have a lot to discuss."

While people moved and settled in the living room, the familiarity of the smells, the overstuffed leather sofas, and homey feeling seized me. It made me want to curl up on the couch and sleep, feeling protected and safe.

Cooper headed to me. "Hey."

"Hey, Coop. Good to see you."

"Yeah, same. Though it has been longer for me than you."

"So I've been told."

Gabby sidled up on the other side of me. Her dyed, black hair had grown out to her chin. The ends looked like they had been dipped in florescent green paint. "Never thought I would say this, but I'm actually glad to have you back."

My eyebrows hit my hairline.

"I know, color me shocked as well. Things have not been pleasant around here the last three years."

"That's putting it mildly." Cooper snorted. "The asshole owes me a new bike."

"What happened?" I flicked a glance from Cooper to Gabby.

"Eli is a jackass at the best of times."

"Yeah, Gab, and you are such a sweetheart," I jabbed.

She rolled her eyes. "I may be a bitch but compared to your boy..."

My teeth clenched. "He's *not* my boy."

Both Cooper and Gabby guffawed.

"Look, I've never claimed to be your biggest fan, but if you can get Eli to be a little more bearable, I will throw you a fucking parade." Gabby crossed her thin, toned arms.

I threw up my hands. "You are Dark Dwellers. Being a jackass is an inherited personality trait. How bad could he have been?"

Cooper brushed his surfer-blond hair back. "You would be surprised. I've never seen him this way. We are dark and, yes, major jackasses, but he hit levels of darkness which even scared us. That's saying a lot. He became reckless and barely stayed in his human form. If he did, he would get drunk and purposely seek out fights with other biker clubs. He sometimes started to shift in front of them. We've had to get him out of extremely sticky situations. Sheriff Weiss even put a warrant out for his arrest."

Sherriff Weiss. The name generated resentment, which gripped my muscles. The mutual hatred of each other was epic. He caused me nothing but grief and misery. What pissed me off the most was he'd been right in his assessment of me but wrong about why. He was certain I started the fires at school. And I had, just not the way he thought. My powers invoked strange things to happen around me all of my life. Light explosions were only one of them.

"We've become Eli's permanent babysitters. Our Second has been on a downward spiral, and the only thing we can attribute it to is you." Gabby pointed at me. "And by your smell, I can understand why he's become such a tyrant." Her nose wrinkled.

If I felt humiliation when Eli brought it up, this took it to an entirely new level. The floor was not big enough. I wanted the earth to swallow me whole.

"You hadn't figured it out?" Cooper gapped at Gabby. "It was pretty obvious after he returned that night."

"Honestly, I didn't really want to think about the two Sasquatches humping each other in the woods." Gabby shrugged.

"Shut up!" My hands covered my face. I was embarrassed enough.

"Yeah, guys." At the sound of Eli's gravelly voice, all three of us spun around. "I think shutting up would be wise." His tone was jarring like someone chewing on ice. Cooper and Gabby quickly dispersed to the other side of the room, abandoning me.

Cowards.

Cole yelled over the crowd, "Everyone is here, so let's get this meeting started." Eli and I didn't move. Our eyes sealed on each other.

"After you." Eli's tone was unpleasant as he nodded toward the sofa. Trepidation filled my lungs. Pivoting, I hurriedly vacated the area and headed to the couch where Kennedy and Jared were.

My mom sat in the corner, her watchful eyes still switching from me to Eli. I hadn't even noticed her come in. She had always been good at slipping in and out of rooms almost undetected. She played a lot of practical jokes on me as I grew up. As a little girl, I looked at my mother like she had superpowers.

It turned out she really did; she was a Fairy, a noble Fay. An "encounter" with a high-Demon had produced me—a hybrid creature known as a Dae. Daes were outlawed in the Otherworld, and almost all had been hunted down and killed. The Queen led most of the Otherworld to believe we were evil and would only kill and destroy. Daes were powerful, probably too much so. But her desire to have us eradicated was enhanced by a prophecy hinting a Dae would kill her with the Sword of Light. I could hear Lars's voice in my head, reading the text:

> *By one of the Light, Darkness will take its revenge.*
> *A bloodline that cannot be repressed will rise to power.*
> *A descendant will take the throne.*
> *Blood will seek to kill you.*
> *She who possesses the Sword of Light will have the power.*

The prophecy was a thorn in my side. I had always thought the Queen was after me for my powers, but her incentive to capture me went beyond this because the prophecy may or may not be about a Dae. For good measure, she wanted to cover all her bases.

Cole took his place at the front of the room. "There's a lot to catch up on, and many things we need to discuss, but let me address a worry you might have." His attention turned to me. "We have redone the security ward around the property. There will be no repeat of Lorcan coming for any of you again."

Lorcan's name brought feelings of hatred to the surface. I longed to hunt him down and kill him. At least I didn't have to worry about him returning to the ranch and trying to kidnap me or take Kennedy again. I had run out of friends and family for him to threaten me with.

"No longer can any of them get in here." Cole shifted his stance. "But the enchantment only warns of unknowns trying to get in, not out. Only the six of us Dark Dwellers are part of the spell, so if you wander off the property, we won't know, and you might not be able to get back."

"Speak for yourself," Cal's voice came from the window. He and Simmons flew in and headed for me.

"Pixies don't count," Eli quipped from the wall where he leaned. "*Sub*-Fae never count."

My hand immediately went to my forehead. This was not something you said to pixies.

"Wh-wh-what?" Simmons puffed up with offense, buzzing toward Eli. "What did you say, sir?"

"He said we don't matter, Simmons." Cal's annoyed voice filled my ear as he landed on my shoulder.

Eli's lip curled up. "What's wrong? Did I offend thee, little man?"

Simmons huffed and blustered from Eli's rudeness. He pulled at the plastic sword, a swizzle stick, attached to his pants. "You have, sir. I challenge you to a duel."

Eli snorted with laughter. "I'll go get some kid's action figure so you can fight something more your size."

Even from across the room I could see Simmons's face redden as Eli riled him more and more. "Eli," I cautioned. "Enough!"

Eli sneered at Simmons but kept his mouth shut.

"Simmons, you're not fighting anyone. He's just trying to provoke you." I waved Simmons to me. Cal had already settled on my right shoulder, ignoring Eli's needling words.

Simmons grumbled and came to me. Of course, when he tried to land, he slipped and fell into my lap, which only roused his ire more. He was a ball of rage. Even Cal was smart enough not to comment on his landing skills. Simmons stomped off my lap and sat on the sofa arm, crossing his arms, sulking. He thought of himself as the best flyer in the realm. He was. His problem was landing.

"Okay, can we get down to business now?" Cole looked at the ceiling, trying to keep himself calm. "Ember, we would like to eventually add your blood to the spell. You are a part of us now, and it would be good for you to know how to get back. Kennedy, Lily, I think you both know it is safer if you don't leave or know how to get back here if you do."

"I think it's wise," Mom responded. "I don't think you need Ember's either. If we leave, believe me, we won't return."

I cast my mother an exasperated look.

"Let's allow Ember to decide." Cole's response was icy.

"Okay," I broke in, turning to my mom. "I think we have more important items on the list. We need to come up with a plan to rescue Dad, Ryan, Josh, and West. Let's concentrate on them and, for a moment, let go of the issues you guys have with each other. I get it. Fay and Dark Dwellers don't like each other. Get over it."

A strange silence befell the room. Magic and tension swirled and slammed into each other like clothes in a washing machine.

Mom cleared her throat. "You're right, Ember. Their release is the most important thing." She directed her statement toward Cole.

He studied her for moment, and then nodded. "Agreed."

"I think the first thing you should do is tell this poor girl what she really is." My mom swept back her long, auburn hair. Every head jerked in her direction. I knew instantly who she was speaking of, but Kennedy looked around the room trying to locate the subject of Mom's comment.

"How did you know?" I asked. Even the Queen hadn't detected Kennedy. How did my mother?

"I smelled her." Mom's hand immediately waved back and forth. "I mean, I sensed it coming off her. Her powers won't stay dormant forever. She's coming of age. Before, ignorance was best, but now she is a part of this, and she can only protect herself with the truth."

My gaze darted to Kennedy who still glanced around with a confused expression. Her eyes grew wide when she noticed everyone watching her.

"What? What is going on?" Her anxious countenance turned to me for solace. "Ember?"

I looked at my hands twisting together on my lap. "Ken... uh... this isn't going to be easy to hear or accept..."

"You're a fuckin' Druid," Eli spat and shrugged at me as I gaped. "What? Now she knows, and we can move on to acceptance."

All attention turned to Eli.

"Seriously, what is your problem?" I glared at him. "You don't blurt something out like that."

"We are wasting time. One of my brothers is being tortured. We don't have time to coddle her."

My fierce glare pinned him. I hated that a part of me agreed. Time wasn't on our side. The Queen could decide to kill or torture them at any moment. Aneira's twisted mind seemed to know no bounds.

"I'm sorry. What?" Kennedy sat more forward, looking at all of us like we had just fallen off the crazy train.

Actually, it's not far from the truth.

Scooting along the sofa, I leaned over, and gripped her hand in mine. "Ken, it is true. I know logically you're going to want to fight this, but you *are* a Druid."

"I'm a what?" Kennedy balked. She had been adopted and always realized her parents weren't her biological ones. She knew nothing of her blood relations, but I don't think she ever expected this.

I squeezed her shoulder. "Believe me; I understand how you feel right now. It seems impossible and goes against everything we've been

16

taught to believe in as humans. But it's real, Kennedy. There are such things as Fairies and Demons as you know now. I'll bet if you let yourself think back, somewhere in you, you've always suspected you were different."

"Different? Different, yes, but a Druid? An actual Druid... no... that never occurred to me." She shook her head. "Druids are human, right?"

"Yes, they have magic equal to Fae but are human. They were members of the priestly class of Celtics and had spiritual powers." Cole could sense her heart rate racing out of control. His commanding tone was calming and soothing.

"Magical? Spiritual powers? Like what? What are they exactly? What do they do?" Kennedy's voice hit a higher notch.

"Each Draoidh family has different strengths, but Druids in general were philosophers, healers, seers. They practiced magic and used enchantments and spells to prepare charms." Cole responded.

"Seers?" Kennedy clenched at her shaking hands. I understood why this one caught her attention the most. She had always been "sensitive" to people, almost knowing before they did what they were thinking or feeling. She was in tuned to everything around her.

"Training to be a seer takes decades, but the gift is in you." Cole glanced at Owen, jerking his head for him to jump in.

Owen jerked forward awkwardly. "Ms. Johnson, Kennedy, I concede this is scary, but you need to know how extraordinary and special you are. You are the last known living Druid. You should not even be alive, but whoever your parents were they went to extreme measures to keep you alive by hiding you with humans."

Cole rubbed his forehead. "Not really helping, Owen."

"I am the last living Druid? What does that mean? Why? Hiding me with humans? I thought I was human." Kennedy wailed. Jared's arm went around her shoulder as he tried to comfort her.

Owen cringed, now understanding his excitement did not extend to her. "Technically you are human, but like Cole said being a Druid makes you special."

"Special? How?"

"For one thing, you will live for centuries."

I could feel the panic boiling under Kennedy's skin. I stepped in before it exploded all over the room and asked, "Maybe if you start from the beginning and explain more about the Druid history?"

"Of course," Owen concurred with a nod. "In pre-Christian times, around two hundred years before Christ, the Draoidhean were responsible for religious teaching and practices. Even though they were human, they knew of the Otherworld and believed in the Celtic gods and goddesses. Their sacrifices and connections to the earth made them grow in power. I personally think the gods started to prefer them over the Fae, and it's why the gods granted them 'special status.' The gods enchanted their blood so the Druids could go in and out of the Otherworld freely. Their lifespans were extended. The higher your rank, the more magic power you had and the longer you lived.

"Just like any group, some wanted to take advantage of this increasing control. The gods did nothing. The Unseelie King also had many Druids working for him and ignored their growing powers. By the time Aneira took the throne, the Druids were more formidable with magic than the Fae. They derived their magical powers from both the Otherworld and the Earth realm. They could create unbreakable spells and curses and hide things even the Queen's power could not undermine."

Owen pushed his glasses further back up his nose.

"The Gaullish were the most powerful of the Druids, which I believe is the blood line you stem from, Ms. Johnson. They were the mediators between the mortal world and the gods, straddling both planes. Aneira feared and hated the Gaullish the most. She tried to annihilate the entire race."

"They're all dead? Why? Because she was scared? How could she get away with something like that?"

Kennedy's questions tumbled out. She had grown up with democracy, justice, logic. The Fae world did not work this way. If the ruler wanted you dead—you were dead.

There was also another reason Aneira hated the Druids. My stay with Lars had opened my eyes to what lengths Aneira would go. They had hidden the Sword of Light. Aneira thought killing the one who crafted the spell would cause it to break or lose power. It didn't. Aneira then killed every Druid, but still the enchantment did not break. Kennedy had survived. If Kennedy was from the elite lineage of Draoidhean and her family snuck her into Earth's realm and hid her among humans, she might be the only barrier between Aneira and this sword.

"The Otherworld is not a democracy. Aneira rules it, and her word is law. She does not take kindly to those who resist her authority. If they do not comply, she finds a way to destroy them." Owen glanced to me, then back to Kennedy.

"So, what about these Gaullish? They were my family?"

Kennedy still looked like a frightened kitten, wide-eyed and ready to bolt.

"It's more a classification of Druids. I do not know for sure what family you come from, but if I were to guess, it would be the family Cathbad."

"Cathbad? Who are they?" Kennedy smoothed her long silky, brown hair. I knew her. This was starting to overwhelm her.

"Cathbad the *Battler* was a seer and warrior and one of the most influential Druids. He worked for the Seelie King because he could foresee favorable days for warriors to go into battle. As far as I recall, he was a good man and faithful to the core teachings of Druidry. He was highly respected and prominent until Aneira came into power. His position as teacher and royal advisor was stripped from him. Druids fell out of favor and became Aneira's foes."

"And she killed them," Kennedy finished for him. Owen nodded. Kennedy's hands twisted together, and she looked at her pulsing veins. "So, my blood is blessed with a spell from the gods and goddesses? This is what lets me live longer and enables me to do magic?"

"Magic has always been in your ancestry, and the gods charmed your bloodline to carry through the generations. If you have children, no matter whom the father, they will be full Druids. The enchantment was to make sure the family's heritage would never become watered down, so to speak. It will not weaken, and in some cases, it could become stronger. The bloodline runs deep in your veins."

"The fact I can pick up on people's auras and feel extreme emotions is not because I am some kind of freak?"

"Well..." I tilted my head. Kennedy slapped my leg but burst out with a laugh. "You walked into that one."

"Yeah, I always do. You'd think if I had such great powers, I'd see those coming."

"Ahh, Ken, it's only because you are so sweet. Still hoping for the best out of me."

"You'd assume I would have given up a long time ago." She grinned.

"Wow. She becomes a magical Druid and gets all sassy?" I feigned hurt. I could sense her calming down, relaxing as we joked, exactly what I'd hoped for. We were us—Kennedy and Ember—still teasing each other. Not a Druid and a Dae with Otherworld abilities.

"But, if I have these skills, why haven't they come out before?"

19

"Like Fae, you don't fully acquire your powers until you come of age, which is around eighteen. Also, you weren't raised in the Druid life. From birth, Druids of old were taught and trained in magic. You should be showing some signs of your magic by now. At first I thought it might have been some spell your parents placed on you. They wanted you to blend and hide among the humans. But I don't sense an enchantment on you. I think it is just you impeding them. You were raised not to believe in magic, and the force of the mind is a strong blockade. I hope since you are now aware of what you are, your powers will come out." Cole shifted back in his chair. "You need to be trained. High Druids are taught for years in one particular art. We don't have this kind of time, so we will be doing a crash-course starting tomorrow."

"Whoa. Wait." I stood. "She has not agreed to this. Unlike me, I want Kennedy to have a choice in what she does. This is her life."

"She can never go back to her old life," Cole argued. "We are lucky she has not been discovered. Eventually, the Queen would notice, and Kennedy would be killed."

"I'm not saying she can go back home. I'm saying she has a right to choose if she wants to be involved with this. To be your guinea pig. At least tell her why you are asking this of her."

Cole clasped his hands, leaning forward. "Kennedy, we were exiled from the Otherworld by the Queen twenty-two years ago. Before she killed what she thought was the last Druids, she had one create the hex banning us. Only a Druid can undo a Draoidh curse. Until you, we never believed there might be one alive to break it. Aneira is torturing your friends and one of our own. We want to be able to get them out. We can only do this if we can get into the Otherworld."

My protective mama bear stirred. "Shit! Can you pull on any more heartstrings there? Tell her what kind of danger you're putting her in."

A hand touched my arm. "I want to do this. Like you, I always knew deep down I didn't fit in. This is who I'm supposed to be. And if I can help them get back to their home and free Ryan and Mark, I'm willing to do anything"

Damn, this girl has such a good heart. Why in the hell did she become friends with me?

Her fierce loyalty to her friends matched mine, so I had no doubt Kennedy would choose to help. My protectiveness still wanted her to have a say. She had a right to decide on her life and not be told what it was going to be. Kennedy and I were so different in some aspects of our personality, but so similar in others. Our love and dedication for family—those of blood or choice—knew no bounds.

I was also impressed how well she was taking this. I hadn't accepted my revelation with as much grace. I had thrown up on the floor. Oh, yeah, baby... that was how I rolled. I was the one who ran around like my hair was on fire throwing myself head first into things without thinking. But Kennedy was a facts person. First came knowledge, then she made a plan.

"When we begin your training tomorrow, we will start with the history and the basics of Druid magic." Cole stood, rubbing his legs. "I think we should take a little break as we could all use one."

A mumbling of consensus passed among the group. Kennedy headed for the door. I heard her tell Jared she needed a moment by herself. He nodded, but his eyes looked woeful as he watched her leave.

"Going for a hunt if anyone wants to join?" Cole stretched his arms as he left the room.

Hunt? A giddy reaction propelled me to take a few steps, following him.

"I do." Eli turned and glared at me. *Don't you dare follow*, his eyes said.

I stopped. As much as my Dark Dweller was pawing on the inside to go on a hunt, I didn't want to be anywhere near Eli. Plus, there was something else I needed to do.

THREE

Seeking solitude in the depths of the forest, I headed out into the warm, evening air. The rich, comforting smells of pine and redwood reduced my worry. Torin had been constantly on my mind, and I wanted to contact him again. The last time I saw him, he was being hauled off on the Queen's order in retribution because he secretly helped me. We weren't as covert as we thought. The Queen was aware of our connection and relationship. Her preferred method of discipline was abuse. She thought of Torin as "hers." Not only did he desire someone else, but betrayed and lied to her for that person. Disgust rooted around in my stomach at what was probably happening to him. Torin had insinuated she mentally and sexually liked to punish him. I could only imagine the sadistic torture she was doing to him. I massaged my temples, feeling bile mounting in my throat.

I slipped down a tree truck and anchored myself. Closing my eyes, I concentrated and called for him. With Torin, even when he couldn't answer me, I always felt him there—as energy, like a life line. Since the Queen had taken him away, I had felt nothing but a cold, dead line.

My feelings for him had always been complicated and strange, and I knew I couldn't take it if he were dead. I would feel empty, and it would always torment me. Guilt would weigh heavy on my heart because he saved me from the Queen. I could not lose him.

"Please, Torin, please don't be dead. All I need is to know you're alive. Give me something, please."

"Is your boyfriend ignoring you, again?" Eli came through the trees.

I grunted a sigh, standing up again. "You really like stalking me, don't you? Is it a cat thing?"

"I am not a freakin' cat." He scowled.

Scoffing, I leaned my head back on the tree.

"I love that you make fun of the exact thing you are now."

I frowned and replied, "My being part Dark Dweller wasn't by choice."

"It was obviously a stupid one of mine."

"Screw you."

"Again?"

Clenching my jaw and fists, I grumbled, "What do you want? Get to the point or get away from me. We seem to have this same conversation over and over anyway. Why not tape one and put it on a loop because I am sick of this shit. Aren't you?" I demanded. "It is so old. You've been nothing but an ass from the day I met you. But since I've been gone, you have discovered a whole new level and grown into an even bigger one."

"I'd like to think I never stop learning and growing."

I was about to go at him with a steamroller of curse words when I stopped. He liked baiting people. He was rattling me, and I was letting him.

Taking a deep breath, I clasped my hands together to stop them from trembling. I smiled up at him, instead. He frowned as though in surprise, and then the confusion turned to fury. His face tightened. I turned the tables on him with one gesture. With a smile. Now that's talent.

He shuffled his feet across the dirt and looked away. "I came here to say that if you are going to dreamscape or dreamwalk with Fairy boy leave me out of it. I don't like forced fieldtrips, especially ones where I'm the third wheel. Usually I'm not standing on the sidelines in a threesome."

Breathe, Ember, breathe, I repeated to myself. "Since you couldn't even handle me, I'm thinking those girls got the short end of the stick. In more ways than one." There were a lot of things I could say about Eli, but being "un-gifted," small, or not talented in bed were not any of them. Still, hitting below the belt made me feel better because, if anything pissed him off, it was a hit to his over-confident ego.

A guttural growl originated from the depths of his throat. "I seemed to remember handling you effortlessly, multiple times. Can you say the same?"

"We girls are good at faking it."

His eyes flickered red, and his pupils elongated. I felt mine mirroring his. My Dark Dweller responded to his, amplifying the already charged air between us. The impulse to take him down, tearing off his clothes as I went, was almost overpowering. The need for sex, for him, rattled my brain. Neither of us moved, both breathing in and out heavily. If I moved, I would not be able to stop myself, which would be a bad idea... really bad. Right? I almost stopped caring when I saw his eyes blaze hotter with desire.

Then he transformed.

I jumped back, startled by this swift change. "What the hell?"

I had seen him fully shift in front of me once when he was protecting me from a blood-thirsty Strighoul. It was fascinating both then and now, as his body burst from his clothes and carved into a sleek, beautiful, and frightening creature. The fur was so black his outline blended with the night. Only his flaming red eyes were visible. He was made for killing, to sneak up on his prey and assassinate them undetected. There was no escaping a Dark Dweller. The moment a victim saw those red eyes, death was only moments away.

Instead of scaring me, it only intrigued me. The razor-sharp bones lining his back reflected the moonlight. They looked like shark's teeth. If you fell on them, you would be sliced in half. Eli's beast-head jerked to the right, sniffing the air. The red blaze in his eyes went green. Dark Dwellers' eyes only turned red when they were at their most primitive. This was either when they were about to kill someone or when they got really, really horny.

Even though I was part Dark Dweller, I would never be able to turn into this form. But I had some of their abilities: my pupils shifted and my senses heightened. I also had Dark Dweller instincts to kill and hunt.

He grunted, and his large sickled claws tore off the last bit of his clothing before he headed in the direction he had been sniffing.

"What? What is it?" I asked.

Though he couldn't use words, it didn't stop us from communicating. We had this strange ability to transmit our thoughts without talking. Even before receiving his blood, we were able to convey what we were thinking through our eyes. It wasn't like I could hear his voice in my head as I could with Torin but more like I understood what Eli was thinking. Unlike Torin, Eli had to be looking at me for it to work. In Dark Dweller form, it only seemed to be enhanced.

I smell Lorcan.

What? Are you sure? I thought he couldn't get in here? I inhaled deeply. It was slight, but I did smell a familiar odor. Eli's senses were way more developed than mine.

He can't, but he is close, and he's not alone. Samantha is with him.

24

The growl coming from my throat shocked even me. My hatred for Samantha overshadowed even my loathing of Lorcan. She had killed my friend, Ian, by coldly slicing his throat in front of me just because she was jealous over Eli. My revenge burrowed deep; I needed her blood.

Eli took off through the brush. His journey was a lot more silent than mine as we headed for the property line. To humans I would be nearly undetectable, but to a Dark Dweller, I probably sounded like a herd of elephants.

I felt the magic of the spell come upon me. Warmth pulsated over my skin like a heartbeat, and I knew the property line was close. The silhouettes of three figures stood on the other side of the line. My eyes took in what was in front of me, but it required a little longer for my brain to really grasp it.

"Kennedy!"

Lorcan's hand firmly gripped Kennedy's throat. His usual smug smile was plastered on his face. He was shorter than Eli but had the same color eyes and hair. "Look what we found wandering all alone in the woods." Lorcan clicked his tongue at us. "You guys make it too easy."

"I'm sorry." Kennedy's eyes watered, fear etched on her face. "I needed some air and didn't realize I had crossed the line." Cole had warned us about boundaries. But because she stepped out, not in, the charm didn't go off to warn the Dark Dwellers.

"Oh, *Damnú air*! Shut up you whiny bitch." Samantha rolled her eyes. "All you humans are so irritating."

If I weren't so scared for Kennedy, I would have laughed. Samantha was the last one to talk about being whiny, bitchy, or irritating.

"Still, I think we might keep this one. She's a special one, aren't you?" Lorcan patted Kennedy on the head.

"Don't you dare hurt her." My muscles twitched. Even if I couldn't turn into a Dark Dweller, the desire to kill was still there.

"Hurt her? Now, why would I want to harm her?" Lorcan grinned. "I came here for you, Ember, but now I will be leaving with something even better."

Eli rumbled, his back hitching up in an attack stance, while he inched closer to the property edge.

"What are you doing here, Lorcan?" I asked. This wasn't the first time he had dropped in unannounced. He was opportunist and used his Dark Dweller stealth to unsettle the balance of power.

He ignored me and faced the midnight-colored beast next to me. "I am a little hurt you kept this from us. Thought we were family, Elighan. This changes everything. Our parents would be disappointed in the way you turned out. Picking a Dae over your own blood and now keeping a Druid from your family." He wiped his hand over his head, in the same way Eli always did when he was frustrated. Lorcan and Eli were brothers and were very different, but you could see the family resemblance in their habits and voice. It could be extremely disturbing. Lorcan was a good-looking guy, but all I could see was a twisted soul. Years of jealousy and anger evolved it into a dark mass of vindictive ugliness. "So as usual, little brother, you pick your dick over your family."

"At least he gets to choose. You are a dick. There is no getting away from that."

"Such a little spitfire, aren't you? Think I am starting to see what Eli sees in you... ahhh... nope, it's gone."

Samantha snorted.

"I have to admit I am surprised to see you here after what happened last time. I tell you your boyfriend killed your mother, and you still run back into his arms." Lorcan swept a hand between me and Eli. "Guess your standards are even lower than I imagined."

"As one of the Queen's lackeys, I'd think you would know I saved my very-much-alive mother from the Queen's dungeon."

"I am not exactly working with the Queen any—"

I kept talking. "You get off on doing shit like this. You're so jealous of your brother you want to hurt him any way you can. Do you get a hard-on by lying and manipulating? Is it the only thing you understand? You are sad and pathetic." I didn't stand firmly behind the sentiment that Lorcan had done it all for kicks. I knew something had happened between them and my mom. But my mother was alive, and Lorcan didn't need to know my doubts.

Lorcan's eyebrow rose. "Really? I'm the liar here? I won't deny I will sway someone to get what I want, but I've never lied to you. Why would I need to? The truth is so much more fun."

He had said many things the night he told me they killed my mother. And when he touched my tattoo, the pain we both had felt had been excruciating. Eli's contact had once been slightly painful, too, but nothing compared to Lorcan's. Since Eli had given me his blood, his touch no longer burned, and only caused a slight buzz. My tattoo was tied to them. Another mystery I needed to figure out. Right now, my priority was getting Kennedy away from Lorcan.

26

"How did you know I was here? I thought there was an enchantment to keep you from remembering this place?"

Lorcan scoffed. "I am smarter than all of them combined. I always have been. Don't look so nervous there, Emmy. I can't cross it, but I can always find my way back here. I made sure of that." I didn't know exactly what he meant, but I didn't doubt him. Lorcan was devious and smart. He would find a way.

"Cross the line, Ember. I dare you," Samantha taunted. "Don't you want to be reunited with your friend here? What was the name of the other stupid human I killed?"

A flash of Ian's goofy smile surged into my mind. I wanted her to pay. I took a step forward. Eli brushed against me, rumbling, and blocking me from Sam.

"Come on, now." Lorcan tugged Kennedy tighter into his body. "Can't we all be one big happy family?"

With a growl, I stepped around Eli. "You don't know the first thing about being a family. I think West would agree with that." Anger burned my words. "Or do you only call people family when they behave how you want them to?"

"Ember, should you really speak about family? When you did nothing to get your dear ol' dad out of the Otherworld? You left him and your other two friends there. Leaving the ones who weren't important? Is it really being a loving friend or daughter to only take the ones who would help you? You let the others die because you are too selfish to step up to the plate."

I snapped. My brain shut off to thought or reason, and I went for Lorcan. Samantha ran at me, cutting off my charge. Energy surged from me, my eyes narrowing. All my different powers wanted to explode out, but the Dark Dweller won.

Kill. Prey. Mine.

Eli moved with me. Not missing a beat, he went for Lorcan when Samantha came for me. Lorcan didn't even have time to transform before Eli ploughed him to the ground. Kennedy went flying through the air, hitting a tree. Her body went limp as she hit the earth, and I hoped she was only unconscious.

I dove into Samantha, and we both went skidding across the dirt. Samantha and I had fought before. Even with all my different magic elements, Samantha was still a match in a fight. She was quick and powerful, and she no longer held back like the first time. By the time I could get my abilities directed on her, she was already on me. My fists balled in retaliation, smashing into her face.

She growled, and her claws popped out, swinging toward me. The Dark Dweller in me responded. I'd been told when this happens, not only do my eyes turn black, but the pupils narrow into a diamond shape. I ducked, barreled into her legs, and knocked us both to the ground. She rolled me over, straddling me. Her arm went back, and her nails prepared to dig into my face.

My telekinetic powers threw her in the air, and her body cracked into a stone surface. She thrashed, spitting and twisting against my mind-hold on her. The strength with which she fought against my powers tired me. Not able to sustain her, she dropped to the ground. She got right up, heading for me once again. Even with my training, she could physically outfight me. She was born to kill, but my mind held her back from actually touching me.

"You bitch! Hiding behind your powers. Fight like the Dark Dweller you pretend to be."

"You think I am gonna play fair?" I laughed. "How little you know me, Sam. I will do anything to kill you."

She snarled, about to respond, when Cooper, Gabby, and Jared leaped from the forest, halting at the property line.

How did they know we were here? As I finished this thought, I remembered they had the ability to talk in each other's head like Torin and I did. Eli probably contacted them.

"Kennedy!" Jared screamed and hurled himself toward her. Cooper and Gabby leaped over the line. They kept in their human forms, but aspects of the Dark Dweller broke through. Their teeth grew long and dagger-like, and their nails became sharp and sickle-shaped.

"Back off, Lorcan." Cooper scowled.

Eli and Lorcan separated. Lorcan stood, rubbing blood from his chin.

I stepped away from Samantha, letting my power release her. She fell forward onto her face, but bounced up with her lip hooked in a snarl. Still, she didn't come after me. We had back-up now, and we outnumbered them.

Jared lifted Kennedy's tiny frame, cuddling her into his chest as he bounded for the property line.

"No!" Lorcan sprung toward Jared and paused at the ward. "Jared, stop. Don't you see this changes everything? I was only using the Queen to get what was rightfully ours. But the little Druid alters things. We can use her." He pointed to Kennedy. "You and I are family. Don't you want what is best for the family?"

"This has nothing to do with family. There is no 'we' in that sentence, only a 'you'." Jared turned away with Kennedy draped in his arms, then looked back. "Oh, and, Lorcan, go fuck yourself."

I couldn't hide my grin of satisfaction. Cooper and Gabby crossed back over the line and guarded Jared and Kennedy just in case Lorcan made a play for her.

"I second it." Eli's voice startled me. His arm went around my waist as he spoke to Lorcan, dragging me toward the ward line. He was in his human form and completely naked. This was something, no matter what was going on, you couldn't help but notice.

FOUR

We ran back to the house at full speed.

"Jared, take her into the cabin. Cooper, go get Owen," Eli directed. "Gabby, find Cole. I need to find pants." He continued to the house. All four of them turned in opposite directions. I followed the figure in Jared's arms. She was now awake, holding tightly onto Jared's neck. He burst through the door; light cascaded down the steps and illuminated the way for us.

"What the hell happened?" I heard my mother ask from inside the room. Springs from the bed creaked as she jumped up. Her outline dashed through the doorway, coming behind Jared to help him.

My feet hit the steps, and I plunged from the darkness into the bright room.

"I'm okay, Jared. You can put me down." Kennedy looked up at him.

Jared's face was set in stone. "You're getting checked. You might have a concussion," he insisted and placed her gently on the bed. Jared was not like the rest of his family. He was the only one born on Earth, and his mother had been human. Half Dark Dweller or not, when it came to being protective of what he considered "his", he became full-blooded.

"What's going on?" Mom looked at me. I was about to respond when Eli, Cole, and Owen clambered up the steps and entered the room. Both Cooper and Gabby were absent. They must have been ordered to stay out; otherwise, Gabby would have been there. Gabby sought out drama like a drug addict. She reveled in it.

"What happened?" Cole echoed. "Gabby wouldn't tell me anything except Kennedy might be hurt."

"I'm fine." Kennedy's small voice was nearly drowned out by everyone clucking around her.

"Eli, why didn't you contact me?" Cole bellowed.

Eli stretched to his full height. "I knew you were busy. I linked with Cooper who brought Gabby and Jared. But Lorcan didn't come to fight. He only came here with Sam. If he wanted to fight us, he would have come with the Queen's army. He wanted to show he could get to us."

Cole stepped closer. "I don't care. You should always call me. He had Kennedy and could have killed her not knowing how special she is. Worse, what if he found out *what* she was?"

Too late. Lorcan already knew, I thought.

"I am the Second. Trust I know what I am doing." Eli eyes flashed.

"Oh, now you want to be Second again? You have been absent from the position for three years. Your choices and decisions have almost exposed us. You have been a nightmare to deal with, unhinged, and erratic." He got into Eli's face. Cole was only six feet tall, but his Alpha authority made him appear taller. "And now you want me to trust you?"

Eli's jaw muscles strained. "Yes."

"Even though you almost put Kennedy and Ember in Lorcan's hands?"

"Everyone shut up." I yelled. "This is not the time to hash out grudges."

A hush came over the space.

"Owen?" I motioned toward Kennedy. He skirted the objects blocking his path and moved next to his patient. While he checked her, I herded the group to the other side of the room. "The rest of you come with me. We don't need your personal shit right now."

Cole and Eli both shuffled and looked away. Cole breathed out, his shoulders relaxing. "Okay, tell me exactly what happened."

"Lorcan happened," Eli puffed out, and the muscles in his face slackened with released tension. Eli and I explained, with Jared and Kennedy popping in with their additions to the story.

"Damn!" Cole scrubbed at his face. "We really didn't need him knowing about her. Aneira will be after her as well."

Eli's head moved back and forth. "I don't know if Lorcan will tell the Queen. At least not yet. I know how his brain works. He's an opportunist."

I rocked on the balls of my feet. "I kind of agree with Eli. Lorcan is not someone to trust, but he made it sound as if he wasn't working with the Queen anymore. He wanted Kennedy so he wouldn't need the Queen."

My mom gritted her teeth. "I don't trust anything coming from Lorcan's mouth."

"I don't either. We need to stay on guard; even if the Queen doesn't know, Lorcan does now. He'll be after her," Eli leaned back against the wall.

Cole agreed. "To be safe, let's run our boundaries. I want to be sure everything is secure and the spells aren't broken."

Eli immediately headed for the door, Cole behind him. Jared sat beside Kennedy, but he looked longingly at the door.

Kennedy placed her hand over Jared's. "I'm okay. Now please go. I want you to."

"No. I'm not leaving you." He pressed his mouth into a thin line, his eyes darting between the door and Kennedy.

"Go," Owen interjected. "She's fine and will be here when you get back."

Jared stood, leaned over to kiss Kennedy on the forehead, and ran out the door. Like me, he could never change into a full Dark Dweller but had the senses and traits of one. He tried his best to keep up with them.

Owen left soon after declaring his patient concussion-free and in good health. Mom went to into the shower to scrub the years of grime and torture from her skin. Knowing I stilled smelled of Eli, I was dying for one as well. It would have to wait; one of us needed to stay with Kennedy. Mom's shower was much more deserved, so I sat on Kennedy's bed, rolling my hair up into a loose bun.

"So, what's going to happen?" Kennedy brushed at the non-existent lint on her pants. "Now Lorcan knows about me."

Pulling my legs under me, I turned to face her. "Cole is still afraid Lorcan might use you as a bargaining chip with the Queen. Eli agrees but seems to think Lorcan will sit on this knowledge till he needs it. Lorcan *is* an opportunist, and he doesn't do anything unless it helps him. What's preventing him from eventually going to the Queen? We don't know. Either way, it doesn't matter. The information about you is out. You really aren't safe anymore."

Kennedy looked down and her fingers twisted around the material of her blanket. A heavy sigh rose from deep within her. "I think I understood from the moment Lorcan kidnapped us I would never be able to go back again. It was something I just knew, without realizing why. I understand more now why you stayed away from us. I don't want anything to happen to my family. My little sister, Hailey... God, I can't imagine if they hurt her. Or my parents." A tear rolled down her cheek. Removing her glasses, she wiped her face. "It kills me knowing I will never see them again."

"Never say never." I clasped her arm. "We don't know what the future will bring, but maybe you'll see them again."

A thin smile turned her lips up. "Thank you, Em, for being here. You don't know how comforting it is to have you by my side during this." Taking my hand in hers, she gave it a squeeze.

"Well, there's really nowhere else I'd rather be or actually am allowed to be." I grinned at her with my "you-know-you-love-me" smile.

She chuckled, but quickly stopped. "God, Ember, what are we going to do about Ryan? Leaving him there, so sick."

"I know. It almost broke me, too. We will get him out. I promise you I won't rest till we do."

She nodded, looking away, and blinked back tears. A little laugh came from her throat. "Who would have thought this would be our fate when we met in junior high?"

"I always knew we were meant for different things. Not sure fighting the Queen of the Otherworld and turning out to be part Demon and part Fairy were among my visions. I was thinking more like animal activists or studying abroad for a year."

Kennedy giggled. "Yeah, not in a thousand years did I think I was from a long, lost line of Druids."

"Well, sounds like in a thousand years you might still be around. Perhaps then you can come to terms with it." For some reason this hit us, and we both started laughing until tears leaked from our eyes.

"Holy cow. This is crazy." Kennedy wiped her eyes with the back of her hand.

"Welcome to my world." I gestured with my arms. We sat for a moment, regaining our composure. The water turned off in the next room; my mom had finished her shower.

Kennedy broke the silence. "Can I ask what's going on between you and Eli? I know he isn't known for his cheery disposition, but he seems like he is going to explode with anger. I could feel it. And it's mostly directed at you."

My eyes rolled up to the ceiling. "If I understood the conundrum which is Elighan Dragen, my life would be so much simpler."

"Yeah, he's a complicated one, even more than the others." She scooted back, leaning higher against the headboard. "So, give me a quick rundown of what has happened since we last saw each other, or at least the juicy stuff you don't want your mom to hear." She looked toward the bathroom door.

"Which would be everything having to do with Eli." I leaned on my elbows. I started in on what happened between Eli and me, brushing quickly past the sex part. But Kennedy got it. Her eyes widen even more when I told her what Lorcan had said about them killing my mom and the link to my tattoo.

"But he obviously didn't. Unless your mother is a ghost, she's alive."

"Yeah, I know. I don't understand any of it. And neither my mom nor Eli seems to be forthcoming with details. Oh, yeah, a warning: Fae are not good at telling you the full truth. Every Fae I've been in contact with tends to be extremely close-lipped. Even telling you a mundane thing about themselves or about Fae in general is like me trying to do math in my head. And you know how good I am at that."

"So nearly impossible." Kennedy smiled, patting my arm. "Funny you say that. You're not an open book either, you know. You have the same trait as well. Probably not as bad as them, but you tend to keep things hidden. Jared, too. He appears all talkative and open, but he's really not. He only me tells the basics of what I need to know."

It always took me off guard how insightful Kennedy could be. Since she now knew what she was, I was going to find it even more difficult to hide from her seer abilities. Playfully, I bumped her leg. "So, what's going on with *you* two?"

Kennedy didn't need to utter a word. The silly smile bursting from her reddening face told me everything I needed to know. "He's so young, though."

"So? He clearly adores you, and the two of you are adorable together. I watched you guys a few times when I dreamwalked. I kind of saw this coming."

Kennedy's eyebrows clenched together. "Watched us? What do you mean dreamwalked?"

Ah, right. "Forgot." I tapped my temple. "You don't know about my freaky abilities." I tried to explain dreamscaping and dreamwalking to Kennedy.

"Dreamscaping is pulling someone into a dream, usually only another Fay. But because of the blood we share, I can bring Eli into mine.

I can fully interact with the person. It feels just as real as when I'm awake. Dreamwalking is the ability, through a dream, to put myself in a place in real life and actual time. But I cannot be seen or interact with people while dreamwalking. I'm a ghost to them."

Kennedy's eyes widened. "Oh, my gosh. There were a few times I felt this strange chill over my skin like I was being watched. Of course, I brushed it off as me being paranoid."

I nodded. "You were feeling me. I saw you react when I would enter the room. I wondered if it was because you could somehow sense me there."

"I did. This is so crazy..." She shook her head. "You talk about Fairies and Fae. What is the difference?"

I used Cole's definitions to me when I had first asked. "F-a-e is a general term for everything in the Otherworld. F-a-y is type of pureblooded fairies. The Queen and her court are pure Fay." I reached out and touched her arm. "You okay?"

Her head bobbed slightly again before her forehead came down on my leg. "Yeah." Her voice came out shaky. "Taking all this in."

"I know this is a lot to deal with." I stroked her hair in a rhythmic motion. The brown silk sliding through my fingers. "If it helps, you're handling this better than I did."

Kennedy gave a small laugh before sitting up again. Her back straighter and stronger. Kennedy may be petite and quiet, but there was something about her which made you pay attention. She had a compelling inner force.

"Now you know what you are so you need to trust your instincts. I think you will come into your powers faster the more you let yourself go and don't try to block them."

"Right. My magical powers." She sighed, looking away. She pressed her lips together and turned back to me. "I am overwhelmed by all this, but..."

"It was like you knew before they told you."

Her eyes widened in agreement. "Yes, exactly." Her face turned serious. "I also always felt, even before I met you, I was waiting for you to show up. The day you came to our school there was a strange connection. There was no doubt I was supposed to know you, and our lives were going to be linked."

I had felt the same. That first day at lunch when I was by myself in the school cafeteria and this tiny thing boldly sat next to me with her friend, Ryan. It was like we were predestined to be in each other's lives. A Druid and a Dae, both orphans of the Otherworld... brought together.

"Okay, enough serious talk. You girls are bringing me down." Mom spoke from the doorway of the bathroom. Turning around, I was startled at the sight of her. She had lost so much weight and muscle, but she was still beautiful. The six years away had not aged her. To a Fae, it was barely a blip on the radar. Her face was striking and sweet. She looked so little standing there. My mother had always been petite, but her formerly curvy, toned frame was now thin from the years of being locked away. To see her standing in front of me again was surreal. I wanted to touch her to make sure she was real. I had always wished for this, but never imagined it possible.

My looks were even in more of a contrast to hers than usual. Being a Dae, I took on features of both my parents, but I favored my biological father—a Demon. I was tall and had jet-black hair with red streaks layered past the middle of my back. My eyes were large and prominent. One eye was a strange, bright yellow-green that illuminated like a cat's eye. The other eye was pale blue-lavender, outlined with electric dark blue and purple.

I was a freak both in the human and the Fae world.

Mom towel dried her hair. "I say tonight we catch up and have some girl-talk and gossip about boys. Tomorrow we can become serious again and get into all the heavy stuff. I think we've had enough for today. Tonight let's forget about everything. Okay?"

"Mom, I don't think talking about boys is the best use of our time. What about Mark and our friends?"

"Humor me. We can't do anything tonight, and I've lost six years of your life, of you growing up. I think Mark would want us to take an hour or two to catch up. Plus, Kennedy looks like if she doesn't get her mind off the hamster wheel, she is going to explode." Mom moved to the single bed next to us and plopped down. There was still a wall between us, but I couldn't ignore how good it was to be near her, laughing and being silly. This was the mother I remembered.

"I'm in." Kennedy sat up, twisting her frame to face my mom.

I nodded slowly. "All right, I'm in, too. But I warn you, Mom, talking boys with me might not be as fun as you think."

"You're right. I am not so blind I don't see there is something between you and Elighan." She grimaced. "Fine, current boy talk with you is off limits for tonight. Kennedy, on the other hand, isn't. I would

36

love to get to know you and hear all about my daughter's exploits since you met her."

I groaned.

Kennedy sat straighter with eager giddiness. "Oh, where do I start?"

"Before we go down that long, cringe-worthy road, who's up for raiding the kitchen? I know where there is peanut butter, extra crunchy." Funny how I told him to just leave me alone, and all I did was spend my time antagonizing him. Going after Eli's peanut butter? I couldn't be asking for it more.

"Peanut butter?" My mom groaned, and her face turned wistful. There wasn't any in the Otherworld. I doubted the Queen's minions gave Mom more than some kind of gruel. I could imagine how much she probably missed peanut butter and other Earth foods.

"Gabby always has cookie dough ice cream in the freezer, too." Kennedy and Mom both perked up. "Let's go, girls. We are invading a Dark Dweller's kitchen."

Several hours later, Kennedy and I took our well-deserved showers and were ready for sleep. All of us were now clothed in outfits I had left here last time I was a "guest." Both Ken and my mom swam in my clothes. My mom was only two inches taller than Kennedy but still short compared to me.

Finally, exhausted from the day and practically in a sugar/food coma from raiding the kitchen, we climbed into bed. I think I was asleep before my lids even closed.

"Torin? Oh, my god. Are you all right? I haven't been able to contact you." I stood up, wildly looking around the forest where he and I had met so many times before in our dreamwalks. *"Where are you?"*

My gaze fell on a huge outline.

"Sorry to let you down."

"Eli?"

"Wow, you got it on the first try."

Disappointment burst through me, not at seeing Eli but at not finding Torin. What was happening to him? Why couldn't I feel him anymore or dreamwalk with him? What had the Queen done? The fear I felt for him was palpable, almost crippling me. It was difficult for me to admit, but I missed our connection. I missed him coming to me. I missed him.

Eli shook his head. "Obviously, I am not who you were hoping for."

"I'm worried about him. I can't feel him at all, and I'm afraid of what the Queen is doing to him."

Eli snorted. "Nothing he hasn't done willingly before."

Resentment boiled in me at his statement. "You have no idea what you're talking about. You know nothing about Torin or what he's been through."

"I know enough."

I gripped my hands together tightly. "Ahhhh!" I gurgled in frustration. Torin had confessed his past with the Queen; most of it was not good or healthy. He had stuck it out with her in hopes of finding me. How could I turn my back on someone like him? Especially for a guy like Eli who strived to be an arrogant prick in life. "For once just shut up. I've only been back for a day, and already I've had enough of you."

"Then stop dragging me into your little nightly fantasies."

"I don't want to." I was frustrated and embarrassed I couldn't stop my unconscious from bringing him in. It made me feel exposed, vulnerable, and stupid, like some little girl who went all goo-goo over him and drew our names in a diary with hearts.

"You want me." He stepped closer to me, his body pressing to mine. "Completely understandable."

He was right. This angered me more than anything. My pride wanted me to come back guns blazing, but I didn't have it in me. Not anymore.

"I will try to learn to control my dreams, but till then you might have to put up with seeing me like this. My mother and I will leave the ranch tomorrow, and you'll no longer have to deal with me in your everyday life. Put us both out of our misery." I strode away from him. As soon as I spoke the words, I knew I was right. Mom didn't want to be here. She made it clear. Kennedy would need to stay; it was safer for her under the protection of the Dark Dwellers, and she'd want to remain near Jared. Mom and I would figure out how to survive. We could go to Lars. He would punish me for disobeying and breaking his contract. It was something I would eventually need to face anyway, but instinct told me Lars would protect me.

Eli moved swiftly to me. "You can't go. It's not safe."

I pulled back so I could look into his eyes. "It is not safe for me to stay. You and I are oil and water, and it's better if I leave. Don't deny you would be relieved. You don't want me here, and I don't want to stay."

His hand reached up like it was going to stop at my cheek, but he jerked it away to the stubble on his head. "Whatever we feel or don't feel, it can't get in the way of your safety. I won't have you leave and get killed or be taken by the Queen because we can't stand being near each other." His words were gruff and harsh. Bitter.

"Well, Dragen, it really isn't your decision."

"So, you'll risk your life to spite me, Brycin?" he snapped. "Damn it, woman, you are the most stubborn, obstinate creature I've ever met."

"Takes one to know one."

"Don't be reckless just to piss me off," he fumed.

"Piss you off is all I seem to do when I am here." I rubbed my forehead. "I can't win with you."

"Em—"

My hand flew up. "Stop talking before more stupid words come out of your mouth. I'm leaving in the morning, and that is final."

"But—"

"No! Not one more word." I backed away from him. Closing my lids, I demanded myself to wake up.

A familiar nauseating feeling came over me. When I opened my eyes, Eli was gone, but I wasn't back in my bed at the ranch. I was inside the walls of the Queen's castle. My unconscious once again dictated who it wanted to see.

"Dad!" I couldn't stop myself from screaming. He couldn't hear or see me, but my need to run to him wouldn't be stopped. He sat in a wooden chair next to Ryan's bed. His athletic body slumped forward. Dark circles surrounded his blue eyes. His silvering blond hair was disheveled and normally clean-shaven face covered with stubble.

Looking around the room, I realized he had been moved in with Ryan. But it was only Mark and Ryan. Where was Josh? What happened to him?

Mark pressed a damp cloth to Ryan's forehead. "When did he become this sick?" Mark addressed someone else in the room. Tearing my eyes away from the gloriousness of seeing my father alive, I noticed Castien leaning against the wall by the door.

"It was not long after they arrived here. Some humans are more sensitive to the transition from Earth to the Otherworld. Ryan appears to be one of those." Castien looked away from my father's direct stare. He shifted, defensively crossing his arms in front of his body.

Whether it was his shielding movement or his lack of eye contact, something didn't sit right with me. Mark obviously felt the same way. "Why don't I believe you?"

Castien looked away with a shrug. "Believe me or not." He fidgeted with the belt looping around his waist. "Whatever I have done was to protect Ryan. I only want him to be safe."

Mark sprang up. "What do you mean?" He took another few steps toward Castien. "This boy is like a son to me. I don't care what you are; I will find a way to hurt you if you harm this boy in any way."

A surge of pride filled me. Go, Dad.

"I saved him." Castien burst from his leaning position on the wall. Mark watched him, his fists still clenched, ready to take on this handsome Fay boy. "He was dying. Between the stress of his cousin's death and the trip between worlds, Ryan's system was slowly failing. I didn't want to see him perish. I did what I had to do to save him. I gave him Fae food to help him live. At first there is an opposite effect. It kills the human immune system before it rebuilds it. They get really sick before they get better."

My stomach gurgled with acid. I knew what this meant: Ryan would never be able to leave the Fae world. I felt guilt, fear, and anger. But I didn't know if it was more at myself for letting Ryan get into this mess or at Castien.

"So, he will be all right?"

"Yes, he actually has been showing small improvements. Ryan will be fine."

Mark plunked down on the bed next to Ryan's with a sigh. My father was unaware of what this really meant for Ryan. I, on the other hand, did not feel relief. I was so grateful Castien saved Ryan but at what cost? Ryan would never see his family, or go to college, or do any of the things he had planned. He had always dreamed about going to San Francisco after he graduated. Now this would never come to pass.

With the knowledge Ryan and Mark were okay, generally speaking, I focused again on Torin. Nothing. Not a good sign. I couldn't bear to think about what the Queen was doing to him, so I tried to find Josh. I could feel him. The connection to him buzzed with electricity and life. He was somewhere in the castle, alive. This was good at least, but for some reason, he was blocked from me. Frustrated, I slipped from my dreamwalk back into reality.

The instant my lids popped open, I was out of bed. Moonlight glinted through the tiny cabin windows, giving the room a spooky glow. Beams of light shone softly over Mom and Kennedy. I let them sleep. There was nothing they could do, and they had been through so much. Revealing what I'd learned would only add to their worries. Mom and I could leave when she woke up. I scratched a quick note telling her my idea and to come find me. *She was going to be thrilled when she reads this*. Since sleep was not going to be my friend, I headed to the place where I could take my aggressions out: the gym.

It wasn't my first choice, but my first choice was no longer an option. My preference required less clothing and slipping into bed with a certain Dark Dweller. My feelings for him constantly ran the gamut between hot and cold—mostly hot.

Dressed in my sweats and a tank top, my hair back in a ponytail, I stepped into the old garage, which had been fitted into a workout facility for the Dark Dwellers. Overstuffed punching bags dripped at different heights from the ceiling. Black, slick mats were on one side and training equipment sat on the other. I grabbed hand wraps from the shelf and went to work on a punching bag. My fears for Dad, Ryan, Josh, and Torin drove into the bag with every punch.

"Your form still is lacking," Eli's rumbling voice spoke from behind me. Without turning, I pressed my head into the bag with an aggravated grumble.

The heat of his body was instantly there as he moved behind me, grabbing my hand. "You are still tucking in your thumb." He curved my fingers in on themselves, placing my thumb over the top. "Now punch." I hit the bag with force. "I know it's uncomfortable, but it protects your fingers and does more damage to your opponent."

The warmth of his body next to mine was tormenting me. Turning to face him, I shifted to the side. "Thanks." My hands fumbled with the cloth tied around my hands. My gaze locked on them to avoid seeing Eli's tall, half-dressed body.

"No problem." He seemed to have no apprehension looking directly back at me. His green eyes glowed vibrantly.

Did he want to torture me? Was his ego so big he knew he could have me on the floor with just a glimpse of his bare chest? Anger took root in my body. I switched my weight between my legs. "Did you want something? Because it would be nice if I could get five minutes without you in my head."

41

Eli's jaw clenched. "Are you still planning on leaving?"

I nodded. "As soon as it's light, Mom and I will be out of your way." I no longer felt as attached to this idea as I had earlier, but there was no way I was backing out of it. Putting space between us was probably the smartest thing I could do.

As Eli stepped up closer, I moved back into the bag, regaining the little space we had between us. A feral smile twisted the side of his mouth. It sent shudders through me. Good or bad I didn't know. There was something even more unstable about him since I returned. Like sanity was something he only dabbled in when he felt like it.

"We'll see." He reached up and touched a strand of my hair, which had slipped out of my ponytail, tucking it behind my ear. He leaned in. His breath brushed against my neck. Against my will, my lids drifted shut as his lips grazed my ear.

A crazed laugh came out of him. My lashes flew up to him standing back watching me. A strange tortured expression on his face. He backed up toward the door. "Have a good workout, Brycin."

And he was gone.

I stood there shaking the hot and cold chills from my skin.

FIVE

I spent the next several hours in the gym, trying to get my thoughts and feelings on the same page. It was barely dawn when another body entered.

"You are not leaving, Ember," Cole stated firmly.

I punched the bag hard. "Eli tattled on me, I guess."

"I am the First. He was conveying information to his leader he thought I needed to know."

"He snitched." I slammed my fist into the bag again.

"Ember, turn around," Cole commanded. When I wasn't in my Dark Dweller mode, they actually had no control over me. Or I liked to believe that. But Cole still possessed power to force me do as he asked.

I stopped. My lungs heaved from exertion. Sweat slid in trails down my face. Begrudgingly, I turned to face him. I knew why he wanted me to look at him. His authority was rooted in his eyes. With my Dark Dweller blood, I would bow to his authority.

Damn Dark Dwellers!

"Look at me, Ember."

I huffed, crossing my arms, looking down at the mat and to the side before finally landing on him. I felt the weight of his dominance instantly.

"You are being foolish and immature. You and Eli need to deal with your problems. Work them out because you are not leaving here. I need you both. There is a war, and I need my strongest players in their top form. I don't really want to know what happened between you two, and as much as you both can drive me crazy, you are stronger together. You are a powerful team." Cole's gaze on me softened. "He has not been the same since you disappeared. I need my Second back, Ember."

My chest constricted. It was rare for Dark Dwellers to ask for help, and here was their leader asking for mine.

"Are we agreed? You'll stay?"

I knew better than to think he was giving me an option. Logic told me he was right. When had I ever listened to logic before? Yet, I found myself nodding. "Yes."

"Thank you," Cole responded and left the room.

Frustration slipped back under my skin as soon as he left. I had made my decision. I wanted to leave, but Eli blocked my way. He didn't seem to want me around, so why wasn't he letting me go? Even when I knew Cole was right, and I had to stay, I still didn't like someone snitching on me. I felt stupid and childish.

I tore the wrappings off my hands and wrists. Cole wanted me to deal with my shit. I was gonna start with my number one problem. My feet stomped into the dry dirt, clouds of dust puffing up as I headed for the house.

"You ratted me out?"

I stormed into the kitchen. Eli was staring at his empty jar of peanut butter, as if willing it to refill itself. A grin of satisfaction grew on my mouth.

Cooper and Gabby stood by the toaster fighting over who got to put bread in next.

"Did you do this?" Eli lifted up the jar. I smiled sweetly. His fists clamped on the plastic container, crushing it.

"Sorry. Do you want me to tremble or swoon?" I folded my arms.

He smashed the jar into the table. "I am Second here. I have duties and responsibilities. I was not going to let you leave without discussing it with my First. We both decided it was an asinine idea." He growled deeply.

"You decided? This is *my* life. Anyway, from what I've heard of you lately, you haven't cared much about rules or responsibility. Why start now?" I slammed my hand on the counter. Mimicking Eli's frustration. Cooper turned to look at me. Gabby took advantage of his distraction, shoved her bread in the toaster, and then set her attention eagerly upon the drama.

"Well, you make stupid decisions. You should not be trusted with making any choices when it comes to men, your safety, or pretty much anything else."

The room filled with energy. The lights flickered. "Why? Because they don't match yours?"

"Exactly."

"Well, the 'men' thing you might be right about. I *do* make stupid decisions." Aggravation thumped in my ears. I had trained for so long to control my powers, to not let them rule me, but when I was around Eli, my restraint went to hell.

"Fairy boy will be so hurt."

Magic slipped from my hold saturating the room. Every light surged, popping with the overload of my power.

"*Fairy boy* was the only one I got right."

Eli's eyes flashed, narrowing. "You'll have to share him with the Queen. Heard she likes threesomes and rough sex parties." The arrow shot right to the center of my weak spot.

There was a high-pitched whine from the toaster before it erupted. Flames lashed out, licking the bottom of the cupboard.

"Whoa." Cooper and Gabby jumped back.

Within seconds, the toaster full of bread exploded. With a loud crack, plastic, bits of metal, and chunks of fiery toast took off in every direction. All of us ducked as burning particles of bread flew at our heads. Pieces of the toaster hit different sides of the room, falling to the floor.

"Breakfast is ready." Cooper yelled as the commotion died down. "Gabby, you like it well-done, right?"

"Enough," Gabby screeched. Her anger catapulted between me and Eli. "Both. Of. You. Follow. Me. *Now*!" she demanded, walking out of the kitchen.

Neither Eli nor I moved.

"You better follow her. She's mad," Cooper said. "I wouldn't mess with her when she's this pissed and didn't get her breakfast."

Eli heaved in air, gave a slight nod of agreement, and started to follow Gabby out of the house. He turned back to me. "Are you coming? I am not the only one getting yelled at." With a grunt I resentfully followed.

Eli and I trailed behind Gabby to the cabin like disobedient kids about to get a spanking. *Mommy was mad.*

"You two, in here." She opened the door of the cabin motioning for us to go in before her. Passing her with my head held low, I stepped into the room after Eli. The door shut with a slam the moment I crossed the threshold. Both Mom and Kennedy were gone. Their beds were made, but my bedding was a twisted heap trailing down onto the floor.

"What the..." I whirled. Wood sliding across the porch could be heard before there was another clatter against the frame.

"What are you doing, Gabby?" Eli rushed up to the door.

"Locking you in," Gabby responded matter-of-factly through the door.

"What? Why?" I moved in next to Eli.

"Because I am sick of your shit."

"Gabby, open the damn door." Eli's fist pounded on the wood.

"Nope," Gabby countered. "Eli, you've always been a pain the ass, but since *she* disappeared, you have fallen off the tolerable boat."

"Gabrielle..." He yelled her name with a dangerous warning.

"Whine all you want, but I am not letting you out until you deal with your shit. I am not the only one who feels this way. I am the only one with the guts to do something about it. We've all had enough of this unrelenting asshole side of you. Coming from us this is saying a lot, Eli. Think about it."

A growl erupted from him.

"Why do I deserve this?" I banged on the door.

"Because you're the problem and the solution," Gabby answered. "So, until there is some sort of progress, I am going to sit outside this door making sure neither of you tries to escape."

Eli leaned his forehead against the door. "I swear, if you don't open this door right now..."

"You'll what?" Gabby retaliated. "Be a dick to me? For the last three years I've been about an inch away from taking you out. Don't cause me to regret I didn't."

"You know I can tear this place down before you could even get out of the chair."

"And you know I'll find another place or another way to lock you up. Don't threaten me, Eli. Don't unleash my true bitch. You know how unpleasant things can get."

This is Gabby's good side? Remind me not to truly piss her off.

Letting air out of my lungs, I leaned against the wall next to the door. "She's just as stubborn as you."

With a gruff laugh, Eli's head turned to me. "Hello, pot, meet kettle..."

My eyes narrowed. "What the hell is your deal anyway? You've been nothing but a complete ass since I've come back. You act like you want me to disappear again. I was giving you your wish, and you blocked me. I thought you'd be thrilled."

"As much as I may want it, you are not leaving here."

"What did I do to you? It's me who should be mad at you. I should detest the sight of you. Not the other way around."

He pushed himself off the door and stepped back, crossing his arms defensively.

"You're the one who had sex with me and then led me to believe you killed my mother." Suddenly, the anger, confusion, and embarrassment I had pushed away were back on the surface, sparking under my skin.

Control, Ember, stay in control.

Eli's jaw set firmly, rage simmering close to the surface, too.

"Answer me. Why would you let me believe it? Why did you say you killed her?"

"I never said I did. Lorcan said it. And you had no trouble believing him."

Blinding wrath came out of my body, blowing out the few lights in the room and dimming the cabin. Neither one of us flinched as glass shards scattered over us, eyes still secured on each other. My heightened senses made it easy to feel his conflicting emotions engulfing the room: the violence, resentment, anger, and even fear. Mine only collided against his.

"You sure didn't deny it." My body strained to keep my emotions in check.

"And what made you think you could go into the Otherworld and face the Queen? You are rash and careless. Did you temporarily lose all logic and thought in that brain of yours? Do you know how stupid it was? Seriously, did you think at all?"

My teeth clenched. Control was slipping from me, emotion taking over. I stepped closer to him. "I don't remember ever needing your opinion or approval. I don't care how stupid you think it was. I didn't do it for you. I did it for my friends and family."

"But you could have been killed. You could have gotten them killed. It is pure luck any of you made it out alive. How would you have felt if you would have gotten Kennedy killed? Or Jared?" His arms dropped to his sides, his fists remained balled, his face etched with fury.

"Ah, so the real truth comes out. I understand Jared, but be honest, your concern is not for me but for Kennedy," I spit back. "That's what you really care about. You would have lost your Druid, your way back into your precious Otherworld, since I am no longer a trading commodity to the Unseelie King."

Eli's chest puffed up with rage. His eyes flamed red, turning into their Dark Dweller state. Energy suffocated the room, choking me. A snarl emitted from deep within him. Eli trembled as his muscles tightened his body.

47

"Shit. Am I gonna have to come in there and referee so you don't kill each other?" Gabby yelled. Eli's anger clearly could be felt on the other side of the door as well. As violent as Dark Dwellers were, I knew he would never intentionally hurt me. Also, I wasn't some delicate little girl; I could fight and hurt back.

"This has nothing to do with Kennedy." His voice strained as he tried to regain control. "This has to do with you." Eli took in a deep breath, roughly rubbing the stubble on his head. "*Ciach Ort!* Have you any idea what I went through when you disappeared?" His tone was harsh and defensive. "I couldn't feel you," he whispered hoarsely and turned away. "I searched everywhere, thinking maybe you were only out of range, that if I went a little farther, I'd be able to feel you. I never did. Hoping you were still alive, I went crazy trying to find you."

There was a loud snort from the other side of the door.

Ignoring Gabby, Eli went on. "I've been on Earth for twenty-two human years now, but nothing felt longer than those three years."

Moisture had evaporated from my mouth. My throat constricted as I tried to swallow. No words formed on my tongue.

In a flash his somber mood turned volatile. His hands wrapped around my biceps as he stepped closer, fingers digging into my skin. "Don't you ever do it again."

My response was automatic. I've never done well with authority. "I can do whatever the hell I want. You have no say." I tried to tug out of his grip to no avail.

"Oh, I have a say when you are doing foolish shit." He tightened his grip, his breath heavy.

My body became even stiffer. "No, you don't. I may be part Dark Dweller, but you cannot command me. I am not something you can control. My choices and actions are my own."

"Damn it!" Eli roared. "Do you have any self-preservation? Any idea with one word or signal from the Queen you and your family would be dead right now? Luck and two pixies are the only reasons you are standing here right now."

"So, I had nothing to do with the fact we're safe?" I screamed back. "You don't think maybe some of my skills and training are responsible for getting us out?" I didn't want to mention the only reason I was actually still alive was Torin had told the Queen I was part Dark Dweller. That knowledge had spared my life. But right now I felt too pissed to be honest.

He barked a short laugh, which only provoked my fury. Without warning, I cinched him closer, my leg hitching around the inside of his, and with a yank I tightened my leg, pulling it back. His feet came out from underneath him, making him land hard on his back, shaking the cabin walls. I leaped onto his chest, pulled the dagger out of my boot, and brought it to his throat.

"Let me ask you again." My words were measured. "Do you really think my skills had nothing to do with getting us out?" His eyes flared red again, but this time it was not from anger. "Don't ever doubt me again." I tilted my head. "If I can have you down on your back without even pulling from my powers, then give me a little more credit than it simply being luck."

"I knew you wanted me on my back again." Lust pulsated through his gaze, making the air grow thick. "Damn. That... that was hot."

I couldn't stop the smile forming on my lips. Just as quickly as I had him on his back, he pulled me down, and flipped me onto mine.

"This works for me, too." He crawled between my legs. His cocky smile thrust my pulse into overdrive. His gaze moved over me, causing me to become dizzy. We didn't move as yearning and desire saturated the room, weaving together so tightly it hurt. We hadn't really cleared anything up, but the need to have a heart-to-heart evaporated when he pressed closer to me.

I acted first. My head rocked forward and my lips crashed into his. With a groan, his hands came around the back of my head and pulled me in tighter. Kissing him felt like finding water in a desert after months. I couldn't stop the whimper of relief and happiness which escaped as I felt his tongue slide over my lips, into my mouth. Our lips were desperate and needy as we inhaled each other. Lust blocked out everything beyond each other. Our hands were already yanking at the clothes obstructing us from touching each other. My fingers tugged the hem of his shirt over his head. His inked lines wound over his shoulder, down his back, and over his butt. Seeing the curved Celtic lines again started my heart to thump faster. My greedy hands tried to consume him. He pulled off my tank in one swift movement. Our hands hungrily ran over bare skin. He was more fit than I remembered. His ass so taut I couldn't stop my hands from pushing their way underneath the jeans. Eli moaned softly, as he hastily tugged at the top of my sweatpants.

He suddenly halted. Before I could ask what was wrong, he yelled out, "You can go, Gabby."

Oh, right.

49

"Awww... it was finally getting good." She snickered, but I could hear the chair creak as she got up. Eli waited for a few more beats before turning back to me.

"Good call." I smiled.

"I'm sure she'll still be able to hear us anyway. We can get kind of loud," he teased.

"We are also capable of damaging property."

"Never liked the stuff in here anyway." Eli grinned; his lips and weight came down on me, laying me back on the ground. He kissed me so deeply everything in me turned to butter. Then he stood and pulled me with him. His arms gripped my bottom, picking me up. My legs wrapped around him as he carried me to the operating table.

"Now you're just getting kinky." I smiled against his lips as he placed me down. "Fulfilling your doctor fantasy?"

"It would be a nurse fantasy."

As I reached for the top of his jeans, he cupped my chin and forced me to look up into his face. His expression was serious. "As I said, don't ever do that to me again. All right?" His words were simple, but I knew they meant so much more. This was equivalent to him baring his soul, letting me see him vulnerable. All I could do was nod in response.

"I told you once I would follow you anywhere, and I meant it." Then his lips were back on mine. I tugged on the belt loops, bringing him in against me. His hands dropped from my face, and stopped at my exercise bra, which he stripped over my head and tossed to the side. His hands roamed over my bare skin, which set it on fire. With a tug, his jeans dropped to the floor. Of course he wore nothing under them. He kicked off his boots and stepped out of jeans without his lips leaving my body. He peeled my sweats over my hips and yanked them off. Only one tiny piece of fabric was now left between us. He climbed up on the table, laying me back. His skin pressed against mine and had every nerve tingling.

"Fuck, I've missed you," he mumbled, his lips and hands exploring every inch of me.

Reaching for my underwear, he once again paused. This time I also heard what had stopped him. The door to the cabin swung open. Mom, Kennedy, and Jared walked in. They paused in their tracks.

I closed my eyes and exhaled.

"Shit."

SIX

"What the *hell* is going on here?"

Nothing is scarier than a mother's fury, and I could feel my mom burning a hole into me; actually, it was boring into Eli's bare ass. I had to give him credit; he did not flinch or scamper off and hide like I wanted to. He stood up grabbed his pants and slipped quickly into them with an amused grin on his face. I wrapped my arms around my bare breasts and willed myself smaller.

Stop smiling. This is so not funny, my eyes said to his.

You're right... it's not funny... it's fuckin' hilarious. He chuckled under his breath.

If my mother doesn't kill you, I will. I shook my head, sliding off the table and grabbed any clothes within my grasp.

Kennedy mumbled apologies and was already half way out the door. Jared seemed caught between embarrassed and entertained. My mother was close to shooting fire out of her eyes.

"We will give you a moment, and then I want to have a few words with you." Rage coated every syllable my mother uttered. She curtly turned, grabbed Jared by the arm, and pulled him out with her to where Kennedy stood on the porch. Eli's eyes still ran over the last of my nakedness he could absorb.

"Crap, crap, crap," I repeated, tugging on what garments I could find.

"Like she didn't know."

"Thinking you know is one thing; seeing it is different. Especially when you're naked and on top of her daughter." A flush of humiliation heated my face.

"Awww, look your ears are turning red." Eli stood over me, his hand cupping the side of my face. He leaned down and kissed the tip of my ear.

51

My mother is right outside the door ready to murder us both. I looked up into his green eyes.

Let her. I am not afraid of your mother.

You should be.

You're the only who can scare the crap out of me. I can handle her.

Where do you think I learned it from? My eyebrow arched.

Mom banged her fist against the door. "Ember, you better be dressed because I am coming in." She only paused a brief moment before entering. I was relatively dressed... at least my sweatpants and tank were back on. Eli was only wearing his jeans, so he swiped his shirt off the floor and pulled it on as she entered.

Arms crossed, she settled herself in the middle of the room. "Elighan, I would like a word with my daughter."

Her commanding tone suddenly made me feel like a kid again. I gulped the panic in my stomach back down.

Eli turned to me. *You're right; she is scary.* He winked before maneuvering his large frame around my tiny mother, who stood like an unmovable boulder, and left me. The sound of the door closing behind him made me wish I could follow.

Don't leave me.

When Mom spoke, it was in the overly-calm, controlled voice which scared me more than if she yelled. "I knew I would have to deal with you having sex with boys, but I will admit not even I imagined you'd be with a Dark Dweller." Her lips turned white as they pressed together. "I don't want you seeing him anymore."

"Excuse me?"

"He is dangerous, and I mean it in the most extreme sense. Elighan is not someone you should be near. You don't know how shady and terrible Dark Dwellers are."

"I'm sorry, but are you telling me who I can and cannot see? The woman who disappeared, who lied to me all my life, who I thought was dead for the last seven years of my life? Really, you are going to stand there and tell me what to do?" I yelled. "What I'm doing with Eli is none of your business. You are a little late for the birds and bees talk. Your daughter isn't a little girl anymore. I haven't been for a long time. I'm an adult and capable of making my own decisions."

"This is what you call making a grown-up decision?" she shrieked. "I'm sorry I wasn't there for you during those years. You don't know how much I regret the time I lost with you, but you will always be my daughter, and I will always want to protect you." The stubbornness in her tone matched my own. "The Dark Dwellers are soulless killers. You do not want to be involved with them. I'm saying this because I love you. Please, trust me on this."

"Trust you? Really? This is so incredibly ironic coming from you." Anger layered thickly in my chest. Needing to move, I went to grab the knife still on the floor from when I tackled Eli. "The Dark Dwellers are not what they used to be, and neither am I."

Mom shifted, keeping me in her sight. "Believe me they are, and they've done terrible things in the past. You need to believe me on this."

"No. Tell me what you know besides what you remember of them in the Otherworld? I already know they were mercenary killers. Is there more to it?" The words fell out of my mouth in a storm of resentment. The two bulbs that still remained intact flickered with my impatience. I took in a lungful of air, trying to compose myself.

Mom's jaw clenched, her eyes looking away.

"Okay, so tell me," I demanded. "You obviously knew them or interacted with them in the Otherworld. Am I wrong?"

"No, you are not wrong." Her finger twisted at the empty spot where her wedding ring used to be.

I could see her debating on opening up to me. She was still hiding things from me. "Mom?"

A crease shot across my mother's forehead before she shook her head slightly. "I understand you are mad. But don't let your anger at me cause you to make reckless decisions."

For some reason this only infuriated me more. A small, crazed laugh erupted from my lips. "This coming from the woman who, when I was three, dated the most wild and dodgy men she could find... any male with a bike between his legs. Guess I take after you more than I thought."

Her eyes narrowed. "This is different, and you know it."

"Is it?" I slammed the knife on the table. Suddenly, I was a teenager rebelling against my parents. "Don't tell me some of those guys you went out with hadn't killed? The only difference is yours were human. Oh, right, not all of them were. You were married before, right? To a Fay who you cheated on with a Demon. Then you married Mark. Is it considered polygamy if you're married to two different species?" I threw out my arms as I churned with resentment. "Yeah, I should really listen to you. I love how you are criticizing my choices when yours have not been so stellar."

My mom gasped. "How do you know about Eris?"

"Eris? Was that his name?"

"Yes," she whispered.

"Did you love him? Did he know about the affair?" I had so many questions tumbling around in my head.

"He did find out about the affair. But it was not as if he wasn't having a string of his own." Every word she uttered looked painful and forced. "Before the betrothal, he was a nice man, or so we all thought. After the marriage, his true personality came out. He was a cruel and abusive man, and he married purely for the title and status."

I felt sick to my stomach. My mother's past was full of hidden secrets and heartbreaking memories. Still, I could not seem to get past my own anger. "Why didn't you tell me any of this? Why did I have to hear this from Lars? It's sad and slightly funny a Demon has been more honest with me than my own mother."

She flinched and took in a deep breath. "I did what I thought was right at the time. Don't judge me. I am your mother."

"Technically... but you haven't been my mother for seven years. Mark has been my mother and father. You have to earn the title," I bellowed. Her eyes filled, and she stepped away from, me, her face drawn and tired all of a sudden. Immediately, I felt guilty. "I'm so sorry. I didn't mean it."

She looked to the side, tears sliding down her cheeks. "Yes, you did, and you're right. I wasn't there for you." She gulped and brushed the salty drops from her face. "I still want you to be my little girl. I want to pretend I didn't miss all those years with you. But I did, and no apology in the world is going to get them back."

My stomach twisted. "No, it's not. But I know you did what you did to protect me." Picking up the knife again, I touched the metal, focusing on the intricate design etched on the blade. I shoved it back into the slot in my boot. "We can't just pick up off where we left off. Things are not so simple."

Mom's head bobbed. "I know. But I want to try. Get to know each other again."

"Yeah... that would be good."

"But first we need to get out of here. We need to find someplace safe. Away from them."

And there went those peaceful feelings that had begun to float down around me. "What?"

"Ember, we talked about this. I know you have feelings for Eli, but trust me. We need to get as far away from them as possible. I thought that was what you wanted as well? Or at least it was before this encounter with Elighan."

"It was. But I came to my senses."

"No. You were right the first time. We need to go."

"Go where?" I threw up my hands. Even though I had agreed last night to leave, now I wasn't sure if I would have gone through with it.

"Up north. I have connections in Canada. We can stay with them."

She'd been planning for this, waiting for me to say the word. The night before I might have left, but things were different today. Maybe I was being more honest with myself. I would have gone out of spite, even knowing I was being stupid. My stubbornness knew no bounds, but neither did my mother's. I could tell she'd made up her mind to go, despite of how dangerous it would be. It would take a lot to convince her otherwise.

"And then what? Aneira is not going to sit back. She will be coming for us. We are being hunted now. We wouldn't even reach Canada. Also, I need to be here for Kennedy and devise a plan to get Mark and Ryan out of the Otherworld. Did you forget about them?"

"Of course not. We can still plan to get Mark and Ryan out up there only without the Dark Dwellers."

"I know what I said in the note earlier. I was angry and not thinking clearly. We can't leave, and you know it."

"Maybe you're not thinking clearly now. Elighan has you wrapped around his finger."

My eyes contracted. "Don't. I am not some silly girl. I never have been. So don't turn me into something because it suits your argument." I sucked in a deep breath. "My stubbornness, which I inherited from *you*, did not let me see the obvious. They are one of the most powerful Fae to have on our side. Having them with us only helps. I am not leaving."

My mom's teeth gritted together. "If it wasn't for Elighan, would you be more willing to go?"

"It doesn't really matter because Eli *is* a part of this... a part of me."

"You may feel this way now, but—"

"No." I cut her off. "You don't get it. Stop making me feel like some daft, dreamy, teenage girl. When I say he is part of me, it is not hypothetical."

Mom's eyes locked on mine. "What do you mean?"

55

"I'm one of them." My arms folded over my chest. "Eli's blood runs in my veins. I am part Dark Dweller now. I won't leave him, and besides, it would be pointless. There isn't a place on Earth he wouldn't be able to find me."

Her head shook back and forth hastily. "It is not possible."

"Yeah, everyone keeps saying that, but here I am. Eli saved my life. I was dying, and Eli gave me his blood. I wouldn't have survived without it. Most thought I wouldn't survive with it, but I did. Owen thinks Daes respond differently to foreign blood. Our blood doesn't reject it but takes it on, molding it with our own."

"Owen's tested you? He knows this for sure?"

"Yes. He salivates every time he can get a needle near me. Last time he checked, I had thirteen strands of DNA. A normal Fae has around eight. I took on Dark Dweller DNA and made it my own. No one knows if this is a Dae-thing or me-thing because Daes keep ending up dead. No one I've talked to really understands or knows the full capability of a Dae," I explained. It felt strange to explain this to the woman who gave birth to me. I guess even having a Dae didn't make you knowledgeable of one. "Guess they didn't have a parenting book on Daes when you were pregnant with me, huh?"

Mom's mouth hung slack. Then she grimaced, looking away.

"Who was my father?" I pulled at my necklace. "Did he rape you?"

Mom's head jolted, looked toward me, and then turned away again. "I don't want to talk about this right now."

"You don't want to talk about it? Don't you think I have a right to know?"

Rubbing her temples, she sighed. "Yes, but not right now. Please, give me a little more time. Okay?"

My shoulders sunk, but I could see the pain on her face. "Yeah, okay."

"You were not conceived in rape. It was purely from love, but it is complicated. I will tell you the whole story... someday. I promise."

Nodding, I looked down at my boots. "So now what?"

"I don't know. This is all too much to take in." Mom looked as lost as I felt. "We'll stay for now."

The gully between us did not feel much narrower. So much divided us. Our once close, loving relationship strained under the weight of what our decisions and fate had dealt us.

SEVEN

Cole and Owen worked with Kennedy for most of the day. Jared was right next to her, also learning about the history of the Druids. I popped in to show my support, but after two hours of an in-depth history lesson, my mind went numb. I still hadn't told Kennedy about Ryan or my dreamwalk. It never felt like the right time to say: "Oh, by the way, our friend will never be able to come back to Earth's realm again." I would tell her; I would. Right then I wanted her to focus on what she could change. She had to concentrate on learning how to be a Druid.

Eli had disappeared after our little morning encounter. Subtly, or not so subtly, I searched the grounds for him.

It was a beautifully rare and extremely hot summer day in Olympia. Cooper stepped onto the porch of the ranch house, a mid-day beer in his hand. The squeaky screen door slammed behind him as he exited the house. "He's not here."

"Where did he go?" To pretend I wasn't looking for Eli seemed ludicrous.

"He's out on a job." Cooper took a swig of his beer. "Since I don't have a bike yet, and all the others are being used, the bastard took Gabby and left me behind."

"What do you mean a job?"

"We still have to survive here on Earth and earn money. We have to work."

The Dark Dwellers went by another name on Earth, the RODs—Riders of Darkness. They were a local motorcycle "club," which controlled Olympia and a lot of the northern coast line of Washington. They were feared by the average population and respected in the biking world. No doubt their Dark Fae aura helped people naturally fear them. At one time their club was larger, but with Lorcan taking some viable members, it had shrunk down to six. Jared didn't go with them yet, but the four large guys and one fierce girl still held a strong presence in Washington.

"What does this 'job' entail?" I stepped on to the porch and settled on the rail.

Cooper sat down on the rocking chair. "You think I'm gonna tell you?"

"Yeah, I do." I swiped the bottle from his hand and took a drink. Ugh. I hated beer. It tasted like skunk piss with week-old oatmeal added.

"Hey. Get your own." Cooper tried to grab it back.

"Nah. I don't actually like beer." I finished off the last swigs of his beer trying not to gag and handed it back to Cooper. "Now talk."

"Man, you are frustrating." He rocked back in the chair, chucking the empty bottle into the recycle bin to his right. I smiled. "But remember, I grew up with Gabby. No one can break me." He returned the smug smile back at me. "We have to get money, Ember, and it is better you don't know how we do it."

"Why? What do you guys do?" My stomach knotted. I had heard stories. A lot of different ones. I didn't want any of them to be true.

"We are Dark Fae. At one time we were hired assassins, mercenaries by nature, and we killed for a living. We don't do that anymore, which is all you need to know."

My mouth opened to argue. Then it closed. Something kept me from exploring this further. A part of me wanted to know, but most of me didn't. I knew it wouldn't make me happy. Eli and the rest of them had been in jail more times than I could count. But to hear the actual words come from Cooper's mouth could change things.

"If you keep hoping to see a nice, good side to us, you should walk away now. Eli is certainly not, and neither are the rest of us. This is us actually trying to be better. Leave it at that."

"I know, but..."

"No buts. We have to make money."

What did I expect? They were Dark Fae. Even worse, they were Dark Dwellers. Was I hoping they would act like good little human citizens? No, that wasn't their nature, but it still bothered me. I couldn't change them any more than they could change me. For better or worse, this was my family, and I would stick by them. I held my head, suddenly really tired.

"I need some water to wash this nasty taste out of my mouth." I slid off the rail and headed inside the house. Cooper nodded and watched me walk off.

The coolness of the indoors eased a bit of the tension, but suddenly I wanted to lie down. Even though I was technically sleeping in the infirmary cabin, I didn't want to go there. Mom would probably be nearby with an unhappy expression and biting comments about Dark Dwellers. I didn't need that right now, especially after my talk with Cooper. Without much thought, I slunk down the hallway toward Eli's room.

Knowing he was out, I slipped through the door unnoticed. I struggled to pull off my jeans since they clung to my skin, crusted with sweat and dirt. When I had grabbed clothes from my house awhile back, it had been cold. I hadn't packed summer items. Feeling like I had dropped ten degrees by being in my underwear and tank, I lay back on Eli's bed. His enticing smell had me curling deep into his pillow. I leaned across and switched on a fan. The cool air fluttered over my skin. My lids closed, and my muscles coveted the relaxation. It didn't take long before I fell into a deep sleep.

Bodies were lumped in piles across the burnt meadow. Ash and smoke hung heavily in the air. Blood soaked into the grass, dyeing it a rich shade of burgundy. The sight of carnage and the smell of charred flesh bore down on my stomach, making me retch. I had been here before. I had stood in this spot. This time there were more bodies and more blood. Death hung in the air, drenching it. The sky was spotted with burning fireballs, the line between the worlds melted into one. Soon there would be none.

"Ember, you have to stop this from happening." A voice spoke into my head. I whipped around, searching for the speaker. I recognized the hooded figure standing deep in the shadows. It was my mother. Even though she never showed her face, I knew. I could feel the unconditional love and connection between us.

"Mom?" I moved closer.

The nearer I got to her, the darkness seemed to close more tightly around us and shielded her even more from view. Her hand stretched out and gripped my hand painfully. "Find the sword, Ember." Her tone sounded desperate and pleading. "Don't let it fall into her control or all will be lost. This will be your future."

I knew she meant Aneira. It was the only thing I was sure of. The figure turned and walked away.

"*Wait!*" *I reached out to stop her. My fingers grasped for the fabric of her robe.* "*No, Mom, wait. How do I find the sword?*"

"*The answer is with you,*" *she said before dissipating, leaving me alone.*

Only the wails of people dying and distant sounds of battle could be heard.

A light knock on the door brought me out of my slumber. My head jerked up. I looked at the door, then over my shoulder. The early dawn light filtered over Eli sleeping next to me. He was sprawled on his back, and one hand lay protectively on my bare thigh. I hadn't heard him come in or felt him climb in next to me. I must have been tired if I slept through the rest of the day and night. The dream left a knot in my stomach. The more I reached to remember it, the more it evaded me.

Another set of taps rattled the door; the memory of the dream disappeared completely. Not wanting him to wake, I slipped out from under Eli's hand. He shifted and turned his head the other way but remained asleep. Adjusting my tank, I tiptoed for the door and cracked it open.

Cole stood on the other side, his expression impatient. "Ember, you need to come outside."

"Why? What's going on? What time is it?"

"Please, come." His tone conveyed this was not the time to argue or ask questions.

I looked over my shoulder at Eli. "Only you," he interjected. "I'll wait for you outside. Please hurry." Cole turned away briskly.

The pants I had been wearing were in a dirty ball on the floor; heat and time kept me from putting them back on. Instead, I reached for a pair of boxer shorts folded on top of Eli's dresser and hopped into them. They were big on me, but I didn't have time to worry about my fashion style. I slipped on my boots and ran outside to where Cole was anxiously waiting for me.

"What's going on?"

"You'll see." He motioned for me to follow him.

With me lagging behind, he headed toward the back end of their property. The sun was scarcely peeking over the mountains. We came to an open field, and in the distance I could see the tiny silhouettes of Simmons and Cal weaving through the air. It took me a moment to realize they weren't alone. Three human forms trailed slowly behind them: two men and a woman. One of the men was being held up by the other two. His arms were around their shoulders as he struggled to hobble forward.

My gaze narrowed on one. All the other worries on my mind instantly dissolved. "Torin," I screamed. My feet struck the dirt as I ran to him. He looked up, his face bloody and swollen. When he saw me, his legs gave out, and he crumbled to the ground.

I skidded to a stop in front of him, and the soil and rocks tore into my knees as I dropped. My hands automatically went to his face, picking up his head.

"Found you." Torin smiled dreamily. He was struggling to stay conscious. His body and face were battered so badly he could barely move or speak, and I could hardly make out his features. One eye was swollen completely shut, and the other only opened halfway.

My gaze flashed and took in the others.

"Oh, my god, Josh. Are you okay?" He was not someone I expected to see again, but I felt so happy I had been wrong. His familiar, sweet face peered down at me with sadness in his eyes. Josh had a split lip, a black eye, and a deep cut on his cheek. Fortunately, nothing that wouldn't heal.

"Yeah. I'm okay."

I recognized the woman on the other side of Torin. She was from the castle dungeon. The one who came up to me, confirming I was part Dark Dweller. It was the only reason the Queen had not killed me on the spot.

"I remember you."

"Yes. I am Thara." She spoke formally, her voice elegant and regal. "Do not fear. I am no longer with the Queen. I helped Torin escape. She would have killed him."

"Thank you." My hands still held Torin's head. He continued to slump further. He had been placed in this predicament and had been tortured by the Queen because of his attachment to me. Even though he was badly hurt, I felt overpowering relief he was away from her. Turning my attention back on Torin, my eyes really took in his condition.

"Dammit..." He was in bad shape.

"*Mo chuisle*," he mumbled. I could tell he had no sense of reality and was fluttering on the edge of consciousness and dreamland.

61

"What the fuck?" A deep voice spoke behind me. Turning, I saw Eli walking to us wearing only a pair of raggedy jeans.

"Simmons and Cal led them here," Cole said.

"We were on guard duty when we spotted them coming out of a door from the Otherworld. We came straight away to tell you, my lady. He stopped us," Simmons declared, pointing at Cole.

"Thank you, Simmons. You did the right thing. Cole was only doing his job as well." Simmons frowned but nodded to me.

There were so many things needing to be answered, but those could all wait. "Guys, we need to get him to the clinic now. Where is Owen?"

"I've already contacted him through our link. He will be waiting for us," Cole replied, grabbing Eli's shoulder and pulling him toward Torin.

Dark Dwellers and Fay were not friends. The term "adversaries" was putting it mildly. This showed even more so between Eli and Torin since they had more dislike for each other than the average Fay/Dark Dweller foes. This demonstration of concern between them was radical. Without question, Eli moved over to him, backing me out of the way. Torin's entire body had gone limp. With help from Cole, Eli flung Torin over his shoulder like a sack of potatoes. Torin groaned in pain, but stayed unconscious. I didn't care how he carried Torin since he wouldn't remember anything anyway. Eli paused in front of me, his eyes moving over my body, a smirk hooked up his lip. "Nice shorts. Think I'll want those back later." Eli turned and headed for the compound.

Already burning on the outside with the oncoming heat, my insides joined in. This was so not the appropriate time, but my hormones didn't seem to give a crap lately what was proper or not. I kept it to myself seeing him pick up and haul Torin to the cabin completely turned me on.

I act like such a girl sometimes.

Cal buzzed down to my ear, a bemused smile on his face and his gaze on Torin and Eli. "Oh, yeah, girlie, things suddenly got fun." He laughed and flew off. Simmons followed, both returning to their posts.

"Yeah, fun," I mumbled and turned to locate Josh.

He stood in the same exact spot; his eyebrows crunched together. He looked vulnerable and preoccupied.

"Hey, Josh. Are you okay?" I moved to him. His gaze lifted. His soft hazel eyes searched mine. The light breeze rumpled his already messy, sandy-blond hair. It was several moments before he nodded and opened his arms. I engulfed him in a hug. "You scared me. I thought I lost you. I am so happy you are here. That you came back."

"Yeah. Me, too," he replied and pulled away. "I think you need to tell me what's going on, and I mean everything."

"I know. I will explain it all. Later. Right now let's focus on you and Torin getting checked out. Make sure you're all right."

By the time Josh and I got to the cabin, Torin was already confined to a bed, still out cold. Owen was bent over him. Mom and Kennedy sat together on a bed still in their pajamas having been woken up by the entourage inundating their room. Cole stood at the end of the bed. Thara, on the other side of him, gripped his hand tightly. Eli leaned against the wall closest to the door; his attention was upon me as we entered.

"Josh." Eli nodded to him.

"Eli." Josh retorted and moved to the farthest wall away from him. Josh had never been a fan of Eli, out of fear or genuine dislike I didn't know. It looked like nothing had changed. Strange. With Josh's love of *World of War Craft* and the fantasy world, you'd think finding out Eli was one of the most feared and ruthless beasts in the Fae world he'd be in awe of him.

Shouldering my way through the crowd, I bee-lined it for the occupied bed. "Oh, Torin." It was still a shock to look at him. The swollen, misshaped face was not one I recognized. His torture was on my hands. "I am so sorry," I whispered hoarsely.

"He will heal." Owen patted my hand. "Slowly, but he will mend."

"You mean the visual wounds will heal." The knot in my throat made it hard to swallow. The room grew hot and constricting.

Owen tilted his head, remaining silent. He didn't want to say it. He was trying to be kind, but the truth was a boulder on my heart. I didn't know what the Queen had done to Torin. Knowing about his past with her and what she was capable of, it had to be awful, degrading, abusive, and painful. Both mentally and physically, she would be sure he felt the betrayal and transgression he caused her. How could he get over all this?

"He needs to rest." Owen hinted at everyone to leave. Only Owen, Thara, Eli, and I remained. My need to stay with him was overpowering. My muscles locked, pinning me in place. My heart and body could not leave his side.

"I will stay, too." Thara's words sounded like a challenge.

My eyes leveled at her, and I growled.

"Thara, I think you need rest and something to eat. He will be all right while you are gone." Owen motioned for her to follow him. She held my stare for a few seconds more and then nodded but watched me the entire time she walked to the door.

Eli still leaned against the wall. His expression held no sentiment, but his presence was loud and consuming. His eyes delved into mine, his jaw set. He thrust himself off the wall, turned and left the room without a word. He didn't need to. His cold, aloof expression told me everything. I ached to follow, but something kept me in place. Sliding a chair over, I sat down next to Torin. I placed his bruised, broken hand in mine. He let out a sigh, and his body relaxed further into the pillows.

EIGHT

Over the next twenty hours, I didn't leave Torin's side, even when they moved him into Dax's old room for more privacy. The infirmary cabin was getting full with Thara, Mom, Kennedy, and me sleeping there. Torin was placed in the room farthest from the other Dark Dwellers, which seemed the best idea. It was built to hold eleven Dark Dwellers. Now only six inhabited it.

Thara's dedication almost rivaled my own. Owen would get her to take breaks, to eat or rest, but he never could sway me. I would not leave him. The thought made something in me ache.

She had gone to take a quick nap an hour earlier, leaving me to sit vigil by his bedside. His swelling had gone down, but the cuts and bruises were slower to heal. For a Fay, his sluggish recovery was not normal, which only added to my concerns. How damaged was he on the inside that made it so slow for him to mend on the outside?

A figure moved beside me, reaching for Torin's wrist. Blurry-eyed, I glanced up at Owen.

"You really need to at least eat something, Ember." He frowned at me.

Refusing once again, I gripped Torin's hand tighter. A small groan floated from his lips. My head turned to him and back to Torin.

"Torin?" I jumped to my feet and reached to touch his face.

"*Mo chuisle*." The words barely made it to my ear. "Are you really here?" His lids fluttered but didn't open.

"Yes. I'm here," I squeaked.

A smile came to his lips, splitting the cuts on them. "I found you. I can now die fulfilled."

My heart clenched so hard it became hard to breathe. The thought of him dying sent daggers into my core. "You are not going to die." It

65

was more to myself than to him. It was an idea I refused to accept. He did not respond, his head falling heavier onto the pillow. Tears burned, choking my throat.

Owen touched my shoulder. "This will probably happen for a bit. While he is healing, his body will only be able to stay awake for tiny increments before it needs to replenish."

It was like a tsunami. Every moment of pain I caused him and the others careened into me all at once. The room began to teeter, and the floor moved under my feet. My knuckles turned white as I seized the bed sheets. My back arched forward, curling into itself. The walls closed in on me.

"Breathe, Ember. You are starting to hyperventilate." Owen pressed his hand gently onto my back.

"She needs some air and food." Another set of hands gripped my hips and pulled me toward the door. Eli escorted me into the morning air. *When did he come into the room?* I hadn't even noticed. How long had he been standing behind me? Listening?

The ranch was silent and in the deep hours of night. Dawn was still a couple hours away, but during summer this far north it always looked as if daybreak was right there waiting for its turn. Eli moved in front of me. His hands clutched the sides of my face. "Hey, look at me. Calm down."

"Oh, God. I did this to him. Me. I only destroy and hurt people..." Another wave of panic swept me along a long river of guilt. I gulped for air. So many things hit at the same time: emotions of my mom, of Mark and West being stuck in the Otherworld, of Ryan never able to leave, of all the people I killed in Seattle. Torin was another on the ever-growing list. It was all too much. Hot, blinding tears pushed past my defensive boundaries and spilled over the walls. I hated crying in front of people and, at one time, Eli would have been top of the list. Things had changed. He now seemed the only one I could show my true feelings to. I pressed my face into him and felt his arms surround me, holding me tightly against him.

"It will be okay." His voice vibrated through his chest against my ear.

"No, it won't." I shook my head, smearing my tears and runny nose over his chest. "Torin's been tortured. Mark and Ryan are still stuck there and along with West."

"Kennedy and Josh are back safe, Torin will heal, and Lily is with you again. We will get West, Mark, and Ryan out." He held me out to look at my face. "I promise."

Wiping at my nose, I shook my head. "Ryan will never be able to come back."

"What are you talking about?"

I hiccupped. "I was in a dreamwalk, Ryan was dying, and Castien gave him Fae food to save him." I didn't need to say more; Eli frowned. He knew what this meant.

He cupped my face and brushed the tears away with his thumbs. "Have you told anybody about this?"

"No." My head moved in concurrence. "Kennedy has been through so much, and she says saving Ryan keeps her going during the really hard moments. I can't take this away from her."

"You're going to have to tell her."

Sighing, I leaned into him. "I know. But not yet."

He lifted my head and kissed me deeply. At first his lips were comforting and sweet, but swiftly yearning soared through my veins. He took away all the pain. Some might say this was not the best time. I disagreed. I needed him—all of him—a shred of happiness in the darkness. His hands slid up the back of my head, and his fingers tangled in my hair. He pressed his lips harder into mine, and his tongue discovered every inch of mine. This time the lack of air into my lungs was purposeful. The need to be closer to him was crushing. He nipped at my lip, which undid me. I grabbed his hand, and with determination of a bull, dragged him to the house and down the hallway to his room.

With the door closed and locked, we turned and faced each other. Our breaths faltered as we moved in closer. My heart thudded against my ribs. He leaned in, and I could feel his proximity encompassing my skin. Desire became so thick I stopped breathing.

His finger skimmed my stomach as he followed the band of his boxers I wore. I sucked back on my bottom lip; my eyes closed at his touch. "I like those on you," he whispered in my ear. "But I'd like them even better off." He gave them a slight tug.

My fingers reached up to the top of his jeans, unbuttoning them. "Ditto."

With a deep growl, Eli picked me up and took me to the bed. We fell heavily on it as our lips ravaged each other. He slid in between my legs, and the friction of his movement against me made both of us grasp one another harder. I couldn't seem to get close enough to him. Panting and clawing, I squeezed my legs tighter around him. Feeling him hard against me propelled my adrenaline to pound in my ears. It drove me into dizzy spells, leaving my mind completely void of anything but the present moment. His lips moved down my neck, making me gasp. My hands tugged his pants over his hips and onto the floor. A rumble emerged from his chest as my hands ran back up over his tight, bare ass. He slipped a finger under the tank I had on and ripped it over my head and threw it aside. Our breathing was short and heavy. I sat up and pushed him down, crawling over him. His hands ran slowly up my body. I let my head fall back with desire, as the shudders of his touch sent tingles rapidly through me. He sat up and brought his mouth to my neck and chest. The warmness of his kisses made me moan.

I smiled wickedly and pushed him back down. I started at his neck and meticulously kissed and nipped slowly down his body, not missing an inch. There were some areas I paid extra attention to, my tongue dragging up the vein in his cock, before I took him into my mouth, sucking hard. Eli groaned, his hips arching, his fingers threading through my hair, pushing me down firmer.

"Fuck!" Eli continued to growl, which sounded more and more animalistic. He grabbed me, tossing me under him as his mouth devoured mine. The sounds of our deep breathing were the only noise in the room as we both touched and kissed each other's sweaty bodies. Ripping off my underwear, he rolled me over onto my stomach. His tongue glided all the way down my spine, parting me. I groaned, my nails digging into the sheets. His body pressed into the back of mine, his breath hot on my neck.

"Please." I begged. "Now." He granted my wish. Sliding my legs further apart, he pushed in deep. There was nothing else but him and me. Pulsating and pounding. Our energy bounced off each other and slammed into the walls, flickering the lights. The need for each other over took any foreplay.

The bed frame cracked against the wall as he nailed me to the bed, the sound of my cries and us together grew louder and louder as our tempo picked up.

"Eli!" My cry broke something in him. Spreading me fully open he pounded into me ruthlessly, dragging me back and forth over the bed, firing all my nerves endings.

"Oh god...harder!" I could feel my body starting to spasm, feel the vein I just was sucking on, pump with blood inside me. "Eli!" The fan above our heads sparked, raining down on us.

He sat up, pulling me with him, slamming deeper inside me.

I bellowed, my pussy clenching around him, the mirror over his dresser shattering into pieces.

"Fuck!" He rammed in even deeper two more times before his hot cum burned into me like a branding iron, spilling so much it poured down my thigh.

It took us a long time to come down, his heavy breath in my ear, his lips grazing my shoulder as he lowered us back down, still inside me.

"Fucking hell, Brycin," he muttered, pulling out of me, falling off me, turning onto his side to face me. We stared at each other. He reached out trailing his fingers through my hair and down my arm.

"Now I really need a shower," I was still panting, my head spinning. My muscles were trembling so bad, I doubted I could move.

"Good place to get you even more dirty." A leer hitched his lips. He rolled off the bed and stood, heading out of the room.

"Where are you going?"

He paused looking over his shoulder. "Thought you needed a shower?" He cocked his eyebrow. "You coming?"

"Um, yeah." Funny how fast I bounded out of the bed. "I'm all about saving water."

"I doubt we'll be saving water." His eyebrow went up mischievously.

"Eli, Ember? Torin is awake." Cooper pounded on the bathroom door. "Time to take a breather. Cole wants you to join us down the hall in five minutes."

Guilt weaved around my conscience. *How could I not be there when he woke up?* Torin had never fully left my mind, but Eli did an excellent job easing my tension and bringing me back from the edge. It did help knowing Thara was probably there.

"So much for saving water." Long ago the water had turned to ice, not that we cared. We had been in there so long everything on me started to prune.

"Told you." Eli mumbled against my lips and reached past me to shut off the spray of water. My tongue found his again, and his arms wrapped around me, kissing me till my toes curled. His hands trailed slowly over my skin.

The bathroom door thumped with knocking again.

"Not stupid enough to think you guys will come out the first time. I'm staying here till I actually see the door open," Cooper yelled through the barrier.

Eli pressed his forehead against mine with a sigh.

"We better go," I said as I watched droplets of water slide down Eli's face and over his lips.

"Yeah, don't force me have to come in there," Cooper shouted. "Actually, scratch what I said. I've seen Eli's bare ass enough, but Ember's would be a nice change."

"All right. All right. We'll be out in a minute," Eli yelled back and turned to me. "Not that you shouldn't show your ass off. It's an extremely nice ass." His hands moved over it.

Smiling, I kissed him once more, taking his hands into mine. "Come on. Cooper will have plenty of other opportunities to see my ass." I directed my words toward the other side of the door.

"You said plural, right? Like in more than once?" Cooper asked back.

"Go, Coop. We'll be there in a few minutes," Eli retorted back and pulled me out of the natural stone and slate shower.

"Five minutes," Cooper said and stomped away.

Eli threw me a clean towel. After I wrapped in it, we hurried back to his room. I slipped on Eli's boxers and a tank and smoothed my hair back into a ponytail. Eli threw on some jeans and a t-shirt and followed me out the bedroom.

The closer we got to Dax's old room, which was on the other side of the extended ranch house, the more my steps became rushed. It was packed. Almost everyone was there. Josh, Gabby, Kennedy and Jared were absent, but the others were stuffed into the small space—waiting for us.

Josh... shit! In my narrowed vision of Torin, I had forgotten about him. I still needed to talk to him and make sure he was all right. I didn't even know where he had been sleeping.

"About time," Cole declared. A blush of embarrassment heated my cheeks.

Mom hovered next to Torin's bed blocking him from view. At my entrance her eyes pierced into me. Disapproval, anger, and disgust darted from me to Eli.

"I'm gonna take a stab in the dark and say Mommy doesn't approve of me or the fact her sweet daughter is sleeping with me," Eli whispered in my ear.

"That would be an understatement," I scoffed, turning my face up to him. "But in no way would I be considered a sweet daughter."

"Not after what you just did. Didn't know you were so flexible. You owe me a new fan by the way."

I shoved him lightly. "Shut up."

"You two want to join us?" Cole's aggravated tone brought us back to the others. This time when I looked, Mom had moved to the side. Torin was now directly in my line of sight. Suddenly, he became the only one in the room. Not able to stop the pull I automatically felt toward him, I moved swiftly to his bedside. "Torin, how are you feeling?"

His one lid was still swollen shut so he craned his neck to look at me. His forehead wrinkled as his attention bounced between me and Eli, taking in our wet hair and the fact half my outfit was Eli's. His lips pressed together tightly. "Because of Dr. Donovan, I feel much improved."

"I'm so sorry I wasn't here when you woke up."

"I told him you never left his side, until I forced you to eat and rest," Owen remarked. He was covering for me, although I'm sure everyone else in the room knew what I had really been doing. I nodded and looked away.

Thara sifted her weight. "I was here." She stood on the other side of him. Her eyes darted to me and then back to Torin. Her expression was stony and tense.

I gave her a tight smile and turned back to Torin. "I really am sorry," I said quietly. This apology had nothing to do with my absence.

Torin immediately shook his head, taking my hands in his. "There is nothing to apologize for. You did not do this to me."

"Didn't I?"

"Ember, I've told you there isn't anything I wouldn't do to keep you safe. It is I who should apologize. I should have been more careful and ought to have realized she was on to us."

"There was no way you could have known. She would have made sure of it." I looked down at our intertwined fingers. "Are you still connected to her?"

Torin once again shifted his head back and forth. "No."

"We questioned Torin while waiting for you to arrive," Cole said firmly. "We cannot have him stay here and still be linked to the Queen."

"She cut all ties to me and took away my position and title." There was sadness and pain in his voice. He was born to be a soldier, and taking it away from him was like taking away his identity. "Thara saved me. She got me out of the castle." He turned to her his gaze full of appreciation and admiration. She smiled back at him and squeezed his shoulder. Devotion to him was clear, but was it out of respect or something more?

"Through our union I was able to recognize what door to use to bring me closest to you."

"Union?"

"Yes. We are linked because of the oath put on us. It connects us. It wasn't until you came of age and out from under Lily's protection I was able to feel it."

The air stopped pumping into my lungs, and I tugged my hands out of his grasp. "Wait. What?"

Torin had told me we had been placed together by the Fae gods and goddesses, and we had been betrothed to each other before I was even born. This was before they learned I was spawned from a Demon instead of my mother's Fay husband. I knew Torin still respected the agreement, but I figured me being a Dae would have made our union null and void.

"I was too weak to contact you through dreamscaping or our mind link. But our union helped me find you. You are my betrothed, Ember. Don't you think I couldn't find my way to you?"

The skin on the back of my neck prickled, and without having to look, I could feel Eli's eyes burn into me. His voice was tight. "You are betrothed to him?"

Turning, I saw his expression matched his tone. I became suddenly conscious of everyone listening to each word being uttered between Torin and myself.

I faced Torin. "When you told me we were attached, you weren't just speaking metaphorically, were you?"

He shifted uncomfortably on the bed. "No."

I had always felt drawn to Torin. Safe. Deep inside I understood we had been meant to be together, even when my heart wanted another. Could all this be because of a bond? Were any of my feelings real? Eli's blood connected me to him. Now I was being told my feelings for Torin were based on an arrangement out of my control. I did not like feeling manipulated or unable to make my own choices. Fear and fury jumbled within me. Lights above my head began to sizzle.

My mother sensed my control teetering on the precipice and stepped toward me to touch my arm. "Deep breath."

"Breathe? You want me to breathe right now?" I exclaimed, my arms waving frantically. "What is it with Fae not telling the entire truth? I am so sick of this shit. Nothing is ever what it seems with you guys."

"Because we know how well you take it," Eli's tone was clipped.

I sent a glare his way. "You are the last person who should be talking right now."

Torin's pained expression stopped me from completely losing it. It was clear my strong reaction had wounded him. Whether it was me or the bond, it didn't matter. The last thing I wanted to do was hurt him. I cared for him deeply, maybe even loved him in a way. Truth be told, if I had never met Eli, I might have accepted this more graciously. Maybe willingly. But I had met Eli. There was no question where my heart belonged. Right or wrong, good or bad.

"Okay, so how do we break it?" I knew I had spoken the wrong thing as soon as I said it, but it was too late to take it back.

Torin stiffened. "You want to break it?"

"Uhhh yeah... well, you were promised to a pure Fay, and I'm not."

"I've told you time and time again I do not care what you are. You were meant for me. This has never changed."

A small growl sounded behind me. *Wow, I sure know how to create an uncomfortable situation.*

Mom tried to reassure me. "You can't break it, Ember. As I told you earlier, it is not making you do anything against your will. It only compels you more to want to choose that person."

"But it didn't cause you want to stay faithful to Eris. You were bonded to him, and you still had an affair with a Demon."

Mom's eyes grew wide before darting away from mine, and a strange expression moved over her face. Bringing up her past caused her distress, but I was starting to care less and less. For once, I wanted to know the *full* truth.

Her voice was quiet, but steady. "Bonded, yes, but then it was forced. Duty. You and Torin are not and never will be forced. If you grew up in the Otherworld, things would be different. Since this is not how life went, you have a choice," Mom replied, her voice distant.

"It's sad it took me being an abomination and being hidden from the Otherworld to give me choices and freedoms."

"Ember, I am sorry this results in your discomfort. It is not what I wanted. I hoped you would want to be with me," Torin spoke softly.

Guilt poured into my chest. "I am sorry. I didn't mean... it's not that

I don't..." Trailing off, I looked around the room. All eyes were on me. Eli's held no emotion, but the intensity of his gaze was enough.

"Yes?" Torin encouraged me to continue.

"Yeah, don't stop there. Finish your thought," Eli commented acidly.

This was a no-win for me. Whatever I said would only hurt people. "Excuse me." I pushed my way through the crowd and jetted out the door.

Only a few steps into the forest, I felt Eli close behind. "Eli, I can't deal with you right now."

"Tough." He walked around to face me. He cocked his head, his arms crossed. "You're dealing with me."

Running my hand frustratingly over my damp ponytail, an exasperated growl hummed in my throat. "What is it you want me to say? I didn't know about this bond. It obviously wasn't something in my control."

"You mean he never mentioned the betrothal to you before?" His tone was more mocking than wondering.

"He did, but..."

Eli stepped over my words. "And did he tell you that you two were bound by the gods?"

"I thought he was speaking figuratively. I mean I always felt something, but I didn't..."

"Do you love him?"

His blunt words stopped me in place and rendered me speechless. Did I love Torin? I did but not in the way Eli meant or Torin wanted. Without Torin I felt lost, but more like I lost my best friend, not my lover. Still, my feelings for him were strong.

"That's what I thought." Eli looked down at his bare feet. "Well, good, he's who you should be with. You and I were never meant to be more than a few fucks anyway."

I shook my head. "Don't do this. Don't try to hurt me because you are pissed or upset."

Eli sneered. "I wasn't."

His words cut me, even if I thought they were a lie. "Look, I can't deny I have feelings for him, bond or not. He has been there for me and helped me when I had no one else." Eli flinched at my jab. "But don't think it lessens what I feel about you. I do care for you, but I..."

The words stuck in my throat. I had never let someone far enough in to "fall in love" with. I cared and loved a lot of people. But being in love was different, and it scared the crap out of me. Even with loving my friends and family, I had still kept walls wrapped protectively around my heart. Love meant loss. My mother's reappearance hadn't changed my reactions. The damage was too far embedded in me. I was strong, but the mere idea of losing Eli or giving him access to destroy my heart... I wasn't that strong.

"But what?"

"Nothing." I shook my head.

"This goes against everything I am," Eli barked. "You will always be connected to him. It's not something that will ever go away. And I don't share."

Fire hydrant. Me.

"And I have the same problem with you," I proclaimed. "Is our connection real, or is it only because of the blood?

His fists and jaw clenched.

"That's not what I meant," I babbled.

"Really? I think it was exactly what you meant." Rage seeped into his words. "Blood may bind us, but nothing else does."

"Eli..."

"Let's make things simple. We're here to get our family and friends from the Otherworld. That's it." He stepped back. "You belong with him, so he can deal with you now." He swung around and walked away, leaving me standing there with my rebuttal covering my tongue.

Holy shit! Can I screw things up.

Words were usually not lost on me, but when it came to my feelings and heart, they were hard to find. I had hidden them deep down, protecting me from the harsh reality. Because of my fears, I could not tell Eli how I really felt. The instant attraction to each other had grown into something deeper. I couldn't deny it, but I also wouldn't admit it. Everything was so crazy, but it only increased the desire to run after Eli and lose myself in him again. Doubt and pride stopped me from acting on it, and I plopped onto the ground with an aggravated scream.

A fluttering sound of wings grew close before Cal landed on my knee.

"Bonded with two different men, huh? Is it fair to call you harlot now?"

I moaned. "Please don't make me laugh."

"You may be bonded to other men, but you know you are really thinking of me and those kisses you owe me."

Pulling my buried head up from my hands, I chuckled. "You're right. You are all the man I need."

Cal blushed and looked away from my gaze.

"Can I ask you something?" I sat back and slouched farther into the tree. He nodded. "I am not a trusting person. I've always been someone who would assume the worst and then reflect later. But with Torin, I never questioned him. I always trusted him even when it went against my nature. Is this from the bond?"

Cal sat on my knee, getting comfortable. "I think so. What I know about bonds is they don't pressure you to love the individuals, but they compel you to be more attracted to them. Automatically drawn to them, trusting them, naturally wanting to help the other. You both subconsciously recognize the other as a mate."

I grimaced.

"Not to say everything goes as planned. It is only supposed to steer you that way. It seems the women in your family have a certain, how do I say, 'stubbornness' to pre-destined fate or to being told what to do in any way," Cal quipped.

"Yeah," I scoffed. "We do have problems with authority, don't we? Even when it's from the gods and goddesses."

Cal and I were silent for a few minutes, taking in the distinct noises of the forest. Crickets chirped a loud, mesmerizing tune through the crackling of limbs and the sound of leaves blowing in the wind.

"Do you love him?" Cal's blunt words wretched my gaze to him.

"Who? Torin?"

Cal tilted his head. "No."

My first reaction was to agree, but then fear held me back—to even hint it. I let out a long breath, hitting my head back against the trunk of the tree.

"Following duty or what you think is right will only hurt you in the end. There is a reason life stepped in with you, even though it came in a form of a dickhead Dark Dweller."

"Ahhh." I dug my face into my hands. "What is wrong with me? I really am messed up, huh?"

"Definitely." Cal patted my knee. "But I still stand by my words. You can't choose who you love; it chooses you."

"When did you get so wise on love?" I asked. "Were you ever in love?"

Cal shifted on my knee with a faraway, and a sad look enveloped his features. When he noticed I was still staring at him, he cleared his throat. "Uh, once a long time ago. Didn't end well." He shook his head and laughed. "What a team we are."

"I think we're a good team." I leaned forward and lightly kissed his cheek.

He flushed deep red. "Now you only owe me one."

"Consider it a freebie."

A loud crunch from the woods had both Cal and me turn to high alert. He flew off my knee when I stood. It was nearly impossible for outsiders to get in, but I still was watchful. Alki had beaten awareness into me. It wasn't Eli who I felt. It wasn't any of the Dark Dwellers as they were silent on approach. This was a human.

A tall, skinny outline advanced from the trees.

"Josh?"

"Hey, Ember."

I rushed to him, throwing my arms around him, but he stiffened under my embrace. Josh didn't push away, but he didn't return my hug either. The poor kid had been through so much, and I had been an awful friend to him since his arrival.

"I am glad you are here with us." I stepped closer. "Josh, I'm sorry. I have been so consumed with Torin I haven't even talked to you. How are you? Where are you sleeping? Do you need anything?"

He looked away. "I'm fine. They gave me some guy named Dominic's room. It's next to Torin's."

I nodded. "I am so sorry I dragged you into this and got you involved with my screwed-up life."

His forehead creased. "Why? You don't think I should be a part of this?"

Confusion wrinkled my forehead. "No, that's not what I meant at all."

"Is it because I am human or because you still think of me as wimpy, pathetic Josh?"

"What?" I floundered. "I don't define you by any of those terms."

"Because I can help. I want to fight against the Queen... for what she did."

My stomach dropped. "What did she do to you?"

"She actually didn't do anything, but she stood and watched as her men beat me up."

"She didn't touch you?"

"No, but queens never do their own dirty work, do they?" He

shrugged, seeming to miss my meaning. "But it's not like I've met too many of them. Well, I've met a lot of queens on the street, but not royal ones." A smile formed on his mouth.

There was a taste of Josh's playful personality, the one I had known in Silverwood. He had changed, but how could he not have? His world had been completely taken out from under him. I missed my friend, the happy-go-lucky kid who I knew back at school. Hopefully, I hadn't destroyed him also, and he would rebound with time. Josh had a bad temper and a rough life. I wanted him to be happy. I hoped this experience wouldn't break him.

"I want to help." His eyes pleaded with mine.

"I don't want you to get hurt. What we are doing is exceedingly dangerous."

"It's too late to think of my well-being now." Anger flickered over his face but quickly disappeared. "Don't cut me out because you think I'm too fragile or weak. You brought me into this fight. I have no home, Ember. It's not like I can return to school, and I won't go back on the streets. You owe me. I deserve to know what is going on and to be a part of it."

I nodded. Fault for his current predicament crushed my shoulders. I did owe him. He had lost everything he had known because of me. Another victim in my wake.

"I think you need to tell me everything, from the beginning."

Again, I concurred. We sat, and I started to talk and continued until the sun was high in the sky, baking the earth.

NINE

Life fell into a pattern over the next couple of days. A few in the group took turns shopping or running errands while the others stayed back. Sometimes a few of the Dark Dwellers disappeared at night. Motorcycles tore through the darkness as they vanished from the compound. I tried not to think about where they were going, but I knew. The gang was "working."

Kennedy, Mom, and I weren't allowed to leave the property at all. Owen and Gabby were the ones to get Mom, Kennedy, and me personal items. Between Gabby's style and the fact we didn't care what they grabbed, we ended up with a fusion of rocker-chick, workout clothes, and cheap polyester. Josh took over wearing Dominic's, which had been left behind. They engulfed him, but he seemed content.

Eli was true to his word: he did not interact with me unless it had to do with Kennedy's training or some superficial question. He wasn't being the psycho dickhead like he had been when I first came back or even the asshole I had known when we first met. He was indifferent. Acting like nothing had ever gone on between us or like he wasn't remotely attracted to me. I had to admit this was worse. I could take the other temperaments. At least then I knew he was feeling something.

To be fair, my stubbornness and hurt did not allow me to tell him how I really felt. My cover had me acting cool and reserved, following in his footsteps.

I knew I needed to stay as far from the draw of Eli Dragen as possible. My return to the cabin the night after we fought caused a few raised eyebrows, but no one said anything. They saw the aloofness Eli and I showed each other and seemed to understand. Torin's presence put a huge roadblock between us. Even though Mom didn't comment, I could see her delight with this new development.

79

Torin was slowly healing. He could get up and walk for a short time. He still had a long way to go. The cuts and bruises on his face remained swollen, but they had healed enough to recognize his beautiful Fay features. Thara never left his side. I had little doubt her faithfulness stemmed from more than duty. She was in love with him. This made things a little icier between Thara and me, and the tension among the Fay and Dark Dwellers was palpable.

The only good thing was since Torin's and Thara's arrival, my mom didn't look at the door every minute like she was getting ready to bolt. Having other Fay around calmed her.

Kennedy embraced her newfound Druid heritage with gusto. There was a strength in her I hadn't seen before. She held her head higher and had a way about her which made you turn and look. Every once in a while, though, I could see Ken appearing like she wanted to throw up or flee.

"How are you doing, really?" I asked her one night when we were alone in the cabin. I folded my legs under me, sitting on the bed with her.

Her gaze drifted to her hands, then back to me. "Better than I thought. You will probably understand this, but I always felt different. I mean really different. I used to think it was because I was adopted. The unknowns of where and who I came from made me not feel normal." Kennedy's soft brown eyes peered at me through her black, librarian-type glasses. She shifted them farther up the bridge of her nose. "I really just knew, like you probably did, that I *really* was strange. I mean I could see people's auras, the actual glow around them, for crying out loud. I would have these strange moments where I would say this prophetic stuff, which I had no idea where it came from, but I knew it was true." She straightened her back, sitting taller. "Now I understand who I really am. It is scary, but I feel good. Stronger."

"You are." I shook my head with wonder. "You are amazing. Even in the last couple of days, I have seen a change in you. I can tell you are scared shitless, but you're jumping in with both feet. I'm in awe of you. It took me a lot longer to accept what I was."

She smiled, and a blush fluttered across her cheeks at my compliment. Her hand pushed against my leg. "Yeah, well at least I'm still human. You'll always be the bigger freak."

"Taller, not bigger! I'm a taller freak." I laughed pushing her back. "I already feel like an Amazon next you. Don't make me feel like an ogre."

"Oh, please, ogre my butt." She rolled her eyes. "Speaking of ogre... what is the deal with Eli?"

I couldn't help but snort when she connected ogre with Eli. My shoulders went up and then fell. "I don't know."

She tipped her head to the side. "How do *you* feel about him?"

"That is an extremely complicated answer." I let out a haggard laugh-sigh.

"No, it's not. It's quite simple." Her stare drove into my soul. Her eyes glazed over. *"You feel the draw toward both. You are connected to them. But one has you, and you have the other."*

My eyebrows curved up.

Kennedy shook her head, breaking her fixed gaze on me. "Oh, crap. I did it again, didn't I?"

"Yeah..." I shifted uncomfortably on the bed.

"I'm so sorry." She touched my arm. "Now that I know what I am, my powers are uncontrollable. The seer stuff is happening to me a lot more often and at the most random times." Guilt etched at the corners of her mouth and eyes. "I really do apologize."

"Don't, Kennedy. You can't help it." I took her hand in mine, looking into her face. "Don't ever apologize for who you are."

A smile grew on her lips. "I won't. Not anymore." Then she bounded off the bed. "Come on. I want to show you something I learned today."

I eagerly followed her outside. The late summer moon glinted high in the sky, leaving it lighter outside than usual.

She walked to a spot on the ground where a few wild flowers had curled up and died. The heat drained and burned the life out of them. My heart tugged. It was the cycle of life, but the earth was so much a part of me I wanted to mourn their deaths.

She knelt, cupping her hands around the plants. Her eyes were tightly closed, and she began to chant. It took a while, but as she ardently recited the strange words, I saw the flowers beginning to uncurl, the colors filling in, and their petals straightening. The ends were still burnt and some parts didn't change, but the flowers stood straight. Alive.

"Holy crap!" My eyes boggled out of my head. "You brought them back to life."

Kennedy sat back on her heels. "No, I can't bring anything back to life, but I am learning to heal. They weren't quite dead."

"Ken, you're amazing," I gushed.

Pride glowed over her features. "I have a long, long way to go, but Owen says I am picking things up faster than he expected."

"I'm not surprised. You've always been a quick learner. You love to study and figure things out."

The sound of the screen door squeaking open brought our attention to the main house. Torin stepped slowly onto the porch, stretching. As if fate really wanted to stir up the situation, Eli moved out from the forest, tugging on some pants. Neither spotted us. Eli probably sensed I was close but didn't know Ken and I were right there in the shadows.

I could see it coming. Eli and Torin had stayed as far away from each other as possible. When they crossed paths, I think everyone froze waiting for one of them to explode. Eli was coming off a run as a Dark Dweller and would already have his testosterone revving in top gear. He'd be looking for a fight.

I stepped forward, wanting to squash the inevitable altercation, but a hand stopped me. Kennedy shook her head. "They need to figure it out," she whispered. Kennedy said this now, but when blood and body parts start flying, she might change her mind. I turned back to the see the guys' paths getting closer.

Eli stopped in his tracks when he reached the bottom of the porch steps. Torin stood rigid with his face like stone. The hatred spewed from them hit the night air, cramming the warm breeze with hostility. Eli took the two steps of the porch in one, his focus on the door.

I felt like I was viewing a horror movie, torn between not wanting to watch and not able to turn away.

Maybe they won't fight.

"She was never meant for you anyway, Dragen. Letting her go was the right thing."

Damn! My lids squeezed shut, my hand coming up to my face.

Eli froze. Even in the dark I could see his shoulders tightening and hunching. Without a word, he turned toward Torin and stepped within an inch of him. Eli's eyes flared red.

My movement was automatic. I could not let them hurt each other. Eli's head jerked at the sound of my footsteps. His eyes latched on me through the dark, pinning me in place. They stayed on mine for a few beats before he faced Torin again and stepped back.

"All. Yours. My. Friend." He spit out and whipped around, yanking the screen door open as he stomped into the house. The door banged so hard behind him the frame cracked.

I let out a staggered breath. "Holy shit."

"I second that." Kennedy expelled a breath. "That was a little intense."

As Kennedy and I slipped back to the cabin, Eli's words rung in my ears. *"All yours, my friend."* It was like a stab to the gut. Whether he meant it or not, it didn't matter; the words lashed across my heart. If I did "choose" Torin, would Eli be okay with it? Could he so easily move on to another girl? Be happy with her? The thought made me want to heave in the bushes.

Being without Eli felt like torture. Being without Torin didn't shrivel my heart into a dark hole. I knew who I truly wanted. My problem was even if I knew how I felt, I was too stubborn to give in. If he was all right being without me, then I had to find a way to be all right without him.

The next day, while most helped Kennedy with learning chants, spells, and healing powers, I took the time to go to the gym and train. I had a lot of aggression to get out. Eli had haunted my dreams the rest of the night. His words turned into vivid stories with him having stunningly beautiful, half-dressed water fairies sitting on his lap and around his feet, kissing him as he laughed at me. I woke up so mad I wanted to slug him.

Working out was how I dealt with those feelings. I also needed to keep my fighting skills in top shape. I had improved but was still far from being ready to battle any soldier. Alki's voice remained constantly in my head: *You are too slow. Not dedicated. When you go to stab someone, be sure about it. There is no redo if he kills you first.*

I kind of missed that tyrant asshole.

While I was practicing, Josh stepped into the room. "Hey, can I join?"

"Sure." I wiped the sweat from my forehead and let the sword's tip lean on the floor. I was surprised I couldn't hear Alki screaming at me from here. *Never disengage. And never treat your sword like a walking stick. You respect it, and it will respect you.*

Josh walked to the wall lined with fighting sticks, swords, and daggers. His eyes were wide with awe. "It's like I walked into a *World of War Craft* fantasy." His fingers trailed along every weapon.

"You should have seen the weapons room at Lars'. Talk about impressive and frightening at the same time."

"He had more than this?" Josh caressed one of the broadswords.

"He's the Unseelie King. He has more of everything." I picked up my blade. "You ever use one of these before?" Josh looked at me, then away, shaking his head. "Well, grab one. I'll show you."

Josh grasped the broad sword. I was waiting for it to drop from his grip. They were a lot heavier than people thought. Surprisingly, he clutched it with ease, fitting it comfortably in his hand. He swung it around directing the tip at me.

"Wow, impressive. You sure you've never handled one before?" I teased.

He let his form go, letting the sword dip. "No, must be those years of playing video games."

My eyebrows drew closer together. "Yeah, not quite the same."

"So, are you gonna keep jabbering or show me some moves?"

A mischievous smile curled my lips. "I love when little boys try to challenge me."

Josh proved to be a quick study. After a few hours, he was parrying with me. I still held back, but he was better than I thought he would be. I'd have to be careful practicing with him.

It felt good to get my anger out. So much in me was black and bleak. Fighting seemed the one time my mind didn't think. I only moved and reacted. It was when I finally experienced any kind of contentment.

Later in the evening, I dragged myself back to the room, my mind and body exhausted due to the heat and exercise. I slipped quickly into a slumber.

My lids opened to a familiar scene in front of me. I stood in the magical forest. Glinting and dreamlike, the trees swayed under the light breeze.

"It feels too long since we have been here together," Torin said from beside me. "I have missed this."

I peered at his face. Here in the dreamwalk, he was fully healed. It was hard to not have your breath taken away when he looked at you. Torin was beautiful.

"You really scared the crap out of me when I couldn't contact you."

"I apologize. I will do my best to never distress you again." Out of my peripheral I could see him staring at me, his eyes full of heated longing. I kept my attention on the trees fluttering in the slight breeze, finding them the most fascinating thing I had even seen.

"Don't say you're sorry for something you couldn't help." I *knocked my shoulder into his, trying to defuse the growing tension between us. He winced. "Oh, sorry. You look so normal in the dreamscape I forget you really are still hurt."*

He rubbed his shoulder. "I am fine. Your touch is always welcome."

I bit my lip, my teeth tearing into the flesh.

"Stop." Torin's hand came up to my cheek, his fingers brushing over my mouth.

My breath caught in my throat. I was torn between pulling away and wanting to stay in his warm touch. His eyes were focused on my mouth. He slowly pulled me to him. I knew how I felt about Eli, but I also couldn't deny the part of me drawn to Torin—the bond which connected us. I always hated those wishy-washy girls in books and movies. They seemed weak, not able to make a decision. But here I was, being the same girl. Annoyance at myself, at Torin, and Eli had me jerking back out of Torin's reach.

His lids narrowed as he watched me pull away. "Ember, don't fight it. You know deep down we are supposed to be together." He was trying to disguise it, but I felt frustration and aggravation skimming his thin facade.

My head started to twist back and forth, "No, no I don't know that." The reason my resentment intensified was because I did have those feelings somewhere in me. I didn't like it. I did not want people telling me what to do or feeling I had no control or choice in a situation. My stubborn instinct wanted to combat it.

"Yes, you do." His fingers wound tightly around my wrists.

"The bond may think so, but it's not how I feel." I shook my head again.

He tugged at my arms roughly, forcing me to look at him. "Stop it! The bond does not force you to feel anything you do not already experience. You are too afraid to admit it." There was a wild note whirling in the pitch of his voice. My heartbeat stepped up, slamming into my chest. I knew Torin would never hurt me, but something seemed off. He was not quite himself. After what he had been through, who could blame him? He might never be all right again.

My expression must have shown some of the concern I felt. His eyes widened. He quickly dropped my hands, moving away. "I am sorry, Ember. I lost my temper."

"It's okay." I licked at my lips nervously. I was okay, but his strangling grip and tone still startled me. He had never been aggressive

with me before. Torin had always been extremely kind and sweet. Patient to a fault. I could feel his patience was now thin and near the breaking point.

It was barely audible, but with my Dark Dweller hearing, I picked up a low, deep growl coming from the forest. I swallowed nervously, scanning the woods. Eli was there somewhere, hiding in the shadows.

I needed to defuse the situation.

"I was about to go dreamwalk on West, my dad, and Ryan."

"Then I will let you go." Torin stepped forward and without warning cupped the side of my face and kissed me. His lips were warm as they softly covered mine. He broke off and leaned his head into mine, whispering hoarsely. "It was nice having this brief moment with you. You were what got me through the pain. Thinking of you during that time gave me hope."

He let go of my face, not waiting for my response, and disappeared into the trees, leaving me dazed and frozen in place.

A branch snapped in the forest and eventually broke me out of my stupor. I could not face Eli or his bi-polar wrath.

I massaged my forehead as I tried to concentrate on West. I wanted to see my dad, but the images of the spikes rammed into West's throat made him my first priority. He was family now, so I focused sharply on him. I wanted to get into the dreamwalk before Eli approached me. I didn't need his indifferent or spiteful comments about Torin or my bringing both of them into my dreamscapes. The connection I felt for them seemed to automatically bring both in whether I wanted them to be there or not.

The queasy feeling was all I needed to realize I had left the forest. I opened my eyes, adjusting to the dark, seedy dungeon. The smell of urine and molding straw did not assault me, but I knew it was there. My nose still scrunched up in memory of the rancid stench.

My vision finally became accustomed to the murky gloom of the cell.

"West..." My feet tripped over themselves trying to move to him.

Blood trickled down his neck, pooling around the collar of his shirt. The blood loss had affected him greatly. Weight had fallen off of him; his cheeks were gaunt, his eyes were sunken, and his face was pale and haggard. His body was burning calories trying to reproduce blood, and he was losing too much to keep up.

"West, I am so sorry." I knelt on the other side of the bars, reaching for his face. "I will get you out of here. I promise." His eyes had been shut, but the moment I touched him they opened. A shiver ran through his body.

He could feel me. His lids blinked, displaying his soft brown eyes. "I have to say you look like crap," I teased, knowing he couldn't hear me.

"You. Look. Like. Crap." A halting voice came from the dark. I jumped, falling on my rear. My eyes scanned the area for the sound.

"And here I thought I had dressed to impress today," West spoke back. His tone sounded rough as he struggled to talk.

Trepidation latched onto my nerves. No one could hear me while in a dreamwalk. Was it just a coincidence? I stood still, wary of who had spoken.

"I. See. You." The voice came again. My heart pounded in my chest. Was it talking to me?

"Well, there goes playing hide-n-seek with you. This was my best hiding spot." West snorted.

My gut told me the strange voice was talking to me, not West.

I moved forward, squinting, and tried to peer through the thick shadows down the prison walk. There was a soft shuffling sound before I saw a short figure. It only came up to my waist and appeared stocky, built like a square with a thick neck and large head. The closer it got, the clearer it became. I could now see the long beard, fat squashed nose, and deep-set, squinty eyes. The time in Lars's library had once again come in handy. The sketches of a dwarf in one of his books almost mirrored the one standing before me. The description had stated they weren't known to be friendly or sociable, kept to themselves, and preferred living in dark, underground places, in mountains, or like this stinky dungeon.

He waddled as he walked toward me, huffing with the effort. Both he and his clothes were filthy. The dirt and grime so deeply set in his wrinkles it looked like he had never bathed. Now I was more thankful I could not smell him as his odor must be horrendous. He carried a pitcher of water and spilled most of the contents as he shuffled to West's cell.

"Do you see me?" I asked.

He didn't look up or even flinch as I spoke, his stout body walked through me without hesitation. Okay, I was losing it. It must have been a fluke he had repeated what I said.

"I see you," the voice said again. This time I saw the dwarf's lips didn't move. He only grunted in response. "But do you see me?"

"I don't need to see you. I smell you," West replied.

Movement on the dwarf's shoulder caught my eye. What I had thought was part of the little man's clothing was a bird. A large one. The raven's inky, black body and bright, beady eyes turned toward me.

The raven had been speaking the whole time, not the dwarf.

"You came back. Fire. You returned home."

"I'd miss you guys too much," West replied dryly. "I think you forgot your medication today, raven. You're being even more nonsensical than usual."

"You see me?" It was less of a question and more an attempt to confirm this was really happening.

"I see all." The creature tilted its head at me.

Crap. The bird really could see me. This wasn't good. It could fly off at any time and tell the Queen I was here. And there was little doubt it knew who I was. My safety felt threatened; the urge to run was strong. I took a few steps, giving one last look to West.

"No. Stay." The raven flapped its wings.

No, I should go.

I slammed my lids shut and thought about Mark and Ryan. I would see them before I left the dreamwalk. I hoped the raven would not tell her right away.

The room spun. When it stopped, I reopened my eyes and examined the area for any potential threat where Ryan and Mark were being held. It looked like no time had passed since my last visit. It probably hadn't to them. Mark still sat in the chair, hovering close to Ryan's bed. Castien leaned against the far wall. Ryan was still unconscious, sleeping deeply. His skin had more color in it, and this time I picked up a slight glow. Oh, holy crap! My friend was sparkling like a true Fairy. The irony of this was not lost on me, and I couldn't help burst out laughing. He would love this.

"So tell me again what a Dae is." Mark's annoyed tone broke into my musings.

Castien exhaled as if this was the tenth time he had answered the same question.

"A Dae is half pure Demon and half noble Fairy."

"So, Lily, my wife, had been married previously to a noble Fairy but had an affair with a Demon?" Mark's incredulous expression told me he was having trouble believing this.

"I'm not going through this with you again."

Mark's blue eyes glared at Castien. "You haven't said yes or no to anything I've asked."

"You need to discuss this with your wife, not me."

Mark's lids lowered.

"Yes, if my wife was alive, and I was not locked up in Fairyland, I would love to talk to her about why she didn't tell me the truth. Why she hid Ember's and her real identity from me. All those years I secretly feared Ember was going insane. I doubted her. I could have been there for her. Goddammit, Lily, why didn't you tell me?" he yelled at no one.

Castien scoffed. "Would you have believed her?" Before Mark could respond, Castien added, "In this world truth can either save you or kill you. In your case it would have been the latter. She protected you by not telling you."

"But you still ended up here. I have to say I think Lily was selfish. Did she think past what she wanted, bringing you into this?" The Queen's voice caused both men and me to jump. Castien straightened, assuming his guard stance. Mark knocked back his chair, standing, defensively putting a hand on Ryan's shoulder.

Shit!

Did the raven tell her I was here? Glancing around, I saw no sign of the bird, which didn't mean it wasn't there somewhere. The only thing keeping me from jumping out of my dreamwalk was the Queen did not look around. Her attention was completely on Mark and Ryan.

"You humans are so amusing. You would put your body in front of his, wouldn't you? Do you not know that would be in vain? Nothing could stop me from getting to him if I wanted, and you would be another dead body I would have to drag out of here." Her voice tinkled like soft bells, but her words cut like barbs of steel.

Mark's hand didn't leave Ryan's arm. I was starting to see it wasn't only my mom I took after. Mark had taught me protectiveness and dedication to those he loved. If I took after even one of his traits, I would be happy. My love for him burgeoned in my chest, almost suffocating me. My muscles itched with need to grab him and take him back to Earth with me.

"You are excused, guard." Aneira didn't take her eyes off Mark.

"Yes, Your Majesty."

Castien bowed and headed for the door. I could see the concern in his eyes as he turned to look at Ryan as he left the room.

"Mr. Hill, may I call you Mark?" She smiled coyly at him. "I have wanted to come and visit you for a while to see how you like your new accommodations. I apologize for my rudeness."

Both Mark and I furrowed our brows at the same time. Mark was

Stacey Marie Brown

no fool. He understood when he was being taken for a ride. Aneira's every move was calculated.

What was she up to?

"You have been comfortable here?" She glided over to stand near him. A musical laugh rang out of her throat. "I know I am such a terrible hostess. I realized I know nothing about you. I don't even know where you are from."

Mark's eyes drifted to her and then darted around the room, like he was waiting for something to jump out. I felt the same. She was definitely up to something.

When he didn't respond, she leaned and gripped his arm, her tone strained. "I asked you a question. You will answer me."

Mark's face relaxed, a slight smile bowed his lips. He looked dreamily at her. She was glamouring him. That bitch!

"Now, where is the one place on the Earth world you felt truly at home and where you had your loving wife and daughter by your side?" Aneira no longer bothered with her sweet voice.

"Monterey. It's where I fell in love with my wife and our beautiful daughter. Lily and I had our first date at a restaurant on Cannery Row," Mark sighed happily.

Aneira let go of him. "See? Was it so hard?"

Mark blinked; a strange expression flittered over his face. He puffed out his checks and took in a big breath. He looked like he was going to be sick.

She smiled, a wide smirk, and strolled toward the door. "You have been most helpful. I look forward to our next visit." The Queen sauntered out the door with her usual arrogant confidence.

When the door shut, Mark collapsed in the chair. I wanted to hug him so much it ached. He leaned over and grabbed a bowl from the table and threw up.

God, I hated the bitch. Watching her made me even more anxious to find the sword and slice it through her neck.

I stayed a few more minutes, but with Earth night coming to an end, I had to leave Mark and Ryan.

Again.

TEN

When I woke, everyone was gone from the cabin. I showered and dressed in jeans I had cut into shorts, a tank, and pulled my hair into a ponytail, then headed to get some breakfast. My stomach rumbled insistently. I walked into the kitchen and stopped. Eli stood at the counter, eating something that looked raw and meaty. His eyes flicked to mine. They stayed neutral. No feeling in them. If he was going to act like he wasn't in my dreamscape last night, so was I.

"Where is everyone?" I held my chin high and continued to the refrigerator. I opened it, looking like I was searching for something.

It took him a few moments to respond. "They're already with Kennedy. This is her first day outside trying spells."

I nodded. "Right." I closed the fridge and headed for the cupboard where the peanut butter was. I paused. The peanut butter belonged to him. I shifted direction and grabbed an apple out of the fruit bowl.

"You can have some peanut butter," he said, not looking in my direction.

"No, it's okay. An apple is fine."

He scoffed but shoved another bite in his mouth.

"What do you know about ravens?" I nervously rolled the apple around in my hands.

Eli straightened, his eyebrows furrowing at my question. "Ravens? Why?"

I shrugged. "Just read something about them and got curious."

He studied me, looking like he didn't know if I lied or not. "They are incredibly intelligent. Known to be tricksters, but really what Fae isn't?" He paused, thinking. "Ravens are also considered protectors, bringers of magic, and dream guides."

So that's how the bird saw me. I bet it was a dream guide who probably could see or walk through anybody's dream like it was real. I might have been as real to him as West was.

"Are they Light or Dark?"

"Ravens are neutral to sides. But, if anything, they are considered more Dark Fae than Light." He set down his fork. "What is the real reason you're asking me this?"

"No reason." I shook my head and drifted closer to him, examining his plate. "What are you eating?"

He knew I was changing subjects, and his eyes penetrated mine before shaking his head slightly. "Venison and eggs."

"Looks like raw venison." Out of habit, my lip pulled up in disgust.

"I like things raw and unrefined."

My tongue salivated for the meat. I didn't even realize I licked my lips till I saw him staring at me. His eyes were fixed on my tongue and lips. Warmth flushed my cheeks and neck. He cleared his throat and found his plate exceptionally fascinating.

"Do you want a bite?" he said, back to being detached from feelings. "You can't deny the Dark Dweller part of you wants it."

Again, my chest ballooned with heat. Oh, yeah, my Dark Dweller, Demon, and Fairy sides all wanted it. But, wait, he was talking about food. I suddenly found his plate exceptionally interesting, too.

I shrugged. "Sure." Acting like I didn't give a shit was guaranteed to fool him. Right?

He scooped up pieces onto his fork and pointed it toward me.

What the hell? He's going to feed me? Crap on ash bark.

I opened my mouth, and he steered the fork in. I tried gracefully to get all the food off the fork and into my mouth. But when had I ever been known for my grace? Some pieces dribbled out and onto the floor, my hand clasped over my lips, shoving the rest in.

So hot.

The pieces of meat exploded on my taste buds, and I groaned with happiness. I had never really liked red meat before Eli had given me Dark Dweller blood, and now I was eating it raw. Raw and loving it.

"Tastes good," I mumbled through bites.

His eyes raked over me. His lips hooked in a half grin, his eyes full of want. The coldness he displayed all week was gone. We stood there. My chest constricted, and my lungs forgot to move air in and out. Every inch of my skin prickled with craving. I thought of him pitching me up on the counter, everything crashing to the floor, as he took me right there. I tightened my muscles to stop from acting on it, but they didn't listen. I stepped closer; only a hair separated our bodies. His breathing went shallow, and my body tingled at the proximity of his. We didn't look each other in the eyes, but I could feel his roam over every curve of my form. I reached out, lightly touching his shirt, his stomach muscles rippling under the fabric. Slowly he bent in, leaning down. His lips were only an inch from mine.

And then they were gone. He jerked back, his hand going to his head.

"What's wrong?" Panic instantly rushed through me.

He pressed his temple. "It's Cooper. He's trying to use our link, but he's not making any sense."

I could now hear the roar of a motorcycle engine resonating through the house, vibrating it. A squeak of brakes rung, like the bike had been parked in the living room. A warning was delivered deep into my stomach. They usually parked their bikes in the shed, away from the house. I rushed to the family room with Eli on my tail. Through the screen door, I saw Cooper bound off Eli's black Harley and rush up the steps to the house.

My body started to pulsate with the tension. Something was clearly wrong. I could feel it in the air, coming in waves off Cooper. Like a bull he tore open the screen, his nose flaring. "Turn on the TV."

"What?" I stared at him.

"What's going on? I couldn't understand you. The girl you were with last night already go stalker on you?" Eli teased Cooper, but his voice held a note of alarm.

"You need to see this." Cooper, not being able to wait for me to comprehend his request, dove past me to the remote and clicked on the TV.

The screen burst to life with images: empty lots; collapsed rubble resembling structures; houses floated down the road back out to sea. People screamed and wailed as the cameras scanned the scene around them.

"What the..." My hand went to my mouth.

"Aneira," Cooper turned to me. "She attacked over an hour ago. I heard it on my way home."

My brain was processing the pictures. The logical part understood the basics it was seeing, the mayhem and destruction, but every other part of me was numb and slow to comprehend. My eyes latched onto the words on the screen, the location of the place.

Tsunami hits Fisherman's Wharf in Monterey, California.

"Oh, God... no." My throat grew tight, and I was barely able to get out the words.

It was the place where Mark had grown up. My home. Aneira wanted to make her attack personal—to hurt me by harming others I knew and cared about. Even though Mom and I moved around a lot, as soon as she met Mark, we moved to Monterey to be with him. My happiest memories took place there. The nice old woman who babysat me had lived there. I learned to ride a bike on our street. Mom, Mark, and I would get clam chowder and go sit on the dock to watch the otters swim in the ocean. My school friends and I played hide-n-go-seek on my lawn.

My legs began to sag. Eli grabbed me as I hit the floor.

"Get Cole and everyone. They should be outside at the training site," Eli commanded. Cooper responded quickly to his Second's order and ran from the house.

"She did this because of me." Crushing guilt squeezed my lungs, and the weight of it curled me into a ball.

Eli shook his head. "It is not your fault. Yes, she made this personal, but with or without you, she would have done this anyway. Maybe even to a bigger city." He was trying to get me to feel better, but it didn't work. I wondered how many lives had been lost and how many victims I had known. More lives had been taken because of Aneira. Because of me. He sat me up, pulling me to his chest. No tears came. I couldn't cry; I could no longer feel.

Feet thumped up the steps to the house. Cole was the first to enter with Cooper and Mom right behind. Everyone else trickled in.

"Holy shit!" Gabby exclaimed.

I sat on the floor, lost. A strangled cry broke from my mother's lips. Her eyes were also glued on the information written across the screen.

"No... no... no. Our home." She had one hand on her stomach and one at her mouth. Her disbelief at what she was seeing was written all over her face.

Cole didn't say a word as he walked closer to the TV. Watching. Absorbing. "Guess there is no avoiding a war now."

A spike of anger shot me to my feet. "How many times will she destroy a city, killing thousands of humans, for any of you to care? It's been three years since she attacked Seattle. What have you guys done? Nothing. And what about the infamous, all-powerful Unseelie King? Why does he continue to let her do this? What is he waiting for?"

Cole turned and looked at me directly. "You."

"What?"

"Ember, you have to understand Fae," he said. "We may be

94

constantly provoking, bickering, and fighting small wars between us. But with a huge, all-out war like this, we tend not to provoke it unless we know we can win."

"And you don't think you can beat her?"

"No. And I think the Unseelie King knows this. It is why he has held off until he locates the one thing that can destroy her. For good." Cole's eyes leveled at mine, hinting at more than what he was saying.

"The Sword of Nuada... the Sword of Light," I whispered.

Cole smiled bitterly. "I see your time with Lars was educational. I figured he told you about the prophecy."

I sucked in air. "You know about the prophecy? About the Sword? How?"

"I was not fully honest with you. Kennedy is not our only way back to the Otherworld." Cole looked between me and Kennedy. "A Druid is one way to break the curse on our family. It will take years before Kennedy can obtain that level of magic. The other way is if *you* kill the source of the curse. The magic breaks, and it will die with its possessor." Cole's boots clumped hard on the wood floor as he moved to the back of the sofa. "Exterminating her is our fastest way in. It is also killing two birds with one stone, so to speak. But since no one could find the sword, we had to keep with the plan to either trade you to the Unseelie King or now use Kennedy's abilities. The trade with you would have included a stipulation that we be involved with locating the sword. As you know that trade never happened." He touched the back of the worn leather couch. "Like the Unseelie King, we make it our job to know our enemies' weaknesses. We know the Sword of Nuada is hers. We searched for years, fruitlessly. Until you.

"If you are the prophesied one, we think the location would be connected to you. Or in something which would stay with you." Cole's eyes darted from me to Mom.

I followed his eyes, his meaning sinking in. They had known about the sword and the prophecy this whole time. Another thing they kept from me. "It was why you were so happy to let me go home and get my clothes the last time I was here. This became your chance to look for whatever you thought I had." The night I had eavesdropped on Cole and Eli, and they had talked about hunting for something they thought was hidden in my house. It all made sense now.

"We could go look at your house anytime, but we hoped it would show itself in your presence somehow. We found nothing."

"Why do you think the location of the sword is connected with me?

Why would I have it?" There was something about that night and what I had overheard which kept me glancing back at my mom. "Do you know anything about this?"

Her arms were folded defensively, and her eyes narrowed on Cole. "No. I have no idea where the sword is located."

Cole tilted his head. "Are you sure, Lily?"

Her face flushed with fury. "I don't know anything, and neither does Ember. Leave her out of this. If you want to go look for this sword, then go. Don't drag my daughter into it."

He grimaced. "I think you and I both know Ember is so far in this there is only one way out. You know she's the one, Lily."

Mom's jaw tightened and her hand touched her lips. She did this when she had to decide about something. She glanced at the TV showing the footage of people screaming and crying for help as houses and buildings floated down the streets. Her shoulders dropped, her head went into her hands, and she nodded. "Yes, I know." Her words were barely audible before she turned and ran from the room.

The sounds from the TV only set my teeth on edge. "Thousands of homes and buildings were lost today. As of now the death toll is over thirteen hundred. Many are still missing. We know the total will only rise. Tourists and locals had no warning. Scientists are stumped as to the cause since there was no major earthquake recorded anywhere in the world today. Some think this might have commenced from plates shifting in the middle of the sea to trigger this kind of devastation. Some doubt this claim as no other towns or areas close by were affected in any way."

"Wow." Josh's face was void of any emotion, but I knew he kept things hidden. "The Queen is really capable of doing this?"

"Yes," Owen replied. "Though this kind of destruction is more than I thought her powers were able to do."

I clenched my fists. "She had help." I continued to stare at the images. "Her little amplifier, Asim." He was the boy who "helped" me destroy Seattle. I once had compassion for him. He could not touch anyone without devastating effects. What a lonely life—never to be touched or hugged.

My feelings quickly changed after what had happened. He had been brainwashed at an early age and thought working for the Queen was a privilege and an honor. He had no empathy for the human lives he took.

"She'd also have to use a water fairy for help. Aneira has no power over water or fire. She can assist, but for this kind of devastation? The water fairies don't like her, but somehow she would make sure they aided her." Cole moved closer to the TV, drinking in every picture flashing on the screen. "Her power is air. She can create hurricanes and tornados, but real devastation is usually with fire."

"It's why she wants me. The water fairies can only damage places along water. And her air powers aren't strong enough to destroy like fire can. We need to act." I aimed my statement at Cole. "We need to do something. Now!"

"What exactly do you want to do?" Cole threw up his arms. "Go back to the Otherworld and ask the Queen to stop?"

"I'm sure she will comply if you ask nicely," Eli tossed in.

"Shut up," I yelled at Eli. "For once can you not open your mouth?"

"You want to take this out on me? Would that make you feel better?" Eli took a large stride towards me, his anger rising.

"Okay, whoa... think everyone needs to calm down." Jared held up his hands, and Kennedy nodded in agreement.

"Calm down? How can I when thousands of lives were lost because they happen to come from the town where I lived! Where Mark grew up. This was because of what Mark told her."

"What does Mark have to do with this?" Kennedy asked.

I looked at her. "Everything. I should have seen this coming, known what she was up to, but I didn't. I let this happen."

"What are you talking about, Ember? You're not making sense." Kennedy regarded me.

"I dreamwalked on Mark and Ryan, and Aneira came in. She glamoured Mark and asked him where he considered home."

"And he said Monterey," Cole guessed.

"I knew she was up to something. I didn't understand what. How could I not see it?"

"It's not your fault." Kennedy walked closer to me, but my rigid body kept her at arm's length.

"It is, and I have to do something about it."

"The only thing that will happen is you'll die if you go to her now. If you truly want to avenge those people, let us find the sword. Then we can stop her for good," Cole said.

Another hushed lull came over us.

"So..." Josh broke in. "This sword. None of you has an idea where it is?"

We all stayed silent, glowering at him and each other.

"How are you going to find it then?" Josh looked around at each one of us, waiting for an answer.

It was not something that had an answer. Not at this time anyway. The aggravation in the room mounted. All of us were frustrated and discouraged.

Where do we even start?

ELEVEN

"You okay?" Kennedy asked me a few days later. I had been barking and screaming at the others while they tried to train her.

"I'm fine."

"You don't seem to be yourself the last few days. I am worried about you." She stood confidently, staring at me. Suddenly, I felt like the child. Something in me recognized the roles of our relationship were changing. She was changing, which made me feel uncomfortable and agitated.

I snorted derisively. "I wouldn't worry about me; worry about yourself. You need to advance faster than this."

Her mouth tightened, and her jaw clenched before she spoke. "I *am* trying."

Trying wasn't helping us. Trying would only get more people killed. "Try harder." I started to spin away and walk off when I heard my mother.

"Ember." Her tone sounded shocked and embarrassed.

I rounded on her. "Oh, sorry. It's not the way you raised me. Oh, right, you didn't raise me. The only thing I've learned from you is pain and to guard myself from really letting anyone in."

I gave her no time to respond to my words before I swung around and stomped off. Even then the guilt of what I said and how I treated them both only made me angrier with myself and them. Uncomfortable, I itched in my own skin. I wanted to act, to do something to stop Aneira, and to help those poor people in Monterey.

Who would be next on Aneira's list?

The news only got worse. The number of deaths rose to over fifteen hundred, and the damage was far more extensive than originally thought.

I couldn't eat and bypassed meals to go straight for the gym. Josh met me often to talk and spar. He continued to shock me at how easy he was picking it up. I guess those years playing *World of War Craft* did help.

"You're really good." Josh panted, leaning on his sword.

"Alki would say my form is dreadful, and my concentration is appalling." I returned the sword to the weapons wall.

"Sounds like a bastard."

"Definitely, but he's a good teacher."

"He helped with your powers, too?"

"Yeah, but mostly he trained me physically. Maya and Koke helped train me in my other powers."

"Right, because one isn't nearly good enough." He bobbed his head. "You got telekinesis, pyrokinesis, and you can acquire powers from the earth. You sure you don't have a cape and an acceptance letter to Hogwarts?"

"That would be cool." I grabbed a towel off the table, wiping my face.

"Wait. I forgot the most important. You are also part Dark Dweller."

"I'm a mutated mutt." I plopped on the table and took a drink of water.

"I'm curious about your Dark Dweller powers." Josh took his water off the table and sat next to me.

My mouth flattened into a thin line.

"You don't have to tell me." Disappointment made his shoulders sag.

I exhaled. "No. It's okay. None of my attributes are as strong as theirs, and I can't shift, but all my senses have heightened."

"That's it?" His gaze darted to me.

"My pupils go cat-like as theirs do when I get really pissed off or protective." Josh was my friend, and I trusted him, but I felt uncomfortable telling anyone this stuff. My instinct was warning me to shut up. Funny, I complained about the Fae not being open, and here I was doing the same, just as Kennedy had pointed out.

"I thought I overheard you say your DNA has changed and iron doesn't affect you like normal Fay?"

I didn't recall telling Josh anything about my immunity to iron, but there had been so many things going on, who knew what I'd said. I could have told him I slept in Strawberry Shortcake Underoos till I was six. "Uh, yeah. It still hurts like hell, though." Again, my throat closed up on saying more. I had always been guarded, but this was different. When had I truly accepted my "Fae-ness"? I couldn't recall, but I wanted to protect and defend our secrets with everything I had.

"How long does it take to wear off?"

As I was about to dodge another question, a piercing wail assaulted my eardrums. With a cry I slid off the table to the floor and covered my ears.

"What's wrong?" Josh jumped down, squatting next to me. "What happened?"

The headache-inducing whine raged in my head, rattling my teeth. I groaned and pressed my hands further into the sides of my head. "The sound... you can't hear it?"

"No. What sound?" His gaze looked me over critically.

"It-It's a high shrill sound." I cringed again as the wail reached another heightened level.

"What? Are you hearing dog whistles now or something?" Josh's voice sounded a little too harsh for it to be completely a joke.

"No..." I paused and looked out the window. "No. Not a dog whistle but a security breach." I jumped down and moved to the door. The Dark Dwellers had added my blood to the spell surrounding the property so I could tell when someone tried to break through.

"Where are you going? Wait." Josh followed me.

I didn't stop. My legs carried me toward the warning alarm. Halfway there the noise stopped. The relief was instant, leaving the air around me peaceful. I continued to walk to the property line and spotted Cole and Eli before I saw who was on the other side.

Lorcan.

His frame dominated the area surrounding him. He wore dark jeans, a black leather jacket, and a cocky smirk as he stared at us.

Why am I even surprised?

I slowed to a swift, walking pace as two flying objects headed for each of my shoulders.

"My lady... whoaaaa!" My hands snatched Simmons before he tumbled off, and I placed him squarely on my shoulder.

Cal fluttered down with grace. "We couldn't miss the party. Hope you brought the booze and the floozies." Human slang sounded funny coming from him. They had been hanging around us way too long.

I glared at Lorcan. He stood alone, but I spotted two figures lurking behind him, slightly hidden in the shadows. Dominic and Dax. He didn't bring Samantha along this time.

Awww, too bad. I'm really in the mood to kill her.

The voices rumbled in low murmurs and became clearer the closer I got.

"You don't think I don't have my own tricks for finding you guys each time. You're not the only ones with friends." Lorcan repeatedly threw a pebble up in the air and caught it.

"How's being a domesticated lap dog going for you? Does she give you treats and brush your coat until it's all shiny?" Eli sneered.

Lorcan's face pinched. "Domesticated? Think you should look at yourself, brother." Lorcan's eyes flickered to me as I walked up to Eli.

It would cause Lorcan extreme pain, but he could cross the line if he really wanted to. Unless he had more than Dominic and Dax behind him, he knew it would be stupid to try. I still didn't take my eyes off him.

"Before you get all bitchy and demand why I am here," Lorcan gave a dramatic pause, "I have come to make a deal. I would like us to become business partners, as you would say."

My loud snort sounded sharp against the quiet surrounding darkness. "Oh, Lorcan, you are always good for a laugh."

He glowered at me. "Shut up, you disgusting revulsion. I can smell you and know you are part of the spell here now. The fact you are becoming more and more Dark Dweller is a disgrace." He focused on Eli. "There is no worse shame on us. You sicken me, brother, allowing a Dae to become a Dark Dweller." His face showed pure abhorrence.

Eli clenched his teeth, his jaw becoming tight. "Shut the hell up." His eyes shifted, and his shoulders started curling as he began turning into his Dark Dweller form.

"Who are you really mad at, little bro? Me or because you know deep down I'm right?"

Cole's hand went out to block Eli from reacting. "Lorcan, go away. You are no longer a part of us or are welcome here, and we certainly won't be making any deals with you."

Lorcan snarled, but slowly his face softened into smug amusement. "Oh, I think you will change your mind when you realize what the Queen really has planned. You think Seattle and Monterey are the extent of her schemes?" He continued when he knew he had our attention. "I may no longer be working with her, but I know what she is intending to do. You need us, and we *all* need the Druid. Sorry, Ember, you are no longer the most important, though your powers will come in handy. The Druid can break the curse, but we'll also have powers Aneira can't touch. We can stand together and fight her. Like we used to."

The deep need to protect Kennedy stewed in my gut. I pushed it away along with all the other emotions I had this week. Lars was right: feelings were a weakness and would only be used against you. "What is she planning to do?"

"You think I am going to tell you without something in return?" Lorcan cocked his head at me. It was equivalent to patting my head and saying, "Awww, aren't you adorable? Cute, but stupid as hell."

"Do you want me to do a fly-by and poop on his head?" Cal whispered in my ear. I couldn't help but laugh. Everyone turned to me.

"Pixies?" Lorcan looked dumbfounded. "You allow pixies here, too? Well, I guess when you go as low as a Dae, everything else pales in comparison."

Two pissed-off winged creatures burst into the air. "Excuse me, sir? You do not offend my lady." An affronted Simmons puffed up.

Both Eli and Cole looked up at the sky with annoyance.

"Guys." I tried to grab their legs, but they zipped out of my reach.

"I challenge you to a duel," Simmons spouted.

Lorcan, Dax, and Dominic responded with a hearty laugh. This only incited Simmons more. Cal stayed quiet. He was no doubt silently planning something.

"Goddammit, Ember. Get those little fuckers away from here!" Eli boomed at me. Rage flaming his eyes.

At the worst moment possible, Josh, Torin, Thara, Mom, and Kennedy broke loudly through the brush. "Ember? Are you out here?" Kennedy yelled. Mom tried to shush her, but it was pointless. Humans could be heard from miles away. Only the Fae eased into the clearing quietly, though Torin with his cane and limp couldn't pull off stealth quite as easily.

I cringed.

"Hey, there you are. Josh told us you took off this way..." Kennedy stopped and her eyes widened, finally seeing the assembled group.

There was a pause as Lorcan took them in. An expression flittered so quickly over his face as he looked at my mom, I couldn't place it. Then his eyes narrowed when they landed on Torin.

At seeing three Seelie Fairies, one being the ex-First Knight, on Dark Dweller land, Lorcan stepped back and shook his head. "I was wrong. You did sink lower."

Dax and Dominic stepped from the trees, either in utter disbelief or in response to our numbers having more than doubled theirs.

"What has happened to you guys? You can't even call yourself Dark Dwellers anymore." The words shot out of Lorcan's mouth. "I always knew you were the worst leader, Cole, but this is disgusting. You run a halfway house for the Light now? Oh, and let's not forget for humans as well." He nodded to Josh. "You knew nothing about being a true leader, and you became one only by default. No one else old enough was left alive. Look at what your leadership has done." Lorcan motioned around. "This is not who Dark Dwellers are. You have made us look soft and weak. You are becoming human, Cole."

In the Fae world this was one of the worst insults.

Cole and Eli stayed quiet, their arms crossed, their heads held high and defiant. There was no doubt they agreed with some of what Lorcan said. Harboring Light Fay and humans was not in their nature. It went against everything they once stood for. But they did it—mostly because of me.

Lorcan shook his head. "If this is what you guys have become, this will be an extremely easy win for the Queen." He took a few steps back; Dax and Dominic followed suit. "I've said this before, but I didn't realize how true it was: our parents would be ashamed. We were once respected and feared. Now look at the fluffy, little bunnies you guys are." He turned to walk away and stopped, looking over his shoulder. "The Queen might have the right idea in taking down the wall between the two worlds, exposing us, and making the two worlds into one. It would only be an improvement."

They slipped into the shadows and disappeared.

TWELVE

My stomach felt like it had been dipped in acid. Lorcan's words rolled around and around in my head. The Queen might have the right idea in taking down the wall between the two worlds exposing us, and making the two worlds into one. The Queen didn't only want to take Earth back; she wanted to mesh the worlds together and have it all under her ruling. She wanted to kill or enslave the humans and reveal us, the Fae. Magic would rule.

It was like sandpaper against my skin. This knowledge would create hysteria the world could not handle. Everything that anyone had ever known would be gone. Seattle's chaos would be paradise compared to what would happen if Aneira's plan materialized.

My fingers slid up the bridge of my nose, pinching my brows together. When Cooper, Jared, Owen, and Gabby returned from running the property line, we spent an hour in a "house meeting" that consisted of us yelling at each other. We circled the same argument till Eli stomped out of the room declaring he couldn't stand another minute of the pointless conversation. I agreed. We were getting nowhere. Eli probably felt Lorcan was right. They had become soft here. I didn't think it was a bad thing, but Eli would.

My skin crawled with a need to go for a hunt or run till all my problems were behind me. I headed for the thick of the forest but stopped when I heard angry voices.

"I know we don't like each other, but for Ember, for this war, we need to try and work together."

"I don't need to do anything for you or her. I'd prefer if you actually left and never came back." Eli's tone was strained and full of below-the-surface rage.

"I will not leave her," Torin replied sharply. "Where she goes, I go."

"Why? You think you two will live together blissfully with little half-breed Fay children running around? You're more delusional than I thought."

I still couldn't fully see them, but I could sense the strain mounting between them. The surrounding trees held in their tension, like a thick bubble.

"I am not the one who is delusional. She was not meant for you. You know this. So let her go." Torin's irate voice drifted through the darkness. "You can never truly make her happy."

"And you think you're that man? You think you can handle her? You think she is the happily-ever-after type?" Eli indignantly flung back. His voice was tightening. It would not be long before he snapped. "And to confirm... I did a pretty good job of satisfying her. I sure can cause her to quiver and scream. Can you say the same?"

"Stay away from her." Torin made an unsteady lunge, challenging Eli, who towered several inches over him. The past week everyone was at each other's throats, but these two had been the worst.

"What are you going to do about it, Fairy boy?" Eli smirked, not even bothering to drop his arms.

Seeing the fire building under both men's edgy façades, I hurried to put myself between them. "Stop it. Both of you."

"No. Let him go. Let's see what Twinkle Toes here can do," Eli taunted.

"Eli, shut it." I turned sharply to him, warning him more of *my* temper than Torin's. As he looked into my eyes, Eli moved back, his arms up in a mock surrender.

I turned back to Torin. "You should be resting. You're still healing. You need to go back to the house."

Even though Torin's strength wasn't back to its fullest, he stood there fuming. His hand gripped the cane so hard his knuckles turned white. My focus was locked on him. I could feel the bond pulling me to him, wanting to take care of him. But my body was keenly aware of the heat radiating off Eli standing behind me. It was like magnetic energy making me long to step back and feel his body pressed against mine.

"Yeah, you should go back and take it *easy,* Fairy boy," Eli taunted.

"Eli." I stepped away so I could turn and face him. At the same time Torin's temper snapped. He took advantage of the little space I gave him to reach Eli. He lunged, his fist crashing into Eli's face. Only Eli's head jerked back in response. His body did not move an inch. I yelped in surprise. I would have expected this from Eli, but not Torin. This short, violent temper was not him. Torin swung in for a second hit which never made contact. Eli darted out of the way, pushing me back. His reaction and fight techniques were quicker than Torin's. There was no contest. Eli could easily kill Torin. Eli ducked and barreled forward, his shoulder slamming into Torin's stomach. Torin's walking stick flew from his hand, almost hitting me in the head.

"Stop!" My voice rang.

They didn't hear me or didn't care.

Bodies tumbled to the ground, leaves and branches crunching under their weight as they fought. Blood sprayed from Torin's nose as it collided with Eli's elbow. Torin struck at Eli's face with the heel of his palm. A crack of Eli's jaw told me the contact had been full force.

"Stop it!" I screamed again. I tried to concentrate to move them away from each other with my mind, but nothing happened, except a few branches flew through the air. Grunting and swearing, they rolled, kicking and hitting each other. In the dark shadows of the forest, I saw Eli's eyes flash red as Torin took another swing. My stomach plummeted. Eli's eyes only flashed red when he was ready to kill.

My lids squeezed together, digging deep inside me. I needed to pull them apart. Now.

"Stop!" A strong clear voice rang behind me. Torin and Eli ceased instantly.

I swung around already knowing who it was.

Kennedy stood there with hands on her hips and an expression I had seen a few times when she had been mad at me and Ryan.

"That is enough." Her tiny frame was commanding as she strode toward the guys. "You two should be ashamed of yourselves. This is not the time or place. People are dying and our friends and family are locked up and being tortured."

Even though I hadn't been the one fighting, my head lowered in shame. She had a certain way about her. Kennedy could be silent for hours and utter one word completely changing your world. My guilt came from having been selfish and cruel to her all week. I had forgotten I wasn't the only one hurting, scared, and frustrated.

The boys climbed to their feet, blood gushing from their noses and lips.

Kennedy picked up Torin's walking stick. "You most of all should be trying to heal and get stronger for the real battle, not fighting for something which cannot be won. Neither of you will win this. It is given, not taken."

Kennedy always said odd things. In high school people considered her "weird" when she said things like this. Now, her strange insights and mysterious phrasing made more sense. It was the seer in her coming out, her Druid nature working its way to the surface.

She had power over the guys. They stood there looking at her with this strange awe. She could have told them to march straight to their bedrooms, and I had little doubt they would have obeyed.

Her spell broke the moment I opened my mouth. "What were you thinking? We don't need you at each other's throats right now." My arms waved frantically. "I want you to stop this now."

"You definitely didn't say those words the other night." Eli wiped the blood from his lip. The knowing, smug smile on his face caused fire to rise up my neck.

"How can you so blatantly disrespect and embarrass her like you do?" Torin took a wobbly step toward Eli again. "You are not worthy of her."

"I never said I was." Eli crossed his arms.

"Seriously, enough both of you," I yelled, having met my limit of their shit.

Kennedy stepped up to Torin and placed his cane in front of him. "Let me walk you back."

Torin's nostrils still flared with anger, but when Kennedy repeated his name he nodded, looking away from Eli and me. Kennedy took Torin's free arm and started him toward the house. She gave one last look over her shoulder, her gaze drifting to me, then Eli. It was quick but full of meaning. *You two deal with your problems* was the basic translation. Her head swiveled back before she and Torin slipped into the darkness.

As soon as they were out of sight, I turned sharply, facing Eli. I moved inches from his face. "What were you going do, beat the crap out of someone who is wounded and sick? Is that what kind of *man* you are?"

His face held a fierce expression, not flinching at my nearness. "Funny, because I think he came after me first. Torin is neither weak nor vulnerable." He moved his lips only inches from mine.

I was suddenly too close to him.

"And don't forget, *little girl*. I am *not* a man. I know you enjoy the fact I can screw you like a beast." His fingers brushed across the crotch of my pants, the friction shooting tingles through me. Fervor vibrated in my stomach and moved lower. My lids shut briefly, stifling a moan. "See? It likes the beast, too."

Knowing he could have me on my knees anytime he desired fueled rage in my gut. I wanted him to take me right there—so hard I didn't know the difference between pleasure and pain. I bit the inside of my cheek. "Do not piss me off tonight. I am not in the mood for your *shit*." My words flew at him with so much fury and pent-up sexual frustration he staggered back one step.

He quickly regained lost distance, his chest bumping into me. The warmth of his skin underneath his shirt and the feel of his hardness pressing into me kicked my desire up a notch. "Why is it you're the only one who scares me?" Eli tilted his head, his lips curling in a smile.

"Because you want your beast parts to stay intact."

His eyes glinted and fastened on mine. Desire, want, need throbbed between us, filling every molecule in the air. I kept my gaze strong and leveled at him. He lifted his hand to my face, but stopped before it touched me. Eli glanced to the side, letting his arm drop. His flirtatious mood altered. He stared at me, his pupils growing vertical. With the way he looked at me, I could sense frustration battering within him. A harsh growl emitted from the depths of his throat. He swung around. A violent roar bounced off the canopy of trees. His clothes ripped from his body as he altered into Dark Dweller form. His dagger-like claws ripped into the earth as he tore away.

I stood there after he was gone, my breathing shallow in my chest. Finally, I turned the opposite way and started to move. My need to run and bounce off rocks was essential for my sanity also.

Tearing through the trees, I jumped from boulder to boulder with precision. My connection with nature mapped the lay of the land in my head. I felt the strongest here. Both my Dae and Dark Dweller sides melded into a peaceful union. I felt more liberated than I had in a long time. Both Lars's and the Dark Dweller's compounds might allow more freedom than the prison at the castle, but they still confined me. I wanted out. I needed to run with no boundaries or limitations.

My legs tore across the terrain jumping, spinning, sprinting, and smashing through the property, taking out all my aggression.

I finally stopped, panting and sweaty. It was a beautiful, clear night, and the stars above shone down on me. I lay back on a rock staring up at the never-ending space.

For a brief moment, I let the threat of the Queen, the deaths, and hidden, magical swords float toward the sky. Leaves lifted off the ground, drifting toward the direction of my gaze. They flipped and twirled as my mind moved them around like chess pieces. They looked like spaceships darting through the night sky. The notion of little green men, aliens, coming to invade Earth was laughable. The real threat was here, dressed and looking human.

Humans never thought of Fae as being real—the true danger. If the invasion of Fae did come, Earth would no longer exist. Magic would tear it apart and leave everything in ruin. I had to stop Aneira. I just didn't know how. The only thing that could stop her was the Sword of Light, and we were no closer to it than we were a month ago.

As my mind dove deeper into my thoughts, I felt a tiny prickling on my skin. Someone was there. Watching me. My "Spidey" senses were in full bloom. I sniffed deeply. The scent was familiar, but nobody or nothing I could place. The leaves fell from my mind-hold as I sat up. I tried to see through the dark shadows looming thickly around me. The boulder turned into a slide as I slipped soundlessly to the ground.

Twigs snapped. My gaze darted and roved over the brush. Swallowing, my heart thumped in my throat. *Who could get through the border?* My nose examined the air again. All Fae smelled different, but powerful magic had a particular odor. Humans also had a distinct scent I was starting to recognize. This didn't smell like any of them.

Keeping low to the ground, I skulked closer. At one time I would have stayed in one spot shaking like a little girl. Those days were over. I pulled out the knife I kept in my boot. The blade glistened under the bright stars as I slipped soundlessly into the throng of shadows.

My focus centered on a darker silhouette under the trees. A figure stood looking at the boulder where I had been sitting. Gripping the knife tighter in my hand, I sprung at the form, dagger ready. The body whipped around sensing me. The face became unmistakable.

"Dammit!" I tried to pivot at the last moment, but still collided into the object. His arms grappled onto me as he slammed back into a tree.

"What the hell, Ember?"

I straightened up and got my balance. "Holy crap, Josh, you scared the shit out of me." My hand clutched my chest.

"I scared you? You freakin' had a knife going for my throat."

"Well, what were you doing sneaking up on me? Not smart."

He grumbled something and brushed himself off, standing upright.

"What are you doing out here, Josh? Alone."

A snort came out him. "*You're* out here alone."

A frown pressed down my lips. Lately, I felt like he took everything

I said the wrong way. Finally, having a moment to relax, my feelers picked up Josh's scent. He smelled like himself. Teenage boy. But not the odor I had detected earlier.

"I came out to get you for dinner, but I got caught up in watching you jump the rocks and move the leaves around. Seriously impressive." He jerked his head toward the boulders.

"Thanks." I wiped my forehead, tidying back the loose stands of hair. "Many months of training."

"With the Demons." It wasn't a question.

"Yeah." The thought of Lars launched shudders through my shoulders. Strangely, I missed him and the others who had trained me. A lot. Particularly Marguerite. I missed her warm hugs.

"So you haven't contacted them yet?"

"No." I fervently shook my head. "Lars is definitely someone I'm avoiding at present, for my own well-being."

"Oh?" Josh's eyebrow curved.

I smiled thinly. "Never make a pact with a Demon." I grabbed Josh's arm, tugging him toward the house. "Come on, I'm starved."

When Josh and I reached the house, I heard a noise. It didn't take long before Josh was looking around curiously for the source of it, too. It sounded like crackling, thick paper.

"He has insulted me for the last time, Cal." I heard Simmons's voice before I saw him.

"Stop moving, Simmons. You're spilling it," Cal exclaimed.

Following the voices, we walked around the wood stack on the side of the house. Cal and Simmons were on a large, white piece of paper, with leaves scattered over it and a bowl of liquid in the middle. The way Cal hugged and clutched the bowl, I was certain it contained juniper juice. Cal hiccupped and started humming happily.

"What's going on here?" I put my hands on my hips and glared down at the two pixies.

Simmons's chest was puffed up. He tried to pick up his bare feet, but the paper came with his foot and threatened to tip over the container.

"Hey." Cal frowned at Simmons then turned back to his bowl, his face full of pure adoration. "He's sorry, my love. He didn't know what he was doing. He promises never to do it again." He fondled the side with loving caresses.

"What happened?" A smile hinted at my lips. But I had learned when Simmons was offended not to make it worse.

"Your Dark Dweller set a trap for us, my lady. A cruel, evil trap. We're stuck."

I nudged Josh in the ribs when I heard him snicker. He squatted and touched the paper. "It's fly paper. My grandma used to put it out in the summer to catch flies and mosquitoes."

My hand flew up to my mouth, disguising my need to laugh. "Let me help you get off it."

I got some water and, with a little force and some of Simmons's skin, he pulled free of the paper. Cal had a death grip on the dish, so I tugged them off as a united pair. Cal didn't even seem to notice or care he was free. He reclined next to the bowl and fell asleep cuddling the saucer.

"My lady, beware. The fight is on now. No one messes with a pixie," Simmons declared before flying off.

"I'll actually have to give Eli credit. That was pretty damn funny." Josh chuckled as he headed for the house.

I rubbed at my temples as the snores from Cal fluttered over the breeze. Funny, yes, except I had heard pixies were known pranksters. This could get nasty.

THIRTEEN

"Where are they?" A voice boomed. I jumped awake, searching the room for the threat. My blurry gaze settled on Eli filling the doorway of the cabin.

Being jolted awake by Eli tearing into the room like a mad-man was all too familiar. I dug my head back into my pillow with a groan, but Kennedy and Mom sprang up startled.

"Where are those little fuckers?"

Huffing, I pushed the blanket off and sat up, rubbing my face. "What are you yelling about?"

"The pixies... where are they hiding?"

"How should I know?" My eyes had finally cleared enough to see something was all over Eli's shaved head. "What the hell is on your head?" Eli's shoulders widened as he took in a breath. I could now see on his forehead and scalp were a dozen penned doodles.

"Are those...?" I trailed off as my hand went to my mouth.

"Penises, yeah."

I burst out laughing but quickly tried to stop when Eli's eyes flashed red. I did a horrible job; my mouth twitched as a giggle clawed up my throat to get out. I had to fight it even more as I continued to look at the crude sketches of penis shapes on Eli's head.

"You think this is funny?" Eli demanded. "They wrote in permanent marker."

The giggles took over, shaking my body, and I howled with laughter. Finally, when I could talk, I added, "You *were* acting like a dick. You insulted two pixies, and they retaliated. You know pixies are tricksters. You only got what you deserved." I shrugged, trying to hold back my snigger. "Actually, it suits you."

His eyes ran over me, taking me in. For the briefest moment I could

113

have sworn I saw amusement flicker in his eyes, but he turned and stomped out of the room, slamming the door behind him.

A hoot of laughter came out of my mouth.

"Now that was funny," Mom said from her bed. "Think Cal and Simmons are my new favorite people."

My stomach ached from laughing, and tension slid off my shoulders. It was exactly what I needed at the moment. Wiping my eyes, I got up out of bed.

"Where are you going?" Kennedy asked.

"I'm going to go warn Cal and Simmons... after I thank them."

I pulled my tangled hair back into a ponytail as I stepped outside. I was still wearing Eli's boxers to bed. I kept telling myself it was because it was so warm outside, but it was a lie.

"Cal? Simmons?" I ventured off the porch. "You guys better hide for a day or two," I spoke to the trees. I knew they were there and could hear me. In case other people were listening, I kept my tone a little chastising. There was a slight movement in the trees. I winked and gave them two thumbs up. A tiny snicker was my only response.

I guess I should go check on Eli and see how pissed he really is.

The house was empty when I entered. I thought I heard motorcycles revving this morning while still half asleep. Lucky them. They could leave when they wanted and get away for the day. Someone was always around; they never all left, so I moved quietly into the house and down the hallway to Eli's room.

"Eli?" I knocked while opening the bedroom door. I popped my head in, quickly assessing the area. It was empty. His room and his belongings called to me, wanting me to discover their hidden secrets. My curiosity suddenly took over any rational thought. I wanted to know what he had as treasures or keepsakes. I glanced behind me. When I was sure he was nowhere around, I continued in. I had been here only a week earlier, but my attention had not been on the objects in his room. It had been on other items he had. The door clicked behind me as I shut it.

Eli was such a perplexing, ambiguous person. I knew he kept secrets from me, and there was so much about him I didn't know. He had a history with my mom no one would talk about. The Dark Dwellers were exiled, and he had something to do with it. Why was he the reason they had been banned? What had caused those scars on his face or his limp? There was a story there, but he was too defensive and guarded when it came to his past.

114

Hell, I didn't even know what books he liked to read. And, okay, if I were being honest, I wondered what kind of porn, if any, he had in his sock drawer.

One wall was lined with windows, one had closets, and the other held the door. His bed occupied the only blank wall. There were no posters or art on the walls, but there was a shelf with books and a dresser with money, loose paper, and a locked wooden box. I tiptoed to it. I could open it; I had opened locked doors before. The only problem was I couldn't relock it. If I forced it open with my mind, it would shatter the lock inside, and Eli would know. I couldn't break into someone's private stuff so blatantly. I forced myself to turn away and look at his bookshelf instead. That was innocent enough if caught.

The books ranged from *Lord of the Rings* and *Motorcycle Diaries* to *Animal Farm* and *Hunger Games*. The last two kind of worried me. *Animal Farm Meets Hunger Games* was hitting a little too close to home in this place. I moved to his dresser. The top drawer held his socks and other things. Only a few boxers were in there. He didn't seem to put on underwear often. No porn. Maybe it was under the bed.

The second drawer was full of t-shirts. I was about to close it when one caught my attention. The paint stain on it was something I recognized. The familiar t-shirt was one of my favorites. It had been Mark's before I stole it, and even though I got paint on it, I couldn't give it up. It was not one I had brought to the ranch last time. It had been in the dirty pile in my closet. I hadn't had time to get it before the Strighoul attacked me when Eli and Cole had let me go back to my house to get some of my belongings. So why was the shirt here?

I left the dresser behind and went to his closet. Clothes draped from hangers, his boots and shoes below. But something big and bulky sat in the back of the closet. Dropping to my knees, I crawled to the back and dragged it into the light. The box was heavy and large. I lifted the lid and peered in. My hands dug through the objects, not believing what I was seeing. It was like someone punched me in my stomach.

The chest was full of my stuff: my baby books, my art, Mom and Mark's wedding album, and many other things I thought were lost forever. I grabbed my baby book, my fingers glided over the small tear in the inseam, pulling a piece of fabric from its binding. The cut of material was supple in my hand—my baby blanket. Needlepoint silk thread was sewn around the edge. My tattoo symbol. Torin told me my mom had been a powerful Dreamwalker. Had the dreams of my mom actually been dreams, or had she dreamwalked with me? It was another thing on my ever-growing list to ask her. She had been tight-lipped since she had gotten back. Because of what she went through, I tried to let it go until she was ready. I think the time was up; I wanted answers now.

As silent as he was, I felt Eli enter the room. His presence filled the space, but he did not speak. I shoved the piece of fabric into my waistband.

"What is this?" I waved to the box containing my stuff.

He stayed quiet and stared at me, his arms crossed over his chest.

"Why do you have my stuff? My baby book, photo albums, my old t-shirt."

"You and Mark have been gone for three years. Did you think your house would sit there?" He moved farther into the room. "The bank put it on the market."

I turned and looked at Eli. He was fresh from a shower. His only clothing was a pair of jeans that hung low on his hips. Drops of water ran in trails down his chest. He wiped his head with a towel. They had faded a little, but the markings were still there. I looked back down at the things in my hands. "You have my photo albums and sketch pads."

Silence.

"But you thought I died... so why would you get my stuff?"

Eli glanced out the window.

Looking back down in the chest, I picked up a DVD. "The Twilight Zone?" I recalled embarrassing myself when I had first met him and invited him over to watch the series.

"Yeah, someone told me it was a cult classic, and I should probably see it."

A twinge of emotion flickered through me. Eli would probably never admit it, but he thought I died and still retrieved these items from my house. He had wanted something of mine. This meant more to me than if he had actually said *I love you*. I was certain nobody knew he had done this. Showing emotions would be a weakness he wouldn't want anybody to know, including me. More tears ebbed at my lids—tears I had been keeping at bay all week. I bit down hard on my lip.

"Well, thanks." I tried to sound unemotional.

He sighed heavily.

"What?" I stood, facing him. He propped his shoulder against the wall, leaning as he studied me. "What?" I demanded again, infuriated with his muteness. "You don't have a biting retaliation? Seriously? You?"

He folded his arms over his taut chest. His muscles cut in ridged lines across his abs.

Not that I noticed or anything.

"Dammit! Say something. Anything. Yell at me for sneaking into your room, for going through your stuff." My arms flailed, like a dysfunctional windmill. "Speak, bark, meow... I don't care. Just have one frickin' emotion or thought. Don't stand there."

His green eyes sparked, and he stepped forward. I countered his step and moved back. His emotions were unreadable. He had the same look when he ordered takeout or was about to snap someone's neck. Nervousness made my heart beat faster, but I stood tall.

"There she is." He lifted his eyebrows and gave me a steady look.

"There who is?"

"The passionate, opinionated, pain-in-the-ass girl I have come to know." He stepped even closer, aligning our bodies. "She disappeared this week. Became distant and detached. Cruel even."

I blinked. "Wait. You're calling me out for being mean, distant, and detached? That's comical."

"Yes, but those things are my charming personality. Not yours."

My throat tightened. I bowed my head.

"I know you feel guilt and pain. You've been through a lot, but you without your emotions, isn't you. Those feelings make you who you are. Why you love so passionately, protect your loved ones so fiercely, and act like a stubborn mule. It's why people are drawn to you, even against their will."

I snorted.

He pulled my face up to look into his. I could feel the wall, which I had put up to guard me from the latest wave of unbearable pain, start to crumble.

"But I can't take it. It's too much," I hung my head.

"You can because you have to." Even trying to be nice, Eli still didn't sugar coat things. "You have people counting on you. You're the only one who can stop her."

I tilted my head into his chest, letting out a breath. We stood for a moment before I felt his arms wrap tightly around me. We drove each other crazy, but he was always the one who could pull me back from a ledge or let me do what I needed to do to get something out of my system. He seemed to understand how I worked even better than I did. He could get me riled up and calm me down. I knew what I felt for him. I was in love with him, and it was terrifying.

117

Without a word, I pushed up on my toes. My lips met his, and instantly fire rushed through my veins. I sighed; I was home. He kissed me slowly and thoroughly, but the spark between us heated swiftly. His hand gripped the back of my head, crushing me into him. His tongue and lips were enticing and inviting.

Finally, I pulled away, both of us breathing heavily. My eyes burned into his. "I've come to recognize this week that you are a serious pain in the ass. I will probably come to regret telling you this, but I've realized I *can* live without you, Dragen. I just don't *want* to."

A grin hinted at his mouth. "Ditto, Brycin."

He went to kiss me again. I knew how things would turn out if I let it. And this is where the vicious cycle lay. Eli and I never talked about or solved the problems between us.

I drew away. "We need to talk." Even I cringed as the words came out of my mouth. Eli's eyebrows went up. "Yeah, I can't believe I uttered those words either. But we do." My teeth tugged at my bottom lip, gathering my words. "I never wanted a normal guy or a typical relationship. It's not who I am. I wouldn't be happy with a 'nice' guy." I made quotes in the air.

"A nice guy wouldn't be able to handle you," Eli agreed with a smirk.

"We can't keep going around like this. I can't take it anymore not with everything else going on. I want one thing I can rely on." My toe rubbed at the cracks in the wood floor. "Not that we won't fight, be sarcastic, or drive each other mad because it's who we are. I can't take the hot and cold from you. I want to know you are in this... you want this." I motioned between us.

Eli's chest expanded as he took in a deep breath, his arms crossing defensively. He was silent for a few moments before uttering, "I want you."

Happiness, desire, and fear fought through my body. "If you really mean it, we can't have secrets between us. I don't want someone trying to be my protector; I want a partner. If we are in this together, we are in this as equals. I am no delicate little girl. I need the truth all the time. Harsh or scary as it might be."

"Agreed. But, in all fairness, I've never seen you anything but as equal... even times I didn't want you to be."

"Then tell me the truth now. Tell me what happened between you and my mother."

A frown cut across his mouth, and he shook his head. "I can't. It is the one thing I cannot talk about."

Frustration burned up my esophagus. "Why? What happened between you? We said no more secrets. Tell me. Why do you both keep things from me?"

"I cannot tell you. You need to ask your mother." Eli's eyes flashed red, his jaw set. "Decide now if this changes things for you."

I didn't know how to respond. Silence and tension cut through the room, turning icy and volatile the longer I stayed quiet.

Finally, I whispered, "I need *something* from you. Tell me about your past. Anything. Like your clan. Why did they hate Daes so much?" I was willing to take any kind of truth or explanation right then. "Please, I need to understand."

Eli's hand went up to his head. With a huff of air, he sat on his bed. "My not telling you this story had nothing to do with keeping the truth from you." His voice was low, humming tenderly in my ear. "The time haunts me. I've never talked about it to anyone."

I longed to sit next to him but held my ground. He wasn't good at dealing with emotion and being close would make things worse.

"I was around the age of ten in human years. There was a group of Daes who had escaped the Queen's notice and had lived on Earth undetected. It was the late eighteen hundreds, a time when even the slightest hint of anyone hearing or seeing unusual things put them into an asylum. Even worse was if you caused things to happen. Unfortunately, these Daes started to gain attention from wardens and fellow patients. The Queen sent in her soldiers to take care of them, but with help the Daes escaped.

"Aneira needed help tracking them down. It's where we came in. My father and mother were the clan leaders; Cole's parents were second in command. The Queen came to my father, paying us a hefty sum to kill the Daes." His green eyes darted to mine. "Remember, my clan was different in the Otherworld; we protected each other fiercely. Nothing and no one else mattered to us. We were born killers, and we took it seriously."

I nodded. I knew this, but it still was hard to hear how cold they were and how ruthlessly they killed. I squirmed, not wanting to know the truth, but I knew I needed to listen to all of it.

"We found their hideout. It was my first real mission, although I had gone out many times before. Gabby, Cooper, and I were too young to actually help with the kill, but Lorcan had been working for several years. Cooper and Gabby were still on lookout, but I got to be part of it on this night." I saw a glimmer of the little-boy pride he must have felt being part of the group.

"We had dealt with Daes before, but this group was different. They were powerful and unstable. They had not learned to control their magic. My father's pride and ego did not foresee how formidable Daes could be, especially when scared and with nothing to lose.

"Things went wrong immediately. An incredibly commanding woman seemed to be the leader. She and her mate killed a third of us before my father pulled back. I was young, stupid, and pumped on my first assignment and thought if I snuck around from behind, I could be the one to kill her. The newest of the clan to ever claim a kill that young..." Eli tapered off. His eyes squeezed shut as uncomfortable memories seemed to stir in him. "Her senses were more heightened than I thought. She knew I was coming and let me get close before turning her powers on me. My mother acted purely on instinct and came at her, ready to destroy the woman. I remember one of the male Daes screaming to warn the woman. Trying to protect her, he went after my mother. His power made her brain and insides burst. She died instantly, a bloody horrible death."

Eli's gaze was far away. "Everything went downhill from there. She crushed my leg but stopped there. I don't know why she hesitated to kill me. It gave my father time to attack, and Cole got me out." His limp and the scars on his face were daily reminders of what happened. "My father and most of our clan were wiped out. Only a handful survived."

My throat closed tightly around itself. "I'm so sorry, Eli."

"Not only had I been raised despising Daes and thinking they were abominations, but my hatred for them only grew after this. I swore revenge on them all." He glanced at me with a sad smile hinting in his eyes. "You kind of threw my plan out the window." He shifted on the bed.

Words detoured off my tongue leaving me mute. I was torn. There was a part of me which understood my own kind and wanted to say they were only protecting themselves. Then there was the part connected to Eli, but not through blood, which wanted to hold him and tell him it was not his fault. It would have probably ended the same.

"There's more," he murmured, stopping my words.

My eyebrows rose as my heart plummeted. I didn't think I could handle much more.

"The name the man screamed... the Dae's name... was Brycin."

Air halted in my lungs. "What?"

Eli's hand went to his head again, rubbing at the new growth. "When you told me your name the first day at Silverwood, I couldn't believe it. It felt like some sick joke fate was playing on me by bringing to the surface every wound I had tried to bury. It made me hate you more. Part of me wanted to kill you right then for it being thrown in my face. I purposely started calling you Brycin so it would remind me of what I went through and what you were to me." Eli's head shook as if he was trying to expel the memories. "Everything was stacked against you. I thought my intrigue was from disgust, but I grew angrier every day because my infatuation for you only increased. It went against my every instinct and desire. I told myself I was only getting to know you, to use you. Wanting to be around you was only because someday my parents would be revenged and my family would get back to the Otherworld. It would have been so simple if those things happened, but they didn't. And I resented you for it."

Why did I demand the truth when it only led to things I didn't want to hear? I had no idea how to respond to his confession. It hurt to hear him say those things, even if it made his treatment of me at the beginning clearer. His feelings might be different now, but it was hard to understand at one time he dreamed of killing me out of revenge because I happened to be from a group who had been deemed outcasts and treated like vermin. It was also difficult to hear about the gruesome deaths of his family by my kind. The Daes had only been trying to save the people they cared about. Both sides thought they were right. Both sides lost.

The other thing that struck me... Was it purely a coincidence my last name was Brycin? I had quickly learned in the Fae world nothing was by chance. So why was I named after this other Dae?

Eli's gaze penetrated mine. "I know what you want to ask, and I don't know. That's something you will have to discuss with your mother. Fae don't have last names; we have clan names. The Fae who live on Earth usually make them up to fit among humans. All of our names here were taken from our father's names. Mine was known as Dragen. I don't know what relationship you have to Brycin, but I don't think it is a fluke."

I didn't either. His eyes were on me, and I lowered my head.

"So this is how I get you to be quiet, huh?" He clasped his hands together, leaning his arms on his legs.

My own hung at my sides, watching my toes move methodically

over the groves in the wood floor. "I asked for the truth. I can't be mad you gave it to me." I took a moment and a deep breath. The revelation felt heavy on my shoulders. "Thank you for telling me." I may understand Eli more, but my past felt more clouded. "I need to talk to my mom."

He responded with a nod.

I opened the door and headed for the one person who could explain and clear up the garbled mess twisted in my gut.

As I walked out the front door, I heard my name being called. Torin sat in a chair on the porch of the infirmary cabin. Thara was by his side. There was no way to pretend I didn't hear him even though I didn't feel like talking to him right then. With an undisguised exhalation, I headed to him.

I nodded at them as I approached. "Have you seen my mom?"

"I think she went for a walk. She said she needed time to herself," Thara said.

Damn. I knew my mom. Like me, she loved to escape deep into the forest for hours. It would be pointless trying to track her down. I would have to wait to talk to her.

"So how are you feeling?" I grabbed onto the rail, looking toward him.

"Almost back to my normal self, thank you," Torin answered. His hands nervously stroked his knees. "Are you available to talk? I would like to speak with you. Maybe a walk in the woods?"

I had my fill of talking for the day, but I nodded anyway.

With a groan Torin pushed himself out of the chair.

"Please, you need to rest." Thara immediately jumped up to help him stand.

"I need exercise. If I stay sitting or lying one more second, I will go crazy." He smiled and patted her arm in assurance. Thara still looked like she wanted to push him back into the chair and tie him up. "I will not go far. I promise." He stepped down the stairs and motioned for me.

Thara watched us go, appearing to fight every impulse she had. Her fists clenched at her sides, her face tight, holding back her disapproval.

"You'd better not trip, or she will be out here dragging you back faster than you can blink," I mused when we were out of earshot.

"Yes. Her intentions are in the right place. She is an especially faithful soldier to me. Maybe a little too dedicated at this time."

I gave him a side glance. "You think that's why she is faithful? Because she's a good soldier?"

"Yes, why?"

An amused chuckle came from my throat. "Oh, Torin, you have much to learn about women." I glanced behind us. We were out of sight from the cabin. "She's in love with you." His eyes grew into saucers. "Oh, come on, you can't be that dense?"

Torin looked over his shoulder in the direction of the cabin. Realization plummeted over his features. "But... but she can't be."

"Why not?"

"Because I am meant for you." He turned back to me, his face set in a stubborn resolution.

"Yeah, about that," I mumbled, stuffing my hands in my pockets. "Can I ask you something?"

"Anything."

"You say we are meant for each other, we are destined. But what is it you actually like about me?"

He stepped back, his eyebrows lowering into a line. "What do you mean?"

"I mean *why* do you like me?"

"That is a silly question." Irritation flicked at the surface of his eyes. His temper surfaced quickly again. It made me sad Torin had changed. The Queen had won in a way. She did break a piece of him, and I couldn't help but feeling I was the one to blame.

"No, it really isn't." I pulled my hands out of my pockets and folded my arms over my chest. "Do you find me funny? Do I challenge you? What do you feel when you see me?"

Torin huffed. "I don't understand what you are trying to get at. Of course, I look forward to seeing you. I take great pleasure in being with you. In kissing you."

"Take pleasure... yeah." A sad smile pulled at my lips. "All you've ever done is your duty. Have you stopped and thought if this is really what *you* want?" His forehead creased as he took in my question. "I have no doubt if I had been born a pure Fay and had grown up in the Otherworld, you and I would probably have a nice life together. But it was not our destiny. It's certainly not mine."

Torin's head wrenched back and forth in refusal at hearing my words. He sounded annoyed. "Ember, you know I don't care what you are. I will protect and love you no matter what."

Frustration crept up my neck. "That's the problem. I don't need protection. I want a partner not a keeper." I took a huge intake of breath.

"Torin, you are so set on 'duty' and 'honor' you are missing the whole point. I swear, even if you felt nothing for me, you'd still be with me only because it was what you thought you should do. It is not who I am and nor what I want. I want passion and love. A best friend *and* a partner." Seeing his face, I quickly rushed on. "There is nothing wrong with honor and duty but not when it comes to marriage or being in a relationship. I want you to honestly tell me you are in love with me. Not because you were told you should be, or it's what you've always thought, but because you actually are."

Torin stared at me, his breath growing shallow. His arms and legs twitched restlessly. "Are you saying this because of Dragen?" Both his eyes and words challenged me to answer, but he didn't give me the opportunity. "You may think you care for him, but he is a Dark Dweller, Ember, a soulless killer. He cannot love anyone. I will not let you get hurt by something like him. He is playing you and will get bored eventually and leave you."

Ouch.

"You have no say in the matter. This is my choice."

Something flared in his eyes, and he turned abruptly, his fist smashing into a tree. Rage tore through his hand into the bark, shredding some of the top layer of the wood. I stumbled back in surprise, not ready for his sudden outburst. "Gods, Ember. How can you not see the truth? How can you not see what he really is?"

My mouth opened and shut, no words forming on my tongue.

"I love you. I am the one who was meant for you." His knuckles bled and dripped down his hand, falling into the soft dirt. "We are supposed to be together; even the gods put us together. We render each other whole."

I always hated that sentiment. Other people do not make us whole. You are whole without having someone else. The person only added to your awesomeness.

"No one makes me whole." I grumbled, but he didn't seem to hear me. "Torin, you deserve more. Someone who truly loves you and you love back. We are not minions of these gods. Our lives are our own to decide, and we control our fate, not them." I could feel my words were hitting a wall. He did not receive anything I said. "You should be with who you want. Both of us should. I love you, but I am not in love with you, and I don't think you are either. Not really."

He limped to me and placed his body against mine. "You are wrong,

Ember. I am in love with you." He cupped my cheek. He was angry, but his touch was soft. "I will always love you. I will let you discover how wrong Eli is for you. And when he leaves you, and he will, I will be there. Because in the end it is you and me." His blue eyes were intense, his focus on my lips. I was sure he was going to try and kiss me. Instead, he dropped his hand with a sigh, swung around, and headed back for the cabin. I let him walk away. My heart twisted with conflict. The bond tugged at me wanting me to go after him. The other part knew it was only because I didn't want to hurt him, not because I was in love with him.

FOURTEEN

"When you're upset, you mumble to yourself. Voices fighting in your head again?" Eli's voice radiated from behind me. Hearing his rumbling tone was like a trigger. I swung around. My heart leaped at his gorgeous, chiseled face with the scar cutting through the stubble on his jaw—so dear to me now.

"How long have you been there?"

Disregarding my question, he strode to me. His body aligned to mine. "You know the difference between him and me? I wouldn't let you find out I was wrong for you." His words were husky and low.

"Would you respect my wishes?" My voice matched his husky tone. He seized my face with both of his hands. My breath hitched. "Even if I demanded you to leave me alone?"

He pressed even closer, his gaze dipping to my lips. "Hell, no." He closed any gap left between us and kissed me so deeply my whole body felt it.

It wasn't until after dinner I got a chance to be alone with my mom. She was on the porch in the rocking chair, using the last of the evening light to read.

"Fae don't have last names so how did we get Brycin?" I blurted, getting right to the point.

Mom looked up from her book, her gaze curious.

"Eli told me there was a Dae, one who killed his family, whose name was Brycin. I know it can't be a coincidence."

She gently closed the book on her lap. "No, you're right. It is not by happenstance. Brycin was the person who helped us escape to this realm without Aneira being able to track us. She helped many Fae flee Aneira's

126

control. A Fae's version of the Underground Railroad you might say. You were a newborn at the time. She got you a birth certificate and all the necessary documentations so we wouldn't be questioned by anyone."

Now the mistakes on my birth certificate made more sense, and why my mom didn't have any pictures of me as a newborn. We'd been on the run.

"One of the busiest Fae doors is the one in Sedona, Arizona. The magic there is so dense it is hard to traffic. She snuck us out and had someone waiting to take us far away from Aneira's watchful eyes. Brycin was an incredible person. Strong, passionate, smart. You remind me a lot of her."

Mom paused, and her voice cracked with emotion. "Unfortunately, helping us led to her demise. She was caught by the Queen and killed because she aided you and me. I heard Aneira tortured her, but she never told her anything." Lily looked away blinking back the tears. "I wanted to honor her. You and I would not be here without her."

Overwhelming sadness swirled in me for a woman I didn't know. She was a fellow Dae, someone like me, and she was killed protecting and assisting her kind. Conflicted versions of both Eli's and Mom's accounts rumbled unhappily together. I felt empathy for Eli's tragic story, but I knew Brycin had only been protecting her own clan. Carrying her name filled me with honor and pride. She was someone I wanted to know more about. The fact she died for me just made one more person who had.

"Why... why would she risk her life for me?"

"She thought the cause was worth it. She was trying to start a revolt against Aneira." Mom's fingers absently caressed the book cover. "Plus, you were a special case."

"Why? Because I was a Dae, too?"

"Partly." Mom looked away, not meeting my eyes. "You are destined for great things, Ember."

"You also believe the prophecy is about me?"

With a despondent nod of her head, she signed. "I had hoped it wasn't you. Part of me thought if I took you out of our old world, it would go away."

"But it's such a vague oracle. How do you know it's me they are talking about?" Even as I said it, the truth scuttled in my bones.

Mom's head turned to me, her orange-brown eyes burrowing into mine. "Because it is."

The railing caught me as I leaned back into it. I also felt it was me. I kept hoping someone would tell me otherwise.

"Can I ask you something?" Her face looked so unhappy. "I was wondering if you had checked on Mark. Do you know how he is doing?"

I looked down at my shoes. It had been a while. After what happened in Monterey, I found it difficult. The disaster pushed the raven incident to the far corners of my mind. Now I was questioning if it even happened. "I need to again." Instantly my eyes welled up. "God, I miss him."

"So do I."

My gaze lifted to hers. "I understand why you couldn't dreamwalk while in the dungeon, but why haven't you since? You could see him yourself."

Her teeth tugged on her bottom lip, grief washing over her expression. "I am the one to blame for what happened to him. I was too selfish to live without him and dragged him into this. If I really loved him, I should have walked away."

"You haven't dreamwalked or dreamscaped with me before, have you?"

She stared at me for a bit before shaking her head, "No. Why do you ask?"

I pulled the bit of fabric out of my pocket. Lily's eyes widened as she leaned forward seeing what was in my hand. "I only found this recently. Long after I got my tattoo."

"Your baby blanket," she muttered to herself, rubbing the material between her fingers.

"Torin told me I acquired my ability to dreamwalk from my mother."

"You did," she concurred.

"Then why didn't you ever try to dreamwalk or dreamscape with me? To let me know you were okay?"

"I couldn't."

I rubbed my head. "A couple nights after I thought you died, and again just the other night, I had a dream. A woman appeared to me. I never saw her face, but I knew it was you. I could feel so much love coming from her. She dropped a necklace in my hand, telling me it was who I was, and it would protect me. It became the symbol I had tattooed on my back, the same one I found on the blanket. If this was a dream, how would I know about this symbol?"

Mom's eyes glistened with tears. "You are incredibly powerful and so is your bloodline. I was a fool for trying to keep you from discovering who you really were. I should have known no matter what it would find you."

We both stayed silent before she stood and walked to me. Her arms wrapped around me, squeezing me tight. I loved her hugs; they had always made me feel safe, protected, and so completely loved. "Do you know how much I love you? You are my world. There is nothing more powerful than a mother's love. Whatever happened in the past or whatever the future holds, will you remember this for me? There isn't anything in this world or the other I wouldn't do or give up for you."

I nodded.

"I love you, *my* girl. So much." She touched my cheek and the swung around, taking off down the steps and into the dusky forest.

That night, Eli slept soundly beside me. With the revelations so raw for the both of us, we did nothing more than sleep next to each other. His hand was always in contact with me, making sure I was there and safe. Being back in Eli's arms soothed me. It gave me the strength of heart to dreamwalk again. Guilt and fear had kept me away from my loved ones for too long. I needed to know they were all right.

I relaxed into the pillow, my eyes closing. In this dreamwalk I wanted to head for Mark and Ryan first.

Surprise rushed through me when I saw Ryan sitting up in bed. Castien sat by his side; Mark stood looking out the barred window.

Impulse took me to Ryan's bedside. Damn. It is so good to see Ryan conscious again.

The glow around him had become even more vibrant. His cheeks were flushed pink, and his skin was back to his normal color.

"What you are saying is Ryan is stuck here?" Mark asked. His tone hinted anger, a quality I had heard quite a bit growing up.

"Fae food saved his life. He was dying," Castien shot back.

"Yes, but now he can never leave here. Never go home." Mark turned facing the two boys.

"I can never see my family again? Never even step foot on Earth again?" Ryan's color drained to pale again.

"You could, but being on Earth would eventually kill you. You can never eat human food again. Your body has changed. It's not exactly

human, but it's not Fae either. Humans adapt differently than we do. We can go to both realms with no problems. We once lived there so our bodies can embrace either. Humans cannot travel between worlds. Now that you have a bit of Fae magic in you, your body will reject Earth. Trust me on this. The theory has been tested thoroughly over the years. All humans have died." Castien leaned to grab Ryan's hand. "I do not want the same fate for you."

I could see Ryan's head bob nervously as he looked at Castien's hand on his. I recalled Ryan saying he had experienced "silent" crushes on boys at school. Only one returned his feelings—behind closed doors. But in front of everyone, the boy made it clear they weren't even friends. He made fun of Ryan, calling him a fag.

The boy had promptly flown across the room and hit the gym wall. Everyone claimed they saw me push him, when in actuality I didn't even touch him. Not with my hands anyway. Now I know my mind powers had done all the work for me.

Fae were not raised to think this way. Gender was not an issue. They liked who they liked and had no qualms about it.

"I've always wanted to be Tinker Bell. Can I get a wand at least?" Ryan teased, but the trembling underneath his words showed his true fear.

Castien squeezed his hand. "There are two times when Earth and the Otherworld come together... our realms collide. Those times you can visit Earth. Otherwise, you will have to live here... permanently."

"Here?" Ryan sat up straighter. "I will have to be prisoner the rest of my life?"

Castien's dark hair fluttered back and forth as he shook his head.

"No. I will get you out of here. I have a place where you will be safe. It is in the Dark Fae side, and it is not much, but it is secure."

Ryan gulped. "You will live there, too?"

"Yes."

Full understanding of what Castien was offering sunk in and showed on Ryan's features: bewilderment, fear, and happiness. He cleared his throat. "You said there were two times I could visit Earth?"

"They are Samhain, which humans call Halloween, and Beltane, which is in May. Those are the only times you can safely visit. If you go any other time, your body will react to the difference and start to fail. But you cannot eat human food even when our realms come together."

Ryan brows crunched together as he processed Castien's words. "So I would live in the Otherworld permanently, with you?"

Castien nodded, a shy, nervous smile tugged at his lips.

Mark broke the budding feelings which were filling the space between Castien and Ryan. "Castien, I can't tell you how thankful I am for what you've done for Ryan, for me. It is weird to say that when I am a prisoner. But this is reality not some sweet fairytale where everyone lives happily ever after."

"I understand your concern," Castien said.

"Ryan, you are like my son. I love you, and I want you to fully understand everything that is happening. I realize you don't really have a choice, but all this won't be as easy as you think."

Ryan pulled free of Castien's hand and stood up. Since the Fae food had completely dissolved into his body, he had grown stronger. Even though he had lost some weight, he still was the same round-faced teddy bear I loved. But now there was a power, a confidence, in him that was different. He didn't say a word as he crossed to Mark, wrapping his arms around Mark's tall, lean frame. Mark hugged him back.

Ryan's father had never accepted Ryan. He had ignored who Ryan truly was, always hoping his son was just going through a phase. Over the years, Mark had grown into more of a father figure than Ryan's real dad.

"I will be okay." Ryan gave Mark another squeeze.

"I know you will, but it doesn't mean I won't worry about you."

It was small gesture, and I wondered if Ryan had even felt it, but I saw Mark lightly kiss the top of Ryan's head. Tears spilled down my cheeks, which I knew were flowing from my real body back on Earth.

Ryan and Mark pulled away, both clearing their throats. "So, what do you think Ember would say about me being a Fairy?"

"Oh, probably something sarcastic." Mark laughed.

"I always knew you had it in you," I replied to myself, wanting to be part of their conversation. The happiness I felt being with them, laughing and joking, filled my chest.

"Yeah, probably something like, 'I always knew you had it in you.'" Ryan chuckled.

Damn, that boy knew me too well.

It was time, but leaving them was so hard to do. I wanted to be there with them, hugging and touching them. I felt better knowing Ryan was aware of his condition. I think when reality really set in, it wouldn't be so simple. But if Castien were by his side, it might take the sting out a little.

Next, I needed to dreamwalk to see how West was doing so my concentration turned to him. He was difficult to visit. The fact I couldn't do anything but watch him in pain, not able to help, went against my nature.

The raven also worried me.

When I opened my lids, the dark, dank row of cells lined the walls. West leaned against the bars with his eyes shut. He appeared even more gaunt and sickly than he did last time. His eyes were sunken, and he had lost more weight. My legs bowed taking me to the stone floor next to him. I reached out and touched his face. He shivered, and his lips flittered open, then closed again.

There were no words I could express. He was deteriorating rapidly. Death was striding up the walk way. "Please don't lose hope. Be the normal, pain-in-the-ass, stubborn Dark Dweller I know you are," I whispered.

"Death comes." A voice spoke out of the darkness. I reeled and saw the dwarf sound asleep in the corner chair; the raven stood on his shoulder. "Death will come."

"No." I said at the same time West mumbled, "Can you tell him to hurry? I am really bored here."

"I know you can see me, raven." I stood.

"Fire. I can see," the raven replied.

"You know who I am?"

"Yes. I know." Its wings fluttered. "Helped fire escape."

It took me a minute before the words registered. "Wait. Do you mean you helped get my mom and me out of here?" My thoughts went back to my recent jail break.

"Only baby escape."

My forehead lined with confusion. "Baby?"

"Shut up, bird. Your voice is grating my nerves." West huffed, his eyes still closed.

"Not speaking to you," the raven replied.

"My wish has been granted then." West mistook the bird's meaning. He repositioned his head, the chains rattling.

"What do you mean by baby?" I asked the raven.

"Help my baby, Grimmel," the bird sounded like a recording of a voice.

"Okay, let's start slow." Frustration begun to strain my patience. "Grimmel is your name?"

"Grimmel I am." It hopped down on the dwarf's knee. The dwarf stirred, but his snores only deepened.

Okay, it was a start. "Grimmel, who is this baby you speak of?"

"You." Grimmel cocked its head at me. Then it hit me. It wasn't the recent escape from jail it was talking about. The raven was referring to when I was a baby, and my mom and I fled Aneira. Were we held in the dungeon here before Brycin helped us get through the door to Arizona? Was he a part of that?

"I thought you were not going to talk," West grumbled.

"Not to you."

Ignoring West, I pressed on. "Did you help my mom and me get away from Aneira?"

"Help only baby." The bird fluttered his wings again. "Baby must live. She asked. I do. Help get baby out. Slinking like fox."

Holy crap! It had been there and had helped get us away from the Queen. The raven was not the easiest to talk with, but there were so many questions I wanted to ask. My mouth opened, but Grimmel flew off the dwarf's lap, landing next to me on the bars of the cage.

"Helped her. Baby should not have lived. Baby destroys." Its black eyes dug into me.

I stepped back from the intensity of its gaze and words. "I don't want to destroy."

"Follow in footsteps."

"Whose? My mother's?"

"Yes." The raven nodded its head. "Go. Others find you. She seeks to kill."

"But..." I looked down at West. He appeared like he no longer had the energy to lift his head.

"Cannot help. He is lost."

"No. Don't say that. He will not die. Especially not here." Fear, sadness, and frustration strangled my throat.

"Hurry, Dae. Dark knight falls."

I felt a shove and a spinning before my lids popped open. I was back on Earth.

I stayed awake for the rest of the night. Eventually, the morning light pushed through the gaps in the blinds. Eli rolled onto his side, facing me. "What were you dreaming about last night? You kept whimpering and crying in your sleep."

Blowing out a breath, I hesitated to tell him. But we decided to be fully honest with each other. "I saw West." I bit my lip, waiting for the outrage I knew would follow. "In my dreamwalk."

"West? What? How long have you been visiting him?" Eli sat up. "Why didn't you tell me? How is he?"

"Not good." I knotted my hands. "The neck device is killing him. When he swallows, the rods dig deeper into his muscles. He's lost a lot of weight..." I trailed off.

Eli's eyes flashed red, then went back to green.

"He's still being his West-self, though," I snickered. Even when West couldn't lift his head, he still could come out with some derisive comments. "You sure you two aren't brothers?"

Eli expression was deadly. "He *is* my brother." I knew what he meant. He was Eli's family, blood or not.

"He doesn't have much time. We need to get him out."

Eli bolted out of bed. "Don't you think I know that?" He began to pace the room. Rage came quickly to the surface with him. "I hate I'm sitting on my ass while one of my brothers is being tortured to death. Don't think for a moment his suffering isn't going through my mind every minute." He took a breath. "Tell me everything."

I filled Eli in on my last two dreamwalks.

"This raven claims to have helped you escape? You trust him?" Eli leaned against his dresser. He was still extremely tense and riled. I knew he'd want to know about West, but there was nothing he could do for him right now. Eli didn't handle helplessness well.

"Yeah, I do. I know he won't go to Aneira. He doesn't seem to like her."

"Get in line." Eli shook his head. There was a beat before he screamed. "Dammit!" His fist slammed into the dresser, and a string of Gaelic swear words erupted. He banged the dresser into the wall again, leaving a huge dent. Eli leaned down, breathing heavily.

I gave him a moment before patting the bed. "Come here."

"No." His chest muscles flexed. His hands clawed the dresser, and his nails gouged deep into the wood grain.

"Eli." I knew what would calm him. With a Dark Dweller, it was either this or kill something. He grunted. He would be turning soon.

I got off the bed and went behind him. My fingers hooked the waistband of his boxer-briefs and slowly slid them down. My heart picked up pace as I felt the monster in him so close to the surface. I wasn't afraid. I shifted his body to face me and lowered myself to the floor. We watched each other. I broke eye contact when I leaned in kissing his inner thigh. He sucked in a sharp breath when I moved up, my tongue running along him. A deep guttural moan came out when my warm mouth took him in, moving slowly. A rumble emitted from him, and his breath became quicker.

He groaned, grabbing onto the dresser as I picked up the intensity. His hand came to the back of my head, holding it tight, moving with me. "I want to burrow myself so deep in you. I want you screaming in mercy." He grabbed me, pulling me up and pressed me back into the dresser. His body was hard against mine.

"Then my job is done."

"This was your strategy to try to keep me in man form?" His voice was thick.

"You're not a man, remember?"

"That's right." His eyes flashed, and his knee went between mine, urging my legs apart. "I'm not."

It wasn't until afternoon that he "calmed" enough to venture past the threshold of his bedroom. The house was still, absent of Dark Dwellers and ex-Fae Knights.

"They're probably out with Kennedy," I replied as I stuffed some raw venison pieces into my mouth. If it didn't taste so good, I would have been completely grossed out. I was starving, and my Dark Dweller side was calling the shots.

"Wow, not even bothering to take the tray out of the refrigerator?" Eli grinned, watching me.

I stood with the fridge door open and shrugged. "Too much effort."

He laughed and sauntered to me. "You know, watching you tear into flesh is a turn on for me."

"Not surprising. You're twisted."

"And you like it." He stood over me.

"I think that makes me even sicker in the head than you."

"Yup." He leaned in, closing the gap between us. His lips drew close to my neck, grazing the skin all the way down to the curve of my shoulder. My breath wedged in my throat. He continued along my arm and then abruptly grabbed a skewer from the plate. "I want one, too." He stood up, wiggling his stick at me.

I frowned, which only made him laugh. "You can't seem to stop waving your meat stick in my face, can you?"

The side of his mouth curled up. "Good one. Clever sexual pun. Well played."

From early in our relationship, we always tried to outwit the other. "Thank you." I bowed my head.

He smiled and bent down, his lips nipping at my neck again. "Thank you for earlier. Certainly helped. The experience was definitely a first for me." He leered at me as my eyebrows arched. "Not that part. Last night... the no sex part. I've never had a girl lie next to me, and we only slept."

I didn't want to think about the others who had laid next to him. "Actually second. We've slept together one other time without having sex."

"That's what you think." His cheeky grin made me laugh.

"Wow, not sure I would brag about it since I didn't even wake up."

"See, you are the one constantly trying to make me prove my manhood here." He grabbed the back of my head. "If you want to screw me relentlessly, Brycin, all you have to do is ask." He winked. "But I want to hear a pretty please."

"Ugh!" I shoved at his chest. "Your ego needs to feel the harsh reality of not getting any."

"Good thing it doesn't look like such a thing's going to happen any time soon."

He had me there. There was no way I could stop any more than he could.

Looking over his shoulder. The window opened to the beautiful, blue sky. Another hot day. "Should we head out to find everyone?"

He followed my gaze, then suddenly blurted. "Fuck! I forgot I was supposed to do a pick up for the club this morning." He shook his head, rubbing a hand over his head. The pen markings were still faintly there, but they were blending more and more into the growth of his hair. "That's where they are. Cooper must have taken my bike and gone in my place."

A blush dotted my cheeks. This meant they all had known he was too "occupied" to go. In the moment, I had forgotten the walls were not soundproof.

Seeing me blush, Eli laughed. "I enjoy you getting embarrassed about that."

"Them hearing us have sex? Yes, sorry, it does make me uncomfortable."

"You don't think I haven't heard all of them one time or another having sex in this house? Even though we had a rule to not bring anyone back here, it still was constant when Dax, Dominic, Lorcan, and Sam lived here."

"Ugh. Don't need a visual, but that's not the point. I have to look these people in the eye every day. Those 'others' were probably kicked to the curb before the sheets even got cold."

"True," he agreed. "But what are you most embarrassed about? Because they know and heard us? Or Torin heard?"

My shoulders tightened. "Torin has nothing to do with this." I wanted this to be true, but as soon as Eli said it, I knew he was right. It wasn't because I wanted to keep this all from Torin. I had made my decision. But I didn't want to shove it in his face. I cared so much about him, and it hurt when I knew I was causing him pain.

"So, this is all about Torin." Eli crossed his arms over his chest.

"No... yes." I sighed. "It doesn't have to do with Torin in the way you are getting at. I know there are no feelings lost between you two, but I care about him. Our bond will never go away, and I will never stop wanting him in my life or being sensitive to his feelings. Hearing us is cruel, and he doesn't deserve it."

Eli's brow arched up.

"He doesn't," I restated.

"Fine. So, you wanna stop having sex?"

I groaned. *Oh, hell no.* "That is not what I mean. I'm asking for us to be a little more considerate around him."

Eli looked away, annoyance flickering over his face. "Brycin, you can do what you want. But I am who I am, and I am not going to tip toe around so Fairy boy can feel better. If I am going to screw my woman, I am going to do it. I don't hold back, wherever or whenever it happens. All others can be damned."

Two of those words, put together, made my stomach drop. It was Eli's equivalent to saying girlfriend. "What did you say?"

"You mean about I am going to fuck you without filters?"

I almost choked on my laugh. "No... the other thing. Did you just basically call me your girlfriend?"

"Would you like fuck-toy better?"

"Oh, yeah, definitely." I put my hands on my hips and tried to keep a straight face. He exasperated the hell out of me at the same time he made me laugh.

"Okay, fuck-toy, grab my meat stick." He handed me another skewer from the fridge. He seized my legs and flung me over his shoulder.

"Seriously, how many sexual innuendoes can you stuff into one sentence?" Laughing, I folded over his shoulder.

"A *fucking* lot." He spanked my ass, sending a zing to my core.

I figured he would head back down the hallway, but instead he turned and went through the front door. "Where are you taking me?"

"There is a small pond at the far end of the property. Think I need to see if my toy floats."

"Will I be deemed a witch if I do?"

He snorted. "If she weighs the same as a duck, and she's made of wood. Therefore? A witch," he quoted *Monty Python and the Holy Grail.*

I adored him even more right then.

"I have to be a witch if I haven't drowned in your bullshit yet."

There was a swift pat to my butt.

"Let me down."

He let me slide from his shoulder. "Okay, but it's only fair I get to ride you later."

FIFTEEN

We were halfway there when we spotted Kennedy and Jared in the meadow. She stood still, her face stern and unyielding with focus. Chanted words flowed out of her like melting caramel. Thick and rich. Jared sat under a tree not far away. Alone in a meadow…and they weren't trying to compete with the rabbits? Eli and I couldn't be more opposite. Kennedy was under a lot of pressure, so sex was probably the furthest thing from her mind. I wondered if I'd act the same. My gaze drifted to the man next to me as we walked.

Nope.

Without thinking, I stopped beside her. "Hey, Ken."

She jumped with a startled yelp and spun around. The invocation just being released from her lips went hurling into my chest. With the force of a sonic boom, my feet tore out from under me, and I collided into Eli. I could feel the spell roll over my skin, enveloping me. Eli and I hurtled through the air. His chin dug into my lower back as we hit the ground. A string of muffled Gaelic swear words projected from Eli's mouth as I lay on top of him.

"Oh, my god! I am so sorry." Kennedy came running to us, helping me up. "Are you okay?"

"Dammit, Ken." I massaged my back, the impression of Eli's chin bruised into my skin.

Jared ran to us, laughing. "Man, you took them down." We all glared at Jared.

"Are you hurt?" She frantically looked me over.

"Yeah, I am," Eli replied, rubbing his nose and chin, trying to sit. "Brycin, that's the second time you almost made me bite off my tongue."

"If only." I turn to look at him and winked. "I keep trying. Maybe next time."

139

His eyes flashed, and a half-grin tugged at his lips as he stood. "There are other ways to keep me quiet."

A simple comment along with a look from him and heat flushed through my body, making me wish we were alone. "Yeah, but this would be more permanent."

Eli cheeky smile grew. "Damn, payback *is* a bitch."

I shrugged and smirked. "Been called worse."

"You'd miss that part of me too much anyway."

"Oh, really?" My eyebrows lifted in question.

"Yeah." He curved his eyebrow at me. His grin only conveyed the memory of where his tongue had been earlier. *Oh, yeah, I would miss that part too much.*

"Not uncomfortable at all." Jared cleared his throat.

Kennedy gripped my hand. "You sure you're all right?"

I turned back to Kennedy. "I'm okay, though your incantations have some major power behind them. I hope it wasn't an incantation to turn someone into a toad or anything?"

"Ember, stop." Eli moved behind me and grabbed my shoulders. Another string of swear words slid out of his mouth, which immediately propelled quivers down my spine. His fingers touched my back. I no longer felt the painful shock of his contact as I had when we first met. It still tingled slightly but felt pleasurable instead of uncomfortable. Was this because I had his blood? I still didn't know what it all truly meant.

"What is it?" I tried to turn my head to look over my shoulder. "J, Kennedy, come here." He swished my ponytail to the side, pulling my tank strap off my shoulder. *Hello, déjà vu.* I recalled the first time Eli saw my tattoo, except then we didn't have an audience.

Jared and Kennedy stepped behind me; small gasps escaped their lips.

"What? What is going on?"

"What is that?" Jared asked Eli, ignoring me.

"It looks like a map." Eli's fingers traced something on my back.

"A map? A map of what? How is it on her back? It was never there before," Kennedy exclaimed.

"Hello? Remember me here?" I said, my arms waving frantically. "What the hell is going on?"

"Stop moving." Eli's gripped me harder and pinned me in place. "No, it wasn't there before. What spell were you working on, Ken?"

"Uh... it was a revealing incantation..." Comprehension made her trail off. "I was practicing a spell to expose others which may be hidden. Like traps and concealing enchantments."

My patience was now gone. I exploded, ripping out of Eli's hold. "Tell me what the hell is going on, right now."

All three blinked, finally acknowledging me. "Someone talk now before I ignite something... possibly you." I pointed at each one.

"I think it's better if you see for yourself." Eli tried to keep his voice smooth, but excitement or alarm emphasized each word.

"I can't exactly see it."

Eli pulled out his phone, motioning for me to turn around.

"It's already fading," Jared stated. "Good idea with the phone."

Eli pulled my tank down farther and took several pictures before letting me pull it up. He tilted the phone screen toward me as I moved close to his side. He had to zoom in, but even then, only a few faint lines could be distinguished.

A gulp of air stuck in my throat. My bare back inked with a black tattoo dominated the screen, but intertwined with it were strange white lines. Odd symbols and shapes covered my back. I didn't know what it was showing, but it was detailed enough to recognize it as a map of some kind with mountains, caves, rivers.

"It's a map?" My finger jabbed at the screen.

"Looks like one to me," Eli replied.

"Why do I have a freakin' map on my back?" My fingers went to my back but felt nothing unusual. I looked up at him. His eyes glinted with an idea. "I know that look. What are you thinking?"

He stroked the space between his brows. "I'm fairly certain we found the location of the sword."

Eli called Cole, and in fewer than twenty minutes the entire group squealed at top speed back onto the property.

"Let me see." Cole charged at me. He had shoved us into the office, keeping the others out for the time being.

"You won't see anything." Eli stood behind me, his hand on my back absently playing with the end of my ponytail. "Kennedy will have to do another disclosing spell. It only seems to last for a minute or two before disappearing."

"Do you really think it's a diagram showing the location of the sword?" Cole focused on Eli with desperation in his words.

"My intuition says yes. It makes sense. It was able to stay hidden with Ember this whole time. It was only by accident Kennedy hit her with this spell, and I was behind her to see it. Otherwise, we wouldn't have found it."

Cole and Owen looked expectantly at me.

"Go ahead, Ken." I waved at her. Eli stepped to the side, letting Kennedy get closer to me.

"I really don't want to hurt you." She cringed as she moved around me.

"I'm tougher than I look." A snort came from Eli, and I pointed my finger at him. "Do you really want to start with me?" He grinned and shook his head.

"Will you please remove your top, Ember?" Owen asked formally. Being naked in this house was normal, and no one thought anything of it. I was raised to be confident in my body, but I still hesitated.

Come on, Em; put your big girl pants on.

At least there were just a few of us. Jared was the only one I felt awkward seeing me topless. Eli had seen it all before, Cole and Owen only looked at me as a science project, and Kennedy was no big deal. I sucked in a breath, tugged my tank top off. I rolled the top and held it against my chest.

"Okay, Ken. Do your worst."

Nothing.

"Ken?" I half turned. She stared at her hands.

"I still don't know what I'm doing. I'm just learning." Kennedy voice had a panicky tone. "Last time was an accident. What if I really hurt you this time? Or worse?"

Jared strode up to Kennedy, taking her shaking hands in his. "It's okay, babe. You can do this. You know this stuff."

She gave him a flimsy smile but nodded. "Okay... okay, here it goes." She took her hands from Jared, held them up, and faced my back.

I turned my head and saw Eli move in front of me. "Just in case you go flying again." I smiled, appreciating the gesture.

Foreign-sounding words flowed naturally out of Kennedy almost like she had grown up speaking them. It was in her blood; they had just needed to be released. When she reached the end of her incantation, magic poured from her hands into my back. The air rippled. A silent undulating wave headed straight for me. I turned and shut my eyes.

Eli was ready when my body slammed into his. I was more prepared this time, but it still hurt. A wall would have been softer compared to his chest. But I didn't mind the comforting arms wrapping around me. Eli propped me up straighter and stood protectively in front of me as Cole and Owen surrounded my back. Fingers started trailing around my tattoo.

"*'S magadh fúm atá tú!*" Cole whispered in awe. "This whole time we didn't know it was literally under our noses. We thought it might be something around Ember, but not enchanted on her."

Owen slowly and deliberately circled me, taking it all in. His persona was always so calming and comforting. "This kind of magic is exceptional and especially rare."

"My mother put it there, huh?"

The Dark Dwellers stopped, each staring at me.

"I heard you two talking the night after we returned from my house, when the Strighoul attacked us. You said you thought my mom would hide something with me." I looked at Cole. "And you asked her again earlier this week. But if she hid this map on me, why wouldn't she know where the location was? Or why would she lie about it?"

"I didn't lie." Mom's voice came from the doorway. We all jerked our attention to her. "I have no idea where the sword is or about this map you speak of."

"I'm confused. Who put this on my back?" My gaze jumped around, wanting anyone to answer.

Mom stepped into the room; her arms crossed tightly around her. "I can't answer the question. Whatever Cole may have suggested, Ember, I didn't have anything to do with the spell on your back. I didn't know of its existence."

"You knew nothing about this?" Cole's tone was doubtful.

"No. I didn't." Mom's chin rose defiantly. It was at times like this I saw much of my own personality reflected at me. I took after her so much.

Cole watched her before he relented. "Well, it doesn't matter now."

Owen had countered every move I had made, following my back like a shadow, poking and prodding at the lines. "It is fading."

"Jared, grab a camera out of the top drawer." He pointed. Jared responded, retrieving it.

With one more invocation from Kennedy, Jared clicked the camera a dozen times before he stopped.

"It fades fast." Cole took the camera from Jared, scrolling through the images he'd captured. "Damn. The lines barely come out. It's hard to see, no matter how close we get to your back."

143

"What do you mean?" I turned to look at him.

"Magic and film don't work well together," Mom stated. "Human-made devices will never be able to capture magic or anything from the Otherworld well. It's a good thing or we probably would have been discovered a long time ago. Most think the pictures showing 'otherworldly' incidences have been doctored or faked because it does not show up on the negative."

"We'll have to draw it," Cole declared.

"I'm not great, but I can draw well enough to get the gist of the map," Jared spoke up.

"That's all fine, but do any of us know where this is?" Eli looked at us. "What is the map of?"

All of us fell silent. The unclear lines and symbols, which I had seen on the screen, were so vague and basic, it could be anywhere. There were no words or anything to define the location.

Cole slumped onto his desk. The air of excitement deflated from the room.

Another roadblock appeared in front of us.

We were all headed to the clearing to work on drawing the map when an overwhelming sensation made me falter. It tugged at my insides to turn in the opposite direction. When I tried to ignore the feeling and keep walking, a dry heave brought me to the ground.

Mom rushed to my side, bumping Eli out of the way. "Ember, are you okay?"

I could only nod my head. Acid felt thick in my throat. Everyone stopped and turned to see me gag again.

Kennedy hurried to my side. "Are you all right? I-I did this, huh? My incantations are making her sick." She looked at Owen.

Finding my voice, I choked out, "I need to lie down. I'll be fine."

Another wave came over me, and I groaned. The pull to move to the other side of the property was so powerful I started to crawl.

"I would like to examine you." Owen reached for my arm, to pull me up.

No. Must go. Alone.

The words ran through my mind, and I shook my head. "Please, I just need to rest." He looked suspiciously at me. The moment I no longer fought against the urge, the sickness eased up.

"I think he should check you out." Mom came to my side, feeling my forehead.

"Really, I am okay." I moved back away from her hand and begin to push myself up. Mom and Owen helped me get my feet underneath me. "You guys keep going; work with Kennedy. I'll go back and rest for a while."

Before anyone could refute this, I turned and began to walk. A solid form was right by my side, moving next to me.

"Eli, I'll be fine. Go with them." My voice rose with the feeling to be rid of him. "I really don't want you around while I'm throwing up in a toilet."

He shook his head. "I don't think so. We can't really do much without you anyway. I happen to find it sexy to hold a woman's hair back as she vomits."

I cringed through a huffed laugh. "You would."

Another violent tug heaved at my arms and legs.

"Please. I really want to be alone right now. I need to lie down, and you would only be a distraction." My desperation had my tone grow sharp.

He cocked his head, and his green eyes burned into mine. I felt he sensed something was wrong, that I was lying, but I didn't give him a chance to figure it out.

"I'll be back soon," I said before he could respond and walked quickly back to the house.

When I got out of sight, I began to run. My legs moved through the woods, ducking past tree limbs and weaving through the foliage.

Faster. My heart thumped. *Faster.*

The nausea subsided but was replaced with anxiety. I was being controlled. Like a ragdoll. My legs pumped harder propelling me closer to the destination. There were only two people I knew who had this kind of power. I didn't know which one I dreaded most.

My skin prickled as I crossed the property line. With a pop, the need to hurry left my body, and I came to a halt.

"It took you long enough. I am a man who does not like to be kept waiting." The cool, commanding voice spoke behind me.

My lids squeezed tight. "Lars." With a heavy sigh, I turned to face him. He stood there as scary and beautiful as I remembered. The air of power and dominance enveloping him was so thick it almost hurt to breathe. He combed his wavy jet-black hair in a neat style. His suit was dapper and probably cost more than a car. But Lars's eyes gripped me the most. He was a Demon and had the same yellow-green eyes I had. Or one of mine anyway. Those intense eyes were narrowed on me now in a look of pure fury.

Crap. No, this deserves an "*Oh, holy crap on ash bark.*"

"Ember," he addressed me. Through the heat, shivers curled over my skin. "It has been a while since I last saw you. Since you left the protected home I so graciously provided you and broke your vow to me."

It was hard not to babble excuses or apologize. The wrath of the Unseelie King was mine to bear. I had breached his contract. I knew the repercussions would come back eventually, and he'd probably kill me. I just wasn't ready for that day to be today.

"Now... tell me what could have been so important to leave us and break your deal with me? An agreement, if violated, has consequences you cannot even fathom."

I gulped, looking at my feet. He would find nothing I said justifiable. Family and friends did not hold the same weight to him as they did for me.

"Just do what you need to do, Lars." I stared straight at him and tried not to flinch.

A thin smile tugged at the edges of his mouth. "No pleading or begging?"

"No. I won't play that game with you."

A short laugh came from his chest. "I am impressed, Ember. Some of the most dangerous Fae have crumbled at my feet begging for forgiveness."

I folded my arms. "Yeah, well I know you better than to think you're capable of empathy." He laughed again. It took everything I had to keep my chin up and not show him my trembling hands. This was a Demon, the Unseelie King, and I had broken a contract with him.

I'm going to be stir-fry.

"How did you glamour me to come to you? I thought I was impervious to it?"

"I didn't use glamour, but telekinesis. I can move your body against your will." It felt like his gaze penetrated into my soul.

I had the power of moving things with my mind, but I could do no

146

more than break open a door or move a cue stick into my hand. To command people to move against their will? That's a powerful tool.

"So how did you find me?"

"Sinnie." He took a measured step to me. "Spells and veiling incantations do not work on the sub-Fae like—"

"Like pixies and brownies." Realization hit me. Cal and Simmons had told me as much when I was trying to sneak into the Queen Aneira's castle.

"Yes. No one ever thinks about lesser Fae possibly being a threat or, in my case, a spy. It took her a while, but between my men and Sinnie, I knew I would find you. She found you a week ago. I was waiting for the opportunity."

A connection finally clicked in my brain. It hadn't been Josh creeping up on me near the boulders. It was Sinnie. That's why the smell was slightly familiar. "It was her that night in the forest. She was the one watching me. You knew I've been back for a while?"

"Yes," Lars stated. "There isn't much that happens without my knowledge. I only needed to find your exact location. I reasoned you would be with the Dark Dwellers, and they would be hiding you."

"So now what? Are you going to kill or punish me for breaking our deal?"

"Kill you?" One of Lars's eyebrows cocked. "Killing you would be pointless. I have greater plans for you. You will work off the debt you owe me."

"Work off?" I swallowed hard. "What do you mean?"

"Well, I did not spend months of my time having you trained for nothing. War is coming, and you will fight by my side. But after the sword is used to fulfill your destiny, you will give it to me."

That didn't sound like a good idea. The Unseelie King, a Demon, having the Sword of Light, one of the most powerful weapons on Earth or in the Otherworld. Would we be trading in one tyrannical dictator for another?

"I have no idea where the sword is."

Lars slanted his head. "Don't disappoint me with lies."

Right. Sinnie had probably been spying on me every day for a week. Probably earlier that day. I cringed at thinking she had been watching my every move, even in the bedroom. She probably overheard us talking about the map and went straight to Lars. "We don't know where it actually is."

A bemused smile thinned his mouth. "But you do have the map to it."

"I do." I sighed. To entertain the idea of pulling one over on the Unseelie King was even too stupid for me to contemplate.

He shifted his weight impatiently. He would know everything that was happening here, down to when I took bathroom breaks, and even the truth about Kennedy. That was how he worked.

"You probably know Kennedy was conjuring a revealing spell and accidently hit me." My hand went to my shoulder. "It only comes out..."

Before I could even finish my sentence, Lars whipped me around, and his finger touched my back. A tickle fluttered over my shoulder. Craning my neck, I could just make out the white lines glowing.

"Holy crap. How did you do that?" It was more of rhetorical question. He was the Unseelie King. What couldn't he do?

He didn't respond, only tugged up my shirt to get a proper look at the tattoo. Damn, I was getting tired of being treated like an object.

"You were smart... more devious than I thought you capable of," he mumbled to himself.

"What?"

"Nothing." He waved me off.

"Do you know where it is?"

He pressed his lips together, his fingers sliding over the lines on my skin. "There is something familiar about it, though I do not know from where." He continued to stare at my back for a few more moments, before he turned me back around.

"While I am looking into these symbols, you will continue to play your little charade. Convince the Dark Dwellers, and whomever else you need to, that you are still following their plan. I am not foolish enough to think they aren't also courting the sword for their own use. After you kill Aneira, it will become mine."

My mouth opened to refute him.

"Make no mistake, Ember. You will be doing this. Remember the little deal we made back when you first came to me? The favor you owe me? Well, I am calling on it now. You are bound to this deal and so is your tongue. You will not be able to tell anyone of it. All loopholes are covered in my deals; you can't even convey it in writing." His smugness had anger firing through me.

"Guess that's what I get for making a deal with a Demon. I won't be making that mistake again."

A small chuckle came from his throat. "A good rule to live by... but never say never. Be thankful I am ignoring your past indiscretion. I told you the repercussions for breaking a deal with me were not something you wanted. You foolishly ignored me and broke it anyway. I could cause you to suffer for it. I am being exceptionally generous. I will forgive the previous misdeed as long as you fulfill the current agreement." Like last time I had made a deal with him, I felt the weight of his words circle down, tightening my throat. "If you break this one with me, I *will* kill the Dark Dweller."

"Kill Eli?" The pain in my chest blazed at just the thought.

"I could also squash those two little pixies you love so much. I am a Demon, Ember. I have been incredibly generous with you. Do not push me. I understand what makes you tick. Threatening you obviously does not work. It is your friends who are your weakness."

"You are no different from her." We both knew the "her" I was referring to.

"I am worse. Do not challenge me. Never forget who I really am." His calm voice sent a chill through my heart. He meant it. I could not let myself forget again he was a Demon and the feared Unseelie Dark Fae King for a reason.

"Do you not think me fair?" he asked coolly. My response was only to glare at him, which seemed to amuse him. "You are so much like your mother. Stubborn to a fault." Lars gave me a small nod. "You will know when I need to speak with you again."

With that, he was gone.

SIXTEEN

"Cal? Simmons?" I stomped toward the compound. "Get your little pixie butts out here now."

Simmons reacted immediately to my call, flying out of the kitchen window where they were probably trying to ferment their own juniper juice in the sink. Again.

"My lady?"

"Where's Cal?"

Simmons looked over his shoulder, embarrassed. "Uh... well, my lady, he's... well..."

"Simmons..." I raised my eyebrow.

"Well, he decided he wanted to go swimming."

"And?"

"He went swimming in the kitchen sink."

My hand went to my mouth. "The kitchen sink doesn't happen to be full of juniper juice, does it?"

"Not much," Simmons defended. "Well, not much now..."

Groaning, I headed for the kitchen. Everyone was still out. *Thank goodness.*

On entering, I found a naked pixie doing snow angels on the counter. "Wheeee... cool air on me tidbits." His Scottish accent was thick with liquor. "Feel all ta prutty colors."

"He's a tad out of it, my lady." Simmons landed on my shoulder.

"You think?"

Cal flipped over and started to swim.

"I had to get him out of the sink so he wouldn't drown. But in order to do it, I had to convince him he was still in there." We both continued to watch the nude pixie doing the side stroke on the table top.

My nose wrinkled. "Remind me never to prepare my lunch there again." I turned to Simmons. "Since Cal is indisposed, I'll ask you."

I sat at the island, and Simmons hopped from my arm onto the counter. "Anything, my lady."

"Are you guys able to sense other Fae?" I didn't want to insult him and say sub-Fae. "Like brownies or other pixies?"

"Brownies," Cal screamed. "Yummy."

Simmons ignored him. "Not really. Not anymore than you could sense another Fae around unless they are really close. Why do you ask?"

"Just curious," I replied. "So, you haven't seen anything like a brownie around here?"

"I have not, my lady."

"Brownie. Yes. Yes." Cal sang out again. He returned to lying on his back, giving up on his swimming moves.

"Be quiet, you drunkard." Simmons waved him off.

"I seeee browwwneee. What a *raicleach*."

"What? You saw her?" I jumped off my stool and ran to Cal. I grabbed a napkin and threw it at him. I didn't care how small his parts were; I still didn't want to see them.

Cal bunched the napkin into a pillow and fell back on it. "Thank ye. Most obliged."

"That's not exactly what it's for." I sighed. "But tell me when you saw her? Was she the only one?" I feared Lars wasn't alone in thinking of this way to find me. Would the Queen contemplate something similar? She didn't seem to think much of anything below her own kind. I hoped she was not as clever as Lars.

"Yes... I saw. Did I say she was a *raicleach*?" His eyes opened slightly, and a smile grew on his face. "My kind of woman."

"Cal, focus. I need you to describe who you saw and if there have been any others."

A rumbling noise erupted from him, and I released an aggravated growl.

"No point in trying to wake him, my lady. He will be of no use," Simmons said apologetically. "But I promise the moment he awakes, I will get all the information you require out of him."

"Thanks, Simmons."

"What the hell?" Eli came behind me. "Why is there a naked pixie on the counter? Where I will no longer eat again?"

"You missed his freestyle stroke," I mused, my face turning to Eli. My eyebrows moved up and down. "Very impressive."

"Hey, I told you not to judge1 that six inches could surprise you."

I snorted. Simmons, upon seeing Eli, turned up his nose and left the room. Cal's drunken snores hummed from beside the sink.

"You feel better?"

"Yeah." I wasn't lying. I did feel better. But I hated keeping the secret about Lars from Eli, especially after making such a big deal about being truthful with one another. I didn't doubt Lars had tied my tongue, but my stubbornness still had to push against the rules. My mouth opened to try to confess. Nothing. It was like I went mute. My vocal chords were unresponsive to the words forming in my throat.

"You got really weird on me... well, weirder than normal." He leaned against the sink. The speculation in his stare drilled into me.

It was Lars. He came to me in the forest. My eyes tried to convey to him. He only tilted his head, waiting for me to respond.

Lars had covered all the bases. I tried to speak out loud again, but my cords tightened down, almost painfully. The more I forced it, the more it hurt. The bond was secured.

I sighed, giving into it. "Between Kennedy's enchantment hitting me and everything going on..." I trailed off, feeling the lie heavy on my tongue.

"Ummm-hmmm." Eli lips pressed together.

"You don't think I deserve to be a little off?" Funny, it actually irritated me that he didn't accept my pitiful excuse.

"Oh, you're more than a little off." He stepped closer to me, a grin curling his mouth.

Ignoring him, I continued on. "I got slammed with a magical curse. Several times. Sorry if I'm not functioning at my best. I feel like I've just been bitch-slapped by Fairy cotton candy, which is not as soft and sweet as one might think." I waved my arms up and down. Eli's eyes only glinted brighter as I ranted. I knew deep down he wasn't buying anything I was saying. That pushed the level of my tirade even higher. "Don't look at me like that. How would you—" My sentence was cut off as he grabbed my lips, pinning then together.

"Shut up, Brycin." His eyes penetrated mine with unrelenting desire. Picking me up, he slid me back onto the surface, undoing the button of my pants. His hands skimmed over my hips pushing the fabric down over my ass.

Breath hitched in my throat. "There's going to be nowhere on this counter we'll be able to eat again."

His eyebrow curved up as he reached over grabbing the jar of peanut butter off the counter. Opening it, he scooped some out. His lips twitched as his finger trailed down my stomach, smearing it down my abdomen. A guttural noise came from his throat, his warm mouth sucking and licked, down my torso. My breath picked up, my back bowing. He went down on his knees, yanking my underwear to my ankles. His palms opened my legs, spreading me wide, smearing peanut butter high on the inside of my thigh.

His eyes glinted up at me as his tongue lapped it up. "Speak for yourself." He muttered before his mouth covered my pussy and devoured me whole.

A kiss on my back woke me. Heat from the morning sun was already heavy in the room. We eventually relocated from the kitchen to the bedroom before everyone came back for dinner. We never made it, and my stomach rumbled the moment my lids lifted.

I heard a snicker as several more kisses trailed along my spine. "Hungry?"

"Starving. But I don't think I can move." I sighed happily.

"I bet I could get you to move again." His fingers glided over my bare thigh.

"Doubt it." My bored tone contradicted the smile twitching my lips.

"Why do you constantly set challenges for me to meet?" Eli mumbled against my skin.

Rolling over, I looked up as he leaned above me. "You'd think I'd be wiser than that by now, but for some reason I can't seem to stop myself."

He set his arms on either side of my head, lowering onto me. "It is a mystery." Limbs and bed sheets began to tangle again when a loud banging bounced off the door.

"Yeah, you guys should be having more sex. Didn't get enough last night or every night, or day, morning, mid-afternoon..." Gabby trailed off.

Eli sighed and pulled back. "Technically you only have yourself to blame. You put us in a room together demanding we get along. We are trying our best to meet your stipulations."

"I think we still have some work to do on that." I grinned.

"Yeah, think I've come to regret it," Gabby replied.

Eli looked over his shoulder at the closed door. "You were the one who couldn't handle me being a dickhead any longer."

"Oh, you're still a dickhead," Gabby piped back through the door. "But now I am not sure which dickhead is worse."

"She's got you there." I shrugged.

He nodded in agreement. "True." He slid off me onto his side, propping his head on his hand. "Gabby, do you have a reason for loitering at my door?"

"Getting tips to produce my own porno video or was it taping the mating sounds of Yetis? Can't remember which one," she said deadpan. "Of course, I do. I mean I enjoy sex, but when I am the participant... not listening to it. Cole and Kennedy are already practicing. He wants Ember to get her ass there as soon as possible. That means now not in twenty minutes."

The screen door slammed loudly as she exited, and her footsteps grew fainter as she headed back outside.

"It's always my ass that people want." I pushed up on my elbows.

Eli's hand drifted under the covers, skimming the side of my butt. "I've invited it out on several occasions, but it keeps bringing you along."

"Shut up." I laughed and smacked him. "My ass has too high of standards to be left alone with the likes of you."

Eli reached for my face. "Good thing the rest of you doesn't."

When our lips met, lust had every nerve dancing again. I begrudgingly pulled back. "I better go. Cole won't be so polite if he has to come get me."

"Worse. He'll send Cooper who has no qualms about dragging you out of bed naked."

"Please. Being naked is more normal to you guys than being clothed." I sat up, pushing the covers off. It was going to be another hot day. This type of heat for this stretch of time in Washington was unusual.

"We're Dark Dwellers. Being naked goes hand and hand with us. So does sex." He threw back the covers and sat up, displaying his physique.

"You guys can all run around naked. I'm quite okay with it. I'm sure Kennedy wouldn't mind, and I don't even think my mother would care too much. She appreciates good-looking, nude men as much as the rest of us. Not sure about Thara, unless it's Torin who is unclothed."

I dug in the dresser for the pair of Eli's sweats I had claimed and made into shorts. I slipped into them, pulling the drawstring tight, then threw on a tank and slipped my hair back into its usual ponytail. Also, something I'd never admit out loud was I liked being in his clothes. Besides his comforting smell, there was an undeniable "we're together" indication that went with it for everybody to see. Sometimes I really hated I was secretly such a girl.

Eli scoffed at my remarks and reached over my shoulder to grab a pair of jeans out of the open drawer. It was something neither of us brought up or discussed, but more and more of my stuff flittered into his room. A couple times I folded laundry and left it in the basket in the living room. Later I'd find it put away, tucked inside his dresser. I never commented on it, and neither did he.

"Coffee?" Eli tugged a t-shirt over his head.

"Is that even a question?"

"With you? No."

"They can wait five extra minutes for me to get my caffeine intake, right?"

"I think they'd prefer it." Smacking my ass, he headed out the door.

"Yeah, 'cause you're such an angel in the morning," I grumbled, slipping on my chucks and following him.

As we walked outside, I continued to feel on edge since at any moment Lars could "call" on me again. I had tried every way possible to tell Eli. But when I attempted to get close to the topic, my throat seemed to close, and no words came out. It felt like being raked over coals, an experience I did not want again. Eli had sensed something wrong, but I brushed it off as still not feeling well.

Almost everyone was out at the training site by the time Eli and I got there. Only Owen was missing, probably in his lab like a freaky scientist, analyzing more of my blood and screaming, *It's alive!*

Josh, Jared, Cooper, and Gabby were stretched out on the grass, watching. Mom sat under a tree, book in hand with Thara next to her. Cole and Torin were standing beside Kennedy as she faced the vast meadow.

Eli put a hand on my lower back, urging me forward to join the group. Torin was busy helping Kennedy but turned when he heard us approach. His gaze went directly to Eli's hand. He looked away, but a flash of heated agony reflected on his features. I stepped away from Eli, feeling guilty. Whatever emotions he had for me were not going to disappear overnight, no matter how much I thought I didn't deserve them. Life didn't work out so simply.

I smiled and approached them.

"You ready for target practice?" Cole smirked.

"Don't tell me... I am the target."

Cole smiled smugly and winked as he brushed away a strand of his shoulder length hair that had escaped his tie.

"We have been working with Kennedy all morning on controlling her direction and intensity. We think she is ready," Torin spoke formally to me.

My regret kicked in when I looked around at all the people working so hard to find this sword. Lars's goal was the same as theirs except I had to hand the sword to him at the end. I wasn't tricking them or even lying, but I still felt uncomfortable not revealing the full truth.

"Funny, it doesn't make me feel better." I frowned. "No offense, Ken."

"None taken." She shook her head, but a smile edged around her mouth. Because she knew she wouldn't hurt me with the invocations, she had lightened up.

"Yeah, you're really distraught over this I can tell," I teased.

"Call it payback after years of your and Ryan's endless taunts." She winked. Kennedy's sweet personality had taken on some spunk. She was coming into her own and finally growing into who she was meant to be. Strong, kind, and a powerhouse in her own way. I loved it.

Sticking out my tongue, I marched into the meadow toward the wooden target they had set up. "Hey. Can I get an air mattress out here or something?"

"You'll be fine. She's really gotten better," Cole shouted. "You ready?" With my back to them, I gave them a thumbs-up.

"This might sting a bit." Kennedy baited me, which made me snicker. *Where did my sweet Kennedy go?*

Bending my knees, I positioned my feet onto the dirt, feeling the earth seeping into me. After hearing the chant sail over the wind into my ears, it was only a heartbeat later when the force of her words hit me. Like a hurricane, the power smacked into me, and once again I was in the air. My face hit the makeshift target, knocking it down as I crashed to the ground.

I lay face first in the dirt, spread-eagle. The sound of feet running to me was mixed with the howling laughter from the group on the grass.

"You okay?" Eli's voice reached me first. His hand touched my arm. "Oooww."

"Oh, Em. I'm sorry." Kennedy came down on my other side. "Again."

I moaned into the dirt. Snickering, Eli rolled me over. "She's okay."

"There's blood." Kennedy pointed at my face.

"Only her nose." Eli pulled me up, using the bottom of his shirt to wipe the blood off.

"I am so, so sorry." Kennedy grabbed my hand; her teasing confidence had vanished.

"No worries. You warned me it might hurt a little." I waved it off and grimaced as Eli continued to clean dirt and blood off my face. I looked into his glittering, green eyes. "I know you are dying to make a bulls-eye joke so go ahead."

Eli pressed his lips together trying not to laugh. "Me?"

"Maybe if you imagine yourself the arrow next time, you'd get better trajectory," Cooper shouted, still howling with laughter. "Become one with the arrow, Em. Be the arrow."

I flipped him off over Eli's shoulder only making the group on the grass hoot louder. I looked at my mom. She had made it halfway to me but stopped. Now seeing I was okay, she was also fighting back laughter.

"Nice, Mom. You, too?" I threw up my arms. "Go ahead... tell me I nailed it."

With that everyone lost it. The situation was hilarious, and I laughed along with them, even though my face hurt when I did.

"All right, Jared, see if you can sketch the map exposed on Em's back before it fades." Cole addressed Jared as we calmed a bit. "Or we're going to have to do it again."

My eyes widened, but Eli had a huge grin on his face. "Seriously. Best day. Ever."

"Remember when you said payback is a bitch?" My eyebrow curved. "Yeah, she's going be one tonight."

"Mmmm... foreplay." He kissed my head and joined Cooper and Gabby.

Since pictures of my back didn't show the true detail and marks of the white tattoo, and we couldn't afford to miss one detail of the map, Jared drew the basic lines, and with his help I would finish it. Josh was right next to Jared, helping him with copying the details of my tattoo. It all seemed to be exciting to him. With the magic and spells, Josh was in heaven.

With my sketch pad in Jared's hand, he outlined what he could before it faded. By the time he finished the detail work, Kennedy had blasted me into the dirt six times. I was sore and achy and covered in soil and dried blood. Torin had been resolute on getting me a pad to fall on, but most times I missed it. Just another day at Camp Dark Dweller.

Actually, it wasn't much different from my days spent at Camp Demon. As I sprawled in the dirt, a memory of when I blew up the training building crossed my mind. Alki, Koke, and Maya lay on their backs covered in blood, and pieces of the building were scattered over the ground all because of my skills needed work.

A strange sadness hit me when I thought of my Demon family, of Nic, Rez, and Marguerite. She would call me her *dulce nina* and hug me so tightly. My mouth began to water at the thought of her cooking. Damn, I really missed that woman. I missed them all, even Koke and Maya who probably didn't feel the same way. Sick as it was, I really missed Alki. They had been my family for six months, and I had felt at home with them.

As the day wore on, Torin, Thara, and Mom eventually left us, going for a walk. Torin had given Eli so many dirty looks, mumbling under his breath, I was relieved to see him go. Eli would ignore him for only so long. Cooper, Gabby, and Eli disappeared shortly after going on a hunt.

Finally, Cole called time and left the last of us as he headed to the house.

"You okay, babe?" Jared shook out his cramped hand, watching Kennedy drag her body to him and plop down next to me and Josh.

"Holy crap, I'm tired." She leaned her head on Jared's shoulder.

"You did well, though. Proud of you." He kissed the side of her head, folding his hand around hers.

"Thanks." She smiled, gazing at him, eyes simmering with love.

They were so freakin' adorable together it almost hurt. She was blissfully happy. Jared was such a good guy, and his adoration for her was clear. They were the "cute, sweet" couple who almost made you gag. But all I could feel was happiness for her. Eli's and my relationship was different from theirs. Neither of us was cute or sweet. We never would be, and I was more than okay with it.

"I hope all this hard work will lead to the sword so we can get Ryan and Mark out." Kennedy sighed, cuddling farther into Jared's shoulder.

"And West," Jared added.

A hard lump formed in my stomach. I was being given the perfect opportunity to tell Kennedy the truth about Ryan. Still, no words came out. Truth clustered on my tongue, debating to leap off or crawl back down my throat.

Her face was so hopeful. Could I rip that away from her? It was supposedly the right thing to do, but was it really? It would break her.

She had lost her family, her home, her life as it had been. All she had was the hope of getting Ryan back with us. I'm sure she still hoped he could go home and be with his family again.

Josh, who was quietly sitting next to me, saved me from my cowardice as he broke the silence. "You don't have any idea where this map leads?" He grabbed the sketch from Jared, rotating it around.

"Nope. Not a clue." It wasn't a lie, but keeping the fact Lars had found it familiar seemed like one.

"Well, we need to figure it out if we're going to find this sword," he stressed. "Who do you think might know?"

"If I even knew who put it on my back, I could start there. But no one seems to even have that knowledge."

"Are you sure your mom doesn't know?" Josh's eyes held mine.

Anger slithered up my spine. "My mom said she didn't, and I believe her. She may have hidden a lot of things from me for my safety, but she is not a liar. She wouldn't lie to me about this now."

"Okay, sorry. Was just asking."

"Sorry, Josh." The subject of my mom did cause me to be a bit snippy.

"You guys finally done?" Cooper, Eli, and Gabby walked to us.

"Yeah." Jared stretched his hands and arms. "Catch anything for dinner?"

"You have to go get your own, kid. Start providing for the little lady," Cooper rubbed Jared's head. Jared jumped up and started to wrestle with Cooper.

Hands tilted my head back, and lips came down on mine. Something tangy and warm coated my mouth.

"Ugh!" I pulled back and wiped my lips. Red liquid painted them. "Is that deer blood?"

Kennedy's and Josh's faces looked so appalled I wanted to laugh.

"Yup." He kissed me again. "I wondered if you'd be able to identify it."

I wanted it to gross me out, like it did Kennedy and Josh. It didn't. It wasn't the best thing I ever tasted, but it certainly wasn't the worst. I grabbed the back of his neck pulling Eli's head closer to mine. I licked the bottom lip.

"Yum." I smiled.

A deep rumble came from his throat.

"Ewww. Emmmber." Kennedy's body shuddered.

"That... that was just nasty." Josh shook his head.

Gabby cocked her head, assessing me. "Okay, she is as twisted as the rest of us."

"Oh, she's even more so." Eli pulled me up. "Cooper, be ready at ten with the truck loaded."

"What the hell? You're not helping me load?" Cooper held up his arms.

"Hey. I have managerial duties. I have to train and educate the new Dark Dweller recruit." He walked backward, tugging me along. I knew where we were headed. You didn't tease a Dark Dweller, especially Eli, and think it would slide.

SEVENTEEN

"When I said I needed to train the recruit, I didn't mean you could come with us tonight." Eli sat up from the bed, swinging his legs down to the floor.

"Well, I did." I sat up, leaning against the wall, pulling the sheet with me. My desire to go with Eli also came from the fact that when I returned to his room, the bed was made. Neat and tidy as a pin. Eli thought I had done it, and I let him believe it. In the precise way it was made, I knew the truth: Sinnie. It was a calling card from Lars. It obviously wasn't urgent enough to puppet me into the forest, but it was telling me he needed to see me soon. I had to leave the property.

"You are not going, and that's final." We had been going around and around the same argument for the past ten minutes resulting in the same outcome.

"I have been captive forever now. First here, then Lars', then as an actual prisoner of the Queen's, and now here again. I'm going crazy. This isn't even an outing in public."

"Doesn't matter. You're being hunted, so you can't leave this property." He pulled on his jeans.

My head banged back on the wall. "Come on. They aren't waiting for me at the property line. We'll be there and back before anyone could possible find out."

"Lorcan could be waiting for you. He probably has soldiers around the perimeter."

He sat down, tugging on his boots.

"But he doesn't, does he? You could smell him and any others before they even get close to me. He said he was no longer working with Aneira. For some reason I actually believe him. Clearly he hasn't told her where I am. Otherwise she would be here. She could be looking for me

161

in Europe for all we know. I really need to get out, Eli." Letting the sheet fall, I scooted in behind him, pressing my naked body into him, talking close to his ear. "Please."

Slowly, I kissed his neck. I wasn't above using *any* of my powers of persuasion to get my way.

Eli grunted. "You have no shame, woman. You really think I am so easily swayed?"

I let my hand drop over his chest, sliding all the way down, unbuttoning his pants, wrapping around his hardening cock, rubbing up and down his shaft growing in my hand.

"I can make it worth your while."

My fingers rubbed harder as I nipped at his ear. He groaned in pleasure.

"You are evil, Brycin. Did anyone ever tell you that? You must be part Demon or something." He leaned back into me, his hips bucking with me, his chest heaving.

"I'll have to get it checked out," I purred, using my other hand to palm his balls, forcing a deep groan from him.

"Fine. You can go." He turned around and threw me on my back, spreading my legs, his fingers dragging through my wet pussy, already throbbing for him. "But you will listen to every word I say. I am not joking." He teased my entrance, making me whimper, as his other hand tugged back down his jeans, freeing his massive erection. "You will not be stubborn or argumentative. Not only is it dangerous because of what is out there for you, but of what we're doing. This is who we are. You have to accept both good and bad." He crawled over me, rolling over my core, arching my back in a cry. "You understand? Every word I say. You obey. No question."

"Eli..." I moaned clawing at him as he dragged his cock through me. "Fuck. Eli!" My pussy pulsed with need. Craving to be filled.

"We agreed?" He pulled away. I arched into him, greedy for his touch, aching for him.

"Please!" I begged.

His dick hinted at my entrance, but he didn't go any further. Driving me over the edge. "Eli..." I growled.

"Agreed?"

I nodded profusely. "Yes!"

"You use sex as weapon against me, and I will use it back on you tenfold. Got it?"

I nodded again.

He grinned smugly before thrusting deep into inside me, His form feral and brutal as he fucked me until I blacked out.

He made sure I knew he was dominant one in this situation. And yes, he left his boots on.

No one was happy about me going. Eli sat back, letting Cole and the others try to talk me out of it, but my mind was set. He'd just snigger the more they tried because he knew it only made me more determined.

Cooper packed Cole's SUV with the merchandise. I never thought I would be part of something like this. I was trying really hard not to judge. I didn't like it, but good or bad this was how they made their money. They were Dark Dwellers, Dark Fae, bikers. What did I expect? For them to have proper jobs and be respectable? Funny in my world the supposed good wanted to kill me, and the bad wanted to protect me. The terms good and bad were relative.

"Eli, you know this is stupid. Why are you allowing Ember to go?" Cole stared at Eli.

"Allowing?" I sputtered, but they both ignored me.

"Have you tried to stop her from doing anything she has set her mind on?" Eli continued to help Cooper load the car. "Plus, she's a good fighter now and has some extreme powers. We can't treat her like she's breakable. She's tough and can handle more than any of us give her credit for."

"Not the point." Cole stroked his chin in frustration.

"I promise I will keep her safe. The Apocalypse Riders won't be a problem. Easy trade. They are the closest to comrades you can have in this business."

A chuckle came from Cooper. "Comrades, huh?"

Eli shot Cooper a look to shut him up.

"I should go instead," Cole stated. "Weiss still has a warrant out for you, and Ember is with you."

"Nah, man, we'll be fine. What could *possibly* go wrong?" Cooper egged Cole on even more. Eli smacked the back of Cooper's head, giving him a shut-the-hell up look.

"Don't worry. This will be fast. It's only a drop off so Cooper and I can handle it. We'll be back and all this worrying will be for nothing,

Mom." Eli teased. Cole was about to interject when Eli hopped on his Harley. He turned to me, throwing me a helmet.

"Climb on, Brycin." I settled the helmet on my head and swung my leg over, scooting up behind him. He leaned back. "You don't know the things I imagined doing to you on this bike."

A thrill consumed me as imagery played out in my head. "You are evil." I poked him in the back. He grinned and started the engine, revving it for emphasis.

Cooper gave a salute, hopped in the SUV, and tore out the driveway.

"My lady, would you like us to follow?" Simmons flew close to my ear so I could hear him over the roar of the engine.

"No, Simmons, stay here. I'll be fine." Simmons didn't look happy, but he nodded. Cal fluttered into my line of slight looking even more displeased with my decision.

Before I could address Cal, the Harley plunged forward. I had to clamp Eli's waist to keep myself from falling off. "Let the good times began." His foot hit the gas as we drove off the ranch.

The wind against my face and the freedom of being outside the property felt exhilarating. A giddy smile wouldn't leave my lips. "Faster," I yelled into his ear.

He toed the pedal into a higher gear and twisted the right handlebar. The bike lunged forward, prompting me to wrap my arms tighter around his middle, fitting my body closer into his. My chest soared, feeling like I was let out of a cage. We flew down the road, and I let my head fall back, watching the tops of the trees zip by as the bike hit maximum speed.

The meeting point was an old, deserted warehouse on the unpopular side of town. No one came here, not even the kind of seedy criminals I had encountered in Mike's Bar, unless they were doing something they didn't want anyone else to know.

We stopped in the middle of an empty lot. "Wow, if this isn't a movie poster for doing shady business." I removed my helmet and slid off the bike. "This is the point in the movie where you yell at the screen telling the girl to get the hell out of there."

"Yeah, but not when the girl is the one who the others should be running from." Eli swung off, his helmet already in his hand.

"Good point."

Cooper rolled next to us. "I miss my bike when I drive this thing. It doesn't go around those corners as sweetly as my baby *used* to." Cooper glared at Eli as he hopped out of the car and came to us.

"Yeah, yeah I get it. After we get the money for this, you'll get your bike," Eli grumbled.

As I started to ask what happened to Cooper's last one, I saw distant headlights bounding toward us. Two cars stopped and several people piled out leaving their lights on blinding me to who was approaching.

Cooper chuckled under his breath. "Oh, man. You are so screwed." His attention was on someone across the lot. His sight and smell were better than mine.

"Shit." Eli lowered his head and muttered under his breath. "I didn't think she would be here."

Eventually, the group moved close enough for me to see them. I scanned the people and zeroed in on a brunette. Immediately, I recognized her as the girl who had kissed Eli at the party in the woods. The night Lorcan attacked me. My gut wrung, suspicion sitting heavy inside my stomach.

"Eli?"

His lids closed briefly. "You can't be mad, Brycin. You were gone *three* years. I went a little nuts. I thought you were dead."

"You were with her?"

"Who left who?" He arched an eyebrow.

Embarrassment and fury burned up my neck. "Don't come at me with logic," I hissed at him. "We're way past that. We've been through too much crap to be sensible." I knew Eli was not the type to go without sex for three years, and I didn't think he'd pine for someone whom he thought was gone, but it still hurt.

His hands came up to my face. "You're right. You and I threw all sense out the window a long time ago."

"Don't be cute." I surveyed the girl who had now noticed me as well. Her face contorted in anger as she glared in my direction. "Let me guess, you didn't tell her you were no longer seeing each other?"

"Well, we weren't exactly 'seeing' each other. I thought if I stopped texting or showing up, she'd get the idea."

Cooper snickered. "You are such a dick, man."

Eli took my hand and squeezed it. "That I am."

Gripping his hand tighter, I glowered at him. "Remind me to kill you later."

One of Eli's drop-dead grins turned up his lips. "Count on it. Now, come on." He tugged me toward the other biker group, only letting my hand go when the leader approached him. I snuck a glance at the girl and saw contempt in her gaze on me.

"Dragen. Morgan." The man nodded at Eli and Cooper. His Second stepped with him.

"Bobby." Eli nodded back. "E.J."

"Did you hear about Hermit?" Bobby asked.

"Yeah, shot. I'm sorry, man."

"Yeah. Good guy. Those bastards in Portland. Heard you guys had trouble with them a few years back. Pock and McNamm, right?"

My muscles tightened. To me it wasn't a few years ago. They still appeared in my nightmares—Pock's hand down my pants and McNamm pinning me to the floor. I wasn't sorry they were dead, but I got uncomfortable with the fact Eli had killed them because of me.

Eli didn't even twitch in my direction, only nodded in agreement and quickly changed the subject. "Would you like to see the merchandise?" Eli motioned him to the car. Cooper turned on a dime and headed back for the SUV.

I was too busy watching Cooper, E.J., and Bobby, so I missed the girl slithering up to Eli.

"I've already seen the merchandise." Her hand jetted out cupping Eli through his pants. "It was more than satisfactory."

Disbelief left me rooted in place. Eli grabbed her hand and shook his head. "Yeah, my mistake, and it definitely won't be happening again."

Humiliation flushed her cheeks. "Why? Because of her?" Her eyes traveled over me. "Don't tell me the infamous playboy has settled down with *that*?"

"Natasha, you knew there were no strings."

Rage discharged from her pores. "You bastard!" She pushed at his chest. "You didn't seem to have a problem when you were screwing my brains out night after night."

The shock, which had kept me frozen, dissipated.

Eli saw me move before I realized I had. "Em..." He obstructed my path to Natasha. "Don't." His hands gripped my arms.

"You. Better. Get. Out. Of. My. Way." Each word bounced off his chest, which blocked me from getting to her.

"Bring it, bitch," Natasha challenged me. "You think he'll be faithful to you? Good luck. Your boyfriend's been screwing me for the last eight months."

"Natasha, stop," Eli bellowed. "You do not want to piss her off."

Natasha put her hands on her hips and sneered at me. "Her? Oh, I think I can take her."

"You think?" I grinned, baring my teeth. "Eli, she thinks she can handle me. Why don't you step aside, and I'll show her what she thinks she can handle?"

"Oh, hell, no." His hold became tighter. "Brycin, she's not worth it."

Those words only pissed off dear Natasha more. She flew at us. Before she could reach me, Eli let me go and grabbed her wrists, holding her back.

"What the hell is going on?" Bobby demanded as he, E.J., and Cooper came around the SUV. "Natasha, I only allowed you to come because you said you wanted to be a part of this transaction."

She held Eli's gaze one more moment before stepping back, pulling free. "You're right, Father. Those are the only goods I'm interested in." She headed for the SUV.

As much as I wanted to despise her, I saw sadness building a strong wall around her for protection, making her more hardhearted. In this life style, she had to have thick skin. I should sympathize, but, nah, I hated her.

Eli's attention returned to me, and his hands were back on my upper arms. "Breathe."

Sucking in a deep breath, I blew it out roughly. "I am so gonna kill you."

"I look forward to it." He wiggled his eyebrows at me.

My eyes looked deep into his beautiful green ones. "If you *ever* cheat on me—"

"Right," he scoffed, cutting off my words. "Remember, I like my beast-parts intact."

I grinned impishly. "And I could render them crispy fried bits and balls."

He shuddered, covering my mouth with his hand. "Shhh... they can hear you." He looked down at his pants. "Don't scare them like that. It's okay boys she didn't mean it."

"Oh, I did." I gave him a withering look. He chuckled, kissed my forehead, and herded me toward the others.

As we were walking, I felt tingling, a tugging in my gut. Panic tore through my veins. *No, not right now, Lars.* I hadn't felt anything all night and hoped Sinnie had just slipped up, not able to help herself from making the bed. That it hadn't been a signal from Lars. My hope was dashed, and now I was being yanked in the direction of the Unseelie King. It wasn't painful yet. "Yet" was the key word here. I swallowed, trying to ignore it and nervously continued to walk with Eli.

We had just rounded the back of car when we heard the others talking. "Looks good. They should be easy to sell on the street." Bobby examined the merchandise. "E.J., grab the case. The amount we decided on—"

Bobby's words were cut off by an outbreak of red and blue lights flooding the area with a glow an instant before sirens began to wail.

"Shit, the cops!" Cooper ran toward us.

Two police cars skidded to where we were parked, enveloping us in dirt.

"What the hell is this, Eli?" Natasha screamed. "You set us up?"

"Don't be stupid."

"Well, someone did." The accusation was directed at me.

"Freeze!" A voice boomed over a speaker. I recognized the voice immediately.

Weiss.

E.J. and Bobby darted for the trees. "I said, *freeze!*" Another cop yelled as he got out of the car.

We all scattered. Everything turned chaotic and frenzied. I quickly lost Eli and searched for him through the throng of retreating bikers.

Right then my stomach gripped in pain, doubling me over. The desire to run in the same direction where the cops were standing burned in my muscles. "Noooo, Lars." I gritted my teeth and fought the notion to act.

"Brycin?" I could hear Eli's voice dimly through the wail of the siren and yelling people.

A dry heave pushed up my throat. "Eli," I replied, but it barely came out a whisper. With everything I had, I willed myself to run. I moved closer to where I had heard his voice.

A fist collided with my gut and ripped breath from my lungs, taking me to the ground. As I landed, a pointy woman's boot slammed into my stomach. "That's for you, bitch," Natasha jeered before kicking me once more. "And that is for your asshole boyfriend."

I writhed in pain from both ignoring Lars's call and the kicks to my stomach. All my control intended to keep humans safe from me dissolved. Anger and pain expelled in wave after wave out of me.

It was in the same instant when I felt myself being yanked to my feet that a spark of my energy lit the vapors from the gas tank and ignited the car's engine. The gun powder and thousands of bullets boxed in the back of the SUV exploded.

BOOM!

The force propelled me off the ground, past the cop cars, and skid me into the dirt. Skin tore against the gravel, and my head slammed back onto the ground with a hard thump.

All went black.

EIGHTEEN

There was a dull ringing in my ears, and my brain and reactions moved groggily through the haze of the dust and debris still settling to the ground. The first sensation I had was of my arms being pulled behind me and metal enclosing them. This type of metal did nothing to me and under normal circumstances I could have broken free.

The second thing I noticed was I no longer felt Lars's pull. Did the explosion break the connection? Or did he stop it? I wasn't given much time to consider either option.

"So, you're still alive, Ms. Brycin. Hiding for the last three years, and you come out to commit a crime? Not at all surprised." Sheriff Weiss' words hissed into my ear. "You are under arrest. You have the right to remain silent..." He went through the mandated Miranda rights before adding his own. "And this time you won't ever leave. I finally have you like I said I would. I knew it was only a matter of time and you'd screw up." He tugged me to my feet while my vision tried to cut through the cloud of dirt whirling around the area.

Eli? I sent out my thoughts. I knew he couldn't hear me, but he could feel me. He would follow.

"You were always trouble, but being with Mr. Dragen has compounded your misdemeanors into felonies. Tampering with lights is child's play compared to black market trafficking."

My mouth stayed shut, and my eyes continued to search for Eli as Sheriff Weiss hauled me to his patrol car. I was still dizzy and confused from being thrown across the ground, kicked in the stomach, and summoned by a Demon. Weiss shoved my head down as he pushed me into the cruiser. The moment he did, I knew I was in trouble. Iron laced the generic metal dividing the front and back of the police car. It wasn't a lot, but it was enough to cause my body react. I sunk back and pressed my pinned arms uncomfortably against the seat.

Weiss grasped his police radio from his belt. "Lambert, copy."

It took a few moments before a voice came back over the speaker. "Copy, this is Lambert. I have Dragen in custody. The others got away."

My lids squeezed together. *Shit.* There was little doubt Eli could have gotten away, but he had probably been looking for me. Knowing him, he'd do something stupid like letting himself be arrested if he knew I had been caught.

"Dammit, Eli," I mumbled. Now through the dark I felt him near. I looked out the window and saw the green eyes first. Glowing and furious.

My own narrowed in on his. *Are you stupid?*

I wasn't the one who blew everything up and then got caught, he retorted.

I was about to curse him further, but Lambert escorted him into the back of the other police cruiser, blocking our eyes from communicating.

There was a part of me, a sick part, that thought, *Oh, how romantic. He got arrested for me.* Our romantic gestures consisted of getting felony charges on our records for each other. The Bonnie and Clyde of the Fae world.

This is not what I had in mind when I think of Eli and me and handcuffs.

Sheriff Weiss slipped into the front seat, turning on his siren. This was not some minor charge we could walk away from with only a slap on the wrist. I really needed my powers so I could get out of this mess, but the iron incapacitated me just enough.

Sheriff Weiss drove from the abandoned warehouses and turned toward downtown Olympia.

"Don't think you are some bad-ass. Do you know how many girls I've seen like you? They all think life with the bad boy is fun and exciting. Until it gets serious, and they find themselves doing twenty to life or worse." He looked at me through the rearview mirror. "If it takes a scare like this for you to get off this path and see the truth before it's too late, then I will be happy."

I shifted to the side so the ache in my arms wasn't so constant. "You've been after me from the beginning. You've probably dreamed about this. What do you care if I get on the right course or not?"

"You're right. I've never liked you and knew you were a bad seed. There was something about you I never trusted, but you also reminded me of someone. Someone I gave up on."

There was something in the way he said it that I knew it was personal.

"Who?"

His hands gripped the steering wheel harder. "A daughter," he said finally.

This made me uncomfortable. The evil Sheriff Weiss was becoming a person. Someone who experienced pain and love. He and I always had a wall of unreserved judgment and hatred for each other. I didn't like him becoming... human.

"You remind me of her. Same stubbornness, same lack of consideration for others. All you think of is yourself, and you give little thought to right and wrong."

I had no idea of his daughter's story or what became of her, but his bitterness was clear. When I first met Weiss, I had a feeling I was being punished for more than just my actions.

"What happened to her?"

"She ran away and got involved with a guy and his gang. She was shot and killed by a cop when she tried to flee a drug bust." Weiss's words were sharp and full of venom. "She made the wrong choices and got what she deserved. The law is the law. She broke the rules and had to take the consequences for her actions."

Wow...

Speechless, I took in Weiss' story. He was a man who thought in black and white, good and bad, pride and honor. Still the pain of losing his daughter had to eat at him. His overzealousness to "get" me was more about his daughter and trying to fix what he hadn't been able to with her. It was sad. It didn't endear him to me, but I understood his actions a little more.

"Shit!" I heard Weiss yell. The police car in front of us, which held Eli, swerved and skidded uncontrollably across the road. Weiss slammed on the brakes, and we slid sideways down the asphalt. Something smashed into us, denting the side of our car, sending it flying through the air.

A sensation of not knowing which way was up wrapped around me. It felt like I had just climbed into the washing machine and put myself on spin cycle. The seatbelt cut into my stomach and shoulder as it held me in place. Both Weiss and I stayed suspended in the air as the car flipped, but the moment the roof made contact with the ground, it crumpled on us with bone-crunching force. My head slammed into the caving roof. Excruciating pain and noise flooded my senses and overwhelmed me. The sound of metal twisting in agony seemed to come from every direction before it abruptly stopped.

Several moments passed as I tried to understand what happened. I blinked and swiveled my head. Hazy moonlight lit the interior enough for me to distinguish the battered and unconscious sheriff. His seat belt held him, but the roof had caved so much his body was huddled against it. I hung upside down, blood seeping from my head. My eyes grew weary, and I wanted to sleep. I craved it like a deep hunger.

Glass shattered and startled me awake, making me retch. A large fist punched through the side window, grabbing the frame of the car door and ripping it off its hinges. I closed my eyes and turned my head unable to block the piercing squeal of metal. I felt hands fumble with my seatbelt. They grabbed me and pulled me from the mangled car. Pain. I felt pain.

Just close your eyes and go to sleep, Ember. The hurt will go away.

I tried to force my eyes open when my body was placed on the rough concrete. It was too dark to see my rescuer clearly, but I could sense he was enormous. His outline blocked the moonlight. My arms were released from the tight bonds constraining them. Blood flooded back into them, making them prickle and ache.

"Is she okay?"

A voice came from behind the man who silently helped me. I knew that deep, male voice. I just couldn't place it with a face.

"Yes," the huge, gruff-sounding man responded. "We need to go now."

Strong arms curled under my legs and back and picked me up like a baby as I drifted off to a place where I felt no pain.

The soft motion of fingers curling through my hair caused my lids to flutter open. I knew it must be a dream as there was no other way he would be here. But why was I dreaming about him? Didn't I have enough boy issues?

My head lay comfortably in Nic's lap. His beautiful, Spanish god-like features beamed down on me. His dark brown eyes fixed hungrily on mine. In a dream, Nic still projected pure, uninhibited sex. He was an Incubus and good at his job. Too good.

I also knew that if I were awake, I would be feeling pain. I felt nothing but a rhythmic vibration making my body rock.

"My little Dae." Nic's lips touched my forehead. Seeing him again was comforting. I had missed them all. But words would not come to my lips no matter how much I tried.

"Shhh..." He kissed me on the lips. "I've got you. Sleep, my sweet Dae." My heavy lids obliged his request. My dreams pulled me deeper into the darkness.

My lashes lifted. A chandelier hung above my bed, glittering in the early morning light. I rolled over and snuggled deeper into the soft blankets.

Shit! I sat up with a start, stunned. It was a *déjà vu* moment to awake here in my underwear and tank top, but this time I knew exactly where I was.

"Lars," I bellowed and flung the covers off as I sprang out of bed. The dresser was still filled with my clothes. Three years later and nothing seemed different. I grabbed a pair of jeans from the drawer. My boots were in my closet. I slipped into them and headed for the door.

Walking down the stairs felt like another day at Camp Demon. The smells of sizzling bacon and rich, cheesy eggs drifted up the stairs. Marguerite was cooking. A sob came from my chest, and I was running before I realized it.

"Marguerite," I wailed like a child as I entered the kitchen.

"*Mi dulce nina.*" Her arms wrapped around me, pulling me down to her short height. My heart burst with warmth as she crushed me to her. Marguerite was like the grandma I never had. She was tough, but her love was unconditional and complete. It was hard to keep the tears back. She made me feel like a little girl, protected and loved. "Oh, we have missed you, *nina.* You must not leave us again."

Right then I didn't want to. With both my mother and Torin at the ranch, things had gotten more complicated and tense. I longed to stay right here, wrapped in Marguerite's love.

"I agree," a voice spoke from behind me. I knew it instantly.

"Rez." I turned and embraced her. I hadn't really realized how much I had missed them. They were my family, too. They were a part of me.

"Oh, I don't know. I certainly was fine without her around." Maya strolled into the kitchen, immediately reaching for Marguerite's scrumptious coffee cake.

I smiled. "Good to see you, too, Maya."

She grunted back at me with her attention focused on the cake in her hand. Alki and Koke entered behind Maya.

Koke moved around me. "If you are back, I will go get extra padding on." She clicked her tongue in annoyance, referring to that time I had blown up the workout room, tossing us yards away, mangled and hurt. Being Fae we'd been okay, but they'd never let me live it down. The room was now built of stone... not wood.

"You don't look as soft and fat as I thought you would." Alki circled me and grabbed my arm. I immediately went into a defense pose.

"To me it's only been a few weeks since I've been here." One eyebrow hitched up, taunting him to attack.

"Oh, no-no-no!" Marguerite waved a spatula between us. "No combat in my kitchen."

Alki looked like he wanted to see if his teachings were still imbedded in my brain and muscles, but Rez shook her head.

"Ember needs to eat and speak with Lars. You guys can beat on each other later."

Alki huffed in disappointment. "Okay. But you come out later. You cannot afford to go soft." He pivoted and headed out the back door, Koke in pursuit.

I smiled, shaking my head. Yup, I even missed Alki.

I need therapy.

"Where's Nic?" I turned back to Rez. A fuzzy dream from the night before hovered in my thoughts.

Rez cocked her head. "Asleep. He was out late."

"Well, it's good to see things don't change around here."

"Actually, he wasn't out for himself; he was helping retrieve you. He went with Rimmon, Gorgon, and Lars's men last night. You didn't see him?"

So Nic wasn't a dream. Without a word I headed for the stairs, for the Spanish god's bedroom.

"My little Dae has returned home," Nic's voice came through the dark when I entered.

"I guess I should be thanking you for that." I stepped farther into the room but kept the door open. Nic was a sexy Incubus and always trouble. Behind closed doors, he was a force I wasn't ready to deal with. His hand reached out from under the covers and pulled the back of my leg. I fell on the bed next to him.

"I've been waiting for you to fall into my bed." He tugged me, keeping me from getting up. We had a brief fling while I had been in the house. We both knew it was no more than that, but it had been fun. The fact I didn't actually have sex with him seemed like a miracle now. Nic was almost impossible not to want. He could still fluster me.

"I didn't come here for this." I pulled away and sat up. He kept his hand on my leg.

"Why did you come here, then?" He sat, revealing more of his bare chest. His dark eyes penetrated mine. Nic was a sex god, and no matter how committed you were to someone, his power drew you in. I was supposedly immune to his charm. If that were the case, no mortal stood a chance. I could feel myself weakening.

"Nic, stop." I got to my feet. "I came here to thank you."

He studied me for a moment, his eyes roving over me. "Well, well, well, my sweet Dae is having sex... a lot of it."

"What?" My cheeks heated up.

"Em, sex is the only thing I am really in tune with. It is how I know who is vulnerable and who to approach. I can tell when someone is really satisfied and when someone is not. You, girl, are incredibly gratified. Those can be fun and a great energy boost, but the humans who are lonely and full of self-loathing are the easiest." He scooted toward me, putting his feet on the floor.

"You are disgusting."

Nic spread his arms with a wide grin. "It's who I am." His eyes bored into me again. "And I'd love to bed you. You would be a challenge."

"You wouldn't get any energy hits off me."

"I'd get another kind of buzz from you. It would be purely for enjoyment purposes. Not work."

I looked away, embarrassed.

"Don't be ashamed for wanting sex, Em. Fairies and Demons are the biggest sex fiends there are."

I didn't want to tell him I was also part Dark Dweller, who could equal an Incubi's need for sex. No wonder I could barely stay in my clothes lately.

"Humans think they need to be ashamed because they want it and like it. You are really enjoying it, aren't you?" Nic leaned back on his arms with a leer. "I am disappointed it's not me."

"You're not upset." I laughed. "You don't like me that much."

He shrugged. "I like you more than most. You've become one of us here." He shifted, only a corner of the sheet covering him. "But you're the kind of girl who wants her partner to be monogamous. I don't and won't ever like anyone enough for fidelity."

"Yeah, well, I just wanted to thank you for saving me." I turned to leave.

176

"You know I wasn't the only one who's missed you. He never stopped searching."

My hand stopped on the door knob. "That's because I broke our contract, which doesn't come without consequences. Lars wants to make sure I pay."

"If that's what you want to believe, but he didn't send out his minions to look for you. He went himself."

I still continued to face the door. "He needs me right now, but I am just a means to end for him."

"When he found you were in the Otherworld, he risked exposing his spies there to help you escape. He even had people keeping your friends and father safe."

I whirled. "What? Who?"

Nic's gaze was steady on me. "Think about it, Ember. Who is in a position to keep your family protected?"

Then it hit me. "Castien. Castien works for Lars?"

Nic nodded. "He is one of several who have risen in ranks under Aneira. Castien is the highest, and the Queen trusts him. He has been a great informant for us, and we don't want to compromise him. He does enough so he won't get caught."

It suddenly made so much sense why Castien had always looked out for my friends and treated them well. I thought it had been because of Ryan, and maybe now it was, but in the beginning it hadn't. How many little things did he do every day to keep Aneira from killing them? Why would Lars bother? He certainly didn't care if any of them survived? I grabbed for the door again.

"Where are you going?"

"To talk to Lars." I gave him a quick smile over my shoulder. "Thank you again for saving me tonight."

"How about you owe me one." He winked.

I chuckled and left the room.

Lars's office was on the other side of the house. I weaved through the enormous English-style home and barged into his office. "Why didn't you tell me you had someone...Castien, watching over my family. Don't you think this would have eased my anxiety?"

He sat in his chair, nonplussed by my entrance. "I could not have you knowing anything about my men there. Your ties to Torin could have exposed them to the Queen. Whatever he learned from you, Aneira could have picked it from his thoughts. I had to keep you completely ignorant, for my men's safety and for your family."

My anger deflated. He had only been protecting the people I loved... from me.

"Why did you do it? I know you don't care what happens to them."

Lars sat taller in his chair. "You are right. I do not, but you do. I needed you to have a reason to fight. I knew as long as they were prisoners you would never give up battling for your family and friends. If something happened to them, you could have gone either way. I was not willing to take the chance."

Manipulation should be the Fae's tag line, but in this case I couldn't get mad. He had kept them as safe as possible.

"Did you know Ryan can't leave now?"

"Yes. It was the only way Castien could save him. Ryan was dying. It was my call."

I wiped the cut on my forehead. "Thank you for saving him."

He nodded. "Now let us talk about more pressing matters, and why I was trying to contact you tonight."

"Was it necessary to flip a cop car, almost killing me in order to nab me? You could have asked nicely. Oh, right, Unseelie Kings don't do that."

"I saved you from being put in jail. You should be thanking me. Again."

"You Fae are so screwed up. I love you think propelling a cop car off the road because I didn't come running is a perfectly normal thing to do."

"You ignored my call. I knew something was wrong." He waved toward the chair. "Please, sit, Ember."

"No. I have to get back. I need to find Eli. Oh, God, is he okay? What happened to him?"

"He is fine. He was able to get away as well."

Relief came out in my breath. "I better go. He'll track me down." I rocked back and forth on the balls of my feet.

"He will not be able to find you here," Lars declared.

My lips curled in a smile. "Oh, really? He did last time."

"What?" Lars stopped, his head darting up. "He was able to find you here?"

"Yes. He couldn't cross the wards, of course, but he knew where I was. The only place he can't seem to feel me is when I'm in the Otherworld. He will find me soon enough."

Lars's forehead creased. "I am aware he does not connect to you in the Otherworld. But I never suspected your tie to him was so strong it carried through our spells and wards." He frowned. "I would have been more diligent had I known he could feel you in our compound."

I shrugged. "You could be as careful as you want, it doesn't stop him. It's kind of annoying, but it won't."

"I am starting to gather as much." Lars scowled.

"Wait. How did you know Eli could not feel me in the Otherworld?" I trailed off; the answer already came to me. "You saw Eli while I was gone. And you knew I was alive the whole time and didn't tell them?"

Lars calmly nodded. "He was causing enough disturbances here on Earth. I needed to control the situation and keep you protected. He would have destroyed my efforts if he knew you were alive."

I groaned.

"You should thank me. Elighan would have gotten himself killed. There is little doubt he would have tried to get to the Otherworld for you, drawing the Queen's attention doing it. He was not subtle or discreet during your absence."

The other stories of what Eli was like during that time only backed his statement. Still, he was going to be so pissed when he found out Lars knew the whole time I wasn't dead.

"Let's get to why you brought me here so I can get back." I crossed my arms.

Lars stood and walked to the glass doors overlooking his sprawling landscape. "It took me a while to realize what I saw on your back." His voice was distant, lost in thought.

"I know the location of the map on your back. I am actually displeased it took me as long as it did to decipher it. I should have known..." Lars cleared his throat, ridding himself of any emotion he might have shown. "It has a great deal of meaning to me."

"Really? Where?" I stared at the back of his head.

"An area near Thessalia."

"Like in Greece? Really? I've always wanted to go there."

"Yes." He turned to face me. "We are heading to the monasteries of Metéora tonight. You and the Druid are coming with me." Of course Kennedy would have to be there. A Druid had to break the curse so we could get to the sword.

179

"Tonight? What about the Dark Dwellers?"

Lars shook his head. "We do not need them."

A sputtered laugh fell from my lips. "Need them or not, they will be coming."

Lars looked out the window and sighed. "I do not want them with us, but I will agree to this only because of your connection to Elighan. He will follow anyway. I suppose they could be an asset in protecting you and locating the sword." Lars walked toward me, his expression severe, and his eyes stared deeply into mine. "But our deal still holds. The moment the sword is no longer needed to dispatch the Queen, it belongs to me, or he dies."

I nodded slowly. "Agreed."

"All right, let us go."

My face scrunched up. I was worried how Eli and the group would take the news about Lars, especially because I'd been keeping it secret.

NINETEEN

Mom somehow sensed my approach since she stood waiting at the property line. My stomach twisted in knots, nervous of what was going to happen. No one would be happy about Lars.

"Ember," she yelled as she ran to me. "We were so worried about you. I was going crazy. Elighan didn't know what happened to you." The strength of her arms crushed the air out of my lungs.

"Can't breathe, Mom," I choked out.

"Good, because I was planning on killing you once I knew you were all right." She stepped back, gripping my shoulders tightly. Her eyes wandered from the top of my head to my feet, making sure I was in one piece. "Don't do that to me again."

"Didn't have much of a choice." I looked around, ready for a raging Dark Dweller to come out of the woodwork. "Where's Eli?"

"He went out searching for you. He said he could feel you but was having trouble locating the exact spot. What happened?" She dropped her grip on me.

"About that... there is something else I need to tell you guys." I cringed knowing how they'd all react.

Mom froze in place, and I saw her nose sniff the air, her eyes growing wide. "Oh, crap on ash bark. No!"

"Oh, yes." Lars stepped from the shadows, addressing my mom with a cool expression. His head gave her a terse nod. "*Sionnach*."

"Lars." Mom nodded in return, quickly regaining her composure. "How disappointing. I was hoping I would never have to see you again."

He sneered. It was one of those icy smiles that always made me squirm in my seat. "You should have come to me, Lily. I could have saved you from a lot of agony. All those years on the run keeping Ember away and then being tortured because of your obstinate nature."

"I wanted to get her away from that life. To keep her safe. You would have only thrown her in head first."

Lars stepped closer. "And did you prevent it from eventually happening? No. You left her ignorant, vulnerable, and weak." Anger punctuated each word.

I had never seen him lose his cool before. No matter how frustrated or upset he'd gotten with me, he kept an air of control. He was always in charge, but something in his tone now made me feel his restraint was slipping.

"She had a life and was loved. Loved more than *you* could possibly understand."

My head snapped to look at my mom. Something in her words and menacing glare caused my stomach to plummet.

"You do not know anything of the kind. You never gave me the chance." He opened his arms before clasping his hands together.

"Oh, I think I knew you both well enough to realize she was better off without either of you."

Fear clung to my lungs. I struggled to breathe, knowing what was coming. I had felt it for a while but never let myself fully accept the thought. Now, I was watching myself being swept down a river toward a waterfall, helpless to stop it.

"She is my blood!" Lars bellowed and his body shook. "*My* blood. *My* family."

Noooo... I was now going over the waterfall into the crushing rocks below.

"What does that matter to you?" Mom stepped closer, her shoulders rising. "You have no idea what family even means. All you cared about was power. You couldn't love anyone but yourself. She doesn't belong to you, Lars."

"And she belongs to *you?*" he snapped back.

My heart battered against my ribs. One idea absorbed my thoughts. Was I listening to my mother and *father* fight? Did my gaze dart between two former lovers? My parents? Everything about it seemed wrong. Lars and Lily together? In love?

My head shook back and forth not wanting to accept the notion. Lars was the exact opposite of what Mom liked. Sometimes opposites attracted, but this was still hard to grasp. I was more shocked and confused about the fact my mom and Lars could have been together than the fact he might be my father. It had been there all along, this possibility. From the moment I had met Lars I felt a strange connection to him.

"Why? Why didn't you tell me?" I looked into Lars's face, searching it for evidence that I came from him. His glowing, yellow-green eyes stared back into mine. His jet-black hair was the same color as mine. I always thought the eye color we shared was a Demon thing. Guess it was more than that. I certainly hadn't got his tan skin tone. My nose and lips didn't seem to come from either of them.

"I did not feel you were ready for this information at the time. There were more pressing matters."

"More pressing matters? Training me and creating a weapon against the Queen was more urgent than telling me you are my father?"

Lars and Mom stilled, both turning to me. A huge gulf filled the space. Dread shot into my gut like an arrow. There was more they weren't telling me.

"Y-You are my father, right?"

"No. I am not your father, Ember," Lars said matter-of-factly.

The rug slithered out from under me. A Ferris wheel in my head was spinning my emotions and thoughts around and around. "Wh-what? I thought... you just said..." I didn't know what I was trying to say anymore.

"I said you were my blood, not that you are my daughter."

Blinking, I stared desperately at him then at my mom when he didn't continue.

Mom compressed her lips together, and sighed. "Ember... Lars is your uncle."

What? My uncle?

"My twin brother was your father. He is dead," Lars stated as he regarded me.

Mom glared at him, "Why don't you tell her how he came to be that way."

Lars's Demon-colored eyes slanted. "There was no other choice."

"So convenient for you, wasn't it?" Mom hurled back at him. "You wanted everything he had."

"Power maybe, but I lost the two things that meant anything to me to acquire it."

"You know nothing of loss. You destroyed the—"

"Stop! Stop!" I grabbed at my head. My entire body trembled with anger, confusion, and fear.

There was a tense silence before Lars spoke. "Ember, do you remember when I told you about the previous Unseelie King?"

It took me a moment before the memory came back to me. It happened the first time I talked with Lars, after I almost drowned and ended up passing out on his land. He had hinted that he had killed and taken the title from the last King. "Yes."

"Your father was the previous King," Lars's body became rigid and his stare distant.

I shook with denial and turned to my mother. "You told me my father lived in New York. I saw a picture of him. Was it all a lie? He wasn't real either?"

"I didn't lie exactly. He was an old boyfriend of mine. You found the picture of us and assumed he was your dad, and I let you believe it. He really does live in New York with a wife and kids. That is all real."

"Just minus the fact he isn't my father. That my father was a Demon who was the Unseelie King."

"You have to understand. I wanted you to have nothing to do with this world or life. I thought I was doing the best thing for you."

"Best thing?" I yelled. "Lying to me? Keeping me ignorant and unaware of what existed out there? I thought I was crazy most of my life."

Mom's eyes filled with tears as she looked at me. "I am so sorry."

"Sorry is not going to change the reality I had to live through your 'murder' and had to be committed for a while because I was seeing and hearing things. Sorry won't bring back my father."

"Mark is your real father for all intents and purposes. Devlin knew nothing about being a parent or caring for a child."

"You never gave any of us the opportunity." Lars thundered, but my mind fastened on something else she said.

"Devlin? Was that his name? You told me it was my father's family name?"

"It was." She responded softly. She hadn't exactly lied about it, but that didn't make me feel any less angry.

I still felt tricked. The whole time I had another clue laughing in my face, like some twisted inside joke that I was never let in on. Ember Aisling Devlin Brycin. My name was one long farce. Every one of the names hinted at who I was or about the world I came from.

"Tell me about him." I hugged myself to keep from exploding.

"Devlin was my twin." Lars shifted his weight to the other leg. "My brother and I shared identical looks and powers, the ones you have inherited. We were very close and did everything together, until he fell

184

in love. Then everything changed." Lars's lids shifted to glance at Mom before they came back to me. She kept her head down, staring at the ground.

So, the Demon Unseelie King, my father, fell in love with a noble Fay, my mom. They had a torrid love affair. When I came to exist, all of their lives went to shit.

How very Shakespearean.

My father was dead. Killed by the present Unseelie King, my uncle. Forget Shakespeare, we should be on a reality TV show.

The notion that I would never get to meet him, to know who he was, struck me. I was sure I should feel something, anything. I didn't. I only felt numb and detached.

"Why did you kill your own brother? To become the King? To be more powerful? How could you do something like that?"

Lars pinched the space between his brows. "I had to. It was not something I wanted to do. He went insane and was no longer fit to rule."

"So, you killed him?" A strangled cry punched out of my throat. "Is that how you solve things? He was your brother no matter what."

His lips turned down, and he bowed his head. There was no sadness or emotion in his voice. "It is how it is done. You never *retire* from being the Unseelie King. It is a fight to the death, and whoever wins is King. Devlin killed thousands of humans and was no longer suitable to be King. He lost himself and became volatile. I remained the only one powerful enough to challenge him. It was up to me."

"Why didn't you tell me this?"

"After what you went through, you were not exactly stable. I did not think it would help you to hear that the former, tyrannical Unseelie King was your biological father, had gone insane, and almost wiped out a country. That your own uncle had killed him and became the current Unseelie King. You needed your human father and friends to focus on. To revenge them. To stabilize you," Lars stated. "It was also unsettling for me to see how untrained and defenseless you were. I needed you to focus on your powers and be able to protect yourself."

For most of my life, I had wondered about the man in New York, my alleged real father. Before Mark, I looked at men on the street and pretended they were my dad. I witnessed fathers pushing their kids on the swing or playing with them on the front lawn. I imagined how it would be to have one. My father would tell me how sorry he was and promise never to leave me again. That he loved and missed me so much.

My daydreams never included him being a Demon. Or an Unseelie King. Or deceased. I envisioned getting together with my father's family over Christmas dinner, not over a thousand-year-old text that prophesized my killing a Fairy Queen with a mythical sword. My dreams had been a little simpler: a dog, a ball, and a lawn.

That was never meant for me. My biological, Demon father was dead, while my true dad was locked up in the Otherworld by a psycho Fay bitch. That was my reality.

Someone has a really sick sense of humor.

Mom held her hand out to me. "Ember, I am so sorry I lied to you. I only wanted to protect you."

"No." I stepped out of her reach. "I've had enough of your idea of protection. It's only brought me pain and heartbreak."

Her face filled with horror and devastation. I didn't care. I pivoted and dashed into the dark night. I needed to be alone. My thoughts were like angry gnats, buzzing around my head. I heard Mom call my name repeatedly, but she didn't come after me. I continued till they were out of sight, then the earth came up to collect me as my legs crumpled.

Breath went in and out of my lungs too quickly. The world around me spun, and I curled into a ball. When the wards went off, it felt distant and far away. Somewhere in my brain it registered Lars must have crossed onto the Dark Dweller's property.

"My lady. My lady. Are you all right?" Simmons fluttered to my face, his expression full of concern and fear. "We have been so worried about you. Sir Torin has been going nuts." Simmons paused, really taking me in. "What has happened, my lady? You don't look well."

I couldn't answer. If I opened my mouth, I would crack open. I was afraid the shards of my heart were too shattered, and I'd never be able to put myself together.

"I will go get Sir Torin. He will help."

"Find Elighan instead, Simmons," Cal's voice spoke from above me. "I think he is back now."

Simmons's chest filled with air, and he frowned as if he would ignore Cal's instructions. But his attention turned back to me before he nodded and flew off.

Cal landed lightly on my shoulder. My arms were wrapped around my legs as I rocked, lost in thought. My father had been the Unseelie King. A part of me had always wondered if it was Lars. Was I disappointed it wasn't? Yes. I had wanted it to be him. Because he was alive. Maybe I'd felt a strange connection to him because my true father was his twin, and he is family.

What made my father go crazy? Is this why there's so much resentment between my mom and Lars? I needed to know so much more now the truth was out. In spite of that, my mind had other plans. It wanted to shut down and forget everything I learned. Cole's voice came back to me: *"Once the truth is out, there's no going back, and you will wish you could."*

"Brycin?"

I didn't respond or move as Eli crouched in front of me. "Are you okay? You scared the shit out of me when you disappeared. Hey, talk to me."

"I have been talking to her for the last few minutes with no response. Think girlie here has finally broke." Cal tapped at the side of my head. "Noodle snapped. No more cookies in the cookie jar."

He'd been talking to me?

"Ember?" Eli said more firmly. "What happened to you? How did you get away from Weiss? Talk to me." He clasped my hands, then looked at Cal. "What happened?"

"What? You assume I know? Like I eavesdropped? Me?" Cal touched his chest, dramatically.

Eli cocked his head and scoffed.

"Yeah, yeah okay," Cal replied. "Girlie here found out her real father was the previous Unseelie King, and the current one is her uncle... who killed her father."

Eli jerked; my lids blinked at the quick movement. His hand went to rub his head. "You've got to be fucking kidding me?"

"I don't kid about fucking." The words were out of my mouth before I even realized I spoke. They sounded robotic, which hit me even funnier. It was something Eli had said to me when we first met, when Mrs. Sanchez put us together to run the ropes course. I recalled how flustered he made me, how sexually heightened and uncomfortable my senses became around him. It had never gone away, but that day felt so long ago. I was a human girl then, blissfully unaware of what I really was and what was ahead.

I began to laugh. Uncontrollably.

"Oh, yeah, the cookie has crumbled. The pixie dust has dissolved her brain." Cal patted my head.

My stomach ached as I continued to laugh.

"Ember, I need you to focus." When Eli pulled me to my feet, Cal catapulted into the air, his wings fluttering keeping him in place.

Eli's green eyes flashed in the moonlight. His face was half shadowed. With his hair just starting to grow, his green eyes wild, and scarred face stern, he looked scary, threatening and ruthless. Sexy and dangerous were addicting qualities. They let you forget the world around you, and I wanted to forget everything I had learned in the last half hour—to stop feeling the gut-wrenching sadness for one moment. My basic need took over.

My lips met his with such force he shifted back. His fingers touched my face, and our lips moved brutally over each other.

"Okay, I think it is time for me to exit," Cal mumbled. "Maybe go see a hot brownie about a woman." He zoomed off.

Eli's kiss deepened. I groaned and started to tug at his t-shirt.

"You know I am never one to turn down sex." Eli pulled back a little. "Ever."

"Good." I smiled and kissed his neck.

"You will tell me what happened with you tonight?"

I tilted my chin up to look at him. "Right now I need a few minutes of forgetting everything I just discovered."

Eli's one eyebrow curved up. "A few minutes? Is that all?"

"Didn't you say there were a few things you wanted to do to me on your bike?"

Both Eli's eyebrows hit his hairline. "What I had in mind will definitely take more than a few minutes."

"I'll give you twelve. Let's see what you can do in that time." I grabbed his hand and tugged him toward the shed where the Harleys were parked.

The moment we entered, his fingers threaded through my hair, yanking me to him, kissing me deeply before he whipped me around facing his bike.

"Undo you pants. Now," he ordered, his voice deep and commanding.

My heartbeat wildly as I did what he said, his breath heavy in my ear, the desire and tension rising.

At the sound of my zipper, he wrenched my jeans down to my ankles, taking them off. He had no patience for my underwear, shredding them off me and tossing them on the ground. The cool night air slipping through my folds, lighting sparks over my skin. Ripping my top over my head, he bent me over the bike, leaving me completely naked and at his mercy.

"Fuck, Brycin. You are gorgeous." Eli's fingers ran through my ass until he dipped into my pussy. "Always so fucking wet for me."

"Eli." I breathed. Pleading.

I heard his own zipper, the sound of his jeans falling, his body moving in closer until I felt his cock pressing between my ass, the tip of him hinting at my entrance, making me groan.

"Hold on." He put my hands on the handlebars right as he seized my hips, then thrust brutally into me. I screamed out hoarsely, my fingers knotting around the bars, holding on as he pulled out, and driving back in again, arching my back. Rolling my hair in his hand, he tugged hard, bowing my back more, pushing me deeper into him.

He let out a growl as I moaned, my pussy dripping as he pounded unforgivingly into me.

"Harder!"

Eli snarled and let any barriers go, his skin slapping loudly against mine, our sounds echoing off the shed. Vicious and violent, it took everything I had to not topple over the bike, my core rubbing over the seat.

"I want your pussy covering it." He growled into my ear. "Every time I ride, I want to smell you on it. Know your pussy was coming all over it." He growled in my ear as he pulled my hair harder.

I started to shake. Enveloped by pleasure, I almost blacked out for a moment, my knuckles curling, my nails digging into the handles, my climax already barreling for me.

"Oh god, Eli."

"No. You can't come yet." He pulled out of me, tugging me up as he moved to the bike, sitting down on the seat. His feet sturdy on the ground, he hauled me back down on him, straddling his lap, my back leaning into the gas tank. His clothed body in contrast to my naked one only added to the charge, the sensual friction against my bare skin.

"I want your eyes on me when you come, Brycin." He gripped my hips, sinking me down on him again, my pussy greedy for more contracted around him, every inch of him was like an electric charge, flicking the light outside the shed. Eli's chest vibrated as I grappled for air, my hips rolling with him, meeting his with the same need.

"This pussy is mine." He drove up into me, upping the intensity, hitting something so deep in me I let out a growl, sounding like a feral animal.

Eli's eyes flashed red. In that moment everything broke. There was no boundaries or limits. We unleashed on each other like feral beasts, letting our true selves free.

189

He reached over, turning on the engine. The roar filled the room as he revved the motor, the violent vibration hitting every nerve in my body, quivering through my core as he continued to pound into me.

I bellowed out, my pussy merciless clamping down on him, my body exploding, ripping my senses from me.

"Fuuucck!" Eli roared, plunging into me ferociously two more times before I felt him release inside me, fluttering another aftershock through me. I went limp, sagging back, gasping for air. Eli's forehead fell between my breasts, his breath fluttering heavily over them. He turned off the engine, but neither of us moved, staying that way for a few moments before he lifted his head.

"That was a shortened version of what I wanted to do. Next time I'm spreading you open and devouring you on it before fucking you." His lips skated over my nipples before he pulled back. "Your twelve minutes are up."

I whimpered when he pulled out of me.

"Stay." He climbed off the bike, zipping his pants back up, as he grabbed a clean rag off the table. He eyes burned with lust as he meticulous cleaned me up, stirring heat through us again.

We were insatiable.

"Come on, before I change my mind and make you ride the engine while fucking you from behind."

Sucking in, my body shook as he tugged me up, his hand swatting my ass to move.

I leaned over the bike to grab my shirt off the ground. It was still wearable, but once again my underwear did not survive. Eli snatched the top out of my hands and drew it over my head, his knuckles sliding down the sensitive skin on my sides. His eyes penetrated mine the whole time.

I shivered, all the images of what we just did blazing through my mind. I wanted to do more.

"We need to get back," I said more to myself than Eli.

Lars was not going to be patient much longer. I was surprised no one came for us already. I needed this time to get my head back on straight, or in this case, lose it completely.

Fuck. I felt a hell of a lot better.

"You need to talk to me first," he said against my neck while he buttoned my jeans.

"Is this your version of talking?" I pulled his hands away and stepped away. "Come on. Lars isn't going to wait much longer." I turned to leave. Eli fingers wrapped around my bicep and yanked me back to face him. His expression turned severe and forbidding.

"Don't play me, Brycin." His grip became tighter; his green eyes flickered brighter. "I know when you're using sex as a distraction. I'm not as simple as you think."

Although I knew he'd never purposely hurt me, a spark of anxiety sizzled up my spine. No matter what we had been through, he could still startle me. The ruthless killer was never far from the surface no matter how "human" he acted.

"You are anything but simple," I uttered.

"I'm a Dark Dweller, so I'm going to choose screwing you over talking. Always. It's who I am. But don't think you can pull one over on me."

I tugged away from him. "Give me a break. I just found out I have an uncle and a deceased father. No one thought to let me know about them even when I was living under their roof." I spit out, fury crackling under my skin. "And even better—Lars murdered my father because Devlin went insane and started slaughtering people right and left. Guess the apple doesn't fall far from the tree."

"Is that what you think?" Eli eyes burned into me. "You are not insane or homicidal."

"I'm sure some would beg to differ."

Eli snatched my wrist again, pulling me into him. "Believe me I know about being a killer, and you're not one."

An overwhelming ache clenched at my throat, emotion chipping away at my wall. I stared at my feet, the ache wiggling into my heart. "They both lied to me. Why would they keep something like this from me?"

Eli watched me. His hands still locked around my arms. "Lily did it to keep you safe."

"I don't know if I buy that anymore."

We stayed quiet for a minute. Biting my lip, I took in a deep breath and asked, "Did you know who my father was?" I had learned all too well Fae loved to keep their secrets. Even those you felt should tell you the truth didn't. Maybe the centuries of hiding from humans and keeping their existence secret from the world kept them so tight-lipped.

"No." He shook his head. "Not definitely. I had my suspicions, though."

My head wrenched up. "Suspicions?"

"You are too strong to come from an ordinary Demon. It now makes sense. It was not too long after you were brought to this realm that the last Unseelie King went insane and was killed. But, no, I didn't know for fact who your father was."

"Do you know why he lost his mind?"

Eli kept his eyes focused on mine, but he paused for a couple of breaths. "No."

I continued to observe him. I suspected he was not telling me the whole truth, but he didn't flinch. I broke first.

"I was always curious about my real dad, but when Mark came into my life, he was enough. I was happy." Tears filled my eyes. "Why can't he still be enough? Why do I care about this man I never met? A Demon who killed people. Why does it make me sad he's dead?"

"Because he was your father." He tilted his head. "You secretly thought it was Lars," he said. Blurry-eyed I looked down at the ground and nodded. "You wanted it to be him."

A strangled cry broke free, confirming his assumptions. At least my father would be alive. Good or bad, it was someone I would know. Now that was lost to me forever.

Eli cupped the back of my head and pulled me tightly against his warm body, enfolding me. Sobs surged from my chest. The protective walls I spent years perfecting tumbled away. He let me cry and held me till I quieted.

"Speaking of Lars, I saw he was here. I'm assuming he had something to do with us getting away from Weiss tonight," Eli said after my heavy tears subsided.

I nodded against his chest. Pulling back, I wiped my eyes. "He caused the accident, so we could escape. He knows the location of the map on my back."

Eli leaned away. "And you didn't think to tell me this till now?"

"I've had other things on my mind." I glared at him. "And don't assume I forgot about Ms. Tits and Ass earlier. We are still going to talk about that."

"Good to see you have your priorities straight, Brycin." He heaved a sigh and put a hand on my lower back, pushing me to the house.

"Oh, believe me, they will become important to you if McTramp comes anywhere near you again."

"Be careful, Brycin, you're starting to sound jealous."

As our feet hit the stairs to the deck of the ranch house, someone yelled at us. "You two are hell to be around."

"Shit!" I jumped.

Cooper sat in the rocking chair on the porch, drenched in darkness. Only his bright, brown eyes showed. "I'm getting really tired of jackin' off. I need to get laid. Now." Cooper got up from the chair and headed toward the door. "I was supposed to get you two a while ago. Let's agree I did," Cooper huffed.

"You got it, man." Eli slapped Cooper's back. "Wait, didn't you get laid by the waitress the other night?"

"Yeah, but with you two around, I'm painfully reminded how even a couple of hours without is too long." Cooper grumbled and moved to the door. It squeaked open revealing the family room abuzz with commotion and people screaming at each other.

Crap.

Cole, Mom, and Lars were bunched together. Their bodies were tense and angry, and voices were raised.

"We are going with you. You think we'll sit back and let you get the sword for yourself?" Cole yelled.

Lars looked calm and in control, but this was when he was his most dangerous. "I never denied you coming. I have come to understand the relationship between Ember and Elighan. It is futile to keep them apart. I do not waste my time or energy heedlessly. But only a few of you need to come, and your job will be to protect her."

"We always protect our own," Cole seethed. "You will not come here and order us around." His pupils stretched vertical. "I don't care who you are."

"I am the Unseelie King. I will have your respect."

"You are not our king. We are not ruled by anyone but ourselves." Cole pounded on his chest.

"If you inhabit Earth, you are under my rule," Lars howled. "I was the one who protected Ember when she was captured and held by Aneira. I do not actually need any of you, except the Druid and Ember."

I saw Eli's shoulder muscles tightened. "You knew the whole time she was there and alive?"

"Yes. Not telling you the truth saved her life and yours," Lars responded.

This is going to be fun.

Eli's movement toward Lars was quick, but I was quicker. I threw myself in the middle. "Whoa! Time out." I had my hands in the T-formation, tapping them together. "I know you're mad, Eli, but that's not what's important right now. It's done. We need to forget everything but getting the sword." I turned to face the whole group and looked at each one in the tight circle. "All of us need to make obtaining it our priority." Eli's hackles were still raised, his fists clenched, but he stepped back from Lars. "Since most think I am the one who is prophesized, I think I get a say as to who goes. Cole, Eli, Kennedy, and Cooper will come with us."

"Oh, hell no! I'm going." Gabby pushed into the circle.

"Me, too," Mom insisted. I was about to refute this when Jared echoed her sentiment.

Josh stood from the chair's arm where he had been perched. "I'm going, also. There is no way I'm being left."

"You might need me. I will go as well," Owen spoke up.

I started to deny their requests.

"My lady. Where you go, I go." Simmons flew up into my eye line. Cal and he had been sitting on the mantelpiece watching the drama unfold.

Cal came up beside Simmons. "You, girlie, will only get into trouble if I don't go."

"Ember, we are in this together. There is no way you are doing this without me," Mom said, determination fixed on her face. I recognized this look, and I knew better than to argue.

I pressed my mouth into a hard line and nodded. "Fine." I turned back to Lars. "We are *all* going. Make whatever arrangements you need to get things in order, but that's how it's going to be. No more fighting or 'my plan is better than your plan' bullshit. We need to be a team. You may not like each other, but we all hate Aneira. We have a common goal. Let's not forget it."

This was probably the stupidest decision ever, but it was made.

Then I started thinking about what would happen when you put a Demon King, an unhappy mother, a group of killers, an unpracticed Druid, and a Dae on a road trip together?

There's no doubt. This is the most stupid decision ever made.

Family time is fun time.

Whoever said this needs a hard slap to the head.

TWENTY

I pressed my face against the tiny window of the plane. The Pindus Mountain terrain spiked and fell in dramatic surges below me. It was breathtaking. This wasn't some family vacation, but I was still excited to be in Greece. I had traveled to quite a few places in Europe, but the center of the ancient wonders of the world wasn't one of them. Though I doubted sightseeing was on the itinerary.

A hand gripped mine in a painful clutch as turbulence dribbled the private jet like a basketball. I turned to look at Eli leaning back in his seat next to me. His eyes were closed, his face white, his jaw clenched, and his breathing was fast and shallow.

"I finally found something you're afraid of."

One of Eli's eyes opened, peering at me. "Not afraid, just extremely untrusting of this human contraption. This isn't natural; it shouldn't be able to be in the air."

"I'm gathering you have never flown before?"

He turned his head forward and looked at the ceiling. "Never needed to. I was meant to be on the ground with my feet touching the earth. I prefer running or riding my bike."

Most everyone in the group agreed using the doors would be suicidal. Aneira would have her soldiers watching them. Since the Dark Dwellers couldn't use them anyway, we decided on other means of transportation. Lars had his private jet prepared for us, and within the hour we were in the air.

The plane was sleek, plush, and installed with all the latest gadgets. Every video game and touch-screen device you could imagine was set up in the chairs. Each one included its own separate pod of gizmos and contraptions. Josh was in *World of Warcraft* heaven. I don't think he closed his eyes once or stopped thumping the buttons on his chair.

Our pilot was Fae and so were the gorgeous flight attendants, Jessica and Melanie. They worked for Lars, and he was their first priority. Lars had retired to his private office in the rear of the cabin as soon as we boarded and had not been seen since. Melanie hovered close to his door and went in and out with refreshments a few times.

It had been a stressful plane ride. All fourteen hours of it. Even after my appeal to "get along," the collaboration of Lars, the Dark Dwellers, and Mom had been less than friendly and cohesive. Lars had declared several times he was none too happy about the extensive entourage escorting us to Greece.

The aircraft dipped again. My hand received another crushing squeeze. "Pansy." I smirked and his grip tightened. "Ow!"

Now Eli smirked.

"You really want to screw with an edgy Dark Dweller? Haven't you learned anything?"

I leaned in; my face was only a breath away from his. "I enjoy screwing with edgy Dark Dwellers."

The corner of his mouth hooked up in one of his bad-boy grins. "Well, I am really tense and edgy right now."

"Ever heard of the mile high club?" I grinned.

"Funny enough, I have." His lips grazed mine as he spoke, sending flutters in my stomach. "And I've always been curious about becoming a member. How does one go about it?"

Heat scorched my skin where his lips brushed. Peeping over the headrest of my cushy, swivel chair I spotted Mom, Thara, and Torin seated in the built-in sofa near the back of the plane—across from the bathroom. Icy blue eyes locked onto mine as Torin returned my stare. Anger flecked with tortured longing appeared in his eyes. I quickly turned to the front.

"Think we'll have to wait." Sneaking back there for a "quickie" would be awkward, embarrassing, and cruel. This wasn't the first time I had caught Torin watching me and Eli with a wistful, furious, or pained look. I felt both sad and guilty. His hurt was hard to take. Our connection wanted me to do everything in my power to make him happy. But the thing that was causing his pain was me and my own happiness. I was far too selfish to give Eli up.

The bond frustrated me because I wanted it to go away. I had been trying to center on where it came from. To see what made me want to protect or go to Torin. When Lars pulled me, it was a physical thing. My arms and limbs moved without thought, and the more I fought it, the more it hurt. My connection to Eli was in my veins, body, my skin... everything. It was *my* need to be near him not a physical pull.

Torin's bond was somewhere in the middle. My brain would shut down, and I would just respond. It was like a code embedded in me long ago, which turned me off and the connection on. I would react first. When I gave myself a moment and forced myself to think, I would realize it wasn't really me who was feeling that way. It was almost like an outside entity had latched onto me, controlling my thoughts and actions. It didn't feel particularly good when I went against it, but it wasn't painful or unmanageable like with Lars.

Eli's hot breath against my neck brought me out of my thoughts. "Are you sure? It would really calm me. You would be doing the community a service," he said into my ear, his hand moving up my leg.

Breath caught in my throat. It was tempting, but I shook my head. "Sorry, guess you'll have to earn your wings on the way home."

A barely audible growl emitted from his throat. "You know better than to tempt me and take it away. You ready for the repercussions?"

I did, and I was. If the plane wasn't full of people, I would gladly let him show me.

"Punish me later."

"Oh, I will. Tenfold." He sighed, giving me a quick kiss before leaning back in his seat.

A crackle came over the jet's loud speaker. "This is your captain. We will be landing shortly. Melanie and Jessica will be coming by to see if you need anything."

Cooper had flirted excessively with Jessica from the moment we took off. They had both disappeared awhile back, and I had little doubt he had gotten his wish to get laid. Probably several times. Jessica came down the aisle straightening her shirt, looking a lot more unkempt than she did at the beginning of our flight. Cooper followed only a minute behind. His strut to the seat was self-satisfied. I wasn't sure if I was jealous or grossed out at the thought Cooper and the stewardess were getting it on in the lavatory.

Josh spent most of the trip playing video games that hadn't even been released yet. Gabby, Owen, and Cole sat in front of us, sleeping most of the way. They were not thrilled to be in the air either. Sitting up, I looked past Eli. Kennedy was curled in her seat, her head on Jared's lap as they whispered and giggled together.

So freakin' cute.

I turned to the window and watched the sweltering tarmac greet the wheels of our plane. Eli kept his eyes shut the entire time. He let out a huge breath when the plane came to halt.

"I want to welcome you to Larissa, Greece. The current time is nine twenty am, and it is already eighty degrees on this August morning," the captain announced.

Larissa had the closest landing strip to the Metéora region, but it wasn't a commercial airport. We were on a military base. Because we could land here told me a lot about Lars's authority and power. Whether it was through glamour, money, or blackmail, I didn't know. I didn't especially want to.

Lars had a luxury shuttle waiting for us as we exited the plane. The trip from the base to the town of Kalambaka was uneventful. No one looked twice as six huge tough-looking Dark Dwellers, three ethereal Fairies, a yellow-eyed Demon, a human, a Druid, two flying pixies, and a Dae exited the van in the middle of town square. I had to wonder if Lars glamoured all of us to look like ordinary tourists, or if the people here saw strange things all the time. No one even looked twice at us. I knew keeping us under the radar from the Otherworld spies was vital.

Lars checked us into the local hotel giving firm instructions. "You have sixty minutes to rest and prepare. We will not be returning. From here on, we will be camping and hiking through some rough terrain." He waved his hand. "Now go. I want you all back here in an hour."

"I need a shower," I grumbled and turned toward the room I had been allotted.

Eli grabbed my waist from behind, pulling me into him. His lips grazed my ear.

"Me, too."

Exactly one hour later, we stood in front of the hotel. I hadn't gotten any rest thanks to Eli, but the shower and he reenergized me. The feeling was quickly fading as the heat pounded down relentlessly. I squinted up at the view, shielding my eyes from the blinding sun. Above the quaint town of Kalambaka, giant rock formations stood strong and prominent, reaching toward the sky. Visible through the puffy clouds, stone pillars balanced a sun-toasted stone monastery high on their shoulders. Worn white-washed stone buildings with red-tiled roofs circled the square, which included hotels, bakeries, restaurants, souvenir shops, and a church.

I was already in love with this area; it felt alive and full of mystery and intrigue. The landscape along with the delectable food brought people here. The scents of tomatoes, pesto, and bread filled the air. I took a deep breath, and my stomach growled with need to taste each delicious smell wafting my way.

"I did a little research on the way over." Kennedy pulled out a piece of paper with her notes. "Metéora means 'middle of the sky,' 'suspended in the air,' or 'in the heavens above.' The six monasteries were built on natural rock pillars. Scientists *think* the pinnacles were created some sixty million years ago, developed from the river and earthquakes. It is said the first people came to this area in the ninth century. To escape everyday life, some eventually settled in small caves, embarking on lives of solitude, and meeting occasionally to worship and pray. As time progressed, the cave dwellers grew into a small community concentrated around the growing number of monasteries."

She never did a "little research" on anything. It was one of the reasons she had been called a nerd and geek through school. She loved facts as much, if not more, than I did.

We now stared at her instead of the stone pinnacles.

"Yes. All quite fascinating, Ms. Johnson, but scientists will never accept the truth. *We* helped create this land." Lars strode up, slipping on his sunglasses. His meaning of "we" was "Fae." So, I was right. This land *was* filled with magic. It was unearthly in its beauty and intrigue. You could feel it all around. I had only been here a few hours, and already I could sense this place burrowing itself in my skin. The history of the town whispered in my ear to come explore, to uncover its secrets. It was as if a siren sang her song to trance me into loving the white-washed stone and red-tiled roofs. I yielded to the desire without question. Even the shops around the square held stories from long ago about the folks coming in and out daily, their happy times and tragedies. The people and their pasts were embedded in the cobble streets under my feet.

The sight of a boy carrying bags of bread, meats, cheeses, and other items brought me back to the present. The local lad obediently placed the items at Lars's feet. Lars handed the boy a wad of money. "Thank you, sir. Anything else you need, you come to me. I will take care of you," he responded in English, then ran off elatedly with his roll of bills.

Lars watched him leave before turning to us. He had changed into cargo pants and an army green T-shirt that fit him perfectly. Even dressed down, Lars projected staggering authority. "I hope you have all rested. We will be hiking and mountain climbing through some especially rough terrain in very hot weather. I have army-issued packs ready for us at our pick-up location."

"Oh, yeah, the fifty-five minutes we had was so refreshing after a fourteen-hour flight," I griped, rubbing sunscreen on my arms. I wore khakis and a black tank with my hair up in a ponytail. Most of us looked like we were about to enter the Amazon jungle or trek across the Sahara. We were dressed in shades of green or tan pants, a tank or t-shirt, and hiking boots, which were a gift left by Lars in each of our rooms. I had to admit he was very organized and prepared. This must have been what he had been doing on the flight here, getting everything ready for us.

"Well, maybe if you spent the time resting, it would have been more beneficial. Remember my room was next to yours." Cooper looked at me with annoyance and then turned to Lars. "This town better be full of single, horny women."

Eli snickered. "When did the need for them to be single ever stop you?"

"True. They only need to be horny."

"Enough!" Lars's voice ripped through the banter. "You are all like prepubescent water fairies. Control yourselves, please."

Lily scoffed. "What's wrong, Lars? Did you forget when you behaved the same? It has been long ago for you, huh?"

Lars's eyes narrowed on my mother. "Hardly. I could put these children to shame, but it does not control my every thought." He gave each of us a pointed look. "I am surprised you are okay with this Lily since it is your daughter who is one of the most active participants in this."

Mom looked pointedly at Lars. "You're right. I'm not, but the more I tell her something is a mistake and will only hurt her in the end, the more she runs head first into it."

That was true. Still pissed me off she knew me so well.

"She does take after her mother, then."

"Lars..." Mom's tone was lethal, and her glare could melt stone. I was glad not to be on the receiving end of those looks.

"As I said earlier, we will not be returning to town. If you didn't prepare yourself properly for the trip ahead, it is not my problem." Lars eyes shifted from Mom to the group. "I have a helicopter taking us up to the first monastery. From there we will trek on foot to our other destinations. We will camp from here on out, mostly in places where it is not allowed."

Illegal for ordinary humans he meant. Not for an Unseelie King.

"I have narrowed the area we will be exploring to a forty miles radius. We will start north of Ypapantis and circle slowly southwest to the town of Kastraki. There are many caves and places where the sword could be hidden. It is a lot of ground to cover, so we need to get started."

The helicopter soared above the monasteries built on peaks, giving the illusion the structures were floating in the clouds. I leaned further out towards the open door on the side.

"This is so freaking amazing."

Helicopters were a lot louder than I imagined. The headphones helped cut most of the engine sounds from piercing our eardrums while allowing the captain to speak to us. Cal and Simmons were a tad too small, so we stuffed cotton balls in their ears. Simmons mouthed something to me and nodded. He and Cal were strapped to my armrest so they wouldn't be pulled out by the wind.

"Oh, yeah... great." Eli groaned into his speaker, his complexion turning pale. This, of course, made me smile. To finally know one of his weaknesses felt like I won the lottery.

"Oh, are you getting air sick, again?" I teased. No compassion here.

His jaw clenched tighter when the chopper swerved right. Lars's "connections" with the military had us in a large, Blackhawk-type helicopters. One that thirteen people and two pixies could fit in. All the Dark Dwellers, Kennedy, and my mom clasped their seats, white knuckled. I could tell Kennedy wanted to look, but her fear of heights had her pressing back firmly into the seat. Josh, Thara, Torin, Lars, the pixies, and I were content with being high in the air.

Looking below I could see tourists swarming the monasteries like an ant hill. Thousands of black dots descended from buses or hiking paths, circling the entrances of the more popular hermitages. The sun pounded down on the earth, cupping it into a cocoon of heat. But up here wind rushed through my hair and top, cooling my scalp and body. It was heaven.

Most people either hiked or took a bus up to the monasteries. Since

Lars wanted to avoid human contact as much as possible, he chose a helicopter. He was starting us at the farthest one, so we could move slowly toward town.

After a while, the chopper settled lower, heading for one of the hermitages. This one was unlike most others built on the peaks of the rocks.

Ypapanti was constructed inside a large cavity of rock. Despite its beauty and brightly painted frescoes, it remained uninhabited and closed to the public. Exactly what Lars sought out.

"Are we landing there?" I pointed, looking at Lars.

He nodded. Normally no one would be allowed to land a huge helicopter beside an ancient monastery. With Lars, rules did not apply.

"Holy crap!" I was giddy with the need to explore the priory. I had wanted to come to this part of Greece since I could remember. By the time we landed, I almost fell out the door, eager to look around and explore.

"This is not a vacation, Ember," Lars pronounced as he exited the aircraft. "We are not here to sightsee."

My lip lowered in a pout.

"However, we will see things no tourist has ever been allowed to, and we will be venturing deep into ruins and learning history kept hidden from the outside world."

My pout turned up into a huge grin.

"Grab your pack. Let us head out," Lars yelled over the sound of the whirling blades. Before we had taken off, Lars instructed us to stuff our travel packs with whatever clothes or personal items we wanted; they were huge. Because Kennedy was so small, she had to lean far forward so she didn't end up on her rear.

The thirteen of us fitted our bags to us and organized who carried the two-people tents and who carted the food. Lars was the only one who had his own tent. Not a shocker there.

The hired helicopter took off, my ponytail lashing painfully against my neck and face. The pixies were zipped into my bag so they wouldn't blow away. We quickly moved toward the empty monastery ready to get started on our journey.

This hermitage was small compared to the others because they built it into the side of the rock. This protected it from weather and being infiltrated from all sides except the main entrance. It wasn't as captivating as the ones built on top of the rocks, but it was more secure.

I stretched out my feelers. Magic hung thickly around this whole area. You couldn't get away from the feeling this place was not completely "natural." Magic was part of this land, making it hard to distinguish it from the enchantments hiding an ancient Fae icon. It wasn't something tangible that you could see but something you felt inside, the tingling of your skin, the prickling of your scalp or gut. It made the area a perfect place to conceal things, but a pain for us to find anything.

Before we started to explore, Lars let us eat lunch of warm bread, meat and cheeses along with some local wine. With my tummy full and happy, I was in an optimistic mood to find the sword.

It was not the monasteries Lars wanted to investigate but the small crevices he considered caves. They were usually in the middle of the mountain, high above the earth. I had taken a few rock-climbing classes, and once or twice I had completed easy levels of bouldering. This was anything but. This type of climbing was for the expert who could scale sheer cliffs to reach a small opening in the middle of a stone pillar. I knew there were people who did this all the time, but it was frightening for me—to put all your weight on one pin, which kept you from plunging to the ground.

Lars wanted Kennedy to go, but her fear of heights caused her to take root far above us, away from the ledge. While most stayed back and watched our belongings, I descended with Lars. He hoped I would feel something because of my connection to the sword. And where I went, so did Eli.

"Hey, this kind of reminds me of that time in the castle when you were climbing those crate boxes," Cal said when I finally made it the lip of the cave. "You took forever then, too." He looked bored as he leaned against the cave wall.

"Cal?" Sweat poured down my forehead.

"Yes?"

"Bite me."

The hot sun on my back, lack of sleep, and strained muscles made my legs shake after my second climb. I wanted to keel over. We had already hiked for miles in between the previous climb and this one. The terrain was getting steeper and more strenuous, but it was the heat that really sucked our strength. It was relentless and stripped you of all energy.

"All right, we will stop for today and set up camp here," Lars declared as I lay flat on my back. Getting any kind of movement from me would take a crane. The group began to move around, setting up our campsite.

"The tent isn't going to build itself." Eli stood over me.

"You really don't want me to help you because I might find another place to insert that tent pole," I grumbled, my muscles simulating wet noodles.

One of his eyebrows went up. "I love when you talk dirty."

"If I actually had the energy to roll over, I would tell you to kiss my ass."

"Then I guess I'll have to start with the front." He leaned down and reached for my hands.

My cheeks reddened as he pulled me up. Funny how I suddenly had more energy.

His lip hitched up. "You know how I like to eat out."

TWENTY-ONE

Since Lars had his own tent, he left the rest of us to figure out the uncomfortable sleeping arrangements. I think Mom hoped I'd come with her, but I made it clear Eli and I would be sharing. Kennedy was becoming less shy by the day. She was the one to tell Jared to get their tent set up. I couldn't help but laugh and think how Ryan would react to this. He might be at a loss for words seeing our sweet, little Kennedy sleeping with a younger man. Thara and Mom ended up roomies, and so did Cole and Owen. Torin and Josh would use the same tent, which seemed strange at first, but they actually had something, or someone, in common—the Queen. They had survived the same trauma and now shared a bond. Cooper decided to sleep outside, so Gabby ended up with a tent to herself. The pixies slept up in the tree near my tent.

With dinner over and a fire roaring in the middle of our campsite, we all sat around looking at the stars and talking. It was the closest we had been to acting as if we actually got along and liked each other. I knew I was the glue holding all these different groups precariously together, and I felt a certain pride in that. It may have been by a thread, but still, when do you get Dark Fae and Light Fae, Demons and Fairies, Dark Dwellers and humans all in the same place without a war? Okay, a war was the reason we were here, but this time we stood on the same side.

I took a sip of my tea and sat back looking at the stars. They felt so close you could bring them down and wrap yourself in their shimmery glow. High up on the cliffs the night turned the air nippy and refreshing from the hot day.

Lars stood and walked deeper into the night away from the campfire and us. He had been in an odd mood all day. Not that anyone else would notice, but I had spent enough time with him to know something was up.

205

I followed him and sidled next to him as he stared at the bright moon floating like a golden disco ball in the night sky.

He didn't look at me, his eyes locked on the sky. "I grew up here, you know. The town no longer exists, but it was near here."

I stayed silent. Getting Lars to speak about personal things was rare. Telling me about his childhood was like getting a unicorn for Christmas. Wait... did they exist in the Otherworld? Maybe instead of ponies, children got unicorns there?

Mental note: must find out if I can get a unicorn for Christmas.

Returning to the present, I tried to picture Lars as a little boy running around these hills under the baking Grecian sun. His jet-black hair and dark olive skin fit perfectly here.

"My brother and I knew every inch of these mountains, and we ran around terrorizing and wreaking havoc. I don't know how our mother put up with us."

Lars had a mother? I had a grandma? I hadn't thought about that. It seemed strange. I knew he had to come from somewhere, but thinking of him as a baby or a little boy with a mother and father took a mindset I didn't have yet.

"Devlin and I were exceptionally close growing up. We felt it was us against the world, and together there was nothing we couldn't do." Lars's expression grew distant. "Twin Demon terrors. We had some good times through the centuries."

"What happened? What made you guys grow apart?" I turned to look at him.

Lars massaged the back of his neck. "It was several things, but the main reason was a woman." He shifted his weight. "We both fell in love with the same one."

"And she chose him?"

"No. She chose me." His words became rigid. "And I chose power." With that he walked deeper into the night, leaving me standing there stunned by his admission.

Days went by, and the excitement and optimism we had felt was dwindling. With every different monastery we searched, the climbing got harder, the terrain trickier, and the sun hotter. Disappointment was bleeding into our moods. I knew it wasn't my fault, but I felt responsible for the lack of progress. Somehow I thought I should be able feel it, to know where it was. I had no clue. Kennedy seemed to be just as frustrated with herself. She had barely learned she was a Druid, and now she was expected to do levels of magic that took others centuries to master.

Even though we had the drawing of the map, Lars insisted Kennedy pull it from me each day in case we had missed some tiny clue. Lars put a lot of pressure on Kennedy, especially training her to sense and break spells. Both Kennedy and I were drained at the end of each day. I spent most of the evenings sprawled on the earth to replenish my strength. Kennedy was connected to the earth and everything around her, but her powers didn't get restored like mine. She would collapse next to me when our torture was over. My energy would be restored and I would feel better, but she'd usually conk out after dinner.

Mom came out to join us under the trees one evening after a particularly hard day. Her hands clenched three coffee cups and something tucked under her arm. "You girls all right?"

"Coffee is not going to help right now." Words fell from my lips, but my body stayed inert.

"It's not coffee; its homemade Greek wine." She sat next to me, placing the cups on the ground. She pulled the bottle out and set it next to the mugs. I saw Kennedy's head pop up.

A chuckle worked its way to the surface. "Oh, suddenly she's alert." I sat up slowly and scooted over so Kennedy could sit next to me. "Where did you get this?"

"I stole it from Lars's bag." Mom gave us a conspiratorial wink. "Thought we could relax and have some girl time."

Mom and I hadn't spoken much after I learned the truth about my father and Lars. I was still having a hard time coping with it and not being mad at her. I didn't meet her eyes as she handed me the wine.

"Thanks."

Kennedy's smile grew wider as she accepted her cup. "This smells good. Like baked grapes roasting in the scorching sun."

I snorted. "You sound like a travel brochure."

"A toast." Mom held up her drink. "To the two girls who have become the most amazing, remarkable, and strongest women I have ever known. I am so proud of both of you."

Tears instantly stung the back of my eyes as we clinked mugs and took a sip. Not only because of what she said, but it was exactly how I felt about them. My mom had always been my idol. Having her fall off

207

the pedestal and become a real person was a hard adjustment. She still was one of the most astonishing women I knew with all she went through and all she sacrificed. She made mistakes, but she did it out of love. For me.

A figure moved behind a tree, causing my body to tighten. I sniffed the air, immediately relaxing.

"Come out here and join us." I spoke to the patch of trees.

Gabby stepped out, her arms crossed, looking bored. "I wasn't spying."

"I didn't say you were." I waved her over.

I saw the edges of my mother's mouth turn down, but she quickly caught herself and nodded along with Kennedy. Gabby had grown up around boys. The only other girl in their group was Samantha, and something told me they didn't have slumber parties or hang out and watch movies, braiding each other's hair. Or in Gabby's case dying each other's hair. She had trouble interacting with other females, and I didn't think she wanted to. I was starting to believe I was wrong.

"Now I see what you are really up to when you claim to be "healing." She stood across from me, making quotes in the air.

"You wouldn't believe the healing powers of wine." Mom stroked the wine bottle like a precious jewel.

"Sit down, Gabby." I patted the dirt next to me. "You can share mine." I handed her the coffee cup.

"That's nice of you, Ember. Sharing." Mom patted my leg like I was five years old.

"Like hell. This is my cup now." I grabbed the remains of the bottle.

"Hey!" Kennedy swatted at me, giggling. "Not fair."

"I'll share. Geez, lady." I laughed back. Gabby held onto the coffee cup, her back stiff as her eyes darted between Kennedy and me. This was all very foreign to her, I could tell. Having "girlfriends" and being silly was not something she understood.

We worked our way through the bottle, and soon Kennedy was standing on a rock with her glass. "Hey, world, I am a Druid. Doooo youuu hear me? A Druid. I do magic and live centuries." She hiccupped. "And I am proud to be one."

"Good for you, Ken. Come out of your metaphysical Druid closet." I stumbled to her. Homemade Greek wine was a lot more potent than I expected.

"Come here." She waved to me. "You, too!" She pointed at Gabby.

Gabby shook her head. "My tolerance is too high to do stupid shit this early. Give me an hour or two."

"Pffffttt." Kennedy swished her hand at Gabby, making herself almost fall over.

I climbed up the boulder. Somewhere inside me I knew this was probably a bad idea. My drunken brain ignored this thought, and I stood next to Kennedy.

"Come on, Em, do it. Yell it out. It feels good."

"I'm proud to be a Druid," I screamed. My mom sat on the ground hunched over with laughter.

Kennedy swiped at me. "Come on, for real."

"I am a Dae." I shuffled my feet higher on the rock.

"That. Was. Pathetic." Kennedy bobbed and weaved into me.

I took in a breath. "I am proud to be a Dae!" I bellowed. Hearing myself say the words hit something deep in me. I did like being a Dae. It's who I am. I was proud of my heritage and of Daes like the Brycin who died for a cause she believed in, for family and friends, for me. I did not want to take it lightly.

An elated smile beamed from me. The gratified feeling lasted but a second before my balance went south. Kennedy and I collided. With a strangled cry, our legs and arms entangled, and we both plummeted from the boulder crashing to the soft soil.

"Owww," I grunted, and Kennedy rolled over with a groan.

"Now that shit was worth coming here for." Gabby tipped her glass at us and downed the rest.

"Are you guys okay?" Mom ran to us. Her voice sounded tight, as she tried not to laugh.

"Yeah. Not feeling so proud anymore," I grumbled, spitting dirt out of my mouth.

Mom let loose, howling. "Oh, no, Ember, that truly is you. And I am so proud of my klutzy, Dae daughter."

"Oh, man..." Kennedy lifted her head and looked at the cup still in her hand. "I spilled my wine."

Laughter echoed from the cliffs, bouncing off the sun-soaked rocks and surrounding us. We all laughed till tears drenched our faces.

"Jumpin' junipers. They can probably hear you girls in the Otherworld," Cal and Simmons flew to us. Cal landed on my leg. Simmons's feet skidded across the ground till he came to a stop, slamming into my back.

"My lady." Simmons pushed away from my shirt, straightening his shoulders as he came around to face me. "The Unseelie King is asking for you to limit your volume."

Cal grunted. "I think his exact words were 'Tell them to shut the hell up before I go there and shut them up myself.'"

I knew there was a real danger of spies being around, but telling drunken people to be quiet was like asking Eli not to be a sarcastic dick. Not gonna happen. I smiled warmly at the thought of him, suddenly wanting to find him.

Drunk and horny. Just the way he likes me.

"We probably should get back. The sun is going down." Mom picked up her cup and the empty bottle. Her cheeks were flushed with alcohol.

"Ahhh, things were just getting good." Gabby frowned, standing up. She was still pretty sober, but was relaxed enough I could see a little chink in her armor.

"Did you spill some?" Cal pointed at the wet spot on the dirt.

"Um... yeah. We fell." Kennedy stumbled as she tried to stand, pointing to the top of the boulder where we had been.

"You wasted alcohol?" Cal's already high voice went up an octave. I cringed at the high pitch. "Glorious, beautiful, magnificent juice of the grapes... lost forever." He went over and patted the wet dirt.

"Come on, Cal, I am sure there is more at camp." I stood. Well, I tried. It took me a few tries to officially stand.

Picking his hand up from the damp spot, he licked it. With a groan I turned to follow everyone else.

Mom came to me and seized my arm, letting everyone else get ahead of us. "Ember." She turned to face me. "I know we haven't had a chance to talk." She swallowed, looked away from me, and whispered, "I am extremely sorry. I know you must hate me, and I completely understand if you do. I thought at the time I was protecting you. I had no right to keep you from your uncle or from yourself."

Whether it was the wine or because my heart understood her actions more, I wasn't as mad at her right then. I wrapped my arms around her. "I know, Mom."

She hugged me back, a sob heaving in her chest. "You are my whole world. The thought of something happening to you..." I squeezed her tighter.

We stayed like that for a while. When she pulled back, she looked directly into my eyes. "When this is all over, we will sit and talk. There is so much I need to explain and tell you—"

I didn't let her finish. "Mom, I'm so happy to have you back. And right now all I want is my mom. We'll worry about the rest later."

She nodded, her eyes glistening with pride. "You amaze me every day. You have grown into such an incredible woman."

"I take after you."

Three out of four of us woke hung-over, sore, and completely useless. Gabby savored this by clanging pots louder and being a lot more "peppy" than I ever thought her capable of.

Bitch.

We soon found out that magic and hangovers didn't work well together. With Kennedy and me out of commission, Lars took off. He was pissed, but it wasn't the first time he left us. He would disappear sometimes. We had no idea what he was doing, or going, but it gave us a free afternoon to relax or explore.

There was something about this area besides the magic it held that drew me close. My real father had been born and raised here so maybe it was in my soul to love this land.

The terrain was breathtaking and unique. Our campsite held court high on a mountain with the valley and river cutting through and around stone peaks below.

I wandered away from camp craving to be by myself and reflect. Wind tickled my face, tangling my hair around my head. Deep, burning red and orange adorned the sky as the sun left us for the other side of the world. I sat and stared at the breathtaking scenery before me. Sandstone pinnacles covered with green vegetation protruded from the landscape till they dropped off into the valley far in the distance.

Sighing happily, I reached for my backpack. I hadn't lost the habit of toting a small drawing pad with me and grabbed it and a pencil. My hand flew over the page. It was like coming home. It had been so long since I sketched. So much had gotten in the way of something I loved almost as much as breathing. This was therapy for me, and it helped me center myself and get prospective.

I sat there losing myself in creating and forgot everything around me except the scenery and my art pad.

"Good to see you drawing again." Eli nipped at me ear.

"Holy shit!" I jumped, slipping forward. His hands grabbed my waist keeping me from plunging to a certain rocky death. Or at least a painful experience. "You really need to stop sneaking up. One of these times you are actually going to send me over the ledge. Literally."

He grunted, softly kissing the curve of my neck. "The family and I are gonna go for a hunt. You want to come?"

"Nah. I'm really enjoying drawing right now." I looked over my shoulder at him.

"Okay." He gave me a quick kiss and stood. "I'll be back later." He gazed down at me. *Be prepared. You know how I get after a hunt.*

"Okay, have fun." I smiled. *Looking forward to it.*

Eli slipped through the foliage and vanished. I shook off the shiver of desire going through me and returned my focus to my drawing. The oranges in the sky blended into the reds, the reds melted into dark blue-violet. *Beautiful.*

So are you. A voice spoke into my head.

I twisted and peered at him. "Eavesdropping?"

Torin stepped forward. His black shirt snuggled against the muscles in his chest. His hair hung loose and blew in the wind. He took my breath away. The man was so beautiful he rivaled the scenery before me.

"I apologize, Ember. I did not mean to intrude."

"No, it's okay." I patted the spot next to me. "Join me."

He hesitated but came toward me, sitting on the spot where my hand had been. "I mean it. You are beautiful."

"Torin..." My heart burned with guilt. "Please, don't say things like that.

"Why?" His eyes bored into me.

"Because..." I shifted my gaze, looking at the darkening sunset. "Because you are making this even more difficult."

He sucked air through his teeth. "How am I making this hard? I am the one who has to watch you and Dragen."

My fingers pressed the bridge of my nose. "I hate causing you pain, and I hate that you are so nice and honorable about all this. You're *too* good."

Torin turned his body toward mine. "Would you prefer me to be a jerk like Dragen? You like being treated appallingly and disrespected?"

"That's not what I meant."

"I am not such a man, Ember. I will only adore you. Honor you. You deserved to be cherished."

Exactly. Like a doll or keepsake. "What about just loving me?" I responded.

He blinked. "Well, loving you goes without saying."

"No, it really doesn't." I brushed my hair back away from my face. "I don't doubt you mean every word, and the girl you end up with will be the luckiest in the world, but..."

"But you are not that girl."

My chest clenched. There was a part of me which wanted to say yes, I was. The bond wanted to claim it. It tugged at my gut, twisting it to act. Yet the pull did not claim my heart. It was like it had been programmed in my brain. But when I thought about it, I realized it really wasn't what I wanted. Still not trusting myself to speak, I shook my head.

"Look at me." I didn't respond to his plea. Fingers came up to my chin, turning my face to his. "Every night the Queen tortured me, I thought of you. That is what got me through. Your face gave me hope to keep living. To keep fighting." His blue eyes stared into mine with such longing and love it ripped away all my will power. I knew it was coming, but I didn't stop it. The warmth of his lips on mine was so familiar; it was like they had been meant for me. His mouth moved against mine, his tongue parting my lips.

No! My soul yanked on my heart and brain. "No. I can't." I stood and moved away.

He followed. "Why?" Something seemed to snap in him. He clenched his fists at his sides. "I have been extremely patient. I have watched and endured you degrading yourself with Dragen over and over. A man can only take so much. You are obviously not seeing the truth fast enough. This comes to an end now." His shoulders squared off, demanding my obedience. "You are with me now." He reached for me.

I pulled back and put more distance between us. "Excuse me? With you now? You have no say about whom I'm with. I am not someone you can control and order around, even if we were together. It is *not* who I am." I shrieked each word with venom, anger charged through my muscles.

This change in Torin was getting harder to sympathize with. The emotional scars of being mentally, physically, sexually tortured had changed him. He was so quick to anger. I wanted to be there for him. To understand. But he was making it exceptionally difficult. I took in a shaky breath. "I care about you. I always will. But it will never be in the way you want."

213

Anger flashed in his eyes. "Dragen has so much of a hold you on that you can't see the truth. He will hurt you and eventually grow bored and leave. I have seen him do this to others over the years." Torin threw his arms up. "We would be good together. I would take care of you, protect you always."

"There it is again. Duty. Honor," I hurled at him, rubbing at my forehead.

"And what is wrong with those things?" His breath sounded ragged, his lids narrowing. He shifted closer.

"Nothing." I shook my head, moving away. I needed to get away from this situation and him. "But it's not what I want. Neither of us would be truly happy in the end. I am sorry, but I don't want to be with you. *Please*, let me go." Not giving him a chance to answer, I whipped around and ran.

"Ember," Torin yelled after me.

I was leaving the man whom I should probably be standing on a cliff at sunset with and heading for the man I had chosen, who was probably tearing into a bloody deer carcass at the moment. I was such a romantic.

Kennedy's words had been right: *You have one, and the other has you.*

Eli had me. Completely.

That night around the campfire, I sat between Mom and Josh. Torin sat next to Thara across from me. I could feel his heated glare, challenging me to look at him. Eli watched with a curved eyebrow. He sensed something was off, but I didn't want to talk to him until we were alone. I didn't feel guilty but disappointment in my weakness for Torin because I kept letting it continue. Even though I wasn't in love with Torin, my feelings weren't cut and dry. I couldn't just turn them off.

It wasn't until Eli and I settled into our tent later when I came clean—or tried to.

"Eli... I..."

"Was the next part of your sentence going to be 'made out with Torin' by any chance?" His eyes burned into mine, frowning.

My eyes widened, and my mouth dropped open. His fingers reached up to click my jaw shut.

"H-ho-how did you know?" I stumbled over my words.

"I can smell him on you." Eli put his arms behind his head, lying back on the pillow.

"Okay, I'm gonna jump over the creep factor and get to the point."

My lids restricted, looking critically at him lying there seemingly relaxed. "You're okay with it?"

He shrugged. "I really don't have a right to say anything."

"So, you don't give a shit who I kiss?" Anger pumped into me. "What about who I sleep with? Does that matter at all?"

Eli opened his mouth to speak, but the train of my fury was already coasting down the tracks.

"What in the hell are we doing then? Are you going to get bored of me and toss me over for another soon? God, I'm so stupid. I am the girl who gets the bad boy and thinks she'll be the one to change him. I thought we were in this together, you and me." My rage only escalated as Eli covered his mouth and tried not to laugh. "What the hell are you laughing at? You think this is funny? Is watching me lose it good for your ego?"

"Honestly, yeah, but that's not why I'm laughing." He sat up.

My rant was over, but the simmering rage underneath slowly rose to a boil. "Oh, please, enlighten me."

Eli's expression turned serious. "Believe me if I had smelled him on any other part of you besides your lips, there would be one less Fairy in the world." He kept his eyes on the wall of the tent. "I have never let myself feel jealousy. It is one emotion that strikes my animal side, and I need to control it. It takes a lot to switch it on, but when it happens, there is no stopping me. I will kill."

I gulped. He had my undivided attention as he continued. "I am not your warden or your mom. You can make your own decisions. I have given up ever trying to control you. I know you will do what is right for you in the end whether it's me or Torin."

My mouth fell open again.

"Don't get me wrong. If it does end up Torin, I will battle him to the death. Until then..." He laid down again. "Besides what I really mean is after the Natasha thing I figured you had a freebie."

A half-amused, half-confused puff of air escaped my lips. "Really? You mean that?"

He grabbed me, flipping me over on my back, crawling over me.

"Fuck, no, Brycin." He pushed his body between my legs, growling into my ear. "If he kisses you or even gets near you again, I will tear him apart. I'm not kidding. I still might." He slid his finger below my sleeping shorts, yanking them down. "Now I have to make sure you and he both know you are mine."

The next morning Lars bellowed across the campsite, breaking the early morning calm.

"You," he roared, pointing at Kennedy. "Get over here."

Her eyes widened for an instance as she popped off the log. She then stopped, hands going to her hips. Her chin went up. "I have a name, you know, besides girl or Druid."

The whole camp froze. No one talked back to the Unseelie King. Well, except me, but that felt slightly different, since I was family.

Lars watched her carefully for an instant before he nodded. "I apologize. Ms. Johnson, if you could come here and assist me."

He still wasn't asking, nevertheless, my eyes opened wide in shock. This tiny five-foot-nothing, ninety-pound girl just put the Unseelie King in his place and won.

Holy crap!

With all that happened to Kennedy since discovering about herself, she now had a strength in her even Lars couldn't deny.

"Ember, you, too." He waved me over and ignored the stunned glances from the camp.

"But my breakfast..." I looked down at the plate of steamy, scrambled eggs. The coffee thermos was still within my reach.

"Now!" He practically stomped his foot with impatience. The niceties only went so far. He had been in a foul mood the moment he walked out.

I threw down my plate on a nearby tree stump. "Does he really want to deal with me before I get my coffee?" I mumbled as I walked to him.

My mom grinned and squeezed my arm as I passed. "Even at two years old you were not a morning person." This brought a small smile from me.

I huffed when I stood in front of him. "What?"

"I want Kennedy to do another revealing spell."

"Again? We've done it every day. Nothing is there you guys haven't already seen. What's it going to do except drain both me and Kennedy for the day?"

"Because I said so."

"Why don't you do it then? Leave Kennedy out of this."

"I am doing my own as well." He jerked his head, "Now, turn around."

Everyone in camp watched, apprehensive of Lars's temperamental mood. I lifted the back of my shirt. Eli came and held onto my arms, making himself my rock.

"Start," Lars directed Kennedy. She nodded and murmured her incantation. Lars touched my back the moment Kennedy finished. The energy entering my back yanked away all my senses. I didn't even feel myself slam into Eli. Then everything rushed back into me like a broken levee. Eli grabbed me as my legs collapsed. I gasped, blinking.

"Holy crap. What did you do?" I hissed.

"I turned Kennedy's spell up a notch. I want to ascertain there is nothing we are missing." Lars brushed lose strands of my hair off my back.

If there was something new to see, I was sure we would have seen it by now. I didn't want to risk angering Lars more, so I stayed quiet.

Cole, Owen, and Mom had moved around me and stood by as Lars inspected my back.

"Sorry, Lars, but there is nothing we haven't seen." Cole sighed.

Lars stayed silent, but I could feel his frustration growing into a force ready to burst.

"Unfortunately, I agree with Cole," Mom said.

"Me as well." Owen nodded.

Jared came around; his cold fingers touched my back. "That's cool. I never noticed this before."

"Noticed what?" Lars asked.

His finger came back in contact with my back. "Right here. It's tiny but consider the white and black lines as one. The bottom of this S-shape and the top of this one connects into an infinity sign."

Several beats passed before Lars let out an oath in some language I didn't recognize. "How blind am I? I have been treating them as separate entities."

"I don't remember ever seeing this mark before. Your power must have pushed it to the surface." Cole was jumping with excitement. "Eli, will you come here?"

Eli let go and walked around me.

"Do you see the marks? They're fading, but what's the design look like to you?" Cole touched the spot on my back.

Eli moved in closer, his finger stretching the skin at the area where they were looking. A hiss of air sucked through his teeth.

"It's the infinity dragon..." he trailed off. "My family's symbol, our sign."

"What?" I turned to face Eli, but Lars grabbed my shoulders twisting me forward. "What do you mean your family symbol? Why would it be on my back?"

Eli didn't respond and continued to touch the image.

"Somebody please tell me what's going on."

Lars swore. "Dragon Cave. That's where it is."

"Where is that?" Mom questioned.

"Dragon Cave is under the Varlaam Monastery, which is several kilometers northwest of here." Lars was already walking away. "Be ready to leave in thirty minutes."

"But..." So many questions went through my head.

Lars turned back sharply and glared. "The infinity dragon is an ancient symbol. It might be related to Mr. Dragen here, but most likely it is not. It also happens to be the figure used for this cave on earliest maps. Now get moving."

With that our army of people dissipated in all directions collecting camping gear.

Eli and I continued to stand there.

"He's right. It probably has nothing to do with me." Eli rubbed at his head.

I peered at him out of the corner of my eye. "Yeah, because things with Fae are always simple happenstances."

TWENTY-TWO

"My lady? The cave is over the next hill. You are almost there." Simmons circled my head.

"Simmons, will you stop screeching," Cal growled, holding his head. He curled tighter in my backpack.

"Is someone a little sensitive this morning?" I teased. The Greek juniper plant grew in abundance here, and Cal was the one hung-over this morning. He had opted out of scouting the area and reporting back. Simmons gladly accepted the role.

The longer we were out here the more alert we needed to be. Discovery by the Queen was always something we had to worry about. Lars helped Kennedy set enchantments in place when we camped, but when we were on the move, we had no protection.

"The area is clear of any humans and Fae, my lady." The tiny man flew at my eye-level.

"Thank you, Simmons."

"Oh, look. I guess they are good for something," Eli quipped.

"How dare you, sir." An angry pixie grabbed for his swizzle stick at his belt.

"Simmons, you know better than to take his bait. Please keep watch ahead. Your lookout is vital to our plan."

He adjusted his sword. "Of course, my lady." He shot Eli a withering look and flew off.

"Why must you do that?" I exhaled.

Eli flashed a smile. "Part of my charm."

"To piss people off? Oh, yeah, you are good at that."

I glanced over my shoulder and saw Torin was in the rear. Since my last encounter with him, he kept a wide berth. Now his eyes penetrated mine, and they were cold and hard. The thought of him hating me felt like barbs stabbing my heart. Would Torin and I ever be okay? It seemed highly doubtful. I also felt the intense stare from Thara next to him, and I quickly turned away.

Josh came beside us, taking my attention away from the personal drama. "You really think the Sword of Light is in this cave?"

"Don't know. I hope so."

A nerve twitched at Josh's smile. "It better be there." He adjusted his heavy backpack. His tone was unusually serious. I stared at him. "I really want to take her down. Revenge for what she did to me. To all of us."

"Of course you do." I nodded. His dedication to find this sword almost rivaled my own. Whatever had happened to him had been more than he told me. My gut knotted at that thought.

The moment we stepped up to the cave's opening, I felt it. Iron. The cave was laced with it. Soil usually contained a form of iron, but it was so diluted it didn't normally have the power to affect Fay. This cave had more than the other caves we had explored so far. Another coincidence or on purpose?

Torin and Thara stepped back cautiously as they felt the metal grope hungrily at their skin. My attention then locked on Mom. She did not step back like her fellow Fay did. She caught my questioning stare.

"Aneira had me locked up in iron for years." Mom took a determined step closer to the cave. "I will be okay."

I turned back on Torin and Thara. "You guys should stay here and keep watch—

Torin's head started to shake before I even finished my sentence. "No."

"You'll be in pain. It could cripple you."

"I am not weak." He glowered at me.

"I never said you were." I threw up my arms. Arguing with him was useless. He wouldn't listen no matter the consequences or how much pain. He would go, and Thara would go wherever Torin did.

"We will not leave either, my lady." Simmons hovered beside me.

Cal, still curled up on my bag, mumbled something in agreement to this.

"Okay." I exhaled and moved forward. "Let's go."

Lars already stood at the imposing entrance of Dragon Cave. The town of Kalambaka loomed in the valley below. Way above us perched the Varlaam monastery. Both the cave and priory were open to the public, but because it was really early, and the cavern was not advertised, it sat empty.

"I read last night in my travel book there is a legend associated with this cave." Kennedy withdrew her notes from the Greece guide and started reading to us. "There's a story told to the children about a dragon that used to live inside a huge cavern underneath the monastery of Varlaam. The dragon went to the nearby village of Kastraki every night to feed on the locals and their livestock. People became desperate and were unable to deal with the creature on their own, so they sought assistance from the monastery of Varlaam. A monk who sensed their desperation sacrificed himself to help them. He cursed the dragon and then jumped off the cliff to his death. Immediately after the monk died, the ceiling of the cave collapsed, and the dragon was killed."

I started to giggle. "Humans think it's a fairytale, but in our world, it probably happened, huh?"

Lars looked at me and turned away. My smile dropped. "It *is* only a legend?" He didn't answer but cocked an eyebrow.

I glanced around to all the other Fae. "Right?" They also looked away from me.

"Seriously?" I exclaimed.

"I told you, my brother and I were troublemakers," Lars replied. "The sacrifice of the monk did not cause it to crumple. He was a religious fanatic who thought he could save the people by surrendering himself to the beast. He got caught in the cave when Devlin and I caused it to collapse. People wanted to use his death as some moralistic story, and the legend arose from there."

"Dragons exist?" I asked.

"Not anymore. They were hunted into extinction long ago." Lars stared off into the blackness seeming to be lost in memories.

"Why did you bring one here?" I looked deeper into the cave trying to picture a huge, fire-breathing dragon sitting inside.

"We were young and bored and thought having a dragon would spice life a bit, especially if we could harness its power. It turned out they were a lot harder to handle than we thought."

I shook my head. Talk about troublemakers. People thought kids nowadays wreaked havoc. Try twin Demon boys with magical powers and too much time on their hands. I wondered if many other so-called legends were based on true stories involving Fae.

Lars clasped his hands together, regaining the group's attention. "All right, enough about my past indiscretions. You have headlamps in the gear packs I gave you. We will be going past where tourists are allowed. It is dangerous and dark, and we will be venturing into some small, tight places." Lars pulled on his headgear. "Because there will be some constricted areas, we can only bring our day packs, so please switch over now. Leave the bigger packs here." He pointed to a hidey-hole in the wall.

One step into the cave, and I went down on my knees. The feeling of everything being ripped from my gut made me feel weak. Thara and Torin followed. I would eventually grow more immune to the Fay poison because of my Dark Dweller and Demon side; the other Fay would not.

Mom kneeled next to me, and her arm embraced me, helping me stand. She appeared the least affected, so I leaned on her as I got back onto my feet.

"We do not have time for you to acclimate. Push through or stay behind." Lars pulled out his lamp, placing it on his head.

"Okay, I'll stay here, relax, catch up on my tan, maybe draw or do some sightseeing," I snipped back.

He gave me a dour glance. "Except you."

"We all go together." I crossed my arms. "No one is left behind."

Lars snarled and threw his bag into the cubby hole. "We are heading out now."

He switched on his lamp, turned, and led the way along the passage.

"Damn, someone's being a prick today." Cooper said, putting on a head lamp.

"I seem to be permanently surrounded by them." I lifted my eyebrow at him. Already the effects from the iron were starting to diminish. Gabby strolled up behind Cooper. "Oh, and a few bitches," I added.

"Damn right." She nodded proudly. She had already put her other gear away and leaned forward on her toes, as though ready for the adventure into the unknown.

Most everyone had moved out, following Lars. Josh was one of the first, eager to begin. Thara and Torin struggled. Because they were slow to switch over their packs or even move, I went over to lend a hand.

"Don't." Torin scowled. "I can do it myself."

I jerked my hand back from his bag. "I know. I only want to help."

His lips went into a thin, white line, pressing together tightly. His expression was hard, but sadness flickered in his eyes. He didn't want *my* help.

I backed off with a nod. "Okay." Sorrow got caught in my throat, and I had to turn away before he saw it. I grabbed my smaller pack, threw the other one in the hole, and rushed after Lars.

Eli slipped up next to me in the dark. His fingers brushed mine. He didn't say or do anything else, but I didn't need him to. It was enough.

Hours went by or what felt like hours. I had no concept of time—only more claustrophobic darkness and oppressive iron-laced walls. It kept me drained and struggling. The passageway was rough and sometimes disappeared altogether. It was pretty clear it had not been used in decades. It was worst when we had to crawl on our bellies, slithering across the sharp rocks. Spiders, bats, and huge bugs moved over the walls, floor, and ceiling around us. We were in a tight crevice. The walls closed in on me; the air was thinner and harder to breathe.

"Relax, Em," Kennedy said from behind. "I can sense you freaking out. Your aura is going very dark."

I reached back and gripped her hand in mine.

She gave it a comforting squeeze. "So, my weakness is heights and yours is confined places."

"With no windows... or light... or way out." *Die. We are going to suffocate and die here.* I could feel the panic burning up my throat, rousing my arms and legs to run. Or rock in the corner.

"Just keep breathing. In and out... in and... ahhhhhhh!" Kennedy screamed, and her finger pointed at my backpack.

"What?" I demanded wildly.

"Spider! Huge!"

Simmons tore off my shoulder into the air; Cal stayed asleep. "Where?" Simmons pulled out his sword. "I must kill it."

Eli leaned around me and brushed it off. It fell with a thump in the dirt and ran across Kennedy's foot. She kicked and screamed, which sent off the bats overhead.

"Enough!" Lars yelled down the tunnel to us. "Kennedy, I need you to stay focused. You, too, Ember."

"Okay." My words came out strained as a centipede scuttled up my pant leg. I waved frantically to Eli to get it.

"You're such a girl." He rolled his eyes and flicked it off.

I leaned up to his ear. "But I screw like a Demon." A naughty grin hitched his lip.

"Hurry up." Lars shot as us, shaking his head.

Lars's impatience with our slow pace was hitting new highs. He constantly was probing Kennedy to see if she felt or sensed anything. When she shook her head, Lars's frustration only swelled. Surprisingly, he didn't take it out on her; his wrath found another outlet. His ire turned toward Torin and Thara who could barely keep up. A few times we had to stop and wait for them. Being in this cave had to be torture for them. The iron constantly brought them to their knees, but they never complained. Owen stayed near, helping when he could. Torin accepted his help with more ease than mine.

Finally, Lars halted. The cave had opened up into a massive cavern, but then the footpath narrowed into a foot-wide ledge. On one side there was a smooth wall; the other was a drop off into a deep void. Cole pointed his flashlight into the vast abyss, but the light never reached the bottom.

"I hear water down there." Cole tilted his head.

"There is a river running through this cave," Lars said. "This passageway is dreadfully narrow and doesn't look stable. The rocks are loose around the edge. Please be cautious. It is a long drop."

I peered down into the chasm. My stomach rolled at the notion of falling.

Lars started along the trail, followed closely by Josh; Thara and Torin brought up the rear. Simmons and Cal rode on my pack. Cal snored most of the way, and Simmons was still twitchy from the spider incident. Big spiders look at a pixie as a delicious meal.

As I stepped onto the ledge, my heart picked up its pace. It was so tight most of us had to walk sideways. I learned an important lesson fast—don't look down. I gulped, shoving my head back onto the wall.

Pairs of hiking boots slid along the restricted walkway like a train. My pack was now set on my front, and my back pressed rigidly into the stone. Fragile bits of rock crumbled with every step we took. Behind me Kennedy whimpered.

"Don't look down, Ken. Feel with your feet and keep your head looking straight ahead." I reached sideways and squeezed her hand.

Her thin fingers gripped mine back. She bit her lip and nodded. My gaze drifted to Torin. The iron was affecting him the most. After what the Queen had done to him, it was clear he would never be the same. It appeared only determination kept him standing. My hatred for her pushed through the pain the iron still caused me. The thought of killing her was becoming an exceedingly welcome idea. She would pay for everything she had done. The weapon of her annihilation was almost in our reach.

As I turned my attention to securing my footing on the narrow path, I heard Thara cry out.

"Torin!" His name echoed off the walls. My neck whipped back. Torin stumbled forward, losing balance and hit the ground sliding halfway off the ledge.

I screamed his name, but in a split second the unstable edge absorbed his fall and reacted. It began to deteriorate under him, generating an avalanche of stone.

"No," I cried, pointlessly reaching out. Rolling debris swept his body off the cliff. Then he was gone. A roaring noise in my ears cut any sound other than the rocks and my thumping heart. The shock had yet to kick in when more of the trail buckled, and I watched as Owen, Jared, Gabby, and Thara plummeted from sight.

I turned to Kennedy but saw her slipping. "Kennedy!" My heart jumped up my throat as I surged for her. My fingers locked around her wrists and yanked her toward me. The earth began breaking off bit by bit under her shoes. My grip slipped as another piece of trail disappeared under her.

"Ember," she screeched as she began to drop from my grasp. I fell forward searching for her hands. An arm slammed me back onto the trail, reaching around me. Eli dived for Kennedy before we lost her to the black pit. There may have been water down there, but that didn't mean she would survive the fall. Eli lay across me holding onto her tightly. Kennedy wailed and thrashed, which made it harder for Eli to hold on.

"I've got you, Ken." Eli voice was soothing and confident. "I won't let go. I promise."

Her eyes connected to his, and she stopped screaming.

"Remain calm. I'll pull you up."

"Okay," she whimpered and let her body go limp.

I leaned over and clutched her other arm. I could hear voices behind me, but I couldn't understand anything in particular. My only focus was on the three of us and the crumbling ledge. Eli easily pulled Kennedy's tiny frame up with one arm. Her arms wrapped in a death grip around him.

"You're okay," he murmured.

Her teary eyes looked up at him. "Jared."

"We need to move out." Lars's voice boomed toward us. "The ledge is still precarious."

My lamp spotlighted his face. "Give us a moment."

"All water leads out. They will not die from that fall. They are fine. We need to keep moving."

I narrowed my eyes at Lars. "You were complaining about them holding us back. Did you do that? To get rid of our 'baggage'?"

"Don't be ridiculous," Lars replied, whipping around, and moved farther down the ledge.

That really wasn't an answer.

"Jared's a strong kid. He'll be fine." Eli steered Kennedy to walk in front of him.

She nodded in response, but she still looked like she wanted to cry or throw up.

"Simmons? Cal?" I called out.

"Yes, my lady?" Simmons darted in and out of my headlamp.

"Please, go make sure they're all right."

"You want us to leave you, my lady?"

"I will be fine, but your role in securing the safety of our fallen soldiers will be immeasurable."

His body immediately straightened. "Yes, my lady. I will not fail you." He bowed and zipped down the dark ravine.

"Wow, what a bunch of troll dung." Cal snorted from my backpack.

"Yeah, I know," I said.

Cal moved onto my pack. "I'll follow to be sure he doesn't end up falling into the water and drowning." He sighed and took off.

"Thanks," I called after him just as I heard a rumble in the ground next to me.

"Shit," I shouted at the same time Eli yelled for me. He had moved slightly ahead with Kennedy. "Go." I waved them forward. "Run."

The solid ground under my feet turned soft and powdery. The knowledge that I wouldn't die from the fall didn't stop the terror I felt as the ledge gave way. The iron drained me of my full strength so my legs didn't seem to move fast enough as the trail crumbled.

I could see Lars and Josh had reached the mouth of the cave. Cole was close to it, helping Cooper and my mom to safety. Eli picked Kennedy up and chucked her to Cooper like she was as light as a soccer ball. To them she probably was. It made me feel better knowing at least

Kennedy and Josh were safe. They were the only ones who would probably die from the fall.

The mouth of the cave was almost within reach when the disintegrating footpath beat me. Air filled the space under my shoes, and I began to drop.

"Brycin!"

"Eli!" Cole screamed as Eli sprung in my direction. Like a choreographed routine, Eli slid on his stomach and his arms reached for me. Cole jumped on Eli's legs, holding him from going over with me. His fingers brushed my arms, missing me. My stomach rolled with the sensation of freefall. Abruptly, his fingers curved into Dark Dweller claws. Sharp and lethal, the sickle nails were long. He stretched farther, the claws clasping and digging into my upper arms.

I screamed as pain erupted through my arms and traveled up my shoulders. It hurt like hell, but I was no longer falling. Sweat trickled off Eli as I hung there by the tips of his talons. I latched on to bright green eyes. They became my lifeline. If I stayed connected to them, I'd be all right.

Pain kept the shouting voices at a distant. I could see Cole and Cooper move to either side of Eli. He had to lift me a little so they could reach me. My skin ripped as his claws dug further into my biceps while he inched me up. I'm sure I cried out, but I felt and heard nothing at that point.

Two sets of hands gripped me under my arms.

"You have her?" Eli's voice strained.

"Yeah, go ahead."

"Brycin?" Eli grunted my name. "I'm warning you this is gonna hurt a lot." And with that he pulled his nails out of my skin and backed way.

The agony was so awful my scream was lost in my sheer will not to pass out. My head lolled back as Cooper and Cole laid me on safe, stable ground. Blood oozed from the holes in my arms. Of course, the one time we really needed Owen, he was floating down some Grecian river.

"Ember." Mom was on her knees beside me, putting my head in her lap. I wanted to fall asleep in her warm embrace. It reminded me of when I was a little girl, and we'd watch movies on the sofa as she tickled my back or stroked my hair.

A sting burst across my cheek. My lids reopened to see Lars on the other side of me. I didn't even remember closing them. "You must stay awake. You will heal yourself in time, but I can numb the pain till then."

"You can numb pain?" I repeated. Well, that's what I wanted to say, but it came out garbled.

227

"I am the Unseelie King and a Demon. There isn't much I can't do."
Countless times I had been in agony after lessons with Alki. Bleeding,
bruised, and singed. He never dulled that pain.

"Neber nub me 'fore," I croaked out.

He scoffed, "You need to experience everything. It builds character,
and you develop a higher tolerance to the amount of pain you can handle."

I tried to stick my tongue out at him, but it was too much effort. I
ended only licking my bottom lip.

"If Ms. Johnson were better trained, she could fully heal you. Such
skills are for more advanced Druids," he commented and placed his hands
on my arms, closing his eyes. He mumbled words I didn't understand. As
if he had stuck a syringe of anesthetic in my arm, a sensation warmed my
veins and muscles and turned the pain to only a slight throbbing.

I exhaled realizing how the anguish had taken all my energy. "Oh,
yeah. Thank you." I felt somewhat dizzy, so Mom helped me sit. My
brain spun.

"Go slow." She held me close, and I cuddled against her. It hit me
intensely on how much I had missed her, how much we had missed
together. I needed to let go of my resentment and not take for granted she
was back in my life.

"I love you, Mommy," I whispered.

Her arms tightened around me. "You are a little high aren't you,
sweetie?" She chuckled and kissed the top of my head. "I love you, too."

Eli moved through the crowd circling around me. I broke away from
Mom and tried to stand. It didn't go well.

He didn't wait for me to try again. He grabbed the front of my top
and hauled me to my feet. His hands seized the sides of my face bracing
me for the force that came. His lips crushed mine. He breathed me in,
stopping any oxygen from entering. I didn't give a crap. Breathing or
having people around me were completely irrelevant.

With the same intensity as when he kissed me, he pulled away, spun
around, and stomped toward the entrance of the cave. I could only smile.
That was Eli.

Mom tucked her arm in with mine, helping me to keep standing. She
sighed heavily.

"I've lost the battle against him for sure."

"Sorry to tell you, but you never had a chance with that one." I
leaned into her, nudging her shoulder. "Too much like my mom."

"You sure are." She laughed then sighed. "More than you know."

TWENTY-THREE

Mom and I were the last to enter the next area. There were four tunnels veering off in different directions. The map on my back showed only a general location of the cave. Once on the inside we were on our own.

Still feeling dizzy, I walked to Lars. "Please tell me you know which one to choose."

He glanced down at me. "I was hoping you could inform us."

My light bounced down each tunnel as I considered each one. "You don't feel any magic?"

Lars shook his head, then looked over his shoulder. "Kennedy, please come forward." Kennedy swiftly moved to his side. "You and I will be doing a different version of a revealing spell."

"Okay." An excited glint reflected in her eyes. I recognized that look. It was the same expression I had after truly discovering my powers. You start craving magic.

Lars's elegant fingers reached for Kennedy. She hesitated but took the offering. "Focus on every word and repeat each one I say exactly. I mean exactly. Do you understand?"

Kennedy nodded, standing straight.

"Okay, let us start."

Latin swirled out of his mouth, every syllable clear but unfamiliar to me. Kennedy recited every phrase precisely. A warm sensation floated from them, creating a light. It swirled and curved through the air pointing toward each one of the tunnels. It circled and finally landed in the opening of the one that veered off sharply to the right.

"That's it. We got it," I cheered.

"Good job, Ms. Johnson. Excellent pronunciation." Lars nodded toward Kennedy who was smiling ear to ear.

I gave her a thumbs-up, and she beamed more.

The light disappeared the moment Kennedy and Lars broke contact, but it didn't matter. We knew which tunnel to use.

Our diminished group marched forward through the long, winding passageway. I hated moving on without the others, acting like they weren't lost down a black hole. It was easier knowing they were all Fae and would be fine. Who knows, maybe they had floated back into town by now and were laying by the river with a drink in hand, eating pesto for lunch. Damn... Eli should have let me drop.

My enthusiasm in being on the right route dwindled the longer we walked. The tunnel seemed never-ending, taking us steadily down, deeper into the earth's crust. The dirt walls enveloped me, sitting on my shoulders, crushing my lungs. Eli became my anchor. His hand in mine and the solidness and warmth of him saved me from losing my mind. Lars had to numb my pain once again so I could stay up right. With the iron, I was slower to heal.

After what seemed like hours, the passage leveled and expanded. This chamber was the size of the Dark Dweller's family area. Not tiny, but definitely not the size of Lars's enormous living room.

"I feel something." Kennedy stopped, closing her eyes.

"What?" Lars moved to her.

"I can't explain it. It is nothing I have experienced before, but at the same time, it's something so familiar." She shook her head, her lids still tight together. She began to walk and stopped a few feet away from the wall.

Josh shone his light toward Kennedy and gawked. "Look!" He pointed, bobbing up and down on the balls of his feet.

Over Kennedy's shoulder I saw a small, infinity shape etched into the surface. You would miss it if you weren't looking for it.

My boots took me to the wall. My fingers traced the symbol, and I could feel the outline of a dragon head in the middle of the carving. Time had taken away any true detail.

We found it.

Emotion prickled my eyes. There was a part of me that thought this would never happen. But we did it. Elation lifted my soul like a balloon. My excitement was tainted by the thought that the others weren't with us. We all had worked so hard to get here. They should have been here to experience this victory.

Lars stepped next to me. "Your fate is about to be sealed. I hope you are ready."

I sucked in an uneven breath. "Me, too."

Josh motioned wildly. "Come on. Let's start to dig."

Lars's lids tapered on Josh. You did not tell the Unseelie King what to do. Ever. Especially if you were human.

"We will not be able to dig until Kennedy shows us the exact spot and breaks the Druid curse. The Druids would have made sure it was fully protected." Lars replied. His words were sharp and crisp. Lars motioned to Kennedy to move in closer. "I had you work on this spell all week, but it was in practice. This time it will react. Enchantments are alive, and this one will try to fight you at first. Are you ready?"

Kennedy compressed her lips and gave a sharp nod as she took several steps before she landed on a spot. "It is here." The tip of her boots dug into the dirt. "Everyone back away, please." We all gave her space.

She opened her arms and started chanting. The words meant nothing to me, but I could feel their power. Energy and pressure built up in the room the more firmly she spoke. Beads of sweat dotted her hairline, and her face crunched. The heaviness in the chamber became almost intolerable.

Her words became tighter and more forced, and she moaned in pain as her legs began to wobble underneath her. I felt something new as I watched her: awe at her power. But seeing my friend suffer also had me restless and edgy.

"Do not stop." Lars yelled to her. "You must push through."

Even though she was the only one making noise, it was deafening in the cave. Through her chants, Kennedy wailed in pain and dropped to her knees. Her teeth clenched, tears and sweat poured down her face as she screamed the words.

Then, like a balloon had been popped, the room's pressure dispersed. Kennedy curled onto her side, breathing heavily.

It was done. She had broken it.

Lars got to her first. "Good job, Ms. Johnson. That was extraordinarily impressive. Your clan would be proud." He placed a hand on her. "Since you are mostly human, I can only help you a little with the pain."

A wave of magic went over her, and she let out a relieved sigh. I helped her sit. "You kicked ass, girl; I'm so proud of you." I gave her a tight hug. "And remind me to never piss you off."

231

She laughed weakly and pulled back.

"Yeah, if Ryan could see me now. Think he'll be a little shocked when he hears about this."

"Our sweet one has got a bite to her." I laughed.

"You can converse later." Lars broke in. "Right now we need to excavate."

As we dug, the Dark Dwellers turned their hands into clawed shovels. *Convenient.* My small hand shovel was doing very little. It was tiring and frustrating.

Fifteen minutes later, I dug my tiny spade into the deep hole. It hit something harder than dirt, and my hand ached from the vibration of the metal shovel.

"We hit something." Cooper yelled, his claws scraping at the top of the solid object we struck. "It feels like wood."

"Maybe it's in a box," Josh spoke up behind Cooper.

We continued to wipe and dig until the object became distinct. It was not a box, but more like a small, narrow, boarded-up door.

Lars moved closer and placed his hand on it. "I feel magic on the other side of this, but it's being blocked."

Cooper grabbed the axe from Cole's backpack. "Move back, guys." He looked giddy holding the sharp weapon. We all reacted swiftly as he swung. It took him a couple whacks before the wood splintered.

"Stop." Cole put his hand out, preventing Cooper from taking another swing.

Cole sat and slid closer to the wood plank. "Cooper, Eli, grab my arms." They both surrounded Cole, holding him as he stomped on the splintering timber. After his third jump on the door, there was a sharp crack. The wood gave way, leaving his legs flailing in mid-air. Light filled the cavern, emanating from the hole like a geyser.

"Holy shit." Cooper got a better hold on him. "Good thing we had you. It looks like a long fall."

I peeped into the hole. The warm light blinded me from seeing the true bottom, but it was definitely far down.

"I think we found it." Josh smiled with excitement. "Whoo-hoo," he yipped through the cave. His enthusiasm was so contagious it made me laugh. The cave erupted in cheers and excitement. It was better than striking gold. We had found our ultimate treasure.

"We certainly have." Lars was cool and collected, but his eyes were coated in self-satisfaction. Lars stood next to me. "Ember, I think you are the only one who can retrieve it. Since you are the one in prophecy, only *you* get it from its holding place," Lars added.

I bit at my lip, looking back down at the glowing hole. We could see something that might be the sword sparkling at the bottom of the pit. "Okay."

"Wait." Eli retrieved a harness from his pack and had me step in it, tightening the straps. He unfastened the rope from his pack and leaned over clasping the metal clip onto the front of mine. His fingers brushing the skin of my stomach. "This feels familiar." He winked. "Who would have thought back in Silverwood the ropes course would come in handy later?"

His touch still burned my skin with the ability to send my pulse racing sky high. "I still think putting us in the same room should come with a warning label."

A wicked smile hitched the side of his mouth. "We should come with several warning labels."

Someone cleared their throat, breaking the heated looks Eli and I were exchanging. I stepped away from him.

"Okay, Em, Cooper and I are going to lower you slowly. Let us know when you're at the bottom." I nodded and sank into the hole, holding onto the wall before Cooper and Cole took my weight.

"You ready?" Cole asked.

"Yeah, let's do this."

"Crap on ash bark. What if something happens when she touches it? What if she's not the one, and it hurts her?" Mom rambled, her gaze and questions pointed at Lars.

Lars waved his arms toward me. "Lily, you know she's the one. Stop fighting Ember's true heritage and destiny. Let her be what she is meant to be."

Pain and sadness flashed over my mother's features, but she nodded.

I had secretly been nervous to touch it, too. Now the fear spread further into my stomach.

Come on, Em, no turning back now.

I let go of the wall, and my body fell a few yards before the rope and the boys' hold caught up with each other. The jolt cracked the joints along my spine. As they steadily lowered me to the ground, the brightness grew to a blinding level. I didn't even see when my feet hit dirt.

"Okay, I've reached the bottom," I yelled. They dropped a few more feet of rope so I had freedom to move. I secured my footing before I turned and fully took it in.

It lay on a raised mound of earth. The blade was etched with Celtic symbols and decorations. The carvings swirled, intertwined, and infused in a gorgeous design. As close as I was, I realized the glow around the sword had begun to pulse. As I took a step toward it, the pulsating picked up. The light was warm and inviting and beckoned me. With every step I took, the more it reacted to me. There was no denying it knew me—wanted me to hold it. The power of it brought me to my knees. I kneeled in front of it like before an altar. I was not religious, but the ancient power this sword contained affected me like nothing I had ever known. Heavy with life and memories. I could feel it brimming with the existence it had lived.

I touched it. My fingers hit the outside of a bubble of light. My body drank in the magic, igniting my insides with power. I was no longer aware of anything but the light taking over my body. It filled every corner, pushing out thought and emotions. No longer aware of space or time, I heard a voice in my head:

If you have this sword, Ember, it means the worst has come to light. It is you who needs to end her reign. Time to end the darkness we have dwelled in for far too long.

Abruptly, I was back inside my body, down in a hole in the ground. My lids pried apart, and I blinked several times. It was pitch black. The glow around the sword was gone. I sat stunned for several beats and heard the voice replay. It was such a comforting sound. I wanted to bask in it, though I could no longer recall if it were male or female.

Shouting from above crept into my conscience. "Ember?" Mom's voice screamed the loudest. Other calls tangled around hers. "Are you all right? Answer me!" Dots of light tried to shine down on me, but the flashlights couldn't quite reach the depth of the cave.

"Yes. Yes, I'm fine," I yelled, switching on my headlamp and pointing the light back on the sword. It was beautiful, but the metal no longer called to me. It hadn't been the sword drawing me near; it had been the spell that enchanted it. I could still perceive its daunting power, but it no longer cared if I held or possessed it. It was neutral to me.

My fingers wrapped around the handle, bearing the weight as I picked it up. The thing was heavy. My hand slid up the metal, caressing the engraved features. It was not iron or any other metal I felt before. It was something that did not belong to Earth.

"Em, what is going on?" Cole bellowed.

Begrudgingly, I stood and gripped the sword tightly against my body. I had come to accept the prophecy and what part I played in it. I felt possessive. It was my destiny, and I was going to fulfill it. "Okay, I got it. I am ready to come back up."

They gradually lifted me to the top. Arms grasped me as I neared the surface. Eli grabbed the weight from my hands, lightening Cole's and Cooper's load. They lifted me and placed my feet on the ground.

"Let me see it." Lars demanded Eli. Eli held it out in his palms while everyone quickly surrounded the sword, ogling it.

Kennedy stepped closer. "Wow, I can feel it. It is alive."

Many things in the Otherworld tended to be alive, like books and weapons. They held history and the life they had experienced. If you are quiet and patient enough, they might tell you their story.

Her finger stretched to touch it. The moment she did, she hit the ground.

"Ken!" I dived after her. She blinked and shook her head. "Are you okay?" I helped her sit.

"Yes. I don't know what happened. I felt like it tried to talk to me. It was too much."

My attention turned back to the sword in Eli's hand. "Eli, do you feel anything?"

He shook his head. "No."

I frowned. I was the prophesized one, the one who should have the connection to it. Why didn't it try to communicate with me again?

Everyone took turns placing their hands on the blade. Nothing.

"Kennedy, if our theory is right about who you are, the Druid who put the curse on it is from your family line," Cole said. "Maybe that's why it is interacting with you and no one else." None of us could refute his reasoning.

Lars turned back to Eli. "Let me have it. I will carry it."

I cringed. I knew what the reaction would be to this. Protests bombarded Lars's declaration.

"You think we'd be stupid enough to let you have it?"

"I don't think so."

"There's no way in hell you are going to hold it."

"Everyone shut it," I screamed, silencing the combating voices. "It is my burden to bear, and I will carry it." My proclamation was not ready for the reality. I swiped the sword out of Eli's hand and went face first into the dirt.

"I don't know about you guys, but I'm feeling better about this." Eli sounded way too amused for his own good. "Glad you're handling this, Brycin."

"Shut up," I mumbled into the ground. He came to my side, helping me roll over.

If you ever want to see me naked again, you will zip those lips right now. I glowered at him.

He smiled and motioned sealing his mouth, the glint in his eyes bright with humor.

"I really do hate you," I muttered as he pulled me to my feet.

I glanced down at the sword. Most of me wanted to kick it, but with my luck I would break my toes in the process. "It'll be fine. I wasn't ready for how heavy it is."

"How about I carry it on my back?" Eli held up his hand stopping the coming rejections to this idea. "I will only carry it until we get out of here. Then Brycin will take it. Believe me, I have no desire to obtain this sword. Plus, if I did anything, Brycin here would kick my ass."

Also, I really want to see you naked again. His eyes met mine. *Wearing only the sword.*

I blushed and looked away. No matter how familiar we became, he could still make me tremble. When I looked up, I noticed Lars backing away from the group. His body rigid. A look of urgency twitched his features as he looked around. Something was wrong.

"What?" I took a step toward him. Everyone near me was distracted by the sword, oblivious to Lars. His eyes turned so bright yellow they were almost neon. In that instant he whipped around and ran for the cavern exit.

"Lars," I called after him. Where was he going? My feet began to follow him out of the heart of the cave and down the tunnel. The light from my flashlight bobbled on the walls and floor of the cave as I picked up speed.

"Lars!" I yelled desperately. Why did he leave us like that? He was gone. Not a sound of footsteps or trace he had been there remained. He was as stealthy and sneaky as the Dark Dwellers.

"Let him go." Mom came up behind me.

"Let him go? But he brought us here. Why would he run off?" I looked back at her, her headlamp blinding me. I shielded my eyes.

"He disappears usually when you need him the most or when he needs to save his own skin. He's a Demon, Ember. He only thinks of himself. He always has."

I shook my head against her words.

"I don't understand, though. We just got the sword. This is exactly what he wanted. Why would he disappear now?"

"I don't know why Lars does anything. There are many reasons I kept you from him, but right now I am most worried about you getting hurt. I don't want you to believe he is more than what he is." There was more she wasn't telling me. This was about the past, not the present. Their connection, like her relationship to Eli, was shrouded in mystery. A secret I would eventually learn, but not at this moment.

Abruptly, I felt a prickling across my skin. A warning. Something was coming.

"Do you feel that?" I took a few steps back, grabbing Mom's arm.

"Yes. The smell is awful. What is it?" She strode back with me toward the group.

I took a deep breath. She was right. A rancid, rotting-corpse stench wafted to us. "I-I don't know." I couldn't place it, but it triggered a deep-seated fear in my gut. We both started to run to the core of the cave.

Something bad was coming for us. Was this why Lars had taken off? His powers would have smelled or sensed this sooner than the rest of us. Was this thing so bad he knew to get out before it reached us? My heart wanted to believe he wouldn't leave us.

Even if he didn't care what happened to me, he would care about the sword. He wouldn't leave it, right?

My thoughts did not have time to focus on him. It didn't matter. He was no longer here to help fight what was coming.

I raced back into the room. "Guys, something is approaching." Everyone stopped and turned to face me. Eli had secured the sword to his back. Even though I hadn't said no to his plan, instinct made me want to grab it away from him and guard it myself. It was mine. My destiny.

Before anyone could react, a voice came into the tunnel. "How many of you *does* it take to screw in a light bulb?" The tone sounded smooth and confident. "I mean there are fifteen of you, counting two pixies, to retrieve a single sword, and yet it took you several days. What does it say about you as a collective intelligence?"

Shit! I knew that voice all too well.

TWENTY-FOUR

Lorcan stood at the entrance to the cavern, the light catching his green eyes. His usual leather jacket and dark jeans were replaced with dark green camo-pants and a fitted black shirt. The death stench had covered up his smell so he was able to sneak up on us undetected.

His hand rubbed his shaved head. Dax stood next to him, dressed similarly. The rest of them were in Dark Dweller form and created protection around the two men. I knew right away which was which. My connection to them let me feel their auras and know them even in their beast form.

"With so many of you, it wasn't hard to track you. Might as well have sent me a postcard from Greece saying, 'Wish you were here.'"

Samantha's beast form stepped closer to me. My eyes narrowed on her. I growled at her in warning.

"Easy there, Emmy," Lorcan derided. I hated the belittling way he said my name, and he knew it. It was all a game. A game of power.

Eli and Cole both stepped closer to me, walling me in. Seeing this, Samantha's lip curled into a sneer.

"Why don't you tell your little kitty to pull back her claws?" I seethed.

Samantha snarled, but with one look from Lorcan, she stopped.

"Oh, look, she's housebroken now." I nodded toward the Dark Dweller.

Samantha growled and paced forward.

"Samantha," Lorcan yelled. She continued to growl softly but moved back. "I wouldn't antagonize her again, Ember. I won't stop her next time."

Funny none of us asked how or why he was there. By now we had learned with Lorcan if there was a way, he had the will.

"You are outnumbered, Lorcan," Cole spoke up.

"Outnumbered?" Lorcan laughed, cutting off Cole. "I spotted half your group scrambling out of the river two miles back. I thought you finally got wise and attempted to get rid of the Light, but seeing Owen, Jared, and Gabby climb out had me reconsider."

Relief filled me. They were all right.

A small sigh came from Cole before he turned a stony expression back on Lorcan. "You are still outnumbered here, and I know you are much shrewder than to come to a fight you can't possibly win. So why don't you get to the reason why you are here."

"Oh, this will definitely be a fight I win," Lorcan responded. "But, you're right, let me get to the point. I came for one last appeal to get you to change your mind. I will get what I want one way or another. I hoped you would come to see how much better it would be working together, against Aneira. We have Ember, the Druid, and now the sword. Everything is in our corner."

As much as I hated to admit it, there was a small part of me that agreed with him. All of us together would be stronger, but I could never work with him or align with Samantha or Lorcan. They had killed my friend, kidnapped me, and traded me to the Queen. I would kill both of them first.

"Let me guess. You want the sword for your own." Eli tilted his head, edging closer to me.

"What can I say, brother? I follow the trend. I want what everyone else wants." He held out his arms. "Now, give me what I want."

Eli smirked. "I don't think so."

"You're not getting anywhere near it." Cole moved next to Eli with Cooper and my mom following.

Had he really thought we would agree to work with him? His narcissism was beyond belief.

Lorcan sighed, looking down at the ground. "I did ask nicely. I came to you, tried to form a deal, but once again you have disregarded my offer. Now, I will do what I should have done in the beginning. Take what I want. This teaches me to try and play nice."

He held up his hand and snapped his fingers. For one brief moment nothing happened, but the anticipation kept me on edge. Abruptly, the quiet ended when a high-pitched war cry sounded behind him, and bodies flooded the tunnel of the cave, running toward us.

My lungs stopped pulling in air when I realized what I was looking at. Fear tugged at every nerve in my body.

We are going to die.

Waves of red-eyed Strighoul plunged into the opening, wailing, with their needle-like teeth bared and ready to fight. None had weapons, but they didn't need them. They were their own means of combat. A shiver cut into my bones as I recalled Vek tearing into my throat the last time I had come across the Strighoul. Just their blood-thirsty gazes had me wanting to cower in the corner. Each was a tall, skinny creature with pasty, white skin. Veins and scars lined their bald, patchy, scalps. Sharp, pointy ears protruded from their heads. Dressed in Goodwill rejects, they flew at us.

I widened my step, swinging a weapon out from the holster on my back.

All our Dark Dwellers, except Eli, shifted into their forms. Eli had the Sword of Light strapped to his back, and if he shifted, it would rip off. We couldn't lose it now.

I knew Mom could handle herself. But Kennedy stood there completely frozen in fear. Cooper jumped in front of her, blocking the Strighoul. Her powers were too new and unsure. Fear kept her from assisting in the fight. She could do one mean revealing spell, but that wouldn't really help us now.

Besides Kennedy, Josh had been the other one who worried me. He had not trained with the rest of us making him an easy target. But when I looked over at him, he held his sword like a pro. He screeched his own battle cry as he dived into the swarm of Strighoul. Swinging down, he sliced into the head of a Strighoul, splitting it in half like a melon.

Holy shit! When did Josh learn to fight like that? When we had trained together, he had been pretty good, but this was different. He possessed instincts that I didn't think he'd have. These only came from hardcore training, or maybe all those hours on his video games did help.

Not having time to think about it, I went into my own battle stance. Four Strighoul ran at me. My blade met with the first one's stomach. I pulled it out, twisting in a full circle, giving the sword momentum to slice the next one in half. Blood and matter splattered my face and body. I whirled back around, carving into another Strighoul. In the small cave, no one dared to pull out a gun since bullets could ricochet.

Lorcan's Dark Dwellers did not join the fight against us. As my weapon plunged into another screaming creature, I noticed Lorcan moving closer to Kennedy. Cooper was too busy fighting the Strighoul to notice their infringement.

I thought Lorcan would go for the ultimate prize, the sword. He wasn't. Instead of going for Eli, who had the sword, Lorcan headed for the Druid. Then it hit me: this was all a set up. Lorcan was using the Strighoul to distract us from what he really wanted.

Kennedy.

Cooper must have finally sensed the evasion because he moved in closer to Kennedy. Backing her up against the wall, he guarded her body with his.

I also needed to protect Kennedy. I would not let them take her. I could feel my body fatigued as it tried hard to fight the iron around me as well as the Strighoul, but they just kept coming. I would only get one step forward when more came at me, pushing me two steps back.

From the corner of my eye, I noticed the Strighoul begin to head for Cooper. While Cooper was busy fighting them, Lorcan slithered up and grabbed Kennedy. She struggled against Lorcan, but he easily dragged her toward the opening.

"Kennedy!" I screamed across the cave. I hurtled toward them, pushing through the bodies fighting around me. I couldn't hear anything, but I saw Kennedy's mouth open, arms reaching toward me. Dax pulled out a gun. My stomach sank. *Oh, please, don't hurt her.* He pistol-whipped her across the back of the head, and her body drooped in Lorcan's arms. He turned toward Dax, and I could see him shouting something at him. Lorcan's eyes flared red. Dax shrugged as Lorcan picked Kennedy up, throwing her over his shoulder.

"Eli," I wailed, looking around for him. He was in the midst of fighting two Strighoul. Still he found contact with my eyes. *"Lorcan!"* I pointed. Eli threw off one of the Strighoul and looked to where my finger indicated. When I followed his gaze, the spot was empty. All Lorcan's team was gone. Like the night, they could slink in and out almost without detection.

Nooooo! I didn't have time to react as three more Strighoul came at me.

"She's mine boys," a nasally voice shouted and hands clamped on my arms. I recognized the voice—Drauk. The Strighoul coming for me stopped, listening to their leader. Distracted by Kennedy's capture, I had let my enemy sneak behind me. Alki would be ashamed. The first lesson I learned: never let your guard down.

"Brycin." Eli's voice rang in my ears. My gaze lifted, meeting his.

I am so sorry. He ripped apart several Strighoul trying to reach me.

"I wouldn't take another step, Elighan." Drauk's hand wrapped tightly around my throat. I twisted and saw his mouth open, baring hundreds of daggered teeth. Eli stopped. The fighting within the cave continued, but the three of us were in our own little bubble.

"Vek got a tasty hit off you last time. I think it's only right I have the same." Drauk clutched me closer to his body, his lips nearing the vulnerable area where the shoulder and neck meet. His breath was moist on my bare skin.

"Don't touch her." Eli unsheathed the sword from his back and swung it over his head. Eli could get to Drauk, but not before Drauk's teeth sunk into me first. He hesitated, gripping the sword tighter.

"Dragen, you know the world of Dark Fae. All is fair. And I think it is only right I get a taste of her." Without hesitation Drauk bit down, tearing into my flesh. A scream vibrated off the walls of the cave. Pain crippled my legs, rendering them useless. The sound of metal hitting the stone floor echoed in my ears. Spots dotted my vision as a fully-shifted Dark Dweller dived over my head. Its sickle claws burrowed deep in Drauk's chest. Both of them collided with the ground, knocking me flat on my back. My headlamp flew off and rolled into the dark corner of the cavern. I lay dizzy and disoriented, with the sounds of the fight far away and dreamlike. The sharp smell kept me from allowing myself to pass out. It reeked of blood and iron. Death and fear.

A roar came from Eli as Drauk chomped into his side. Eli sliced Drauk across the face with his claws. Bits of skin and tissue stayed in Eli's nails. A ragged cry broke from Drauk's lips. He huffed, and my blood and skin dripped off his lip. A deep chuckle came from his throat. "Keep trying, Dragen, but I can feel the Dae's flesh digesting in my system. Even a little of her powers will make it easy for me to defeat you." Drauk hurdled back at Eli.

As they continued to fight, I tried not to throw up. Lars's magic was wearing off, and pain pulsated through me. The muscle and veins Drauk had torn throbbed with agony. The desire to shut my eyes and fall asleep was almost too much. But my family was battling, maybe dying for me. I could not let them down. If I were to die here, it would be after I got the sword to safety.

Ember, get up. Don't die now. You've come too far. I mentally nudged myself to sit. Acid coated my tongue, and vomit rose to the back of my throat.

The sword lay at my feet. Everyone around me was too busy fighting to see the most powerful thing in the world was there for the taking. With my good arm, I tugged it to me while blood bubbled from my shoulder.

A strangled cry came from Drauk. He pulled away from Eli, bending over in pain. "What is happening?" He gripped at his stomach and fell to the ground. Eli growled but stepped back. Even in Dark Dweller form, Eli's face showed his confusion. Whatever was happening to Drauk was not something Eli had done.

I immediately understood. It was me. When Drauk bit me, he had taken in a small amount of my powers. But my powers came with a price—something he hadn't thought of. Picking myself up, I clutched the sword in my left hand and dragged myself to him.

"This is what you get for biting a Fay in an iron-laced cave." I sneered at him. "Iron poisoning." He looked at me, with real fear flittering through his expression. Like any Fay's first contact with this metal, it was debilitating. You could not move, making you vulnerable.

Fighting through the pain, I gripped the handle of the sword with both hands, swinging it up. I made a throttled cry and dropped the sword with everything I had. The blade cut through his neck like a cucumber. His head popped off and rolled across the room. Spinal fluid and blood trailed behind. Adrenaline pumped through me, giving me a dazed high. I stood there stunned.

Holy shit! Did I just chop off someone's head?

I hadn't even finished the thought when there was a horrid scream from across the cavern. I turned to see more Strighoul entering. All the Dark Dwellers were in their beast form, tearing and slicing into the Strighoul. Lars was gone. Kennedy was, too. There was only a few of us left fighting the mass infiltration of Strighoul. Panic ebbed in my stomach when I didn't see my mom anywhere.

I was working completely off adrenaline, and I needed to ride it until I collapsed. I couldn't lose much more blood. Eli's head nudged my leg, bringing me back to him and almost knocking me off balance. I looked down at the flaming red eyes belonging to him.

Run, Brycin. Get yourself and the sword out of here. His eyes locked on mine.

I don't want to leave you... any of you. There are too many Strighoul. Pure anguish of losing any of my family bolted my feet to the stone ground.

I need... we need... you and the sword safe. Don't let all this be for nothing. We can take care of ourselves.

I swayed on the soles of my feet, hesitating.

Brycin, run!

Run? It was harder than I thought. I stumbled during the first couple of steps. The iron slowed me, as did the lack of blood. It dripped down from the curve of my shoulder and trailed the length of my arm. My sheer will to get the sword away from the Strighoul kept me going.

"Come this way." Josh motioned for me to follow, his eyes wide and frantic. I faltered before heading toward him. He focused his headlamp and directed me toward a small hole on the far side of the cave. "Go." He nodded toward the opening.

If it weren't for the fact we were running for our lives, I would have laughed.

Yup, Alice is finally going down the rabbit hole.

Tucking the sword under my arm, I glanced back one last time and saw the small space filled with Strighoul. Dark Dwellers jumped through the air, slashing and biting. All the movement made me woozy. Right as I turned my head, I thought I saw out of the corner of my eye a small, reddish animal jump onto the head of a Strighoul, clawing at its face. I blinked, and it disappeared in the throng of bodies.

Great. Delirium is setting in, and I'm starting to see things.

Hands pushed at my spine, turning my attention back to getting through the hole. There was only enough room to crawl. Single file. It went for about fifteen feet before it opened into another room. All sounds of the battle were blocked by the thick cave walls. I pushed myself up, and Josh caught me as I wobbled to the side.

"I really hope there is an exit here." I glanced around the room. The only light came from his headlamp.

"Yeah, me, too." He let go of me and started walking the perimeter of the new chamber.

"I'm so glad you're all right." I watched him investigate. He had several cuts and was developing bruises over his skin. Other than those injuries, he seemed okay. "How did you fight off the Strighoul? I could barely do it. Impressive."

Josh snorted. "With a father like mine, you learned to fight and survive."

I knew I should be helping him, but it was all I could do to keep upright. I leaned against the wall, breathing heavily. "Yeah, but Strighoul are quite a different enemy."

Josh swung around. "Are you upset I survived? That a human boy could actually hold his own against a Fae?"

"No... that's not..." I shook my head. I had no energy for this. "Ignore me. I'm out of it right now."

He took a breath. "Yeah, sorry... me, too. Come on. I think I found a way out."

I bit into my bottom lip with wave of determination. I took a step. *You have to keep going, Em. For your family... for the ones being held prisoner,* which now included Kennedy. Revenge and anger burned enough in my veins to keep me moving. Josh lit the way, and I slid through a narrow crevice and entered a long tunnel.

"This has to lead out." Josh pointed his flashlight down the corridor and took off at a brisk walk. "Up or down as long as it takes us out of here."

I couldn't argue. Keeping up with his pace took a lot out of me. As blood trickled down one arm, the sword became heavy in the other.

I felt a pull on my arm. "Let me carry it for you."

"No!" The response was quickly out of my mouth. *Protect the sword at all costs. Don't let anyone else touch it.*

Josh's eyes slanted down. "I was trying to help. You're injured and slowing us. Now let me carry it for you."

I stepped back. "No."

"Let me have it." He lunged for it.

A growl came from my throat as I put my body in front of the sword.

Josh pinched the bridge of his nose and sighed. "You're being stupid. Let me carry it."

I didn't move. Everything in my core told me not to let go.

"I really didn't want it to happen this way. I really didn't." Josh shook his head. He unsheathed his dagger, pointing it at me. "Let me have the sword."

What the hell?

"Josh... Josh, what are you doing?"

He charged forward, slamming me into the wall, his knife to my throat. The lamp on his head blinded me. I could only see the outline of his face. "What I was sent to do. To take you and the sword back to my Queen."

"Your Queen? What are you talking about?" I sputtered. The utter deceit knifed into my back like the steel at my throat. *Oh, God, no.* "Sh-She is not your Queen, Josh. You are human."

His expression darkened. "You don't understand. You never did. You pretended to care and be my friend, but you're not. You never have been. Deep down you really consider me a lowly human. I'm beneath you. Everyone has made me feel inferior all my life. No one thought of me for much of anything. My own family considered me worthless." Sprays of anger spit from his mouth as he spoke.

"That's not true. You are my friend. You're anything but worthless."

"Shut up, Ember. I'm not stupid. Don't you think I couldn't sense how all of you felt about me at the ranch? How I was a nuisance? And Eli and the others really wanted me gone. I was below them. Even back at Silverwood, Eli treated me like I was a parasite."

"Don't take it personally. He treated me like that back then, too," I retaliated.

"But you are special. You are something. I'm still a pitiful human."

"Is that what you think? Why you are doing this? To be something more?"

"The Queen saw something in me. She wants me to be her First Knight. I *am* something worthy to her."

The knot in my throat moved down to my stomach. Her First Knight? I knew what this meant, what it entailed.

"Josh, you can't. You have no idea what it means. She's only using you."

Wrong thing to say.

The edge of the dagger whipped back up to my throat. He moved in closer, pressing it to my jugular. "You must really think me stupid. Poor dimwitted, gullible Josh."

When we were at Silverwood, I had learned as sweet as Josh seemed to be, he had a temper. His dad had been the same way and had beaten Josh excessively growing up. Josh used to hate his father for it. Now he was becoming the same person.

"You are not dumb." I was trying to defuse the situation, but everything I said seemed to only enrage him.

"Shut up! Just shut up! What's funny is I was the one fooling you. Even when I slipped up and showed you I could handle a sword, you still believed me helpless. Don't you think she trained me? The whole time I was with you, I was getting information for her. How easily you gave it, never thinking I was the one thing you should fear."

That bitch did it again. She took someone else I cared about. Josh was susceptible. Aneira didn't need to glamour him. He only needed someone to tell him he was special. He fell happily into her web. What better way to get to me mentally and physically than to use someone I trusted and cared about? A spy in the nest.

Pricks of fear shrouded my skin. "Oh, Josh, what did you do?"

He pressed the knife deeper. "I'm helping to create a better world."

It was almost as if her voice came out of him. She had done a good job of brainwashing him.

"Please, see what is right in front of you. She is trying to take over and render humans the inferior race. She will destroy Earth." I rambled on, trying to break through to him. "She is using you and will kill you as soon as you're no longer helpful. Please, Josh, don't do this."

He shook his head. "Believe me I am not worthless to her. She cares about me and wants me to be great. She and I are a team and will make things right again."

My lids fell shut. I swallowed the huge lump in my throat. The edge of the blade pierced my skin. She had gotten her hooks in him. She had wrapped Josh in a powerful blanket and had given him everything he needed, all he craved and lacked.

"How long have you been working for Aneira?"

"After you left the Otherworld, my Queen graciously took me in. She didn't see a lost or helpless boy. She saw a future warrior and trained me. We came up with the plan to let Torin go, but to have him think he escaped. For appearances she had a guard beat me and put me in the room with him. It was *me* who planted the idea in Torin's head on how to escape. Here was this all-powerful First Knight, a Fay, and he gobbled up my subtle hints. It was so easy." Josh's eyes glinted with pride and giddiness. He relished knowing he had tricked a Fay and that he was smarter and better than them. Josh was being the exact thing he hated.

"My Queen and I set up the 'escape.' We knew Torin would lead me straight to you. She was so pleased with me when she learned you were going after the sword, and I knew every step you guys were taking. You did all the work." Smugness vibrated off Josh.

Fear must have shown on my face because Josh smirked. "That's right, Ember. The Queen knows all and has been with me almost every step of the trip." With his free hand he tapped at his head.

Of course. Torin told me the Queen had the power to dreamwalk and connect to her First Knight's thoughts. A solid block of ice slithered down my back.

Dammit!

"Your job was to let us find the sword, then separate it and me from the group." His deceit hardened my heart.

"Of course. Let's go." The Queen would prefer us to be outside the cave walls. Funny, for beings so strong and powerful, a little iron, and you're helpless. Guess the human wins here." He grabbed my shirt with one hand and pulled me forward.

Keeping the sword to my throat, he clamped down on my good arm and tugged me forward. I didn't know why I hadn't noticed earlier how much he had filled out. He was not the scrawny, clumsy kid I'd met at Silverwood. He had changed. I had been so caught up in my own shit I overlooked what Josh really had needed. Someone to notice him. A friend. Now it was too late.

I was more trained than him, but the iron and loss of blood caused me to stumble and trip over the smallest pebbles in the cave. All I needed was to reach the mouth to get away from the iron and let the earth fill me with its healing power. Then my strength would come back. That would be my opportunity. The sword and I needed to stay out of the Queen's hands by any means possible.

Josh's headlamp bobbed down the dark cave, giving us only enough light to see a few feet in front. My eyes followed the light, but I didn't need it. The path and space mapped out clearly in my head.

The passageway suddenly ended, leading to what appeared to be a dark, endless drop. The path picked up on the other side of the fissure about one hundred feet away. A thin rope-bridge suspended in between. I gulped and paused at the approach to the bridge.

"Ladies first." The sword nudged into my back.

"Now I can say you have literally stabbed be in the back."

"Funny." He responded with another shove. "I said go." He pushed me toward the thin, twined rope. There was only one cord to walk on and one to hold. I took a deep breath and stepped onto the twine. It wobbled and swayed, and my one arm held on with everything I had. When I got my balance, I slid my feet and inched across the bridge. The rope creaked with protest. Josh tucked the sword into the back of his pants and stepped out behind me.

"No, Josh, don't!" The instant the words were out of my mouth I knew it was too late. The cord unraveled and snapped under our combined weight, causing us to plummet into the dark abyss.

TWENTY-FIVE

Falling, with no idea where you are going or how far the ground is from you, is bizarre. When you can see the ground, you know when the end will come. You can anticipate it. But this was a sickening loop of "Is it now? Now? How about now?" All you know is your death is at the bottom, and you will meet it faster than you want.

It was only a split second before I splashed when I perceived what was below us. The speed and force with which I struck the water was like hitting a brick wall. My skin burned on impact, and the water scraped me raw. It was only a few seconds after I immersed when I felt a disturbance next to me which had to be Josh. The chilly water wrapped around and closed me in its deadly clutches. The darkness penetrated so deep it didn't seem to make a difference if my eyes were opened or shut.

Air! My lungs screamed. I started to swim, hoping I was going the right way. Kicking and thrashing, I finally breached the surface and gasped for air. I blinked and wiped the water from my eyes. A splinter of light far in the distance cast ghostly impressions through the cave.

Light meant a way out.

Realization that nothing moved next to me twisted my gut. "Josh?" No response. *I can't let him die. No matter what he's done.*

Taking a panicked breath, I tried to map the space around me. I detected a mass floating near me. Blindly, I headed for the object.

"Please, don't be dead." My hands felt the back of his head, and I rolled him over. The sword was still tucked deep into his pants, weighting Josh down and pulling him below the water.

"Shit." I grappled for his clothes and tugged him. Terror caused my breath to falter; the edge of the underground lake was quite a distance from us. I couldn't do CPR here. I hooked him under my bad arm and side-stroked toward the water's edge. Between him, the sword, my bad arm, and depleting strength, it was touch and go to keep my own head above water.

Finally, my feet brushed up against something solid. I thought being able to stand on the ground would be better, but getting his weight on dry land was still difficult. A wave helped push us enough so I could lay him on his back. Water lapped, bobbing his body back and forth.

Using all my senses except sight, I tilted back his head and started CPR. I compressed his chest and blew repeatedly into his mouth. "Come on, Josh," I wailed. "Breathe." Frustrated with the lack of results from my efforts, I thumped my fist into his chest with as much force as I could gather.

Josh sputtered and choked. I could hear water erupting from his mouth as he turned to his side, spitting up. He vomited, but at least he was alive. I sat back on my heels, shaking.

"You saved me?" His voice was raspy.

"Of course."

He didn't respond, but rolled on his back with a groan. "Are my eyes playing tricks on me, or do I see a little light in here?"

I turned to look at the glow. "There is some kind of opening over there. It's enough to let water out. Let's hope it's suitable for us."

Josh pushed himself up and stood, which started another bout of coughing. With his hand he pulled me to my feet. "Let's get out of here."

I nodded and turned toward our sliver of freedom. Both of us moved slowly, hobbling with pain. I was surprised neither of us had broken anything, though Josh clutched his chest as though he had cracked a few ribs. If that was all, it would be a miracle.

We eventually rounded a corner, and the splinter of light turned into a gaping hole, enough for us to hike out. Josh let out a sigh of relief.

As we climbed over the rocks and moved closer to the exit, Josh grabbed my elbow. "Em, wait. No matter what... thank you for saving me." The expression on his face was pinched, whether due to pain or guilt, I didn't know. He turned and crawled over the boulder through the exit to the outside.

I had no choice but to follow.

The hot, glaring sun blinded me as we ascended from the dark, cool cave. Instantly, the heat encased me. My strength was depleting rapidly with blood loss, and the temperature only aggravated it. The earth called to heal me, but there was still too much iron around. Josh grabbed my arm and dragged me across the threshold. The oppressing iron that had been in the cave lightened, but it still wasn't enough. My power only tapped at the soles of my shoes, not breaking through.

"Keep walking." Josh hauled me forward. Guess our truce was over. The Sword of Light glimmered in the sunlight against his back.

"Seriously, I save your life, and you're still going to turn me over to her?"

Josh's eyes narrow. "Oh, should I be eternally grateful to the all-powerful Dae?"

I shook my head. Just a minute ago he was like the Josh I had known. That boy was gone, again.

With every step away from the cave, I felt better. Blood clotted, trying to heal my open wound, although I was still too drained to fight Josh. Sleep and a complete day lying in the woods would help, which was not an option. My brain was full of cobwebs; I couldn't even plan an escape.

I lost track of how far or how long we walked. The unrelenting heat sucked our energy before it even started to dry our clothes and hair.

We stumbled down the mountain, and his grip on me tightened. When we reached a forested area, the shade felt like heaven. The relief did not last long, as a new sensation hit me instantly. Magic. It was so thick and powerful my lungs clenched, and I felt woozy.

A dozen guards suddenly appeared and positioned themselves around Josh and me. Aneira stepped from behind them. She was the most beautiful thing I had ever seen. Probably the most extraordinary Fay who ever lived. She stood tall and elegant with deep red hair that fell to the middle of her back. She had pale violet eyes and alabaster skin. Breathtaking. Ruthless.

I shook my head. Her glamour usually didn't work on me, but I was weak and susceptible.

"Your Majesty." Josh pulled the sword from his back, laid it flat across his palms, and kneeled in front of her. "I have done what you asked. I have brought you the Sword of Light."

"Thank you, Joshua. Once again, you have proven you will be a great First Knight." She touched his shoulder gently. "Please rise."

Josh stood, his hands still displaying her awaiting gift—the precise thing I had fought so hard to find and keep from her. Everything we worked to achieve for was now gone. It was as if someone gutted me from the inside out, tearing out my heart. My legs shook under me as a whimper escaped my lips. It was gone. All gone.

Aneira's fingers extended to touch the carved markings on the blade but stopped. Her hand only hovered over it. Her eyes flickered bright, and her face showed both desire and dread. She had wanted it for so long, but perhaps she feared it even more. When Josh stepped closer to her, she stepped back. She was terrified of the blade. And she should be; it was the one thing that could kill her.

She stared at it greedily before she snapped her fingers. Guards rushed to her side. "Three of you please escort my remarkable First Knight back to the castle and see this is properly sealed away." Her gaze never left the sword.

Josh didn't seem to notice, and he continued to stare at her in awe. Her praising words only made him stand taller, happiness etched on his features.

"You honor me, my Queen, with this task." Josh bowed his head. Every word he uttered sounded like it came from his video games or some movie. He was living his fantasy and blinding himself to the truth around him.

Aneira finally looked at him and gave him an adoring smile. "I trust you completely, my knight."

"Ugh. I am gonna vomit listening to this artificial crap." I couldn't stop myself. It was such bullshit. How could Josh not see through her? Unfortunately, this brought Aneira's unwelcome attention my way, and she glared at me with a look of hate.

"Joshua, please go." Like an over eager puppy, he bounded forward so fast the three guards had to run to catch up. About three hundred feet away, he disappeared into what seemed like thin air. Humans, unless they were seers, could not see the Otherworld doors. Josh did not hesitate. He had known it was there.

"You look astounded, Ember." Aneira mocked, moving closer to me. "You wonder how he knew the door was there. Once humans go to the Otherworld, it changes them. Their minds open, and they see things they never allowed themselves to imagine before. Humans like to be ignorant of us. We scare them." Her smile widened. "Like they should. They are weak and stupid."

"Tell me how you really feel?" I crossed my arms. Every minute I delayed her, my powers grew stronger.

"You may be Fae, but you are exactly like them. Actually, you are worse... a Dae who thinks like a human. What did I expect? Lily raised you," she sneered and turned to her guards. "Cuff her."

Two guards clutched my arms, pinning them in front of me. Another pulled on gloves as he took the iron handcuffs from his belt. I was having a *déjà vu* moment: another country, on another hill with a different guard but otherwise it was the same. That recollection brought back awful memories. Trepidation ate at the lining in my stomach. I could not afford to lose more strength.

I bit down hard, grinding my teeth as the guard placed the cuffs on me. The arms hooked around mine and kept my legs from collapsing. I tried to swallow back the pathetic moan that came up my throat, but I couldn't. My lids fell, my body wanting to join them. *Sleep. I just want to sleep.*

"I know you have been keeping something from me, Ember. Shame on you." She shook her head like I was a naughty child. "To think your little Druid friend was a prisoner in my castle. She may have gotten way, but I already have men tracking Lorcan. It is only a matter of time before she is mine again. Having both a Druid and a Dae?" She trailed off, her eyes flickering with excitement. "The possibilities are endless. Then, after I'm through with you, I'll have the sweet pleasure of killing you both."

I bared my teeth, "Leave her out of this." Strangely, I was suddenly glad Lorcan had Kennedy away from here.

"I think you know me better than that, my dear girl." The Queen laughed giddily. Now she knew about Kennedy, she would not rest till she captured her.

"I know you are also aware of your family connection to Lars. Do you see now why I enjoyed using you against him? Utilizing his niece to destroy his kingdom bit by bit. Ripping him from his throne, destroying everything he and his brother built. It would have been even better if it was the prior Unseelie King. Not that it matters. They are both the same to me, and their blood runs in your veins. Lars was in love with your mother as well. He was her first love, but his need for power pushed her into Devlin's arms. Knowing your disgrace of a mother, she slept with both. Who knows? Lars *could* be your father. Either way, this has been most enjoyable for me to use you against what they created."

The thought of Lars possibly being my father had crossed my mind, but I had quickly shoved it away. Now it was in my face. Images of Lars and Lily being together slammed into my brain. She had been with him before she fell for his twin? Everything I had seen between them seemed to dispute it. Even when I had first thought Lars was my father, the thought of them together seemed wrong. Time and anger did funny things to people, but it still didn't seem right to think of them as an item.

"Like Lars, you are all talk. You speak and devise plans to overpower me, but when it comes to actually putting up a fight, you crumble at my feet." Aneira looked thrilled as she revealed this to me. "Lars was here earlier. He came to stop the big bad Queen from taking the sword out from under him." She opened her arms, gesturing around. "You can see how well that worked for him. He is gone now."

"Gone? Did you kill him?" The thought of my uncle dead tightened my chest. Not the Unseelie King or the Demon, but my uncle. I had barely learned the truth about him being family when he was taken from me. He had come here by himself to stop Aneira. That was why he ran from the cave earlier. Not because he was deserting me, but because he wanted to stop the Queen from getting me. I was ashamed of myself that, as usual, I thought the worst of someone. I hadn't believed the Unseelie King as someone who would run from anyone, but my trust in people was so low it made it hard to automatically think the best of them.

"He thought he could beat me. What a fool. I am the most powerful Fae. No one can defeat me, especially now I have the only weapon in my possession that can conquer me."

The sickness in my stomach rolled. Between the news about Lars and Josh and the effects of the iron, I won't deny I was a blubbering mess. It became too much. She had won.

Broken. Enough. My head fell forward and tears leaked down my cheeks. "What do you want, Aneira?"

"I want revenge." She said this quietly, but every syllable was resolute. I forced myself to look at her. My body was trying its hardest to fight the new dose of iron poisoning. The earth was helping me as much as it could, but it was not enough. Opposing sides gave and took at the same time, tearing trenches into my gut.

"Against whom? Humans? For taking Earth from you? Is that what all this about?"

She watched me carefully. "You have no idea what it is like to live in fear of something that should fear you. We were here first. This was our rightful home." She spouted and then took a breath. "But you are part of my revenge. You should never have existed. I want to destroy you and everyone you love... slowly and painfully... as they did to me."

Her fingers gripped my chin, squeezing hard. Her fury was pointed at me. This woman truly hated me with every fiber of her being. There were other Daes who had existed. Had she despised them this much?

"Using you to destroy the precise thing your mother tried so hard to keep from me renders it so deliciously perfect." With a maliciously beautiful smile, she stepped back from me. "Let us go *home*, Ember."

The guards had only taken a stride forward when my blood ignited, tearing through my veins. My feet dug into the ground and stopped our group from progressing. I couldn't see him, but I knew he was there.

"No..." I muttered to myself, looking around. Even if the idea of him being near comforted me, I did not want him here. I wanted him safe.

A solid crunch of gravel broadcasted Eli's arrival. He could slink up on someone in the middle of the day without a hint he was there. He wanted to be heard.

Aneira stopped and turned, glancing around. The guards became twitchy, looking for a new threat.

"I hope I am invited to this little soirée." Eli sauntered up. He was bleeding everywhere; cuts and teeth marks pitted most of his body. Chunks of flesh had been taken out of his side and shoulder. Battle wounds from the Strighoul. "Fairies do know how to throw a party. Please tell me someone invited the nymphs and water fairies." Eli rubbed his hands together. He kept his attention off me, purposely not looking my way.

What is he doing?

"Elighan, it has been a while. The last time I saw you, blood covered you as well." Aneira replied with disgust. "What brings you here?" The Queen pressed her lips together and looked at me, then back to him. "Please don't tell me it is for *her*." She frowned.

Eli was naked, which became more and more apparent the closer he got. I guess I should be flattered he didn't stop to change before coming after me.

Aneira was not immune to his nude physique either. Her annoyance flipped the closer he got to us, changing into a look I recognized. It was the expression I saw on most women who looked at Eli. Her eyes flared with desire. I had gotten used to him being naked, but I still didn't like her seeing him exposed.

"If I had known you would grow up so sexy, and large, I would have kept you as one of my pets." She sashayed up to Eli; her hand reached to his face. His body stiffened under her touch.

"I'm not really good at being potty-trained," Eli retorted, looking bored. But I could feel his tension raging underneath.

Her hand drifted down from Eli's face to his chest. "My, you have grown. I can imagine you would be a real beast in bed."

My hackles rose, almost choking me with anger and possessiveness.

"You'll have to ask her about that." Eli nodded toward me. His eyes finally met mine.

What are you doing? Are you completely insane?

Yeah. I told you, Brycin, where you go, I go.

You are nuts. My lids blinked double time trying to keep the tears back.

I think that's been well established. His mouth stayed neutral, but his eyes held the glint of a smile. *I am not letting you go in there alone, again. Cole went to find the rest of our group and then they will go after Kennedy. I came for you.*

My mom?

I convinced her it would be best to go because she could help more from the outside.

I let out a sigh of relief. I could not fathom the idea of Mom returning to Aneira's prison. I didn't know what happened to Lars, but there was this annoying bit of hope in my gut that said: *He's the Unseelie King. He cannot die easily.* But if he wasn't dead, where was he?

"I'd prefer to see for myself." Aneira's comment brought me back to the present. Her lids lowered hungrily as she took in his crotch. She continued, salaciously looking him up and down. "You will be much more fun than your brother. Harder to break. I love a challenge."

The implication was not at all subtle, and she was not one for empty threats. Since my mother's "death," I knew I was capable of handling a lot, much more than I thought I could. This was not one of them. The thought of her having Eli—oh, hell no—things would go down. I charged forward, the guard behind grabbed me, drawing me back into his chest. The Queen didn't even flinch; her attention was still on the male in front of her.

"You're not really my type." Eli shrugged indifferently.

There was a brief flicker of annoyance on her face before a twinkle of laughter filled the air like music.

"I am everyone's type. I will be glad to show you." Her eyes glinted with a challenge.

Like the pop of a balloon, my fury erupted. Through the iron, my power dredged up from the depths of my soul. The thought of her touching Eli or using him like she had Torin drew a curtain of red. I didn't see anything. I only felt.

With a gust of energy, Aneira was torn off her feet and thrown back through the air. A hard thud sounded as she landed on the rocky terrain and skidded across the ground. The silence that came after was deafening. The soldiers stood in shocked muteness as they watched their Queen lying flat on her back.

Crap...

Eli obviously felt the same. His head sagged forward, swearing under his breath, as he shook his head back and forth.

"My Queen." A guard ran to her, waking the other soldiers out of their daze. A handful scrambled to her.

She lifted her head. "Get off of me." She stood without help as rage ignited her eyes and burned into me.

"You disgusting half-breed..." She persisted with a slew of insulting words, but it was in Gaelic, so I only understood the angered, biting tone. Power thundered off of her as she barreled toward me. The guard behind gripped me harder, keeping me in place. Her hand flew up, colliding with my face. A torrent of pain slammed through my cheek, and I stumbled to the side. Spots dotted my vision.

A deep growl came from the form next to me.

"Your girlfriend here needs to learn her place, as you do." A handful of my hair was yanked up. Cool, blue-lavender eyes met mine. "If you ever do that again, Ember, I will kill you." Her voice was icy-calm. She was back in control again.

I straightened. A fevered anger still locked my muscles. "And if you *ever* touch him, I. Will. Kill. *You.*"

Another blinding sting ripped across my face as she hit me again. "I touch what I want, you insolent girl. You will respect your Queen."

"You are no Queen of mine." I never could keep my mouth shut. She hit me again, and this time I tasted blood.

Eli snarled and launched himself at her. In that moment the Queen pulled something from the folds of her dress and sliced her arm toward Eli. A torrent of blood spurted from his neck in a gush. Eli's body crumbled to the ground.

TWENTY-SIX

"Nooooooo!" A scream so guttural and primal ripped from my throat. I pitched forward. "Eli!" I wailed. Horror cut across my heart, cleaving it in half. Guards immediately seized my arms and hauled me to my feet, away from Eli. He tried to gasp for air but gurgled, choking on his own blood. Panic reached deep into my soul. All my senses went primitive. Spitting with rage I bit at my capturer's hands. I fought against them snarling like a beast. I twisted and screeched, and the world spun underneath me. I did not know which way was up or down. My only instinct was to get to him.

Violent cries kept coming from me as I watched more blood soak the earth beneath him. It was almost like I was twelve again, and my mother's body was lying in a pool of her blood. Tears rained down my face, filling my mouth as I continued to yowl in agony.

The Queen turned my face up to hers. "Silence."

My chin pointed toward her, but my eyes would not leave him. He took a shallow breath. A whimpering sob reverberated in my chest. His neck gaped open, and muscles, tissue, and veins protruded from the vast hole. Bubbles of blood oozed out of his mouth and neck as he struggled for breath. My nose picked up the strong smell of blood and the magic from the Queen's blade that had torn through his skin. It was a Fae-welded blade. He would die.

Nails dug into my chin as Aneira forced my attention back on to her. "You can save him, Ember." Her lips twisted into a cruel smile. "Your Fay powers can heal him."

It took me a few seconds before her words registered. I could heal him. My earth powers had done it before when he had been shot by a rival gang. A surge of hope filled my chest.

"Please, let me save him," I sobbed as I struggled to move to him. The soldier's grip on me was ironclad.

"Let us make a deal." Her voice curled around me like a venomous snake.

"Anything. I will do anything you want. Please let me save him." The thought of losing him, of being without him, left a void in my heart so big nothing could fill it. I had barely lived through my mother's death. I was pretty sure I would not get through his.

"It's what I was counting on." A smug grin twisted her features. "This prophecy has been a thorn in my side for years. I lost count of how many Daes I obliterated over it. But you are the one who is supposed to fulfill it, aren't you?" It was not really a question. "I don't want to destroy you right now, Ember. You are valuable to my plan, but you will no longer be able to touch the Sword of Nuada. Unbearable pain will come to you if you try to take the sword for your own to use against me. And he will die on the spot." Her head motioned toward Eli. His breath had grown so light I could no longer see his chest moving. "In exchange for this, I will allow you to try and save him. You better decide quickly, Ember. He only has a few moments of life left. Then he will be lost to you forever."

A new flood of panic burst through my chest. There was no question what I'd do. She understood that. Even if it meant the chance to kill her was gone for good, I would do it.

"Do we have a deal?"

"Yes. Yes. I'll do it. Whatever you want." Tears trailed down my face.

A weighted energy skimmed down my skin. It prickled and reminded me of when I made a deal with Lars, locking me into the transaction. Breaking Lars's deal had been excruciatingly painful, and he had gone easy on me for violating the contract. Aneira would not. The bond she cast would kill Eli in a blink of an eye, and she would enjoy it. This was a contract I would not and could not break. Ever.

Aneira smiled complacently. Her soldiers still held me.

"Let me go," I choked through my tears. "Please... I agreed to your bargain." I struggled to get free.

Aneira paused and then gestured to her men to release me. When their hands let go, I gave no pause and flung myself to Eli's dying body. He had lost so much blood.

"Please stay alive. Do not dare die on me." I tried the best I could, with my wrists bound, to grip the sides of his face, my hands marinating in his blood. I brought his mouth to mine. The blood he gurgled stained his lips. The salty taste of my tears mixed with blood and the raw, masculine taste of Eli coated my taste buds. All I could focus on was pouring every ounce of energy I had back into him.

My filters were down and panic kept me from processing all this clearly. I called on the earth's power, and it came in abundance. I tugged ruthlessly at it, wanting more. It filled me with warm light. Plants crawled and slithered to me, hearing my cry.

Energy poured from me into Eli, but his body lay still. No movement or response. I moaned, pressing my lips harder to his. The warmth in me built hotter and hotter. I could feel Eli's muscles and skin molding back together. Blood stopped seeping from his neck, but there was no life in him.

"Don't you do this to me. You have to live," I hissed at him. "For once don't be so damn pigheaded." My lips came back down to his. My energy was waning, but the heat inside was growing, becoming painful.

Goddamn you, Eli. Sit up and fight me.

He didn't move. His chest stayed level.

"You ass. You are not allowed to die on me." I pushed at his chest. Uncontrollable sobs shook my shoulders. The buzz my blood normally got when he was near had dissipated. It was growing so feeble I could barely sense it. It would soon be gone soon. For good.

"Retrieve her." I heard the Queen order her men. A hand came down on my shoulder, lugging me back on my butt.

"No! Noooo!" I screamed. "You told me I could save him."

"Yes, and you tried. I did not promise he would live." Aneira tapped her nails impatiently against her arm. "A minor detail you missed. Now, get her up." She motioned to her men.

With a heartbreaking wail I wrestled away from the guards, crawling over to Eli.

Hands fumbled to pull me. "He is dead, Ember," the Queen said.

My mind shut down. All I could see was him. The connection between us was no more. I felt nothing from him. My blood was silent. This was not the way we were supposed to end. We had been through too much together. My heart and soul were completely his.

I will not lose him.

From depths I didn't know existed, I dug into my core and summoned the earth. When my lips touched his, energy went through me like a sonic boom, stripping me of my senses. I tumbled in the air, landing in a crumpled ball, a few feet away. The Queen and her men stumbled back from the pressure. Eli's limp form flung back, hitting the rocks with a crack. His mouth and eyes popped open on impact. He took a gasp of air. The liquid in my veins hummed back to life.

"Eli!" Drained and dizzy, I zigzagged to him, collapsing on the ground at his side. "You're alive."

He swallowed a few times before he spoke. "I always knew you'd be the end of me." He winced in pain. His voice was low and ragged. Blood soaked his chest. The scar across his neck was enflamed, but already starting to heal. The wounds from the Strighoul had also healed.

Hearing his voice again submerged me in happiness. I let out a relieved sob. "Don't you ever die on me again. You got that? Ever!" My eyes continued to water.

Eli's hand gently wrapped around the back of my neck. "For future reference, the next time I'm about to die, I want to go out fucking you. Only way to die."

I hiccupped a laugh. "Duly noted."

His green eyes met mine when I touched his face. Our eyes hungrily scoured each other. In a rare moment, Eli's expression became serious. He pulled my ear to his lips and whispered hoarsely, "When you are about to kill that bitch, I want to be there. I want to help tear her apart, limb by limb."

My lips went into a narrow line. I dipped my head and nodded. I would tell him of the pact, just not now. It was devastating for me think about coming all this way for nothing. *No!* I don't know how I was going to do it, but Aneira had to die. Right now Aneira had the sword. That was the first thing I needed to deal with. The second would be getting us free of her. Third was freeing me of that bond.

"This is absolutely nauseating," Aneira said behind me.

I hadn't forgotten she was there, but Eli had a way of blocking out the rest of the world. I swung around and stood in front of him. Eli rose, using the rocks as his support. He was weak, but he held his head rigid trying not to show it. I was shaky and exhausted, but if the Queen came after him again, I would rip her apart with my own hands.

"Oh, I am so pleased you are all right, Elighan. I was disappointed to lose a play toy like you. Such a waste." Aneira brushed her long, red hair off her shoulder. "Though, I wonder. Would Ember have tried to save you so fiercely if she knew the truth about your past?"

My head whipped around to look at Eli. His eyes flickered red, pushing off the rock with a growl. I knew Eli still held secrets about his past, but Aneira enjoyed provoking people. Right now I could not let her get into my head.

"Eli." I flung out my arm to stop him. He looked at me. His pupils elongated and burning with rage. *Stop. She's only trying to goad us. She has the sword now. We have to get it back,* my gaze conveyed to him. He held my stare. I could feel he wanted to destroy her. Letting out a breath, he shook off his fury and stepped back. I knew how hard such a thing was for him. It went against his nature. Once his anger was out, it was hard to get it back in the box.

"Well, well, well... how interesting. You are able to communicate with Eli like you are one of them." My head whipped back to Aneira. She was looking curiously at me. "When Torin told me you are part Dark Dweller, I was astounded at how that could possibly be. I was intrigued. Would you take on their traits? Would you become more invincible? I never imagined having Dark Dweller blood would enable you to communicate with him or become immune to iron."

She let the last remark hang in the air, her gaze on the handcuffs that still wrapped around my wrists.

Shit. I had been so consumed with defending and saving Eli, I completely forgotten the implications of using my powers through the iron cuffs. I had a sinking feeling her knowing this information was not going to be good for me.

"Joshua told me of this possibility. Elighan gave me the perfect way of testing this theory. I knew if you could do it, you'd use it while trying to save him."

"That was a test?" I exclaimed. "What if I couldn't?"

"Then he would have died, and I would have known your limitations." Her lips pressed together in a devious sneer. "However, I was right. You are going to be exceedingly useful to me, Ember."

A snake of anger and dread wrapped around my gut just thinking that I might not have been able to save Eli. I shook my head trying to clear my mind of the thought.

"Whatever is in his blood that has made you immune, I will be interested to discover. To never have to worry about iron poisoning. To have this Fay weakness eradicated." Aneira's eyes glinted with possibility. "Yes, I am especially interested in your blood."

Nope. Not good for me.

"It still won't help you. I lived through the blood exchange. Will you be able to say that about yourself? I am a Dae, a species that is even more formidable than your Fairy ass."

Why, oh why, can't I ever keep my mouth closed?

Instead of the anger I thought would furl my way, she laughed, throaty and alluring. "You remind me so much of your mother, passionate and stubborn to a fault and for all the wrong things." She put her hands on her hips. "I will not be transferring your blood, but your power."

"What? How?"

"I know of a way that I can transmit your powers to me without a blood exchange." She smiled like a Cheshire cat. I had no idea what she was talking about. Whatever it was it didn't matter if I understood or not. She did. And she was giddy with this knowledge.

"You want to transfer my powers to you? And I am simply going to let you have them?"

"You will." She replied confidently. "Getting you to do it will be easy enough. Not that I am asking." She eyed Eli again. "Iron may not perpetually control you, but your connection to him and the others still back in the Otherworld do. That is your failing. You will help me, Ember. Have no doubt of it. Now let us go see how your *dear* human father, that other Dark Dweller, and your chubby friend are doing."

"You bitch," I spat at her.

Aneira stepped up to me. "Be careful, Ember, the more you act out, the more I act out on him." She patted my cheek harshly, igniting my bruised face.

She stopped, and a huge smirk broke over her lips. "Or maybe you would like to go in her stead, Lily?" The Queen kept her head in my direction, but her words were not for me.

Lily? Oh, no.

"You know I would, Aneira, but I know you too well. That option is not actually on the table." Mom stepped from behind a massive stone. She also showed signs of a battle: her tank top ripped, her army pants torn, her clothes peppered with blood, and her face bruised and scraped. My legs almost gave way.

The Queen pivoted, facing my mom. "Am I becoming so predictable?"

"Yes," Mom retorted.

What was she thinking? She had gotten away. Why would she come back? I could barely stand from the outcome of saving Eli's life. What if Aneira hurt her, using her against me, too?

"Mom, w-what are you doing here?"

"I was wondering the same thing, Lily. What are you doing here? You afraid of what I might do... or say?" Aneira asked.

My mom's jaw tightened. "Ember is my daughter, and I will do everything in my power to protect her. Like I said, I know you, Aneira. I want to be here."

The Queen howled with laughter. "Ohhh... so many things in what you said amuses me. This is going to be enormously entertaining." The Queen swished her hand. "All right, if you want to tag along, who am I to deny you?"

It was all a show. She would never let Mom walk away. I fought between throwing up and being furious with her. Why would she go back so willingly? She couldn't help me if she got locked up again. Why would she risk it?

Then it hit me. *Mark.*

Not that my mom didn't want to protect me, but it was a stupid move. She was up to something, so this was intentional. Before I could make eye contact, guards surrounded her and blocked my chance to see any kind of answer in her eyes.

"Well, today has been an especially productive one." The Queen nodded to her men. "And give him a robe. He is quite distracting." She motioned at Eli. One of the guards took off his cape and flung it around Eli's naked body. She began to walk towards the door. The guards took the non-verbal cue and pushed me and Eli forward. My head turned to where he walked next to me.

We will get through this. His eyes were filled with strength and certainty.

My heart suddenly surged with emotion. After almost losing him, there was no question how I felt. Even in the middle of this mess, he could soothe me, cause me to feel stronger. I could take on the world if he were by my side. Whatever was ahead of us, we would get through it—together.

I love you, my eyes said to his. My cheeks flushed and my stomach dropped. I had never told anyone that before, besides my family and close friends. This was different.

Eli's pace faltered. He looked up at the sky, shaking his head. A strange, pained emotion flickered over his features. He eventually looked back at me. *You shouldn't.* He gritted his teeth; his expression had become stiff and callous. *I'm not worth it.* He then turned away.

Embarrassment coated my face. *W-What?* That was not the response I expected. My humiliation converted to anger. Heated words simmered on my tongue. They were about to be dumped on him, but my mouth stayed shut.

I felt him again. Not just sense, but I could feel his emotions. The last time it was this strong was right after he had given me his blood, after I almost died from Lorcan's attack. I don't know if it was because I consumed more of his blood as I was trying to save him, but it was there and his emotions were all over the place. Angry to euphoric, miserable to pissed off, with himself and me.

I swallowed my hurtful words. Judge a man by his actions, not his words. He had almost died for me, and he was still by my side.

The guards prodded us at a steady pace to the Otherworld door. My experiences with the Otherworld did not make it a happy place to go back to. The only good thing was it brought me closer to Mark, Ryan, and West, to help them escape. But how could I take Mark and West and leave Ryan behind? I couldn't leave him. There had to be another way.

We neared the door. I was getting better at spotting the wavy air pockets now. While the guard's attention was on the Queen getting safely through, a humming sound tickled my ear.

"I leave you for one moment and look what happens." Cal landed on my shoulder. "Covered in blood again," he tsked. My ponytail had completely fallen out of its hold, and he hid easily underneath my thick hair.

A small smile inched up my face.

"Simmons is staying back with the rest for now. Our dysfunctional family is all back together, figuring out how track the Druid girl. Figured you'd want Simmons to stay with them."

I gave a small nod.

"I won't leave your side, girlie. Not like you can function without me anyway."

I loved Cal. He tucked tighter against my neck as guards tugged me through the door.

Here I go again. It was no longer a rabbit hole, but a never-ending black void full of constant lies and secrets.

Kennedy was in the hands of Lorcan. The Queen now had Mark, Mom, Ryan, West, Eli, and me. Josh was Aneira's brainwashed minion. Lars was either dead or had run off. At least Torin, Thara, and the rest of the Dark Dwellers were safe and, hopefully, on a plane heading back to the states.

Aneira now held the only weapon capable of destroying her. My destiny was to kill the Queen, which now was no longer a fate I could fulfill. But some way, somehow, I would destroy her. With or without the Sword of Nuada, I would take down the Queen of the Light, plunging her into the darkness—for good.

No one fucks with my family.

Thank you to all my readers. Your opinion really matters to me and helps others decide if they want to purchase my book. If you enjoyed this book, please consider leaving an honest review on the site where you purchased it. Thank you.

Want to find out about my next release? Sign up on my website and keep updated on the latest news. www.staceymariebrown.com

Blood Beyond Darkness
(Darkness Series Book #4)

The Sword of Light, the only weapon capable of killing Queen Aneira, has been found. Ember's destiny is to end her reign and become the new Queen.

Or so she thought.

When Eli and Ember are taken by Aneira, she is forced to make a deal to save the man she loves. A curse is placed on Ember that if she uses the sword against the Seelie Queen, Eli Dies.

A price she might not be willing to make.

The fight for Earth is on, and old grievances and enemies must work together to stop Aneira from bringing down the wall between Earth and the Otherworld, making humans servants to the fae. And those who oppose her reign, will parish.

When deep secrets are revealed, Ember's world and heart is ripped apart even more. Ember must go beyond anything she could ever imagine, making the ultimate sacrifice, saving millions of innocent lives.

Not all fairytales have a happy ending...

Book 4 Available Now!

Acknowledgements

I would like to thank all the fans who have continued to support me so whole-heartily. Or at least support Eli! You have amazing. I hope you will continue to love these books and characters as much as I do. I can't believe there is only one book left in the series!

Again, to my Mom. These books are just as much yours as mine. Your help has been so fundamental. There are still not enough thank yous in the world to repay you. I love you!

Linne, "L," and Colleen for being my beta readers. You girls are amazing! Your input and advice have helped make my story even better. And your "extra" notes, L, always make me laugh. You really do get into Eli and Em scenes. I am so thankful to have you in my life.

Emily Mork for your beautiful tattoo designs and always being inspiration to me. Love you!

Jay Aheer for making the most beautiful covers!

Jordan Rosenfeld. Thank you again for all the hours you put in to help shape and develop my book. I absolutely adore you! http://jordan rosenfeld.net/

Judi at http://formatting4u.com/. Thank you! You have made the stress of getting my books out on time so much easier.

As always, a big thank you to my family and my friends around the world. Don't think you're in the clear! Your part in my stories will be told someday—soon. I love and miss you all so much.

Glossary

A ghra: Gaelic for "my love."

Bitseach: Gaelic for "bitch."

Brownies: Small, hardworking Faeries who inhabit houses and barns. They are rarely seen and would do cleaning and housework at night.

Ciach ort: Irish for "dammit" or "damn you."

Cinaed/Cionaodh: Irish meaning "born of fire."

Dae: Beings having both pure Fairy and Demon blood. Their powers and physical features represent both parentages. The offspring of Fairies and Demons are extremely powerful. They are feared and considered abominations, being killed at birth for centuries by the Seelie Queen.

Damnú air: Irish for "damn it."

Damnú ort: Irish for "damn you."

Damnú ort bean dhubh: Irish for damn you black-haired woman

Dark Dweller: Free-lance mercenaries of the Otherworld. The only group in the Otherworld that is neither under the Seelie Queen nor the Unseelie King command. They were exiled to Earth by the Queen.

Demon: A broad term for a group of powerful and usually malevolent beings. They live off human life forces, gained by sex, debauchery, corruption, greed, dreams, energy, and death. They live on earth taking on animal or human form, their shell being the best weapon to seduce or gain their prey.

Draoidh: Another term for "Druid."

Draoidhean: Plural for Draoidh.

Dreamscape: Dreamscaping is pulling someone into a dream, usually only another Fay. But because of the blood they share, Ember can bring Eli into hers. She can fully interact with the person. It feels just as real as when you're awake.

Dreamwalk: Dreamwalking is the ability to put yourself in a place that is happening in real life and actual time. But you cannot be seen or interact with people while dreamwalking. You are a ghost to them.

Drochrath air: Gaelic for "Damn it" or "Damn you."

Druid: Important figures in ancient Celtic Ireland. They held positions of advisors, judges, and teachers. They can be both male and female and are magicians and seers who have the power to manipulate time, space, and matter. They are the only humans able to live in the Otherworld and can live for centuries.

Fae: A broad group of magical beings who originated in the Earth Realm and migrated to the Otherworld when human wars started to take their land. They can be both sweet and playful or scary and dangerous. All Fae possess the gifts of glamour (power of illusion), and some have the ability to shape shift.

Fairy (Fay): A selective and elite group of Fae. The noble pureblooded Fairies who stand as the ruling court known as the Seelie of Tuatha de Danann. They are of human stature and can be confused for human if it wasn't for their unnatural beauty. One weakness is iron as it is poisonous to the Fay/Fae and may kill them if there is too much in their system. Also see "Fae" above.

Gabh suas ort fhéin: Gaelic slang for "Go f*ck yourself."

Glamour: Illusion cast by the Fae to camouflage, divert, or change appearance.

Gnome: Small humanlike creatures that live underground. Gnomes consist of a number of different types: Forest Gnomes, Garden Gnomes, and House Gnomes. They are territorial and mischievous and don't particularly like humans.

Goblins: Short, ugly creatures. They can be very ill-tempered and grumpy. They are greedy and are attracted to coins and shiny objects. Will take whatever you set down.

Incubus: Male. Seduces humans, absorbing their life force through sex.

Incantation: An incantation or enchantment is a charm or spell created using words.

Kelpie: A water spirit of Scottish folklore, typically taking the form of a horse, reputed to delight in the drowning of travelers.

Mac an donais: Gaelic, for "damn it," literally meaning "son of the downturn"

Mo chroi: Gaelic for "my love."

Mo chuisle/Mo chuisle mo chroi: Gaelic for "my pulse."/Irish phrase of endearment meaning "pulse of my heart." Can also mean "my love" or "my darling."

Mo shiorghra: Gaelic for my "eternal love."

Ni ceart go cur le cheile: Gaelic for "There is no strength without unity."

Ninjuitsu, pankration, or bataireacht: Forms of martial arts. Bataireacht is Irish stick fighting.

Otherworld: Another realm outside of the Earth realm where the Fae inhabit.

Páiste gréine: Gaelic for "child born out of wedlock."

Pixies: These six-inched Fairies are mischievous creatures that enjoy playing practical jokes. They are fierce and loyal and have a high "allergy" to juniper juice.

Pooka/Phooka/Phouka: Irish for goblin. They are shape changers that usually take on the appearance of a goat.

Pyrokinesis: The ability to set objects or people on fire through the concentration of psychic power.

Raicleach: Irish for vixen; "easy" woman.

'S magadh fúm atá tú: You're kidding me.

Seelie: The "Light" court of the Tuatha De Danaan meaning "blessed." This court consists of all the noble (pure) Fairies and Fae. They have powers that can be used for good or bad, but are thought of as more principled as the Unseelie. However, "light" does not necessarily mean "good."

Shefro: A type of male Fairy.

Shuriken: Traditional Japanese, concealed, hand-held weapons that are generally used for throwing.

Sidhe: Another name for the Fae folk of Tuatha De Danann.

Sionnach: Gaelic for "fox."

Striapach: Gaelic for "whore."

Strighoul: "Cannibal" of the Fae world. They consume the flesh of other Fae to gain their powers. Will eat humans, but prefer Fae.

Technokinesis: The ability to move an object with the power of one's thoughts.

Téigh trasna ort féin: A Gaelic swear word with the approximate meaning of "Go screw yourself."

Telekinetic: The power to move something by thinking about it without the application of physical force.

Tuatha Dé Danann (or Danaan): A race of people in Irish mythology. They are the earliest Fae/Fairies.

Unseelie: The "Dark" Fae of the Tuatha De Danaan. These are considered the un-pure or rebels of the Otherworld and do not follow the Seelie ways. Nocturnal and have powers thought to be more immoral. They can also use their shell to seduce or gain their prey; however, "dark" does not necessarily mean "bad."

Wards: A powerful, magical spell primarily used to defend an area and is supposed to stop enemies from passing through.

About The Author

Stacey Marie Brown works by day as an Interior/Set Designer and by night a writer of paranormal fantasy, adventure, and literary fiction. She grew up in Northern California, where she ran around on her family's farm raising animals, riding horses, playing flashlight tag, and turning hay bales into cool forts.

Even before she could write, she was creating stories and making up intricate fantasies. Writing came as easy as breathing. She later turned that passion into acting, living and traveling abroad, and designing.

Though she had never stopped writing, moving back to San Francisco seemed to have brought it back to the forefront and this time it would not be ignored.

When she's not writing, she's out hiking, spending time with friends, traveling, listening to music, or designing.

To learn more about Stacey or her books, visit her at:

Author website & Newsletter: www.staceymariebrown.com

Facebook Author page: www.facebook.com/SMBauthorpage

Pinterest: www.pinterest.com/s.mariebrown

Instagram: www.instagram.com/staceymariebrown/

TikTok: www.tiktok.com/@staceymariebrown

Amazon page: www.amazon.com/Stacey-Marie-Brown/e/B00BFWHB9U

Goodreads:
www.goodreads.com/author/show/6938728.Stacey_Marie_Brown

Her Facebook group: www.facebook.com/groups/1648368945376239/

Bookbub: www.bookbub.com/authors/stacey-marie-brown

CPSIA information can be obtained
at www.ICGtesting.com
Printed in the USA
LVHW050900190723
752643LV00051B/13